RYAN CREEK

BOOK 1

H J Pettersen

ISBN 978-1-957943-11-4 (paperback)
ISBN 978-1-957943-12-1 (hardcover)
ISBN 978-1-957943-13-8 (digital)

Rushmore Press LLC
1 800 460 9188
www.rushmorepress.com

Printed in the United States of America

FOREWORD

Thank you always to my perfect partner and wife, Kat. Thank you, Freida (Brinkman) Howard, otherwise known as Granny, for the love and kindness you so generously gave to your extended family. And finally, to Mother Pettersen, thank you for your trust, even in the darkest moments of your youngest child's life.

CHAPTER 1

The young boy could feel springtime shooting through his whole body. With only a couple of weeks of school left before summer break, Gunner ran out of the hot, dilapidated, one-room schoolhouse at mid-morning recess to the swings. As he pumped his legs as hard as he could, the swing climbed so high he could feel the sweet, though brief, weightlessness of floating before gravity grabbed him again.

The old lady teacher watched, frowning. Her eyes hard, her mouth set in a tight clenched line. As she rang the bell, the kids skipped and ran back to the old building with peeling paint and broken gutters, on the small island across from Anacortes. It was the best they could do in the child's most formative years in the late 1950s. One-size-fits-all was the only option for education on the small island.

The floors creaked with the footsteps of twenty children attending grades one through three as they shuffled into their shared desks. The teacher smacked the desk with the wooden ruler and looked at Gunner as the children immediately sat still. "Gunner, you were swinging too high, again. Go out to the entryway and wait for me." That was the hallway in the center of the schoolhouse. With a glaring, twisted smile, she said, "I'll be right out. You wait there for me."

Now in Gunner's eight-year-old way of thinking, he never did see a line drawn that you couldn't go past while you were swinging. "Not too high" didn't give him a mark. So, he gave himself one. By the teacher's thinking, that was too high.

The teacher and Gunner flat out did not like each other. It was like mixing oil and water when it came to these two. Looking back, it made an excellent recipe for disaster in young Gunner's life.

As everyone knows, there are no doorknobs on the child's side of the door. The teacher was a warped old bag in Gunner's view—definitely past her prime. He was sure she should have been put out to pasture long ago.

It never made sense to Gunner, how she would cut him out of the herd and ride him the way she did, right in front of the other kids. It's the same way his old man did.

Gunner knew what was in store for him. Going out to the hallway meant the old bag was going to hit him with the rubber garden hose again. Gunner thought, *It's that damn hose or the old man's belt. What's it going to be, Gunner?* He made his decision in a flash and with no regrets.

The hose didn't hurt that much. It was more embarrassing with the other kids watching him from their desks. They listened to the beating out in the hallway, including all her insane yelling.

Not this time. He decided from that moment on, she would never hit him again. He chose the old man's belt over the old bag's hose. Gunner could take the belt, but not the hose from someone that didn't like him and took pleasure in hitting him. He wasn't sure that Dad didn't get the same satisfaction using his belt on him.

Gunner did as he was told, walking over to the corner door and out into the entryway. He glanced back over his shoulder at the other kids. They stared at him, knowing what was coming. One thing he never could understand was that none of the other kids would go home and tell their folks the teacher was beating on him. They all knew that if Gunner said anything at home, his old man would beat him twice as hard. He guessed no one wanted to get involved. Dad had a reputation for being mean.

He closed the classroom door quietly behind him, his classmates watching his backside going through the door. He walked straight over to the coat rack that lined the wall, took his coat off his hook, and picked up his Roy Rogers lunch pail and hat. Gunner didn't miss a beat. He acted like it was time to go home. He put his hat on and zipped up his coat. He turned for the front door, not looking one way or the other.

If she came through the classroom door, he planned to keep on going out the front door just like he was. Gunner was ready to fight his way out that door. He hoped she would not dare to stop him. In his gut, he knew what he had just started. There was no turning back now. Gunner had made his mind up to head for home. That was where the wrath of a mean father waited for him. So be it.

Maybe, just maybe, he could talk to Mother before Dad got home on the last ferry. She would understand. Mom loved little Gunner and would listen to what was going on.

With those brief thoughts shoring up his decision, Gunner got clear of the old schoolhouse. He was out the door for home, never looking back. If he had to return to that school in Gunner's mind, it would be over his young dead body. Most likely, someone else would be dead too.

He slipped around the back of the school next to the woods so the other kids couldn't see which way he went and rat him out. He ran across the field and finally made it to the woods. No one could find him now unless he wanted them to.

CHAPTER 2

Gunner headed toward home, five miles as the crow flies. The walk gave him time to think over his situation and sort out what he was going to tell Mom. He did not want to make her believe he was a bad kid. All he wanted was the teacher to stop hitting him.

Mom always came home on the five-thirty ferry. Hopefully, Dad wouldn't be home until the last ferry at six. Gunner knew he had to drag his feet, taking his time so Mom got home before he did. Good timing was needed, and he knew he had to work on Mother first.

He considered he could be sleeping outside tonight if Dad got all wound up. For sure, all hell would break loose. In their house, you never knew what was going to happen.

With summer coming on and the sun warming things up, Gunner was enjoying his walk. The trees and fields were wonderful shades of vibrant green and the sky bright blue, peppered with white puffy clouds. Gunner was happiest out in the fields and forest.

He stopped at Paterson's Pond to eat his lunch, then skirted way around the house because he knew Mrs. Paterson was home during the day, and he didn't want to be seen. Once past the farmhouse, it was clear going all the way to his house.

Gunner spent every spare minute he had out in the Pacific Northwest backwoods that surrounded his parents' small 10-acre farm on the eastern side of the island. The farm wasn't much. They leased out the field in the back of the house for haying and kept a few sheep in the orchard immediately south of the tiny house. That is a whole other story, those blasted sheep. The evening was coming on much faster than Gunner wanted. The plan he decided on was to go straight into the kitchen once Mom got home.

Gunner just didn't want the teacher to beat him anymore.

As Gunner stepped through the back porch door, he could tell Mom knew there was something wrong. *Boy, that was awful fast for just getting home. Mom knew everything!*

Then he saw him. The old man was propped up in a chair, his huge forearm resting on the kitchen table. He seemed crouched, as if waiting to strike.

Gunner readied to take flight. The old man was taking a deep breath to start yelling. It was his every-day-mean self, showing up faster than usual.

It appears the school had called Mom. All Gunner wanted was to explain his side of the story. Spelling it out for her was easy. Mom was patient with all her kids.

Telling the truth was the only way Gunner could go. His lying was of poor quality. Besides, Mom would know if he tried to lie anyway.

First the teacher, now the old man was his second problem for the day. He was making noise and talking over Gunner, so he couldn't get a word in edgewise. Gunner knew the old man would get all the facts screwed up before you could say, "No, that wasn't the way it happened."

Then he would launch into a yelling spell, "What do you mean 'No?' Who are *you?* You don't tell me no!" That meant he was going to throw a fit of some kind right then and there. What usually happened next was everyone would run for cover except for the one that was taking the reaming. That was most likely little Gunner.

Then out came the belt. One time, Dad beat big brother with his belt buckle making marks on his bottom. Brother's P.E. teacher at school asked where he got the scars. Brother lied to the teacher and joined the Army the day he graduated from high school.

The old man was the problem this time too. It was too hard for Mom to hear Gunner talk, with the old man going crazy and making all the noise and comments he was. That was when Mom laid down the knife. She had been chopping vegetables on the counter cutting board. She came over to the table and sat down, facing Gunner. It gave Gunner a chance to stand in front of her and tell his side of the story.

Mom calmly said, "Now, Dad, I can't hear what he is trying to say with all the noise you're making." Once Gunner finished telling his side of the story, Mom said, "You go wash up now and get ready for dinner." That's all she said, nothing else.

There was no hitting going on. Gunner thought it could be that there was enough of that going on back at the schoolhouse. Gunner couldn't be sure what was going on. Mom's face showed no expression after all that Gunner had explained. He wasn't sure if she was mad or was waiting for the teacher's side of the story. Gunner wasn't sure about the old man either. Could he be getting ready to launch, or what?

Couldn't Mom see mistakes came early in life? Young people need some time to sort things out and move on. Couldn't they see he had a lot of sorting to do?

The old man spoke up, "Gunner, you need to bring in your stove wood for the night before you clean up. Go on out to the woodpile, and you start splitting kindling for the morning fire. Then fetch your wood. I'll be along to check on how you're doing."

He gave Gunner that same sly smile Gunner had seen earlier from the teacher. Gunner knew what was coming, and he wasn't sticking around to take another pounding from the old man or anyone else. Well, maybe Mom could beat on him. He would be ok with that.

"Ok," Gunner lied with a smile. He headed for the door of doom for the second time that day. Stopping outside the back porch door to listen, he then ran to the cabin out back of the house where he and his older brothers slept. In the cabin, Gunner yelled to his brothers, "This ain't right. Mom didn't say I done wrong. Now the old man wants to beat on me." He hurriedly blurted out his situation. Big brother asked, "Whoa there, slow down. How do you know the old man wants to beat on you?"

"He told me to go split some kindling out at the woodpile, and he would be along to check on me. Give me a break!"

Stopping to gulp for air, Gunner continued, "He might as well have painted me a picture of him pulling his belt off to start whipping my backside." Staring at his older brother's face, Gunner said, "You know how he is."

"But how do you know he's going to beat you? You did walk out of school today, didn't you?"

"When I went out on the back porch and leaned down real quiet like to listen in, I knew the talk would be about me . . ."

"Tell me what they said."

"Me leaving school. Mom bought my story. The old man thought I was lying because I always lie." Exasperated, Gunner said, "The only reason I lie is to not give him a reason to beat on me."

Gunner took a quick breath. "You know that. All of us do that one way or another. Even Sister, as good as she is. She doesn't want to be in trouble with him either." Gunner waited for his big brother to say something. Brother didn't speak up fast enough, so Gunner filled the space.

"I'm done here. I can't do it, no sir. And I'm not going to take a beating from that old rag teacher. I can't do it." Gunner looked up to his big brother's kind face and kept talking, "I can lay low out in the woods for a month. Then he'll be gone fishing in Alaska for the summer. Mom will let me come back in. Besides, she doesn't hit as hard as him."

Big brother gave a big grin that relieved the tension in the cabin. Even the middle brother, sitting at the study table, gave a short laugh, trying to keep clear of what was going on.

"Can I borrow your 4-10 shotgun, some shells, and your camping kit? Oh yeah, a couple of your traps would help also."

"Hold on, where are you going? You can't just take off. You know Mother would flip out."

Gunner was frustrated. "You don't get it. I am walking out of here just like I did at school. I have had my fill."

Big brother's mouth was set in a tight line as Gunner continued, "This is it. I've had enough of the old man's belt too. He will have to catch me first. You know he is too fat and slow to do that in the woods."

"Jeez, Gunner," Brother finally spoke up. "This is crazy. Are you going up to the mountain?"

"Yea, you know where I'll be. First, I need to get out of here before he comes out to the woodpile, to 'check on me.'"

Gunner walked over to where his brother kept his camping kit and gun. "He will be on the warpath! You want to help me or not?" Gunner looked back over his shoulder to his big brother as he reached for the kit.

"Yeah, you know I'll help you. Here, take the gun, and I only have one box of shells. You use my gear all the time anyway."

Brother paused, a smile spreading across his face. "You know where the traps are. Just don't get caught stealing grain out of the Grandy's silo." Brother paused again. "You remember how to grind grain up and make flatbread, don't you?"

"Yea, sure do."

"Ok, get going. Once he fights off Mom, he'll be at the woodpile looking for you."

"Thanks, Brother, for everything." Gunner gave a short laugh. "Hey, if I drag my feet, maybe he'll drop his pants to his knees with his belt in his hand looking for me."

"Just go now. I don't want the old man to catch you."

"Come by when you get a chance," Gunner said as he threw the bedroll over his shoulder, hefted the shotgun in his left hand, and dove for the door. A long look from both brothers followed him out.

CHAPTER 3

The darkness outside was heavy with silence. A few stars braved the early twilight, shining gently as the dew gathered on the hayfield grass where Gunner lay, a hundred feet south of the outhouse with a good view of the woodpile. Dad would stop here first, looking for him like so many times before.

Quietly watching, Gunner waited, pondering the day's events and his current situation. *I don't want him to beat on my brothers for covering for me. If he takes the belt to them, I'll go back in and put myself between them. Whatever the price. This is between me and Dad, not them.*

He reached down and felt the 4-10 shotgun next to his leg. *You know all this was bound to happen. That old bag teacher and her garden hose, she never liked me anyway The old man is always telling me they had the family all planned out with the three kids. Then I had to show up. Those are the hard-cold facts around this house, and ain't nothing going to change until I'm gone. Thank you, Brother, you taught me how to survive out in the woods.*

Right then, Dad came storming out the back door, pulling at his belt as he rushed down the porch steps. There was no Gunner at the woodpile. He ran for the cabin, his belt halfway out. The only door to the cabin was on the backside, and Gunner couldn't see what was going on. He heard the bang of the door as it slammed open.

Gunner laid still and listened as the old man bellered like a wounded bear. "Where is he?" he yelled. There was only silence. "Is he gone? Where did he go? I will find him. You know I will. Then that little smart mouth will pay."

Gunner could hear Big Brother's calm but firm voice, "Why don't you let him be? He's had a bad enough day."

"Bad enough?" Dad bellered. "He hasn't started having a bad day. When I get my hands on that little sass-mouthed squirrel . . . Now for the last time, tell me where he is."

"He's gone," Brother answered.

"Gone? Where the hell did he go? We live on an island, and there's nowhere to go. I'll find him. This island isn't big enough for him to run from me."

"Dad, he went to the woods. You won't find him there. I think that guy is part wolf. You might think he's there, but he's not." Brother couldn't keep a small smile off his lips.

"You might be the oldest here, but that doesn't give you the right to be smart-mouthing your father," Dad yelled. "Don't you forget you still need to hold that mouth of yours." A long silence followed, and Gunner could picture them glaring at each other.

"Alright, I'm going into the house. When he comes in tonight, you tell him if he knows what's good for him, he'll come into the house and see me."

Brother's calm voice carried out to Gunner, "I don't think he is coming in tonight. Or any other night as long as you want to whip him."

"Like I told you, watch that mouth of yours. You can still take Gunner's place with the belt." Again, a long silence, then the door slammed. Gunner laid there wrapped in the safe, quiet security of the evening darkness in the damp hayfield.

Right then and there, he knew this was it. It was like earlier today at the schoolhouse. He had better start making plans to stay out until the old man left for summer fishing in Alaska.

Now, for something to eat. Gunner's stomach was talking to him, and he knew Mother stored spuds and onions in the dirt floor basement under the house. He would need to slip in there and get a handful of something to eat. *Don't forget the carrots hanging in the rafters that Mom bought in town. Best do this when they sit down to eat, and I can slip in and help myself.*

Sure enough, Sister came down the back porch steps to fetch the brothers out of their cabin for dinner. Gunner could hear the knock at the door and the call to dinner. He watched the three of them walk by the woodpile in the dim yard light and up into the back porch.

Gunner's stomach was growling loudly now, and that got him to make an early raid on the cellar. He was hoping they would think he was gone. Brother might guess he was in the basement collecting things to take with him to eat. They had done it many times before when they went camping together. He ran to the old basement door and worked it open, just far enough to slip in. It was pitch black in the familiar, damp, smelly cellar. Mother always had him fetch what she needed out of there, so it was easy for him to feel his way. He scooped up a half dozen spuds and put them in an empty onion sack. He could hear the family talking above his head through the floor as they ate dinner at the kitchen table. The old man was doing all the talking, and it wasn't all that good. "When I get my hands on that little weasel, I will tan his hide good like never before."

Mom spoke up, "Dad, he's gone, for now. I don't see why we can't enjoy our dinner, please?"

"Ok, but I will hunt him down. Bill, what are you smirking about?"

"Dad, you could be standing 10 feet from him in the woods, and you'd never know he was there. That guy is good at blending into the forest."

"I don't want to hear it. I've worked in the woods most of my life, and I can smell a varmint that's up to no good out there. He won't slip by me by God."

Mom's patient voice came through again, "Dad, let's eat our dinner. We can talk later." Gunner could hear the finality in her voice, and things went quiet around the table.

Gunner put two onions in the sack along with a few carrots hanging from the rafters. *That should do.* He slipped out the door, closing it softly behind him. He hurried back out to the field where he had left the shotgun next to the bedroll and collected up his gear. There was a gnawing feeling in his gut telling him it would be a long time before he ever saw home again.

Now, he needed to get over to the Grandy's grain silo for half a sack of grain. That would hold him over for a month and by then, the wrath of the old man would be gone to Alaska.

CHAPTER 4

Heading for the Grandy's farm in the dark, Gunner knew he had an hour's walk ahead of him. If it were daylight, he could make it in half the time at a fast walk on the road. *At least, it isn't raining, just cold.* He stayed off County Road thinking the old man could be in the family car hunting for him. The Grandys rented the family's field and there was only one fence that separated the two places. Cresting over the slight hill, Gunner could see the barnyard light. *Wish I could talk to Justin. Just can't go up to the house. That would be trouble for him.*

Justin was a couple of years older than Gunner and two grades ahead in school, but that didn't stop them from being friends. Tonight, he could only visit with their barnyard dog, Ben. He wouldn't bark at Gunner as he walked up in the dark. Sometimes, Ben would come all the way over to the Gunderson's to visit with Gunner and play. Gunner's dad would yell at him and the dog and make him take Ben back home. Dad, as usual, didn't understand that Ben was his friend and only came to visit. He would go home on his own, come dinner time.

No wonder Dad didn't have many friends. He was just plain unfriendly.

As Gunner approached the barnyard, Ben came across the field to greet him. He was happily wagging his tail and leaned against Gunner's leg to get a scratch. They walked across the barnyard together, stopping at the tool shed to pick up a gunnysack for the grain Gunner needed.

He and Ben walked to the trap door on the silo. He would only take what he needed. Sometimes, Gunner would help Justin with his chores in the evening and Justin would have Gunner go to the silo to retrieve grain for the livestock.

Ben stood quietly, watching, as Gunner filled his sack halfway, hefting it a couple times, making sure it wasn't too heavy to carry. The barnyard light was just enough to let him see. He said goodbye to Ben and headed out for the forest.

Eventually, he would find the cave up on the mountain his brother had shown him last summer. Since then, they had been there many times. Brother Bill had told him that miners prospecting gold in the late 1800s had dug the mine. Only a few other kids knew where the cave was, hidden on the side of the mountain.

He continued his walk north across the field to the bend in County Road, then crossed into the forest on an old logging road. Gunner had a hard time seeing as the night got a whole lot darker the deeper he went into the woods.

He stopped and sat on a log, his stomach still growling. He knew he needed to think things out as carefully as he could. One more time, he knew he would not go back home. He knew the beating would be twice as bad. Then, he would be sent back to the old bag teacher. She would do him worse than before, teaching him a lesson not to make trouble for her again.

Don't Dad and the old bag realize they aren't teaching me a lesson? I will dig in deeper and fight back harder anyway I can. The beatings will stop here and now. It ain't going to happen to me anymore.

Gunner reached into his onion sack and took out a couple of carrots. They were sweet and helped to fill the empty pit in his stomach. He knew he couldn't see the trail even if he wanted to keep walking in the darkness. *It's been a long day. Think I'll put out the bedroll behind this log. For sure, there aren't any bears or anything that will bother me in the night.*

He guessed if Dad came looking for him, he would go up the skid road left by the loggers in front of the house. No worry, even if he came here, Gunner could easily hear him coming. In the morning, Dad would go to work in town, then be busy getting the boat ready to leave for Alaska. Mom had to work in town and his brothers and sister needed to go to school in town. Gunner figured things would move along as usual without him. Come the weekend, Brother would find him. Maybe Justin and Ira Paterson would stop by for a visit.

Crawling into his bedroll behind the rotten log, Gunner was comfortable with the shotgun next to him. The blankets warmed him from the cold night's dew. Within minutes, he was fast asleep, wondering what the next day would bring.

CHAPTER 5

Gunner woke with a start, forgetting where he was. *No, there's nothing out there.* The dim morning light peeked through the tall forest trees. He snuggled deeper into his bedroll, waiting for the warmth of the bright morning sun to dry the morning dew, before looking for the cave and setting up his new home.

After drifting back to sleep for an hour, Gunner got up, collected his gear and grub sacks, and started up the logging road. *It will be a great day, no rain.* Brother would tell him when the coast was clear, and Dad had gone north.

The walk was longer than he expected. Finally, there it was, waiting for him. Nothing had changed or disturbed the area around the cave since the last time he and his brother were there.

The mine had been dug and blasted out of hard rock. It would keep him warm and dry. They had made a fire in the mouth of the tunnel the last time, and it was ready for a new fire. All he had to do was build it inside the ring of rocks they had made.

Deeper inside the cave, the light was dim, but his eyes adjusted quickly. The first thing he could make out was the evergreen boughs he and his brother had hauled into the cave to make a soft, warm bed. The boughs would need to be replaced. He was pleased with how things were working out, and he knew he would be just fine here.

A quick thought went through him like an icicle. Mom. She didn't deserve the old man running their lives the way he did. Gunner knew he would apologize to her for the wrong he did by running away. He would remind her there would be no more beatings by Dad or anyone else. Gunner might be smaller and younger, but it didn't give Dad the right to beat on him.

Gunner got a fire going, replaced the boughs for his bed, and now could get to grinding grain on the flat rock. Big brother had used the stone, showing him how to scrape the rocks together with the grain between them. That made a rough flour for flatbread. Using his brother's tiny fry pan from the camp kit, he could bake the bread over the fire.

Darn, I need water. He would have to hike down to the creek at Square Bay to fetch some. Then, he could make flatbread and bake one of the spuds wrapped in tin foil by the fire. *Yep, this will work out just fine for the time being. There is no one to bother me up at here. No siree.* Gunner set about to make up his home.

* * *

It'd been four days now since Gunner had left home. That would make it Saturday, he figured. He was keeping track of the days in his head. Maybe Brother or Justin would come for a visit. Gunner was surprised how lonesome he was with no one around.

Gunner hiked down to the small stream at Square Bay to fetch more water for the day. Standing on the shore, he wished he had brought his fishing pole. Fresh fish would be great to eat and that thought made him hungry. He could hear an outboard motor in the distance and looked out on the water. A small boat was coming around the point at the mouth of the bay. He jumped back into the underbrush next to the shoreline. As the boat got closer, he recognized Justin and Ira.

They were headed straight for him. He knew they couldn't see him and he wanted to keep it that way. He watched to be sure no one had followed them. Fifty feet off the beach, Justin called out, "Gunner, are you there?" He called two more times as they came closer to the beach.

"Gunner, dammit, answer me. It's okay. We're all alone." He shut off the outboard motor and the boat silently glided in the water, barely making a ripple, as silence returned to the bay. A pinecone dropped to the ground from a tall fir tree in the still of the morning. The sun was rising higher in the east behind them.

Before the boat hit the beach, Gunner stepped out from the bushes with a big grin. "Morning, boys. How'd you know I would be here?" The boat gently slid up on the gravel beach.

"We talked to your brother Bill," said Justin. "He was worried about you. We decide to come looking and bring you some fish we caught this morning."

"That sounds great. You got some matches? We can build a fire and cook them up right here and now."

Getting out of the dinghy, Ira spoke up, "Gunner, you need to be careful. Bill said your old man was getting the Dolmen brothers to bring in their hounds to sniff you out."

"That doesn't sound good. Let's get a fire going. I'm hungry." The fish was soon cooked and devoured. Both boys could see Gunner was hungry.

Ira asked, "How long are you going to stay out here?"

"Until the old man goes north. I won't come in until then."

"When will that be?"

"A couple of weeks. I'm counting on Bill to tell me when the coast is clear."

Justin broke in, "What about the hounds? Those brothers have them trained good. My dad was telling me about them."

"I have Bill's 4-10 shotgun with slugs. That is, if they come for me." Gunner paused, thinking over what he just said. He never wanted to kill a dog. "I'll have to kill them dogs if they try to tear into me, don't you think?"

"You be careful," Justin said. "They think the world of those darn dogs. God only knows what they would do if someone put a slug in one of them."

"I guess we'll wait and see what happens. I don't want to be tracked down and caught by those two drunks."

Justin stood up. "I got some canned goods for you in the boat. Bill thought you might need more grub," he said smiling.

The sun was high in the sky now. Ira stood up. "We need to get going. It's a long way back to the beach house."

They pushed the little boat back into the water and got in. Justin handed a heavy sack of canned goods to Gunner. Both boys had brought canned food from home to add to what Bill had sent out. The boys waved as Gunner stood on the beach, watching them backing away from shore.

Justin looked over to Ira as he was steering the outboard motor. Talking loud enough to be heard over the motor, he said, "Damn, that guy has a lot of guts to do what he is doing. He won't take a beating from anyone anymore. That rotten old bag has hit us both." Justin waited for Ira's thoughts.

Ira thoughtfully said, "Yeah, you're right, but that still hasn't got anything to do with him out here living like a wild animal. He's all by himself. Besides, you know he's two years younger than us. I don't think I could do it, even as old as I am."

"Yeah, I know what you mean," Justin commented, lost in his thoughts.

Gunner had a full stomach and thought he would go back up to the cave to rest up. His mind was abuzz with all the information the boys had given him. What would he do if the dogs were let loose on him? *Those stupid mutts could sniff out anything. Wonder if they would bite me?*

He thought he could club them, striking for a knockout blow. That wouldn't kill them, but the brothers would take them home and leave him alone.

No, what if I missed one swing? There are two of them.

Gunner thought about the dogs all afternoon. He decided they would probably come tomorrow because Dad and the brothers had Sunday off. He needed to hustle and get things ready somehow. He spent the rest of the day preparing for Dad and the dogs. He could run, but the dogs would follow him. No, here is where he would make a stand and fight.

First, he rigged lines and set out clubs along the route he planned to take. Second, he moved all his gear out of the cave and stashed it out of sight in a tree southeast of the cave. Gunner knew the dogs would follow him. He had read about how hounds have such a good sense of smell. He made circles from the cave in different directions, leaving his scent on the trails.

Finally, Gunner went out on the rock cliff at a place called Lovers' Leap. The rock cliff was shear straight up and down. There was a narrow shelf of rocks thirty feet down and the water's edge lay below that another fifty feet. The Madrona tree that hung out over the cliff would be his last chance to dump the dogs. Here, he could grab the heavy rope hanging down at an all-out run and swing way out over the cliff. It was a scary move, but it might just work. Then he would scamper up the rope into the Madrona tree and back down again to safety and freedom. He and Brother had hung the rope last summer, so he knew it was secure.

With preparations made, evening was approaching and Gunner fixed corned beef and hash from the food the boys had brought him. *That tasted wonderful!* He ate the whole can and one of Mom's carrots. That night, he slept outside the cave under a sky filled with stars, just the way he liked it. If he was caught inside the cave, he would be trapped and have nowhere to go. As he went over everything one more time in his mind, he decided they would come up on the logging road from the south. The dogs would find his scent there and follow one of the circles he had made earlier.

CHAPTER 6

Gunner got up with the sun. Patiently, he watched, waited, and listened. He reaffirmed that Sunday was the only day they could come for him.

Soon, he heard hounds, baying and howling as they do. Then, he listened to the Dolmen brothers hollering at the dogs. He laid quietly in the bushes on the hillside where he had stashed his gear and slept last night and from his position, could easily see everything. The two dogs came into sight, hooked up to his scent and took off like a shot, making a beeline straight for the mouth of the cave. From the sounds the dogs were making, the brothers figured they had cornered young Gunderson. The dogs waited outside the cave, barking and baying, raising quite the ruckus.

Gunner changed to a sitting position. The first to catch up with the dogs was his old man, puffing and gasping, out of breath, with sweat running down his cheeks. The creased red lines in his face told Gunner he was hopping mad. When he faced the mouth of the tunnel, Gunner could see the sweat seeping out the back of his shirt.

The old man also figured he had Gunner cornered. He ran into the cave like a half-crazed animal, screaming at the dogs, still yelping, to get out of his way. Their barking and running back and forth showed they weren't interested in what Dad wanted.

Finally, the brothers showed up, also out of breath and drenched in sweat. One of them had a shotgun slung over his shoulder. Both collapsed on the ground calling the dogs to them, but the dogs didn't come. They kept barking and running around, noses to the ground. They would howl, then run around the mouth of the cave again and again, working themselves into a frenzy.

Gunner laughed to himself. *Stupid dogs, they are so confused.* It was apparent they were trying to figure the circling around Gunner did to spread his scent. *Looks like it paid off.*

The old man came out of the mine, a savage look on this face as he looked out at the hillside. He roared, "Gunner, I know you're out there. You need to come in. I brought my belt, and I will tan your hide." He listened intently. "You know we'll catch you today."

No, not today, old man, no never, as long as you want to use your belt on me.

Dad hollered at the brothers, "What's wrong with your dogs? Why are they all screwed up?"

The older brother laughed. "Your young squirrel was expecting us. He's a smart one, that youngin' of yours. He drag scent around this area."

Pausing to catch his breath, the brother said, "It appears to me he drew a circle so the dogs can't pick up on one scent. We need to catch our breath, then split up and see if we can get a single scent for the dogs to follow."

While the brothers rested, the old man was getting madder by the minute. He thought Gunner was running and would get away.

Still watching from a distance, Gunner stayed still, not moving from his original spot. He knew it was time to start working his way for the rope over at the Lover's Leap tree. *Patience,* he told himself, *it won't be long now.*

Gunner pulled back through the underbrush as quietly as he could. He half trotted and ran toward the rock cliff. Just like he figured, he could hear the hounds howling. One was closer than the other. Gunner could hear the older brother's voice, also getting closer. He was yelling and cursing at the dog as he did before at the mouth of the cave.

Suddenly, there was a scream and more swearing from Filbert. *Darn, he must have run into a low hanging limb. Too bad.* The limb had smacked him square in the middle of the forehead, almost knocking him out as he let go of the dog leash and screamed for his brother. "Delbert, come here quick and help me. I done lost the dog."

The dog was free now and charging straight for Gunner. Gunner was running as fast as he could, not looking back. The rope was still where Gunner had hung it over the edge of the cliff. Before he reached it, he glanced back behind him. Yep, the hound was on his heels, exactly how he wanted. Gunner continued running flat out, closing in on the tree. He leaped at the last second, kicked hard with every muscle in his legs, reached out, and grabbed for the rope with both hands. With a gorilla grip on the line, he hung on for his life.

The dog was so bent on catching what it was chasing, it kept running right off the cliff edge. Once in midair, a shrill yelp escaped from its mouth as it fell down the thirty feet to the outcrop of rocks below. Swinging on the rope, Gunner looked down and saw the dog lying on the rocks, motionless. As he swung back and forth on the rope, there was a sharp ache in his heart for the dog. He knew it was his fault the dog was lying there, motionless, dead.

Gunner knew the others were close behind him. With a couple of quick pulls, he was up on the branch heading for the trunk of the tree. He scurried back down to the ground and away as fast as he could. He slipped back into the underbrush, making himself invisible, then climbed a fir tree to sit on a low branch. From this position, he could easily see the rope.

First, the old man showed up. He ran up to the tree where the rope was still swinging from the branch and looked over the side of the cliff. He stood still, staring at the dead dog below, shaking his head.

The second dog stopped next to the old man. He started howling, looking over the edge to see his sister laying there motionless, thirty-five feet below.

Delbert, the younger of the brothers, stepped out of the trees and stood next to the old man. The old man pointed down over the edge of the cliff to the dead dog. Gunner was close enough to hear Delbert groan. "Oh my God, oh no. What has that little bastard gone and done to our dog?" He bent over to catch the dog beside him and put it on a leash.

He turned toward the old man as he stood up, then looked back as Filbert stepped out of the brush. The gash in the middle of Filbert's head was plain as day. With blood streaming down onto his face, Filbert asked, "You got a rag on you?"

Delbert said, "Look what that little bastard did. He plum ran old Queenie off the cliff and killed her."

Filbert yelled, "What the, how did that happen? She's too big to let him throw her off the cliff."

"No, Sir, that ain't right. She plumb run off the cliff a 'chasing him."

The old man had no patience. "Can we get back to finding my kid?"

"We're done here, Gunderson. I need to tend to this here gash in the front of my head. You can find him yourself. I think sooner or later, you'll need help to come in and drive him out."

Filbert stopped to sop blood off his face. "Right now, we are a dog short. We come out here to help you and give the dogs a chance to do some tracking."

Delbert asked, "What about Queenie?"

"What about her? She's gone, and we hired out our two dogs. Sorry, Gunderson, we got to go. You coming with us?"

The old man grumbled, "Yeah, we ain't going to catch him today."

They all turned and walked back down the trail away from the big Madrona tree at Lovers' Leap. Gunner knew the old man was cagey, and he would come back again, just before dark.

As Gunner sat in the fir tree, he knew he had a couple of hours before his dad returned. That would give him enough time to make it back to the house at a fast walk on the cleared logging road before it was completely dark.

Gunner's gut feeling was not good. He felt terrible about the dog. It hurt when he heard Delbert call the dog "Queenie." Gunner had done what he needed to do to survive and not get caught.

CHAPTER 7

The sun was heading for the west side of the hills a few hours later. Just as Gunner figured, the old man popped out of the underbrush. He took a quick look around and dove back into the woods. He had to hurry as he would be running out of daylight soon and he was determined to find his youngest son. He decided to search toward Square Bay.

Just before dark, Gunner came out the edge of the woods and walked to the big Madrona tree. He wanted to look over the edge to the ledge below. Gunner wanted to know if it was dead or not.

He laid on his belly with his head sticking out over the edge of the cliff. He watched the dog for a full minute in the dim dusk light, the coolness of the ground soaking through his shirt.

Did he see some slight movement down there?

Yes, I did see movement. How did it live after a 35-foot fall? She's not moving much, but she is moving! How am I going to get her out of there?

He took another look over the edge, his mind churning ideas. *Wait a minute. Brother had a hiking rope with his camping kit. Yeah, it's with all the gear I stashed outside the cave.* The dog moved its head again. *It'll be dark soon. I'll come back tomorrow. If the dog is still moving, I'll pull her out with Brother's rope.*

He slid back from the edge, dusted himself off, and started walking.

Gunner needed to get the gear he had moved from the mine and make a new camp, just in case the old man or the brothers came back to the cave one more time. Now that they knew where the cave was, he needed a new place to live. For tonight, he would sleep by the cliff.

Gunner and Brother had found an old hollowed-out cedar stump a quarter mile deeper into the woods down the skid road northeast of the Grandy ranch. It was huge and would make a good home. *I'll set up camp there tomorrow.*

"I'm tired. Better eat and get some sleep. It's been a long day," Gunner sighed to himself. He retrieved his gear from its hiding place and spread out his bedroll. He laid down and looked at the beautiful stars in the sky. Gunner questioned himself over and over if he was wrong for running away.

Was I a bad son? Mom doesn't need a lousy kid in her life. She always cared for and loved me no matter how stupid I was acting up or doing dumb things. The old man liked to beat on us kids, or it could be he didn't want us. Gunner's mind was wandering as he gazed up toward the sky full of stars.

Brother will come and tell me when the old man was gone north. That should be in a week. Then and only then I can go home and be safe. Most of all, there won't be the threat of beatings anymore. Well, not until fall when he comes back.

The stars were long gone now. Gunner could feel the warmth of the morning sun on his face and on the full length of his bedroll. He laid there, soaking up the comforting warmth on his tired young body, sore from yesterday's escape work and the dogs. He was hesitant to return to the tree at the cliff, but the dog was there, and he was the reason. He had to get it out.

Once at the tree, he inched up to the cliff's edge on his knees. Slowly, he peeked over to where he had last seen the dog the night before. *Yup, she's still there. Look, she's sitting up now.* The dog looked up to him as if to ask, "Would you please help me out of here?"

Gunner had brought the climbing rope from Brother's camping kit. If he could, he would save the poor dog. It was stupid for running itself off the cliff. He didn't feel he had outsmarted the dog by any means. It was just following its instincts, like Gunner.

Gunner talked to himself as he made a plan. He knew he had to do this by himself. First, he had to go down and get the rope around the dog. Next, he had to climb back up to the tree on the line. Then he would pull the dog up to the tree and find out what was broken, that is, if it had broken anything at all. Hopefully, it wouldn't be worse, only bruised up. He couldn't imagine there weren't any bones broke after a fall that far.

He tied the rope off to the tree. Brother had showed him how to wrap the line around himself to slack it off and safely lower himself down. Inch by inch over to the edge of the cliff, then foot by foot, down he went.

Is fifty feet long enough? He didn't want to run out of rope and drop to the outcropping where the dog was. He saw the end of the line barely touch the bottom when he threw it down. Not only would the dog be stuck there, but Gunner would be too.

I'm sure this rope will work. Gunner needed just enough to wrap around the dog, then he could pull himself back up the cliff.

When he arrived on the ledge, the dog didn't move or make any sound. He hoped she knew he was there to help. The line had snagged on a bush when he threw the slack over the cliff. He cleared the snagged rope and that gave him and the dog plenty of extra rope to get the job done.

Gunner talked quietly to the dog, the same way he would talk to old Ben, his barnyard buddy. The harness he had fashioned out of the end of the climbing rope wasn't the best, but it would work. He put the harness around the dog, and there was still enough slack for him to climb out hand over hand. Gunner used his feet to dig in against the sharp gray granite rock behind the thick moss on the face of the cliff. Gunner fought his way up the rope with only a couple of slips of his boots on the rock face. He crawled the last few feet using his bare hands, digging his fingers into the soft moss and dirt at the top, then pulled himself over the edge.

Gunner was panting as he rolled over to lay in the sun and catch his breath. Getting up on his knees, he could see the dog sitting on the ledge, looking up at him. Queenie still had that look on her face. *"Well, aren't you going to pull me up and out of here?"*

Gunner took a bight of the line, pulling it around his backside. He stood up on his feet and started leaning against the line, walking backward, step by step, ever so slowly. *One step at a time, you can do this.* He guessed the old girl weighed about seventy pounds.

Finally, he backed into a sapling and tied off the rope. That let him take another bight of the line at the edge of the cliff. He knew he would make it this time. He continued to back up, holding the line. Ever so slowly, he dragged her over the edge. She laid there motionless.

As he laid the rope down and walked over to the dog, she looked up to him with that same sad, hurt look in her eyes. Gunner felt her legs and ribs for broken bones. There was nothing obvious, as she did not yelp when he ran his hands gently over her body. She seemed weak from lack of food and water and bruised up badly from the fall, but overall, nothing serious.

Gunner sat next to her on the edge of the cliff and pulled a can of spam out of his backpack. They shared the entire can of spam in the morning sun.

She needed water after the spam was gone.

CHAPTER 8

Gunner couldn't help but think about his new friend. *We need to get out of here and move all the gear to the cedar stump. It will be safe and dry for us there.*

Gunner, big for his age, had no problem hefting the dog up on his shoulders, bending his legs, then standing at the same time. She only whimpered and wiggled a bit with pain.

Gunner walked gently through the woods, carefully stepping over roots and rocks to not jar the injured dog. Queenie didn't make a sound stretched across his shoulders. Soon, they reached their new stump house.

"Welcome home, old girl. It ain't much, but at least we'll be dry when it rains."

He carefully laid her down on a bed of cedar boughs he had made for a mattress earlier. She laid quietly where he put her.

Gunner looked her over. "For someone that was barking so loud when the chase was on, now you can't mumble a tiny yelp. Okay, you stay here. I will be right back with our gear, and we can move in."

He spent the rest of the day making two trips to get all the gear moved, then fetched water from Square Bay. That was his third trip down and back to the bay. The sky was clouding over with thick gray-black clouds bulging with water to dump somewhere. He thought they would have rain tonight as it quickly got dark in the deep forest on the way back with fresh water.

Their stump was a perfect house with massive roots extending into the sky, making it the ideal place to crawl into for shelter. It would keep them dry when the rain came. That night, the sky opened, and buckets of rain fell to the earth. Queenie laid tight against Gunner's legs, and never moved. Come morning, Gunner gave her water and more of his canned corned beef and hash.

As he scraped the last of the food out of the can, he said, "Queenie, this has to change. You will eat me out of all my canned goods in no time." He gave her a long look, and she looked back up to him, trying to understand what he was saying.

"So, what are we going to do? Ok, here's a thought. Old Ben is the barnyard dog at Justin's house. The Grandys keep his food down at the barn. Maybe I can borrow some for you. Then, when you can walk on your own, we'll take you home. How does that sound?"

Gunner could swear she nodded her head in agreement.

There were extra things Gunner had to do now that he was going to the Grandy barn. He knew he would be back before dark, and Queenie would be okay while he was gone. He still made sure there was plenty of food and water left out for her and he hung the grain bag high up on the limb of a fir tree.

He knew what time Justin did his chores at the barn and planned his arrival to meet up with him. They could do some catching up and Gunner would ask for dog food for Queenie and more grain for his flatbread. Most importantly, he needed to get a message to his brother that he had moved. Justin was a good friend and could be trusted.

Gunner arrived at the farm before dark, laying low in the drainage ditch on the big hay barn's backside. Soon, Justin showed up for his chores. "Hey, Justin, can you hear me?"

Justin stopped dead in his tracks, not sure he had really heard anything. Then, he gave a big smile. "Where are you?"

"Over here in the ditch."

"Okay, slip on over to the barn loft. I'll be right along, lots going on around here."

Gunner was sitting on a bale of hay up in the loft when Justin showed up. Justin sat on a hay bale across from him so they could talk. Justin said, "You sure have stirred things up around here on the old island."

Gunner frowned. "Yeah, like what?"

"Well, for starters, the brothers are claiming you killed their prize dog, Queenie."

He stopped to chuckle, "On top of that, they wanted your old man to pay up for the dead dog you outfoxed."

"Oh boy, what happened then?"

"Seems your old man told them to go to hell, right there, at the ferry dock. You wouldn't believe it, but about half the island was standing there."

Justin paused. "You should've seen them. Your old man said they didn't catch you, so he wasn't going to pay. He didn't get anything and wasn't going to pay for anything. Now, this is where it got interesting. He told them, 'If you two drunks don't like it, I would be happy to kick both your sorry asses into next week somewhere.' It was great! You should have been there. Second thought, you probably shouldn't have been there. It was because of you, and there was almost a fight."

"Did anything else happen?"

"Yeah, your brother told me to tell you if I saw you that your old man will be leaving Saturday noon for Alaska."

"Great. Is Bill coming out to tell me when I can go home?" Gunner paused to think. "Could you tell him I moved to the cedar stump deeper in the woods? He'll know where it is. He's the one that showed it to me."

"Sure, I can do that. Do you need anything?"

"If you don't mind, could I bum some of Ben's dog food?"

"Don't tell me you're taking to eating dog food?"

"No, not for me. I pulled Queenie off the cliff. She and I have become best friends. What a great dog. She's waiting up at the stump for me now. I think she's only weak and sore, and that's all that's wrong with her. It was a hell of a fall, you know. I'll have to tell you about it sometime."

"Yeah, I heard the brothers' side of the story. You'll have to tell me about it later. I have to get going. The folks will think something is wrong."

"Hey, how about some of Ben's food, please."

"Sure, help yourself."

"Can I get some grain to make flatbread for myself also, please?"

He grinned, "Ok, go ahead. We'll put it on your bill from the last time you were here." Giving a half laugh, he turned and headed for his chores.

Gunner loaded a small bag of dog food and more grain. He was gone just like he came, a small ghost in the setting sun.

It was completely dark inside the stump house when he got home. "Queenie, you here?" He felt her nose against his hand, telling him she was hungry. He held out a handful of dog food. She was so hungry she ate it right out of his hand, then licked his fingers. Gunner was too tired to eat. Sliding into his bedroll, he thought it was too hard walking in the woods with only half a cloudy moon. "Goodnight, Queenie." She laid close to his legs all night, and that kept them both warm.

Queenie was healing fast with Ben's food. Gunner would mix in some water to make gravy, well, dog gravy anyway. She would woof it down like it was her last meal.

He tried to figure out what day it was. Tomorrow, she would be able to travel and could go home to the brothers. Gunner was thinking of the route they would take. As the crow flies, it was eight miles. There were lots of logging skid roads he could take.

The brothers lived south of the schoolhouse about a mile. He knew it would be a long day's walk for both Queenie and him. She had been a lot of good company and they had become good friends living together in the stump. He would miss the old girl.

That night, the stars were out, not a cloud in the sky, and they laid out under them. Looking up, his hand on Queenie, he realized he missed his mom, sister, and brothers.

Gunner kept asking himself, *Did I do the right thing by running away?* He knew he had "walked out" on his family. Now, someone else would have to split the kindling to build the morning fires to keep the house warm. Gunner fell into a fitful sleep.

"Good morning, Queenie. Today you go home to be with your brother. Anyway, I think he's your brother." He packed them lunch and put his grub sack up on a branch with a rope to keep the forest critters from helping themselves.

The sky was bright and clear as they started on the long walk ahead. Both Gunner and Queenie would be walking to the middle of the island where the brothers lived. Once they came out of the woods, they would be across the road from the brother's house.

Gunner had to be extra careful, hoping no one would see them next to the county road.

These island people have awful big noses, and they didn't let anything get past them. He would prefer to not be caught, not yet anyway. The sun was high overhead by the time they came out of the woods. Crouching down in the underbrush, Gunner hugged Queenie and said goodbye as he slipped the piece of rope from her neck. She headed straight for the brothers' run-down shack. Queenie's brother started baying when he saw her in the front yard. Gunner had pulled back into the forest to not be seen. Delbert came to the front door to see what the commotion was. "Well, I'll be! Hey Filbert, lookie who come home."

As Delbert stepped onto the porch, he called to his dog and examined her. "Hey, Queenie, you look good. No scrapes or broken bones." Filbert looked at her as well. She was wagging her tail, happy to be home.

"Our girl isn't hurt at all," Filbert said. "You're right. She looks terrific. You ready for some food, girl?"

Gunner smiled. Now she would be with her family, like he wanted to be someday.

CHAPTER 9

Gunner walked back toward the stump, cautiously passing the Paterson's place not to let Mrs. Paterson see him.

Once he was over the hillside, he started to cut across Grandy's hayfield. Seeing a cloud of dust on the road ahead, he crouched and kept walking.

There's that blasted school bus, throwing up a cloud of dust.

The school bus had just dropped Justin off from school and started up the road again. Then, he heard the brakes screech as the bus came to a thundering stop. Gunner dropped to the ground. He carefully peeked through the tall grass. The driver was staring out toward him. Gunner knew he had to get out of there and fast. He was very familiar with the fields around there from helping his brother run muskrat trap lines.

Gunner cautiously crawled on his belly toward the ditch, finally crawling over the edge. The ditch was about 6 feet deep, and all dried out with the start of summer. The trench was like a runway for Gunner's young, strong legs as he started north at a dead run, not looking back to check on the nosy bus driver. The ditch ended twenty feet from the county road. Gunner knew this part would be tricky. He could hear the bus' grinding gears around the corner over the thumping of his racing heart.

No, don't go, not enough time! Yes! Go! They might stop at the ditch to look for him. No, wait! Gunner knew if he made it to the woods, they would never catch him.

It has to be now or never! Now! Gunner leaped up and ran as fast as he could. *Only twenty feet to the barbed wire fence and the edge of the road!*

He grabbed the top of the fence post with both hands and catapulted his legs over the top row of barbed wire. His feet barely touched the ground, as he started running flat out across the dirt road, diving into the small row of bushes on the wooded side of the road. It was soft enough to land on his chest and hands. Gasping for air, he could feel the rumble of the rickety old yellow bus through the ground, trundling by him but not stopping. He had made it!

Thank you, whoever you are, for your help.

Gasping for big gulps of clean, crisp air, he knew it was over. He could relax now. He pulled his knees to his chest, wrapping his arms around them, making it easier to breathe. It was time to get going. Gunner knew he would not dare do that again. He kicked himself for being so stupid. He knew what time the bus would be coming by.

Why didn't he wait until it passed? Maybe the old man was right. You are stupid, Gunner. The conversation with himself continued all the way back to the stump house.

After fixing a small dinner, Gunner lay on his bedroll. He was methodically going over everything that had happened to him this spring. His next thought was about his food supply. What if he ran out of food? Gunner knew where the small island deer grazed. He also knew where they went for fresh water and where they slept. He would work on that idea in a couple of days.

Gunner had fallen asleep and the cool of the evening woke him. Slowly, he dragged his bedroll into the center of the stump house. His young body was sore from all that went on today. Spreading the bedroll out on the dirt floor, he buried himself inside it, and young Gunner was sound asleep as soon as his head touched the blanket.

* * *

Three days ago, he had taken Queenie home. He liked that dog and sure did miss her. Today he was returning from Square Bay with fresh water. As he approached the stump house, he could hear people talking. He froze in his tracks and listened, not allowing himself to breathe.

Gunner began to smile. It was his brother's voice, but who was with him?

Careful not to make a sound, Gunner crept closer and stopped. There, he could see who was with his brother.

Bill sat on the log in the front of the stump house. On the other log was his uncle-in-law, Uncle Martin. Gunner liked Uncle Martin and trusted him. He never wronged Gunner in any way. *Why is he here?* Gunner crept closer.

Laying low in the underbrush, Gunner called out to his big brother. "Brother, come out and talk to me." He paused, "Hello, Uncle Martin, nice to see you."

Martin said, "I don't see you, Gunner. Why don't you just come in, and we can sit and talk for a spell?"

Gunner didn't move. "Thanks, but no thanks. I need to talk to my big brother."

Brother spoke up, "It's okay, I'll be right back. He's just careful."

Brother yelled out, "What direction are you, Slippery Squill?"

"Brother, walk on out in the underbrush. I'll be there." Gunner gave a laugh. This was fun for him. He knew it was time to go home, and he was glad it was over.

Brother walk into the brush until he heard a voice behind him. "You can turn around now." He turned, Gunner was sitting on a stump.

Gunner was quietly laughing, "Gotcha."

Brother smiled, happy to see his youngest brother. "You little varmint, I should skin you and hang your hide on the shed wall."

"No, Mom wouldn't let you." Gunner laughed again. Then, his voice turned more serious. "What is it, Brother? Why is Uncle Martin here?"

"He wants to take you as crew on his fish boat."

"I thought Cousin Jill was going with him. That's only right. That's his daughter. She should have the job, right?"

Bill explained, "She changed her mind, didn't want to be gone all summer. I think she has a new boyfriend from church camp. I'm not sure about the details. Besides, Unk needs a real worker on board, not someone who worries about her nails and hair all the time."

"Makes sense. Is the old man gone to Alaska? You know, after him coming up with the brothers to the cave, he would skin me way before you can."

"I watched him leave this morning. You'll be leaving this evening if we can get you going."

"Alright, but if the old man steps out from behind a tree, I will run away again. Then I'll have to go grow up someplace else." Gunner paused. "Once I'm all grown up, I'll come back and whip you. You hear me?"

Brother shook his head. "Come on, Mr. Tough Guy. Let's go talk to Uncle Martin."

They walked into the small camp together. Martin was sitting on the same log where Brother left him.

"Hi, Gunner."

"Hi, Unk."

"Did Bill tell you what I want to do?"

"Yeah. You can count on me."

"Okay, get your gear. We can talk on the way to the house. We need to catch the next ferry as soon as we get out of here."

"Unk?"

"Yes, Gunner?"

"Can I stop and talk to my mom for a minute? I need to tell her I'm sorry for running away on her."

"Yes, you can do that." Uncle Martin smiled. "I think that would be a good idea, so let's get going. I want to catch the evening tide out to the Straits tonight."

Gunner asked, "Brother, would you give me a hand?"

"Why am I always picking up after you, Squirrel?"

Once at the house, Gunner went straight to his mother. He needed to apologize for being so much trouble.

Mother smiled. "We've worked all that out. When you get home, it'll be a few days before school, and we'll be living in town by then. You'll be going into the fourth grade at the school on 12th Street."

Gunner asked, "What about Dad? Will he use his belt on me?"

"No, we talked about that before he left for Alaska. He wanted me to tell you there would be no more beatings. I promise you'll be safe when you come home."

"Thanks for that, Mom. I just don't want to have to run away anymore."

Mom smiled and hugged young Gunner. "Now, you go have a good summer working for your uncle."

CHAPTER 10

Gunner's life settled down for the next few years. A change had come over him from his island experiences and they would shape the rest of his life. He had stood up for himself and took care of himself as needed. He fought back at the meanness around him and won through cleverness and his own determination. He knew what it would take to strike out on his own and make his way in the world. The biggest lesson was at what level he had to meet the things that were coming at him. These lessons were tucked away in Gunner's young mind, safeguarded to be used at another time.

As Gunner would tell it, "Some things right, some not so right came from living on the island." The next thing he would say was, "Never look back, keep looking forward. The world can always be a better place with a brighter tomorrow. I know the sun will come up, and I want to find out what's waiting for me."

Whether Gunner's accomplishments were to be large or small, they would be his own. And he owned them, right or wrong. He knew this to be true. He also learned early to keep true to himself. There was no letting others influence him or keep him from believing in himself. His "bottom line" would always be there. Gunner would tell people he refused to apologize for being "Gunner Gunderson."

Life, for Gunner, was like the Cascade Mountains, a lot of ups and downs. He made it to the late spring of 1962. Now at the ripe old age of fourteen, things weren't quite shaping up as he had wanted them. School was still a problem. The school folks never wanted him to be in the grade he was. They said he was too young, and they talked Gunner's mom into holding him back a year.

No one wanted to dig up the skeletons in Gunner's closet, with the abusive teacher on the island for three years. To Gunner, it didn't matter one way or another. The damage was done. All Gunner wanted was to move on and live a quiet life far away from where he was raised.

Being held back a year weighed heavily on his mind. He kept thinking he should clear out once and for all and head to Alaska. It was time to be on his own. He could work and live up North.

Life in his father's house wasn't working out for him either. With that and school always staring him in the face or pounding at the back of his mind, Alaska was looking better all the time. Gunner was sure all he had to do was sneak onto a northbound boat and never look back. As he had been fishing with Uncle Martin since he was eight, not only did that keep him busy and out of trouble for the summers, but it made him strong and mature for his age. He was working in a man's world, as they called it then. And fishing gave Gunner freedom from town and home.

His father was gone during the summers, fishing in Alaska, then logging or finding other work during the winter. Gunner knew the old man's view of him hadn't changed any. He and his brothers were there for free labor. All paid for with room and board. That made the father the supreme leader and tyrant-in-charge. Work was a critical part of life from early on. Being a kid was not an option in their house or on the boat with Uncle Martin. There were very few opportunities for Gunner to be a growing kid. All the children in the house had it beat into them early to succeed. Mom did everything she could to support her offspring while the old man was busy commercial fishing.

Dad was always grumbling about the extra mouth to feed at the table. He was a crude, but complex person and it took Gunner a long time to figure him out. Life was complicated enough without dragging the old man's baggage along with him. Brother Bill preached he was a product of his environment. So was Gunner, and that would be there at every corner of his life.

Gunner saw it as having two different sides. It is hard as nails on one side, then a kind, thoughtful, solid young man on the other. Confusing, huh?

Living in town wasn't the same as the island. No trees, no beaches, and Gunner missed both. On the island, he could be outdoors working or exploring all the time.

School was a never-ending embarrassment to him when the family moved off the island. Even back in the fourth grade, when he came home one day with a problem he needed to sort out. First, he needed to talk to his sister Christa right away. Gunner figured she was the only one that could help him out of this embarrassment.

He caught her coming through the door from school. He said, "I don't know how to write cursive, and all the other kids do. I don't want Mom to make me take the fourth grade over again. Sis, would you please help me?" She didn't realize that he couldn't write but only print. Her answer was yes, she would help him.

He repeated himself, "Please don't tell Mom. She'll hold me back a year. Then it will take forever to finish school and get out of here. I don't know how long I can last in the old man's house the way things are going."

Sister said, "Bring your books home every afternoon. We'll work on them before Mom gets home from work."

Gunner knew she would do it. When they were younger, she always wanted to play school. He was the student, not much of one, mind you, but she was willing to work with what she had. That worked for him. He wanted to play soldiers, go hike, climb trees, and walk the beach. There weren't many kids on the island, so he and his sister kept each other entertained. Christa was three years older than Gunner and had a head start on life. And she was favored by the old man. He had a soft spot and was kind to Sister.

Back to learning to write. It didn't take long with the cursive alphabet in front of Gunner. Sister and guilt were pushing him forward at a rapid pace. After about a month, he could write cursive, but his sentence structure was still wrong. Hopefully, the other kids wouldn't look at him like he was so stupid anymore. Sister started making him read more. That got boring, and out the door he would go. He had made a few friends, so it was easier to slide along in school.

Now, about that sliding along. Gunner knew the day would come where he would have to pay up for being neglectful of school studies. That gut feeling of uneasiness visited him every day in the classroom. He developed a sturdy, quiet façade to cover it up.

That year, Gunner was out of the fourth grade and again, he went fishing with Uncle Martin. The next three summers were the best of his life, out on the coast fishing.

Now, he was wrapping up the seventh grade. Time had flown by. Gunner's grades were still terrible. Mom and the school "pencil necks" decided he needed to do the seventh grade over again.

Gunner asked his mother, "How about summer school?"

"No, that is out of the question," was Mom's reply.

Grinding back through the seventh grade again was a bad idea as Gunner saw it, and that did not sit well with him. Maybe now was the time to head for Alaska. Otherwise, it would be another year of trouble with the old man, and he didn't want that. In Gunner's heart, he knew there was only himself to blame when his mother refused to budge.

Gunner decided to go for a walk to the docks where the fishing boats were tied up and think about his problem.

CHAPTER 11

Each summer, Mom would ship one of the three older kids to her mother in Idaho. It would usually happen when they pushed back on the old man and were ready to leave home, no matter what.

Granny had been providing a summer place for Mom and the kids for many a year. You could say she was a pressure relief valve for Mom. This maneuver usually let that particular child make it to graduation. Granny knew Mother had her hands full with the old man.

Now, it looked like Gunner would be on the accelerated plan as Mother was hinting she needed to ship him over to Granny.

Uncle Martin had just sold his boat and accepted a job running a fish buying scow for an Alaska-based cannery in the Aleutian Islands. Gunner was too young to go with him. You may as well have shot a hole in Gunner's heart, leaving him dead in the water.

Going to Granny's was a must in Mother's eyes. Gunner knew she needed him to go to stay out of trouble, or to keep him from packing his bedroll and leaving home. She would still have control of her youngest child by sending him to Granny's.

Gunner wasn't a bad kid in the eyes of the law. He did have an active imagination and was always up to something, but going to Granny's would be a slow death for Gunner. He had gotten used to being a commercial fisherman. He would regularly be taken out of school early and put back into school late due to fishing.

Gunner was younger than his classmates by one year. The school folks attributed his lousy grades to his age and level of maturity. They never considered his formative first three years of school or the house he was raised in. You'd be surprised how an attitude could pop up, having been raised on fishing boats to boot. Then, a heavy dose of peer pressure if you were set back a year in school. After that, you were pretty much on your own in 1962. It was how they did things back then.

And now, Mother was deciding it was time to ship him off to Granny and Norman's for the summer.

Granny's place was a ranch buried in the center of the Idaho wilderness next to the Nez Perce National Forest and located on the Red River.

The time had finally arrived to leave. It was an evening just before supper on the last day of the seventh grade for Gunner.

"Gunner," Christa called as she came through the garage door.

She paused to look at her little brother, three years her junior. He was sitting on a short, three-legged stool on the dirt floor of the old wood garage as he hunched over a tired rusty Maytag gas washing machine motor he had dragged home.

Gunner looked up at her and smiled. His leathery, weather-worn face had come honestly from fishing with their uncle out on the ocean. Being only two months away from his fifteenth birthday, Gunner stood six feet and carried a wily frame of 165 pounds. Gunner's bright blue eyes and unkempt blond hair were inherited from their Norwegian grandfather. He wore his regular work clothes of a worn, checkered flannel shirt with the sleeves cut off at the elbow. His shirt was left unbuttoned, hanging open in the early summer heat. There was an Ed Roth t-shirt with a hotrod painting underneath the flannel shirt and the words "Mothers Worry."

Christa winced as she looked at his swollen, tanned fisherman's hands. Just like his leathery features, they were honestly earned working long, hard days on the decks of the fish boat. Torn, dirty jeans and worn boots completed the picture of who Gunner Gunderson was on the outside. Very few people knew who her little brother was on the inside.

A person would have to know their father to understand. Gunner never had a chance to be a normal kid. Gunner would say, "You had to come out swinging just to survive around this house." He was right and that's what made him so tough at his young age. Christa loved her little brother, even if he had attitude and just plain meanness stored up in him. It wasn't his fault. It was the world he was raised in. Both Sister and Mother knew this too well, and there was no way to stand up in his defense.

"Dad wants you in the kitchen, right now, Gunner," Christa said.

As Gunner stood up, Christa felt the kindness of his smile. She wanted to wrap her arms around him and tell him, "Everything will be alright, little brother."

Christa wished he had never experienced those first three years in the one-room schoolhouse. This moment might never have arrived. Today, he had to face his situation with Dad and the seventh grade.

Gunner's gut knew it was coming for a long time. "Well, let's go in and get it over with," he grumbled.

"Do you know what's wrong? I thought I was lying low and keeping out of trouble lately." He lied. He knew right where he was with school.

Christa shook her head, "I don't think it's a good idea to back-talk him. Dad is mad, so don't make matters worse, please."

Gunner gave a half-laugh, "Sis, do you think I would back-talk our kind, loving father?" He could see a slight smile on Christa's lips.

Walking in, Gunner found the old man hunkered down in his chair at the kitchen table. He always sat like that. He kept his back to the wall, making it impossible to get him from the backside. That let him keep an eye on everything in the room. The old man had a warped sense of insecurity. Nothing could sneak up on him and being the size of a young grizzly bear, he didn't need an advantage.

Gunner knew the old man though, and that gave him an edge.

Mother was at the kitchen counter fixing dinner. Dad had his index finger tapping hard on the tabletop in front of the chair next to him. This meant, "You sit here and don't say nothing." Gunner thought, *Here we go, let the circus begin.*

The old man's voice cranked up about three levels, filled with emotion. "Gunner, what the hell have you been doing? Your grades are garbage, and you're not cutting it at school." The old man paused to compose himself. "Your mother went up there today and met with the counselors."

He was fuming. Gunner could see his fingers twitching as he held his hands on the table. "They all decided you're going to do the seventh grade over again. Gunner, you know you did this yourself. What kind of a dummy are you? I got straight As when I went to school. You are an embarrassment to your mother and me."

The old man straightened up in his chair, and Gunner could see his neck muscles tightening. "Now I'm stuck with you for another whole year in this house! What are we going to do with you?"

Well, that confirmed it one more time, Gunner thought. He was never welcome here anyway. The old man treated Gunner like a rented mule and only acknowledged him when he needed help on the fish boats or around the house.

Gunner could see the old man was working himself into a frenzy, getting ready to take a swing. That meant the flat of his hand on the back of Gunner's head with a loud smack. He knew this was going to happen because he had been there so many times before.

Gunner also knew all he had to do was to give him a small smirking half-smile. Then stare him in the eye, sit back, and watch him launch. They had been here so many times before. It was like when the island teacher hit him. He was ready to dig in. *No, old man, this is the end of the line for me. I have had enough. Think I'll get off here.*

Gunner looked up from the table, staring at him defiantly. With barely a smile, he said, "Never really cared much for that school anyway. They're just a bunch of pencil-necked jerks."

The old man started yelling at the top of his lungs as if someone had stomped on his foot. He bellered, "Who the hell are you to say that? Those are good Christian people trying to do their job!"

Gunner watched as the old man gulped for air, his face turning crimson-purple.

"You are nothing but a smart-mouth kid that can't even keep your grades up. Bob and Christa get straight As. Even your brother Bill makes a C, and you can't even do that."

Gunner purposely gave a heavy sigh, "You don't understand." Gunner knew it would set him on fire. No one tells the old man he didn't understand something. "I don't care about the school or the people in it. I want to go north and live my own life."

Another jab, and this one would tilt him over the edge. One more defiant stare for good measure, and then Gunner shrugged his shoulders. *That worked.* Gunner saw the volcano short-circuit in the old man's eyes. He continued to watch as the old man began shaking as it went through his whole body, not even trying to collect himself. The old man reached back, pulling up his right hand like he was going to smack Gunner.

Gunner jerked his arms up as a defensive move. It would deflect the old man's hand from hitting him on the backside of the head. Gunner knew it had to come sometime. The school discussion was over, and the hitting was about to start. He openly accepted the responsibility of provoking things to go to this level, and he wasn't stopping now.

The old man moaned, "Why do you always jerk your arms up to cover your head?"

Gunner snapped back, "Why are you always pulling your hand back like you're going to hit me?" He raised his hand over his shoulder to show him. The old man got his wires crossed and thought Gunner was going to swing on him. During the Big War, he had boxed in the Navy, so he was fast, way faster than Gunner.

His left fist hooked up and connected with Gunner's face while Gunner watched the old man's right hand, which was just above his head, coming down toward Gunner. The hook took Gunner right out of his chair as if a sledgehammer had hit him. His flight path was a short two feet backward and Gunner landed square into the open refrigerator door that Mom was holding.

Gunner almost tore the door off its hinges with the impact of his body. The blood started pouring out of his nose as he slid down to the floor in a crumpled heap. The old man was upon his feet, dancing around, set to hit him again. He hovered over Gunner for a few seconds, his fists clenched, ready for the next round.

Mother screamed, "Dad, don't hit him anymore!"

Gunner was stunned but figured it was coming. He just couldn't think fast enough. He lay in a heap on the kitchen floor. He needed a second to ponder his situation. *If I get up, he's going to hit me again, and if I lay here, he might leave me alone. Mom could tell him to knock it off. Then maybe he'll get mad and leave.*

The old man grumbled at Gunner, laying on the floor. "You can get up off your ass, take your sorry carcass, and leave. I don't want you around here anymore. Law or no law, I don't have to put up with a smart-mouth kid in my house."

Mom handed him a towel for the blood pouring out of his nose. Once on his feet, Gunner didn't turn his back to the old man. He was never to be trusted. Gunner backed out the kitchen door cautiously, keeping an eye on him. He knew the old man would blindside him if he turned his back, even for a second.

The cold air felt good as he started walking toward the marina. Once again, his safe refuge was where the commercial boats were. He knew he could get some peace there.

Gunner watched the late afternoon sun bounce off the water, thinking about what he was going to do now that he had his own life. After two hours of thinking, he started for home. There was a separate entrance to the basement where he slept next to the furnace. He certainly wasn't going into the house while the old man was there.

Mother came down early the next morning. In no uncertain terms, she informed Gunner that it was time to ship him off to Granny's for the summer. They would leave the next day. That was final, and Gunner knew he couldn't argue with her. She was usually right and meant him no harm.

The next morning came early, and they were ready to leave. Mother had him pack the night before. He didn't say goodbye to anyone other than sister Christa. There wasn't anyone else to say goodbye to anyway. The brothers were busy with their own lives.

The old four-door Ford looked tired in the still-dark morning. Gunner knew the trip would be five hundred long, hot, quiet miles and that his mother had just sentenced him to an extra year of school.

The summer would be spent far away from the water he loved and worse yet, he would be spending the time in the company of people he didn't really know and cared less about.

CHAPTER 12

As the miles passed, Gunner had more time to think about what he wanted to do and what his options might be. All the time, he gazed out the car windows. As he watched the passing countryside, he started to feel better about what would happen to him. He became aware that he was getting farther away from the old man and his mean ways. Mother could be doing him a favor.

He glanced over to watch his mother's face as she held the steering wheel of the ancient ford. She appeared to be at peace. Gunner knew he had a great mom. They were friends, that is, as close as a mother could be to a not-very-happy 14-year-old son.

Without a doubt, he was loaded with attitude, having the father he had. Gunner and Mother had many good times together. He trusted her more than anyone in the world. Mom thought the adventure and distance would help him make it to his high school graduation.

At Snoqualmie Pass, in the Cascades east of Seattle, his mother tried to break the ice. He took the opportunity to try to change her mind. "Mother, why so far away from the place I like? I already miss the water."

"No choice," Mom sighed. "It will be good for you to see new things and work with animals on the ranch."

"Why couldn't I get a job on another fish boat?"

Mom's answer was the same. He had to give her credit, she was consistent.

She added, "No, you know I only trust your dad and uncle to take you fishing."

Uncle Martin was good to me. He was the only adult who didn't talk to him like he was a stupid kid. The last time Gunner saw Uncle Martin, he thanked him for that.

"How about we let me move onto the eighth grade and not do the seventh grade over again? How about that?"

There was no compromising. "You didn't have the grades to pass, and you have to take the seventh grade over again. It is the only thing you can do." Mom continued, "You'll have fun working on the ranch. Granny is fun to be around. You'll see."

"Not sure about a cowboy's life with horses, cows, and haying. I like boats and water."

Mom left it at that, and they were quiet again.

The drive took them across the state to eastern Washington, then crossed into Idaho and the city of Lewiston. After gassing up the old ford, they headed on to the Camas Prairie, meandering through the Nez Perce Reservation. Eventually, they arrived for the night in Grangeville, Idaho.

Aunt Ida lived there with her husband and four children in a roomy, old, two-story house. Ida was Mother's youngest sister. She reminded Gunner a lot of his mother. They both were tall with the same features and kindness inherited from their mother, Granny.

After coffee with Aunt Ida the next morning, Mom was ready to head for the Red River Ranch. The flat hot prairie melted off behind them as they started down the Grangeville grade.

The sign on the side of the road read "7% Grade Ahead." They twisted and turned down through the mountain switchbacks like a roller coaster. Gunner could see how exciting this country could be. He was amazed to see the ragged pine trees growing among the bare rocks on the hillsides and cliffs.

Soon, they were at the bottom of the grade and Gunner first saw the South Fork of the Clearwater River. It was bulging with rushing water headed for the Snake River, then eventually into the great Columbia River. Finally, the water would make its way to the Pacific Ocean that Gunner missed so much. He wished he was standing on the deck of his uncle's fish boat if only to see it again.

This must be snowmelt from the mountains. They passed thundering rapids as the river passed close to the highway. Gunner thought it was beautiful, but the ocean was bigger, better. In Gunner's gut, he knew these people wouldn't understand. They could care less about how he felt about the ocean.

The single-lane road ran on the north side of the river. On the other side stood tall green trees with short scrub brush and steep rocky banks.

Mother started to explain, "This road is called the Elk City Road, and it follows the river for a long way. Elk City is a town of about 200 people. It's a mining town that originally started in the mid-1800s."

She paused, paying careful attention to her driving as a huge truck loaded with lumber was on its way downriver from Elk City.

"Just up here, the rest of the road to the ranch is dirt and gravel. When we get to the unpaved part, be sure to close your window because it will be dusty."

Things were beginning to look a little better to Gunner the further they drove into the wilderness. The land felt friendlier. The river occasionally opened up to a wide valley of wildflowers and green meadow grass, outlined with tall pine trees.

They passed a deserted ranch house and barn along the river meadow as they kept working their way up the south fork of the Clearwater river. He watched the beautiful blue sky with its puffy, white clouds floating like out on the ocean.

Finally, they were in sight of the ranch house. They crossed a short wooden-planked bridge with new concrete ends that spanned a narrow part of the Red River. Looking down as they crossed the wooden bridge, Gunner thought the river looked more like a big creek. The ranch house came into full view on the side of a gently sloped hill with a small herd of horses grazing in the background.

Granny and Norman made their home there as caretakers for a businessman in town. Gunner thought of the ranch as more of a prison than a house. It was punishment for bad grades and back-talking to the old man. He should have headed North and never looked back when all this started. The same gut feeling kept showing up, but Gunner wasn't going to disappoint Mother again.

At first sight, Gunner liked the old ranch house. It was an old log cabin protected by a rusty half-rotted tin roof that held off the winter snow and summer sun as best it could.

Mom parked the car across the road in front of the barn turn-out. Granny and Norman were sitting on the overstuffed couch on the front porch.

Gunner followed Mother, climbing the steps to be hugged by his round, little Granny. She wasn't fat, but she was short and strong-bodied, the reward of a hard-working life as an Idaho woman.

Granny was a cheerful high-energy person. For as long as Gunner could remember, she had curly gray hair and glasses. The best part was she had a warm, friendly personality.

She liked having kids around. *She should*, Gunner thought *since she had six of her own*. Gunner smiled politely, saying "Hi" to Norman and reluctantly offering his hand. Mother had instructed him to do the handshake. Gunner didn't quite understand the why of it.

That done, Gunner slowly turned, taking in the beautiful view of the valley in front of him. He was surprised to think he could get used to this view. The corral used for branding calves was on his far left, west of the house. He could smell sun-warmed pine trees on the hillsides as the day's heat was building. It reminded him of the evergreen trees on the island.

Granny and Norman seemed happy to see them. Gunner thought it's more for Mother than him, but that was understandable. There was a coolness toward him when they looked at him or asked a question. Gunner thought this probably came from them not liking the old man. Taking it one step further, Gunner was sure it meant they didn't like him either. Gunner had experienced this feeling many times before in his life.

Mother was the oldest and had many of Granny's great traits, especially her kindness and patience. She wasn't short like her mother, but tall and slender like her father, who had died of cancer when she was fourteen.

Norman was a tall, strong man of many skills. He had worked as a cowboy, then as a packer for the forest service for many years. He and Granny shared the feeding and caring of their livestock, were happy together, and liked taking care of the ranch.

Sometimes, Norman would do light logging and chainsaw work, which was on the rare side now. Mom said he wasn't feeling well lately.

What Norman did have was a long worklist for an almost-fifteen-year-old kid from the coast. Gunner figured this was probably part of the deal to help pay for his keep.

While Mom was visiting with Granny, Gunner unloaded their bags from the car. Mom would be staying a few days before driving home. He dragged his bag and Mother's suitcases up the front porch steps and through the front door.

Granny and Norman's tiny bedroom was on the right, and the living room on the left. A large rock fireplace surrounded by overstuffed chairs and a rocker for cold Idaho winter nights took up most of the living room. An old crank telephone hung on the wall next to the front door. Granny said the phone worked. You had to make calls with the crank to get the operator, who then put the call through.

Gunner climbed up the narrow staircase to the attic sleeping areas with open log framing used for rafters. His bed was on the left. It had a thick feather mattress and a small desk sat next to the window directly above the front porch. He could see everything that went on in the valley from there. He knew this would be a favorite place to watch the world.

Throwing the bags next to his bed, he returned downstairs. The kitchen took up the entire back of the house with a large round table that could seat a crew of people. Granny's cookstove was next to the back door by the wood box. Gunner knew it would be his job to keep it filled with firewood, just like on the island.

By the stove was a coffee can of empty eggshells. Gunner was to break up the shells and feed them back to the chickens. It helped the chickens make more eggs that Gunner would gather every morning. The window above the kitchen sink took in the beautiful Red River view. It was a peaceful view, made just for the person washing dishes.

Gunner felt uneasy in this strange place as he reflected on the day. He hardly knew these people. They were Mother's relatives, not his. He could feel his attitude harden knowing it was going to be a long summer. But the situation at home wasn't any better. He dreaded the thought of being stuck here when Mother left. He also knew this going downhill had to stop, but he didn't know how to put on the brakes. And, for the moment, he wasn't sure he wanted to.

CHAPTER 13

Chores were first on his to-do list. Granny handed them out like an Army drill sergeant. Gunner was to get wood from the woodpile first thing every morning and fill the cookstove wood box. Granny repeated herself, "This had to be done every morning first thing, no excuses."

He had to feed the chickens while collecting last night's eggs. "Hunting for eggs would be fun," she said. "And don't forget to clean out the chicken coop."

Next was breakfast, and he was starving for Granny's delicious sourdough pancakes. Once breakfast was over, there was cleanup to do and that included whatever Granny needed to have done around the house and barn. Gunner was thinking being a housemaid was not his choice for a life's work. He much preferred to be outside with the animals and man's work, as they called it.

Norman, on the other hand, was a hard one to please. Gunner knew right away Norman had it in for him. He would ride him if he thought he could get a burr under Gunner's saddle. And that happened immediately if Gunner said something that didn't agree with Norman's way of thinking.

Gunner wanted to get along. He even shook Norman's hand to be respectful when they arrived. Seems there was no sense in even trying. It was like Norman wanted to break him like a rebellious young colt. His approach was crude, like the old man. He sure didn't do it with kindness.

Norman would pick a verbal fight so he could laugh at Gunner and feel good about himself. He would blindside Gunner with words not called for. Gunner had been raised with this tactic. He knew the game and what Norman was doing. His response was a deadpan look, defiantly staring straight back at him. The silence would make Norman twice as mad. He wanted Gunner to fight back with words so he could out-talk him. The look on Gunner's face said, "You're stupid, Norman, and I won't play."

Gunner learned this a long time ago from the old man. It just didn't make any sense to fight when you knew you were going to lose. *Once again*, Gunner thought, like at home, *there were no doorknobs on the kid's side of the door.*

Granny would turn a blind eye while Norman was up to his tricks She was like Mother, pretending nothing was going on, hoping it would solve itself.

Topping Norman's list of chores was digging a new hole for the outdoor privy. He had staked it out, not far from the old spot. The outhouse hole was to be four feet by four feet and six feet deep. After digging a while, Gunner's shovel started coming up empty. He had run into hardpan clay. It was a dense layer of soil under the topsoil that was so hard and tightly compacted it wouldn't even let water run through it.

This hardpan clay was like hitting concrete. Gunner eventually discovered it went all the way to the bottom of the six-foot hole.

"At four feet square by five-foot-deep, that calculates to 80 cubic feet of hardpan to dig out of this stupid hole in the ground," Gunner grumbled to himself. It was apparent that moving the hole to the softer ground was out of the question for Mr. Norman.

That day, the sweat was pouring off Gunner's face and his T-shirt was soaked in the Idaho early summer sun. He wasn't making any progress with just a shovel. Frustrated, he scrounged around the barn and found a steel bar with a pointed end. That would drive into the hardpan and break up the clay, no thanks to Norman. He also found a short-handled pickaxe to break up the clay. Gunner didn't know that later in life, all this hole-digging would help him out. Right now, he was hot and sweaty in the small hole he hated, always bent over, picking and shoveling.

The outhouse job seemed to drag on forever. Gunner would haul the ladder in and out of the hole every day, because Norman wanted it put back in the barn when he was done every day. Not only was the hardpan digging next to impossible, but slow, and the worst part for Gunner, it was boring.

When Granny and Norman went into Elk City to shop one day, Gunner wanted to stay at home and work on the stupid outhouse hole. Done working for the day, he cleaned up and sat at the desk by his bedroom window. It was getting dark, and he lit the kerosene lamp to read. Looking out the window, he saw Granny and Norman's headlights coming up the road.

Gunner blew out the lamp and went down to help unload groceries. As he walked out to meet them, Norman flew out of the car and started yelling at him, "Why did you blow out the lamp?" Norman was thinking Gunner was up to no good.

Gunner didn't answer right away, shocked that Norman was so mad about that. His silence, as before, made Norman's anger explode. Gunner stood still in the dark in disbelief as Norman continued to chew on him for blowing out the lamp. Gunner's gut feeling took over and for the duration of the tirade, he remained silent. Not a word came from his lips.

He didn't bother telling Norman that he was raised to turn off all flames as he left the cabin of a boat. At home, the old man leaned hard on the kids to turn off all lights, especially to shut off all flames, and you best believe they did it.

Gunner knew Norman didn't want to hear any of that from a kid from the coast. He was mad and just wanted to pick a fight, again. Later, Gunner discovered Norman was in a lot of pain at the time. If he had known, he might have understood better.

The only thing that might have given him an idea of what was going on was another time when Norman got out of the car, doubled over, and went straight into the house. No one talked, so Gunner didn't ask.

A few days later, when the cousins were coming for a visit, Norman grumbled about the toilet hole not being dug fast enough. The oldest cousin was roped into joining Gunner into the scraping, picking, and shoveling in the hole. They were the same age and were labeled the "Latrine Detail." That gave the adults something to laugh about. Being the butt of the jokes didn't sit well with Gunner. He was tired of jokes at his expense. A few days later, they were finally done with the hated hole in the ground.

Well, they thought they had finished. It turned out the hole had a slanting taper to it. The darn walls didn't go straight up and down after the "inspector" put a plumb bob on it. *Why couldn't anything be right?* Norman had his son Ned straighten it out. The "Latrine Detail" didn't hear a thank you or anything, just, "It's about time."

A few days later, a friend of Granny and Norman's stopped by. Cleo, an old, retired miner, lived up Moose Butte Creek, a few miles from Granny's. He asked if Gunner would like to go up to the hot springs for a swim, then do some fly fishing on their return home.

"You bet!" Gunner chimed in, excited to be off the ranch and fishing. Time marched forward slowly and finally, Cleo came by in his Willys Jeep wagon. After a brief visit with Granny, Cleo and Gunner loaded up and were soon at the hot springs. Gunner swam like a seal in the big spring pool while Cleo enjoyed soaking his old bones in one of the original wooden tubs set up inside the lodge.

After that, they had burgers and were on the road again. Cleo drove to one of his favorite fishing holes on the Red River halfway between the ranch and hot springs. There, Cleo patiently taught Gunner how to fly fish. *He is the best teacher*, Gunner thought. And he knew right away he could trust him. They caught a bunch of fat rainbow trout to take home to Granny.

Gunner grinned from ear to ear all day. When they returned in the early evening and stopped in front of the ranch house, Cleo handed Gunner a worn leather pouch. Inside was a collection of beautiful, intricate, hand-tied fishing flies. "These are my special fishing flies. You keep them for good luck." Gunner was caught short for words. He thanked Cleo and smiled back. Gunner thought this was one of the best things to happen to him since the time spent with his grandpa. *This man is special.* Granny met them at the jeep, happy to accept the fresh fish.

A few days later, Norman was working in the blacksmith shop by the road, next to the garage. Granny had gone to town with Ned, her son, to shop. With his chores done, Gunner was looking for something to do. He asked Norman if he could saddle and ride Janelle, Granny's little filly. The filly was a sweetheart, but she was green and spirited. The deal was, they would let Gunner ride her if Granny or Norman were at home and checked with them first. Usually, Gunner rode the old Arab gelding plug named Butch. The problem with Butch was he had Gunner figured out.

Norman said, "Yes, but saddle her here next to the shop, so I can help if you need." That sounded fair to Gunner. He had just finished saddling the filly and mounted her next to the blacksmith shop where Norman could watch.

Right then, Granny came rolling up the dirt road. Before Ned could get the truck stopped, Granny threw open the passenger door and jumped out of the pick-up truck. She was hollering and running full speed straight for Gunner and the horse.

He had just mounted up. As fast as he could, he dismounted the horse and stood there as Granny shook a fist at him and screamed, "You were told never to ride Janelle unless Norman or I were home."

She stopped yelling long enough to take a shaky deep breath. Gunner pointed to the shop where Norman was leaning up against the outside wall. He smiled as he rolled a cigarette, taking in the show. The whole incident made him grin from ear to ear.

For whatever reason, Granny had finally lost her patience with Gunner. She was not cutting him any slack, even if he hadn't done anything wrong. She said, "Oh," spun around on her heels, and walked quickly to the house.

Gunner pulled the saddle and bridle off Janelle, and would never ask to ride her again. No words were spoken the rest of the evening between Gunner, Granny, or Norman. That night, Gunner decided, Granny or no Granny, there were no friends here for him. Well, maybe the old miner he had gone fishing with.

Once again, in Gunner's short life, things weren't working out very well. *This is it. I've had enough. I'm out of here come morning.*

The next morning, right after breakfast, Granny sat down in front of Gunner at the table. She said, "I'm sorry, but I didn't know Norman was home. He was supposed to be working. That's why Ned took me into town shopping."

"Don't fret none, Granny. I understand why you did what you did. Things aren't working out here for any of us. Think I'd rather go home and put up with the old man's crap. At least I know where he's coming from."

Gunner knew if the old man hit him, the sad fact was, he was used to it. Here, he felt like he was being ambushed every time he turned around.

Granny put her hand over his, her old eyes sad. "There are only six weeks left of summer for you." She paused and looked into his eyes. "Let's wait and see how it goes."

"No, Granny. I can't make anyone happy around here. We all know that. I'm all done here. I'll write to Mother for some money to buy a bus ticket home."

Granny could see Gunner had his mind made up. It must be the German in her, but she wasn't going to take no for an answer. She took one more try. "Why don't you take Butch and go camping up Moose Creek? You can stop and visit with Cleo for a day or so. Besides, you like to camp and explore."

Now, that doesn't sound like a bad idea. "Well, okay," he answered. "When I get back, I'll be leaving." Gunner planned to keep on going once he got home on the coast. It was time to work his way North. The school was no place for him, and he sure wasn't going back to the same grade again, and he wasn't going back to the same house as the old man.

CHAPTER 14

The more Gunner thought about camping and exploring with Butch, the more excited he became. A thousand things were running through his head. This was a big country, and suddenly, he saw the adventure and chances to learn more about it. Maybe he could explore an old mining claim? *Yea, that's it.* That would be his goal. He would probably need to be way up in the backcountry to find a mine.

Gunner got right to it, heading to the barn where all the junk treasures were stored. He was positive he could dig through all the old equipment and find the gear he needed.

Inside the rickety barn, with sunlight streaming through the gaps in the boards, the walls were covered with all sorts of gear hanging in the dust and cobwebs. Gunner would need a camping kit first. He hurriedly started putting one together.

As he laid out his finds, Gunner was disappointed to find so little gear in front of him. *Not much here. I'll have to make it work.*

Granny pitched in some canned goods along with a lot of tips on finding food out in the wilderness, like berries. "And be careful, the bears like them too."

"Thanks, Granny."

Norman was still riding Gunner about the camping trip with the cousins a few days earlier. The cousins and Gunner were camping outside. Everything was fine until Benny started telling bear stories in the dark next to the campfire. They all got spooked, packed up their gear, and hiked back to the ranch house. Norman was surprised to see them again so soon and asked, "What happened?"

Benny ran his big mouth and said, "The bear hair kept tickling his nose." The ribbing started, just like the stupid toilet hole. Norman never let up and he would not let Gunner live it down. That made Gunner even more determined to do this adventure alone. He would prove to Norman and Granny he was up to the task.

The next morning, Gunner planned on tying his gear to the old Army saddle he had used on Butch previously. He would ride out of there, and not look back.

Norman showed Gunner how to hobble Butch so the horse could graze while Gunner was busy exploring. Norman always bragged the old horse was so steady he could shoot an elk while sitting in the saddle on Butch's back. Gunner would jump in and explain the rest of the story because Butch was sound asleep underneath the saddle, so he was standing perfectly still.

Butch was a smart horse, and he knew Gunner wasn't an experienced rider. Gunner was young and just plain not much of a horse handler. What leveled the playing field was that Gunner had discovered the magic of a willow switch. All he had to do was show it to Butch. Wow, that old sway-back rag of a horse would be a good boy if he caught sight of the switch out of the corner of his eye.

Gunner went back to looking over his food pack. *Not much here either.* Gunner suspected that Granny had planned it that way. She knew it would shorten up his trip if he got hungry.

He only had a small .22 caliber Rimfire pump rifle his brother had given him and he scrounged up an old World War II bayonet in the barn. The bayonet was huge, with a fourteen-inch-long blade. Along with it, he found a canteen and an Army web belt to hang the canteen and bayonet on.

Gunner was figuring on eating fat red squirrels he could shoot with the .22 cal. Well, hopefully, they would be fat. Then there would be berries, if the bears didn't eat them first. Don't forget rainbow trout out of Moose Butte Creek. Also, whatever ran in front of the .22 would be dinner too. All this would happen when he was hungry. That, of course, would be almost all of the time.

The evening was coming on fast. Gunner hurried up the hillside field behind the house where the horses and mules were grazing for the summer. Butch, an aged, dappled-gray, swayed-back horse was easy to spot. His coat was certainly a gift from his Arabian-bred mother. Butch stood patiently, munching a mouth full of grass as

Gunner snapped on the lead rope and led him to the barn for the night. Gunner figured that would cut out the time of catching him the next morning and he could load up first thing.

Gunner took another long look at his gear. *This is pathetic. There's just not enough.* He had to fight off the sick feeling in the pit of his stomach. "Damn it, I don't want to quit early. I'd rather starve to death than come back to this place early." If he did come in early, he knew he would have to listen to a bunch of adults giving him a hard time. *No thanks.*

Before breakfast ended the following day, Gunner had laid out his plan to Granny. His first night would be at Moose Butte Creek, then onto Cleo's for the next night. He reassured Granny she could always check with Cleo as to where he was.

Deep inside, he was hoping she would worry a little bit about Butch and him. Quickly, he shoved that thought out of his mind. He didn't think anyone cared one way or the other. Except Mother, she would want to know where her youngest born was.

Gunner had been shoving a lot out of his mind lately, like school, living at home, and commercial fishing. He thought it must have been the adventure in front of him. There was danger in it. Gunner could be risking a lot, like his life, but that was the most exciting part. He felt confident he could do this. On occasion, parts of his youth would seep into the back of his mind. Yes, he could do this. He just needed to be careful. Finally, he was glad to be getting out of there.

"Where you off to after Cleo's?" asked Granny.

"Doesn't much matter," answered Gunner. All he wanted was to get lost in an excellent adventure.

Granny hugged him goodbye. "You may not know this, Gunner, but your Grandfather Prentiss, when he was alive, would often go on hunting trips up in these mountains. I know you'll be fine, and we'll see you when you get back."

Gunner saddled Butch, waved goodbye to Granny on the front porch, and started down the driveway. He didn't look back.

The forest service road led up to Moose Butte Creek. The small creek gave a direction to Butch and Gunner to take as they made their way to Cleo's cabin. It was a well-worn, narrow, dirt road with a beautiful thick pine forest on both sides. The air was still and quiet except for the slow but steady clip clop of Butch's hooves. On occasion, the familiar sound of birds talking in the trees floated on the air.

Gunner's thoughts wandered back to the island where he had done a lot of growing. It gave him even more confidence remembering when he and his brothers lived in the little cabin out behind the house. There, he had so much freedom, with plenty of time to go exploring in the woods. He would take long hikes down to the beach, finding odd washed-up treasures. And he would go camping and fishing, alone, like now.

His time had been well-spent, getting ready for the adventure he was taking off on today. He was comfortable being alone and he didn't need people around. The truth was, he preferred to be alone.

Butch and Gunner followed the winding road next to Moose Butte Creek. He wanted to spend the day catching and cooking up a mess of trout. Then he would have extra food to eat later on the trail.

He found a perfect camping spot ideal for him to catch fish for that night's camp. The wall of a rocky cliff protected them with dense underbrush and trees surrounded them, providing cool shade from the summer sun and a small meadow in front by the creek where Butch could graze to his heart's content.

Setting up camp was fast because there wasn't much gear to set up. He hobbled Butch near the creek so he could get a drink of water as he was grazing, then found the deepest pool in the creek. As fast as he could put a worm on the hook, there was a fish. In no time, he had a dozen rainbow trout on his fish string. He thought about his fly-fishing trip with Cleo and smiled. He wanted to share his catch with Cleo.

Soon, a campfire was started, and those beauties were fried up as well as a small pot of rice cooked over the open fire. After he ate his fill, he was happy to see there was enough left for a trout lunch tomorrow and maybe even a trout dinner later on.

"Boy, it sure takes a lot of time to keep the two of us cared for," he said to Butch. By the time the sun went down, Butch was tied up next to the campfire by Gunner's bedroll. The day had been a good one, and they were both ready to call it a night.

Gunner rubbed Butch's neck and scratched behind his ears. "Goodnight, old boy. Keep an eye peeled for anything coming around. I'll be right here if ya need me."

Around midnight, a loud cracking sound woke Gunner up with a start.

Probably a range cow out in the brush. He noticed the campfire had burned down to embers. He slid out of his bedroll and threw more wood on the fire. He noticed Butch hadn't been alarmed at all by the sound. There wasn't as much as a peep or one of his familiar snorts out of him. Gunner couldn't get his eyelids to close again, so he stayed up a couple of hours tending the fire. He wished he had a gun a lot larger than the little pump .22 rifle.

Finally, he crawled back into his bedroll when he couldn't keep his eyes open any longer.

CHAPTER 15

Daylight arrived too soon. Butch was restless and wanted to start grazing, so Gunner got up and moved him near the creek. Breakfast was the cold biscuit with bacon Granny had handed him on his way out the door the day before.

It took only a few minutes to break camp because there was so little to pack. Gunner decided he wouldn't worry about how little gear he had. There wasn't anything he could do about it, and he didn't want to waste time thinking about it. *Things are what they are, right?*

He hurried along, not wanting to waste any daylight. He loaded up Butch so they could both walk up the hill toward Cleo's cabin and that was easier on old Butch. Progress was slow with Butch stopping to graze at will. Finally, Gunner saw the cabin. As they came around the back corner of the cabin, he saw Cleo chopping stove wood.

Gunner remembered, *you never want to surprise another man when he's busy with his chores, especially when he has an ax in his hands.* Gunner stopped Butch and watched, waiting for Cleo to look up. Butch took care of that with one of his world-famous "I'm tired" snorts. *Darned old plug.*

Cleo raised his head from chopping. A broad smile lit up on his tired, weathered face. He set his ax down and rose from a slight stoop in his shoulders. Cleo was a man's man, tough as nails, with a small stature, maybe five foot four. His body had started to melt away, as it usually does when people get older.

His hands were still strong and leathery from many years of hard work. On top, his hair was thinning, and deep lines crossed his forehead, but he had a friendly smile and always a hearty laugh. Gunner felt he could trust him, and he knew this man was honest as the day was long. Cleo smiled, "Well, howdy there. Where are you two hombres headed today?"

"Hi, Cleo. We want to bunk in your shed a night or two if you wouldn't mind." Gunner couldn't help himself and started blurting out what he had on his mind. "I could use some pointers on staying alive out in the backwoods. I only have a few days of grub but would like to stay out there a while."

Stopping to take a big gulp of air, Gunner continued, "Granny gave me three weeks to explore, then I have to be back. That's not much time to get some real exploring done."

Cleo smiled again, "You bet. I can get you headed in the right direction."

"Cleo, maybe you can point out some of the old mining claims I could explore. I'll need to camp where I can keep Butch fed, watered, and close to me. If anything ever happened to this old plug, Norman would skin me alive as sure as I'm standing here."

He shut up to give Cleo a chance to talk. "Okay, you unpack in the barn over there and hobble Butch out back. There's a fresh pot of beef stew on the stove, and I baked a couple of loaves of bread. My guess is you might be starving by now."

"Sure enough," Gunner answered eagerly, a big grin on his face. He was liking Hotel Cleo. *Yep, I'm starving, as usual.*

Gunner was happy to join in Cleo's world of patience and kindness toward him. Could it be Cleo saw a sliver of his younger self in him? And he enjoyed Cleo's interesting stories, like his grandpa used to tell.

What surprised Gunner was when he was out here with Cleo, he thought only of the good things about home and forgot the bad times. It was a relief not having the wrong thoughts nagging away at the back of his mind like when he first got to the ranch.

Lunch was the best. Cleo insisted he eat two helpings of everything, and that filled Gunner up.

"There's plenty, and later on, I'll teach you how to make a couple of loaves of sourdough bread for the trail."

After lunch, Cleo sat in his wooden rocking chair on the front porch, as Gunner sat nearby on the top porch step. Cleo gave Gunner a stern look and began, "First, I want to know what you have for tools. Better yet, fetch your camping kit. You can lay it out here on the front porch for me. Then we can go over it, piece by piece."

Gunner ran over to the barn to get his small pack. On his return in the noon sun, he laid it all out on the front porch floor, including the bedroll. "Here it is, the whole works, no kidding," Gunner smiled. "I know it's not much to be going out in the wilderness."

Gunner watched Cleo gently rocking back and forth, deep furrows in his forehead. Scratching the top of his head, his hand bent and stiff, Cleo stared at the gear for a long while.

Finally, he said, "Looks like we've got some work to do, so let's get started. The bedroll is okay for summer, but if you are out there in the winter, you should double that."

Cleo didn't slow down. "Your coat is too light. A man needs a good pair of leather boots, gloves, and a hat to keep his head warm.

"Now, don't forget you need a pair of knee-high rubber boots if you do any panning or working in a mine. In fact, what is your plan, young man?"

A little afraid he would not believe him, Gunner hesitated then blurted out, "I want to explore the backcountry, maybe where your old claim was."

"Is that all?" Cleo asked patiently, amused at the young man's enthusiasm.

"I think it would be nice to find an old cabin, if possible, that could keep the rain off my head. It would save me from building a shelter, and I won't have to sleep in a wet, muddy mine someplace."

Cleo smiled, then nodded, "Let me think about that for a while. Okay, what else do you have on your mind for a plan?" Cleo paused for a moment. With a slight smile showing on his face, he said, "You know, a man needs a plan, and then he needs to stick to it. Your success will come from thinking ahead with good planning."

Gunner thought, *I'm a man now in Cleo's eyes and I'll make him proud of me.*

Cleo sighed. "Do you know anything about mining?"

"No, sir, not really," Gunner replied. "I thought you could fill me in on that. Then I can figure the rest out with a strong back, as they say on the fish boats."

Gunner paused to see if Cleo had any thoughts for him. "Could you teach me how to skin a squirrel or possum and cook it for dinner? I'm always hungry."

This time, Gunner could tell Cleo wasn't joking. "Boy, you do have great dreams. But promise me this, if you run out of food or hurt yourself, I want you to come in. You let me help you. Am I clear on that? Promise me now!"

How did I become a boy again? Maybe it was when I sprung all my hair-brained ideas on him all at once. Guess I should slow it down a bit.

Gunner answered in his most serious voice, "I promise, Cleo. I won't lie out there and die on ya. You are my first stop for help. I do understand the risk involved, but I really would be grateful for your help and experience to keep me out of trouble."

Training went on for the next two days. Cleo would talk, Gunner would listen, and when Cleo had finished speaking, then and only then, would Gunner ask questions. That was how he learned on the fish boats, and it worked well.

Cleo gave Gunner a map with an old magnetic compass. On the island, his brothers had taught him how to use a compass and a map.

Cleo also gave him a couple of killing and cooking lessons. Gunner mentioned that squirrel would probably be his main meal. He shot a nice red squirrel and started to dress it out. The old bayonet was dull and made a mess of the poor squirrel. They had a knife-sharpening lesson later in the day. Next, Cleo showed Gunner how to cook pancakes and bread on an open fire. They used Cleo's recipes and the flour and yeast Cleo gave him.

Gunner was beginning to believe Cleo wasn't going to let him go without being fully prepared. "Tools," Cleo said, pointing him in a new learning direction.

"Let's sharpen that machete you have there, otherwise known as a bayonet."

Off to the shed they went. Looking around, Cleo found an old Army web belt with suspenders that Gunner could hang the knife on. Cleo had Gunner put the gear on, then hung the bayonet upside down on the left shoulder strap. There was a hilt latch that would hold the bayonet in the sheath.

"That's where it will live on you," Cleo said. "Working or sleeping, it doesn't matter." Gunner looked at the bayonet hanging on him and asked, "Why upside down on the shoulder strap?"

Cleo patiently explained, "It's so long that it would be in the way if it were on your hip while you're working, and you couldn't pull it out smoothly and quickly if you needed it in a hurry. Now, make sure you practice pulling it out. You'll get used to it. It could save your life if you ever get it sharpened." He gave a hearty laugh.

Cleo drove it home. "In the backcountry, never be more than an arm's reach away from your knife and preferably your gun. See that stone on the sheath?" Gunner nodded yes. "That's a sharpening stone. Keep that knife razor-sharp. It could save your life someday. Do I need to repeat myself again?"

It was as if Cleo was talking from his own experiences.

Gunner didn't want to ask Cleo for any details unless he wanted to talk about it. That was another thing he learned on the fish boats back home. If they didn't want you to know, don't come prying or asking. It could ruin a good friendship.

"Every evening, make sure you sharpen all your tools, understand?" Cleo continued, "So, where is your ax?"

Gunner answered, "Ax? I have a hatchet I can use for a hammer."

"No, you need a long-handled, single-bit ax, and it has to be sharp, just like your knife. What about a pick and a shovel?"

"No, I wasn't planning on digging much. I guess I am going to now, huh?" Gunner grinned. "You wouldn't have a spare I could borrow, would you?"

Gunner could hear a heavy sigh in his voice, "Yes, I do. It's looking like you came with a dream, and that's about it."

Gunner wasn't sure, but he was thinking he might be wearing out his welcome if he had to borrow anything else.

"What about a gun?" Cleo asked.

"There's my .22," Gunner quickly answered. "About all it will do is knock down a squirrel. Honest, when Butch and I camped at Moose Butte Creek the other night, I wished I had something bigger."

Cleo thought a moment. "I have an old single-shot 12-gauge shotgun. You'll need a box of double-aught buckshot and a handful of slugs. That will give old bruin heartburn or knock down a skinny deer for you."

In his next breath, Cleo went on to more lessons. "Don't waste the meat of any animal you kill. Skin it out, wrap it with game gauze, then hang it in a cool place. I got some you can have out in the tool shed. Be sure and don't let old bruin get wind of your meat, or he'll be over for dinner. You should be alright. Got any questions for me?"

"Could you tell me something about the gold process that could get me started?"

"Let's save that for tomorrow," Cleo said. "It's time for dinner now. You fetch some wood for the cookstove and take your gear back to the barn. Don't forget to take care of that plug of yours, then clean-up for dinner and come on in."

Gunner had another million questions during their meal together. Cleo sat there, patiently addressing every one of Gunner's issues.

Gunner felt like he was taking Cleo back to a favorite place in his life. With dinner finished, Gunner cleared off the table and washed the dishes.

Cleo headed to his comfortable chair by the stove in the living room and was fast asleep within minutes. On Gunner's way out, he threw a blanket over him. He cared for Butch in the barn stall and fell asleep on top of his bedroll, thinking it was one of the longest days of his short life. Tomorrow would be even longer.

CHAPTER 16

The fire in the stove had gone out when Cleo woke up with a chill. He looked at the clock but couldn't see it in the dark. He guessed it was close to two a.m. and realized he was still in his comfortable chair. *The kid must have thrown a blanket over me on the way out.*

Cleo couldn't shake his concerns about the kid going off into the wilderness. *Why did I wake up worrying so much about him? It's a real job to take this on at his age. He's so young. You know though, I think he's up to it. He's damn near a man. He has maturity. His time in life doesn't have to do with anything. Age doesn't matter out in the wilderness. What matters is that you can do the job or not.*

Cleo thought about reading on aboriginal and indigenous tribes having rites of passage for their young men. The girls in the tribes had puberty, and it was their rite of passage just the same. The kid needs his, no matter his age, biological maturity, or just plain mental maturity. *I do believe when it's time, it's time.*

I was about the same age when I did darn near the same thing. No one stood around and said, "No, you can't go, you're too young." They said, "Here you go, you'll need some gear and a gun." That was all there was to it. I left the next day. They mollycoddle the young ones these days. It's making a bunch of sissies out of them. That was the best thing that could've happened to me. And when the war came along, I was ready. Both Slim and I agreed that was what kept us alive in the trenches.

Cleo sat in the dark, thinking hard on how best to help the kid have his adventure and survive to talk about it. Rolling the situation over in his mind, he thought about sending him up to his old claim. The old cabin should be good with a little work, and there would be a few tools up there as well.

Butch could have the corral and the shed to sleep. If the kid fixes the fenced pasture he used for mules, Butch will have the field with plenty to eat and drink.

Now let's see, it's been 15 years since I boarded up the mine and shut down the stamp mill. The mill had a roof over it. The shaft wasn't much, but I think he would only need to dig another 20 feet to hit the hard rock. The vein would be there. Don't think he can work his way to the 20 feet in three weeks but maybe six weeks. He'll need to make the repairs first. That will take him time, and he has to do it first, or the rest of it won't come together. Guess that point needs to be driven home.

Cleo was feeling better now that he was working through all the concerns in his mind. *The kid has to keep food on the table. He can't starve himself by working too much. I'd better press him more about taking care of himself.*

He asks many questions, but he is doing pretty damn good, keeping his mouth shut and listening to what I say. Someone along the way taught him that good habit early. He can take it when I drive a point home with him.

I'll keep close tabs for a while, especially if he gets a notion to make a winter of it out there. Things can get tricky and go wrong fast. I do think that's what he's planning, although he doesn't know it yet. He doesn't talk much about it. He doesn't want to go home or go back to that school. Maybe someday, he'll fill me in on what happened there.

Now is there anything I forgot? He could use that new plastic turf at the sluice box. They say it works, and I have a new roll of it out in the tool shed. Think I'll send that with him along with the sawbuck pack and bags. He can leave his saddle here and pick it up on the way out. I better get some sleep and quit worrying about him. It will be another long day tomorrow. This old chair feels good with the blanket over me. Think I'll stay here and skip the bed, beings that I'm settled in already.

You'll be just fine, kid. Don't get ahead of yourself. That's all you got to do. Yeah, we'll talk about all these things over dinner tomorrow night. We need to include going over the miner rules.

Cleo knew he would help the kid on the road to becoming a man and whatever the adventure would bring him.

He closed his eyes and fell quickly back to sleep as if he had never awakened. The tension had left his face. He had the answers he was looking for to help the kid and was more at ease with him taking off for the wilderness to find his rite of passage.

CHAPTER 17

Daylight was breaking, and Butch was up to his old tricks, grunting and snorting. He seemed to like Gunner sleeping next to him. That way, he could tell him when it was time to start eating again. Gunner led him out to the small meadow, hobbled him, and made sure there was a bucket of water close.

Cleo was up and going strong. Gunner could smell the frying bacon and eggs with sourdough pancakes that drew him inside. Gunner thought he had died and gone to heaven. *Wow, that food smells so good.*

"Today," declared Cleo, "we will cover everything we talked about yesterday. We need to drill all this into you. That comes from my Army days, alright?" Gunner knew he had put in his time in the service.

"Also, young feller, I have mining books you can take with you that we need to go over. You'll need to read them all page for page. You won't go wrong." Not taking a breath, Cleo continued, "I want you to go up to my old mining claim. It has a cabin with a corral and a shed for Butch to sleep. Now, the mine should be just sitting there." He paused for effect.

"The stamp mill was working when I shut it down fifteen years ago. As I said, I only shut it down because of my health problems. All you need to do is clean up the stamp mill. Best use lots of lube while putting it back together. Next, pipe the water from the pond to the turbine water wheel, and you should be good to go."

"How far is it from here to your claim?" Gunner asked. Cleo was quick with his answer like he had made the trip hundreds of times before.

"A short half day's ride, maybe a half day's walk. With that old plug you got there, it might be a long day," he laughed. "You'll have to stop and gas him up a couple of times on the trail. Let him have a rest. You got to take care of him, and he'll take care of you."

"Will I need to take his pack off when we stop?"

"No, just ease the cinch around his belly."

"Okay. Where's the claim located?"

"It's on Ryan Creek. I'll show you on the Metsker topo map. You won't get lost. There's a trail that used to be a road once upon a time. You and Butch can follow it if you keep your eyes open."

"Yes, I'll do it," Gunner blurted out. "Then we'll split what I take out. Okay?"

"No," Cleo answered calmly. "You'll need all the help you can get, and that goes for your poke too. By making improvements, it will keep the claim active and between us. That's where it should be. Remember, the mine didn't peter out. It was my health and my age that did. That's why I shut it down.

"You only need to dig another 20 feet. There, the hard rock will be with a vein of gold. I just ran out of energy late in life. You need to take advantage of your youth while you have it. Life is a timed event for all of us, Gunner. One day, it will be your turn in the bucket just like I am now. Things will get complicated later on for you. Trust me on that.

"When I stopped working the claim in the 1940s, there was enough gold for wages. Gold was worth about $340 an ounce in September of 1947.

"I couldn't make it another winter with my health the way it was. Today, hearsay says the price is $280 an ounce. That's $60 less. With your youth, and the new plastic turf I'll send you out with you, it could make up the difference.

"I promise you it will be hard, back-breaking work, day after day." Cleo paused, thinking. "There were a couple of apple trees up there and a plum tree. You can pick and dry them. Pick plenty of berries. Keep an eye out for old bruin. He likes berries too."

Gunner appreciated Cleo's warning, and he had heard this before from Granny. He was starting to think that's what would get him if he didn't watch out.

"Wish I had a dog," Gunner was thinking out loud. "It could let me know when something is coming around that I need to know about."

"I had a dog once," Cleo said, sadness in his voice. "He saved my life. That was when a cougar was going to jump me. The dog got in between us. The cougar killed the dog, but I killed the cougar."

Gunner could tell that dog meant a lot to Cleo, especially since the dog gave its life for him.

"A man needs a dog out in the woods," Cleo agreed.

It's looking like I'm a man again.

The day went by too fast, and it was time for Gunner to pack his gear. Cleo had loaned him a sawbuck pack and bags for the tools he was also loaning him, and Butch would pack it all into the claim.

Gunner would lead Butch so he could carry more of the equipment, not having Gunner's weight on his back. Eventually, everything was packed except his bedroll. He put Butch in his stall for the night. When they were ready to go in the morning, the bedroll would go on Gunner's back along with the coat and leather gloves Cleo gave him. The 12-gauge shotgun would be in his hands like Cleo told him.

Over dinner, Gunner could tell Cleo had more to say. It looked like he had it all thought out before he started talking. That reminded Gunner of the time his coach was giving him his last talk before a big wrestling match.

Cleo began, "What I'm about to say is because I care about you, man to man. You might see these things come in handy sometimes. I don't think you can dig the twenty feet in three weeks. You might in six weeks, and then you would have something. Make the repairs first. You will need to do them, and that will take time. Don't worry about the mine until you have the repairs done.

"Have a good plan and stick to it. That's important. Do you get what I'm saying?"

Gunner nodded his head slowly. He wanted Cleo to know he was listening hard.

"You have to keep food on the table. You can't starve yourself by working too much. That will mess up everything. The truth is you eat like a young mule. If you don't keep your energy and strength up, you could come down with something. Think about these things I've talked about tonight when you go to bed, especially paying attention to detail."

All Gunner could say was, "Thank you for everything, Cleo."

Gunner got up from the table and started washing the dishes while Cleo went to his comfortable chair in the living room by the stove. He was sound asleep when Gunner threw a blanket over him and quietly said, "Goodnight, old friend."

Gunner knew he had received his marching orders. He sure had a bunch of things to mull over in his head. *Maybe a lot of that could be done on the trail tomorrow.*

Daylight arrived early with the warm summer sun. Gunner knew he needed to get going and he chose not to think about the things that could go wrong on this adventure. He took a few minutes to split up extra wood for Cleo's stove.

Gunner was quietly leading Butch past the back of the house for the trail. Cleo came out, "Whoa there, you two. You can't be leaving just like that without some oats and breakfast. Besides, I need you to copy down the miner's rules to take with you and hang in the cabin."

"Cleo, we have a long way to walk and need to make the cabin before dark." Gunner was anxious to be on his way.

"The trail is well-marked, and you have the map. Don't leave on an empty stomach. I know you. There won't be any stopping but to water and graze that old plug a few minutes."

"I didn't want to bother you. I was hoping you would sleep in this morning. We'll be back in less than three weeks."

Cleo wasn't taking no for an answer, and that was final. Gunner thought there were a lot of Germans in this country. Cleo must be one of them. Being hard-headed was one of his best parts.

Over breakfast, Cleo was kind but very stern. Gunner could hear the concern in his voice. He wanted to leave him with one, if not many, thoughts for his trip. Gunner listened carefully to every word.

"Be quick with what you do out there. That edge in the wilderness might save your life and your animal's life someday. You should practice being ready for anything. You never know what's coming around the corner. Some things want to eat you. Never let your guard down.

"You have your youth, so be sure and use it to your advantage. Most animals, and people, figure you aren't as fast as you are. Think ahead. It will keep you alive out there. Show those creatures you have no fear. That is the edge. If animals sense fear, their instinct will make them move on it.

"And do not forget good planning. It will save your bacon every time. Trust me on that."

"Thank you, Cleo," Gunner said gratefully. "I know, keep practicing. That will set you apart from others."

"One last thing," Cleo said. "Start reading the books I gave you. Set aside time every evening to read. You need to keep your mind growing as your body grows in the work and survival confronting you every day."

"Cleo, you said a mouthful. I'm only going out for three weeks to an old mine."

Cleo snapped a quick answer, "You never know, young person, what's around the next corner, and I want you to make it around that next corner. I know you are hearing me, and I want you to remember these things we talked about. Don't forget you live by the miner's rules, and you will never go wrong."

"Thank you, Cleo. We got to get going. Thank you for all your help, and I'll be back in three weeks, okay?" That was all he could say without getting all choked up. It was hard to say goodbye to his good friend.

Gunner went out back, un-hobbled Butch, tightened the pack cinch, and waved to Cleo as he led Butch by the front porch. Cleo stood there, smiling.

"Hey, wait a minute," Cleo said. "I almost forgot. I copied these down for you so you can read it later when you get to the cabin."

Cleo handed Gunner a hand-written list of ten numbered items he had penciled on a brown paper grocery sack. The writing was a little shaky, but he could tell Cleo was pressing hard on the old lead pencil to write it.

At the top, Gunner could see where the two words were scrawled out at the top, "Cowboy Rules," then scratched out and two new words were written under it in bold print: "MINERS' RULES."

Gunner smiled, folded it, and put it in his left breast pocket. As he shook his old friend's hand one more time, he stepped off the porch and picked up Butch's lead rope.

CHAPTER 18

The trail was well-marked, just like Cleo told him.

Butch was a good boy as Gunner led him. He was not jerking back or shying away from branches or bushes. *Could it be because there is a switch in my hand?*

The switch started bothering Gunner. He thought about that old schoolteacher hitting him. He threw the switch away to the side of the trail. Butch watched him do it. That was the best thing he could have done for them. "Come on, Butch. We'll stop soon so you can have a drink and graze some. You do know we still need to make the cabin before dark, right?"

While Butch grazed, Gunner took his .22 and shot two red squirrels for dinner. He cleaned and skinned them the right way. Gunner used the pocketknife Grandpa had given him rather than the bayonet, and this time, the knife was sharp. He did thank the squirrels for letting him have them for dinner. He had read in a book that this was something the Indians did, and he liked that. Besides, Cleo's Miner's Rules # 8 stated, "Be thankful and never waste what God gives you."

"Butch, we got to get going. It is still a long walk to get there, partner."

Gunner remembered what Cleo had drilled into him, "Always watch over your shoulder. This place is not safe. Some things out here will eat you." On the island, it was always safe.

By late afternoon, the sun was at the treetops on the far ridge. Gunner thought that might be the ridge above the cabin and he was excited. They were so close. It was a beautiful view with the mountainsides blanketed with trees sloping down to Ryan Creek at the bottom of the small valley. He could see the trail was still there with one big dogleg gradually going down to the creek, then a cleared road or wide trail. *That might be what Cleo used to bring in a wagon with his supplies and the old stamp mill he was telling me about.* Butch and Gunner carefully descended the steep trail and finally reached the valley floor.

The valley opened up to a lush, narrow pasture along the sides of a creek. A short quarter mile away was the other side of the valley. Gunner saw the cabin, just like Cleo said.

The shed was behind the cabin, and he could make out a lodgepole corral for his partner. An old sagging fence was wrapped around a field with lots of good wild grass for Butch's eating pleasure.

"Butch, I think I see your cafeteria, like junior high school." *Now that's a crummy thought.*

Gunner used his hatchet to pry off the two boards Cleo had nailed across the cabin door many years before. The nails were rusty, and the warped boards almost fell into his hands. With an easy pull, he opened the door and looked inside.

He looked back to Butch. The old horse had started munching on the tall, meadow grass where he stood, the lead rope dragging along as he ate.

Gunner looked for little critters like field mice that might have made themselves a home. Dust covered everything, and the air was musty from being closed up for so many years.

He knew this cabin would work out perfectly with his quick glance. He liked it. With some living in here and elbow grease, he could make it smell and look like a home in no time. The wood cookstove was sturdy and well-vented, so he could use it right away.

A cast iron pan sat on the stove next to the sink with a four-pane window above. The counter had open shelves above and cupboards next to the shelves. A double bunk bed with rusty springs and two worn-out mattresses rolled up to the head of the bunks lined the other wall. In the middle of the room was a rickety wooden table and two chairs.

Gunner guessed the cabin was about ten feet by fifteen feet at the most. It seemed huge for him. He had spent his summers living in small fishing boats.

He walked outside and looked back to the cabin and could tell the outside walls were lapboards. The shake roof was sorely in need of repair. He had seen the last of the daylight coming through the holes in the top before he went outside.

It was hard to see with the sun going down, but he could see Butch patiently waiting to get rid of his pack and doing some rapid grazing before it got too dark. The sweet, untouched meadow grass was just what Butch wanted. Gunner loosened the pack and slid it off as Butch stood munching. Gunner hauled the gear inside and dumped it on the cabin floor.

He found an old bucket that looked like it would hold water and went to the creek behind the shed. He filled the pail with cold sweet water for Butch and his canteen for himself. He tried to look around outside, but it was getting too dark. He led Butch to the shed for the night and received a whinny of appreciation.

Inside the cabin, Gunner stoked the stove and had a friendly fire for the squirrel dinner he had shot and cleaned earlier in the day. His bedroll went on the old, smelly mattress just like it belonged there.

After dinner, Gunner lay on top of his new bunk bed. He was thankful there was plenty of grass for Butch and the small stream of water for them both, as well as the bed in the cabin to sleep on.

He had one last thought before falling to sleep. *Things are just fine, Cleo. We'll be good here. You knew that all along, didn't you? Thank you again. I promise I won't forget the lessons you taught me.*

In the morning, Butch and Gunner began to settle into their new home. Butch didn't seem to mind the hobbles as long as he had plenty of grass to eat. The water was close by, and a shady tree to stand under for his naps during the heat of the day.

Gunner found a broom and started his cleaning chores. The place was already looking better.

Next, he had to prop up the outhouse. Cleo had even left a Sears & Roebuck catalog from the 1940s next to the sitting hole. That would be for his reading pleasure and anything else that paper might come in handy for.

Now came the job of feeding himself again. That turned out to be a bigger job than Gunner thought it would be. Cleo made it loud and clear that he was to take care of himself, and Gunner believed him.

An inventory of his food supplies showed he only had a couple of days left with what Cleo and Granny had given him.

Okay, let's do the easy stuff first. There is not a grocery store down the street. There're supposed to be apple and plum trees around the back of the cabin.

Yep, there they were—beautiful, tasty fruit hanging on the trees waiting for his picking. A bunch of apples and plums went to the cabin to eat later. Gunner was careful not to eat too many, or he would be visiting the outhouse he had just propped up out back.

Gunner hiked over to the dogleg with a small pot from the kitchen in his hand. He remembered seeing berry bushes on the side of the hill in the dusk of evening light. He found the bushes again, and the luscious, juicy berries practically fell into his pot. *That's a good start. Now for some meat.* There was still a little bit of squirrel leftover from last night.

"Take care of the critters first," Granny would say, and she was right. If he got the old fence line mended right away, Butch could roam free as he pleased. Gunner never liked the idea of hobbles. He sure didn't want anyone to hobble him.

Lucky for Gunner, there was an old roll of barbed wire, staples, and a rusty pair of fencing pliers in the shed to help him get started. He shared the big news with Butch, "Looks like a day or more of work on the fence. Then I can get up to the mine, and you, old-timer, can have your freedom in the pasture. That will give me my freedom to make more repairs and not be worried about you."

While tending to the fence line, Gunner noticed a lot of wildlife on and around the field. He saw mice, a porcupine, and a yellow-bellied marmot. That was good news. Now, he wouldn't have to starve after all. There was another critter Gunner could hear out in the woods but couldn't see. And that was the ever-wily, wild turkey. He had read about them. They were hard to see and even harder to shoot. These were crafty birds.

He worked on the fence, keeping the .22 or shotgun close by just in case he saw something to eat. He planned on finishing the fence repairs and rounding up something to eat at the same time.

Gunner kept working on his post hole digging and wire stapling while he thought about how to catch or shoot one of those wily turkeys. Slowly, he came up with a plan. In the early morning, just before daylight, he would put some of Butch's oats by the stream where he had seen turkey tracks. Then, he could hide in the brush and wait with the shotgun to ambush one of those giant birds.

Gunner had seen all kinds of wildlife tracks by the stream. He figured that would be a great place to set up a salt lick someday. On the island and at the ranch, they would set a block of salt out in the field for the cows and horses. There were times early in the morning when Gunner would see a white-tailed deer, or an elk, stop by for a lick or two. He made a mental note to put a small block of salt on the shopping list for town. That would bring deer near to the cabin, and he would take only what he could eat.

It was dark again before he got all the chores done, including feeding himself, cleaning up the kitchen, and getting ready for a good night's sleep. When Gunner went to bed, he saw the moon was out, and he heard the coyotes or wolves howling back and forth. *There could be a wolf pack around here.* He needed to stay alert since their tracks were at the creek also.

Gunner was sleeping so soundly the next morning he almost didn't wake up in time to set his turkey trap. Butch would have to wait for him to get back before he could let him out. Sometimes, Butch was like a big old puppy dog following him around. That wouldn't work while Gunner was trying to get one over on a bunch of hungry turkeys.

He grabbed a cup of Butch's grain and the shotgun. Using the flashlight, he snuck quietly to the creek. He was hoping the turkeys weren't up yet. Finding the tracks leading to the stream, he spread the grain across them then quickly got behind a big log with the shotgun loaded and the hammer cocked. A pine tree bough hid the top of him and the gun.

He was ready just in time. Daylight was breaking, and Gunner could barely make out the wild turkeys. *Boy, they are beautiful.* It was so exciting. *Slow down now, be patient,* he told himself. *Don't hurry, dummy.* Then, he saw him, a mid-sized tom strutting out in front of the flock.

All Gunner needed was one tom. He reminded himself again, *Don't hit the others with the shot. Take your time, deep breath, let it out easy, hold it, and squeeze the trigger slow...ly.*

Boom! Smoke and feathers went everywhere. He could hardly see through the dim morning light. There was the turkey, lying on the ground like it was asleep.

By the time Gunner got the turkey plucked and dressed, half the morning was gone. He enjoyed doing everything and was happy knowing he had dinner hanging, all wrapped up, in the shed, but the whole process had taken a lot more time than he thought it would.

The fence repair was going good except for the dozen big lodgepole pines he had to replace on the corral. That slowed him down. With steady work, finally, the corral was done. Two and a half days he had spent on just the fence, but the chores were caught up.

Now I can go up and see what's going on at the mine. Gunner had started a make-shift calendar by carving a notch on the fence rail every morning when he put Butch out to pasture. *Darn, there are eight notches on that blasted fence already.* Over a week had been used up. *Jeez, where has the time gone?*

"Twelve more notches, and we will need to leave," Gunner told Butch that morning. "That's less than two weeks, and I haven't even seen the mine yet. We got to hustle, boy! I am planning on coming back after I take you home."

Gunner put Butch out that morning and headed for the mine. Even though he couldn't see Butch from the mine, he knew the open space of his fenced pasture would keep him safe from predators. Old Butch would have room to decide if he wanted to fight or take flight.

Gunner enjoyed the walk through the forest. It was north of the cabin and up the hillside about 100 yards. The sky was clear, and the sun was bright. The mine was why he had come, and he was itching to get started.

His first look at the mine showed it was a mess. Gunner thought even that was being kind. *Wow, this is going to take some work and I don't have that much time.*

Someone had broken down the boarded-up door at the mouth of the mine. Gunner wondered how someone could damage a hole in the side of a mountain nosing around. All the bracing timbers were intact, but the mine shaft itself was small. *Could it be because Cleo was a smaller-sized man? In height maybe, but never in stature.*

Inside the mine was a broken rusty four-wheeled muck cart on tracks that needed fixing. Gunner had read that after drilling and blasting, he would need to start the "mucking out" process including loading rock in the muck cart, hauling it out, dumping it, then getting more rock from the mine. Just like that, trip after trip.

Gunner was glad he had brought the old carbide lamp from Granny's barn and had remembered the can of pellets to make the gas. The light would let him see his way into the end of the mine.

Cleo was right again. There was no hard rock all the way in. Now it all made sense. Cleo figured another twenty feet of digging to reach the hard rock and the vein of gold.

Cleo had to be pulling gold out from this loose stuff. So, the dirt and rock had to come out of the mine. It could have given him a grubstake to pay for the gear he would need for the winter.

Gunner left the mine to check on the stamp mill outside. Maybe he could do something there. The stamp mill was mechanical, and the books Cleo sent with him would help. Gunner had a lot of experience repairing mechanical things on the fish boats. *Shoot, I was fixing Sister's bike before I was seven years old.*

Below the mouth of the mine was the old, rusty stamp mill in a sorry-looking, half-collapsed, wooden shed. *Cleo probably left a can of grease in the shed. He did say, "Use lots of lube on it."* Gunner hoped to save the stamp mill but was sure the whole shed would need replacing before the snow came.

A double-jaw crusher sat on the north side of the stamp mill, directly below the end of the muck cart track. By feeding up to twelve-inch rock to it, the crusher would fracture the big rocks into smaller rocks to fit into the stamp mill. The stamp mill had small hammers about the size of a soup-can to crush the smaller rocks as they came from the crusher. The stamp mill made the rocks about the size of a dime or crushed them to "fines," according to Cleo's books.

From the stamp mill, the small fines were washed through the sluice box, which would separate the gold from the junk or "tailings." That would be where Cleo's new plastic turf would go. Still thinking the process through, Gunner remembered what Cleo had said. "Gold is six times heavier than rock, so the heavy stuff, gold, goes straight to the bottom of the sluice box, and the larger stones wash out to a tailings' pile. Then the miner, you, eventually need to move the tailing pile." Gunner could see why Cleo was grumpy with him for not having a shovel.

The equipment could run for a week or two before he needed to clean out the sluice box. It meant sorting the big stuff by hand, rinsing the plastic turf, and finally, using a gold pan to separate the gold from the fines. Those books of Cleo's were worth reading so that he could understand how everything worked.

Cleo said to read the books page for page. After that, Gunner thought he should add "read the books all over again."

He needed power to run both the jaw crusher and the stamp mill. The power came from a giant water wheel geared down to set the stamp mill at the right speed. The gearbox on the water wheel looked like it was out of some kind of truck. Gunner noticed there wasn't any water coming out of the pipe to run the water wheel. *Here we go, one more problem on the road to success. There must be a pond up the hill to hold the water to be piped down to the water wheel.* Gunner remembered Cleo taking the time to explain the process and equipment up above. Cleo made him draw a picture on a brown, paper grocery sack as he talked.

Darn, that's back at the cabin with my gear. I'll pull that out tonight and look it over real close. Gunner sat on a nearby boulder and thought carefully about each piece of mining equipment and what he should repair first.

He decided the sluice box would be first because he needed it to restamp the tailings and take out the leftover gold. His experience working with the old man rebuilding boats would help him with this job. He needed lumber, a saw, and nails.

Gunner's eyes wandered over toward the stamp mill shed. He exclaimed, "Thank you, Cleo!" The shed had enough lumber in it, and with nails, he could fix the sluice box. He knew he had to replace the shed boards before winter anyway. Next, he would need water for the sluice box either by piping it in or hauling it. He liked the pipe idea best because it was already there. The real problem was that the old pipe was rotted out. *Darn thing will need several leaks plugged or patched up before it'll be usable.*

Gunner had a long conversation with himself to convince him that re-stamping the tailing pile would work. He would ponder it over while he was rebuilding the sluice box. He remembered the old man telling stories about his Uncle Fin having a mine during the Depression. He and his partner would only work on the tailing piles and always had money.

Rebuilding the sluice box was about all Gunner would be able to do with the few days left at the claim. Butch needed to go home. Thoughts of working the pile gave him hope. Surely, Cleo had left a few gold specks for him. He wanted to have something to show for his time.

Gunner knew this was a gamble at best. It all could be for naught.

CHAPTER 19

*O*k, fine. The old tailings' pile it is, and that's all the time I have. If there was nothing in the tailings' pile, Gunner would buck up and take Butch home. Then he would turn right around and come straight back up to the mine to dig out the last 20 feet for the vein by hand. Gunner knew not having a drill or dynamite for the mine made the work slower, but he could hand dig the twenty feet.

I'll start by re-stamping the tailing pile and running that through the sluice box using the new plastic turf. Cleo swore that was the new process. He said it was like magic compared to the old days when he was mining.

Gunner's brain began to wander as he made his way back down the hill to the cabin. He was tired, and the sun was going down fast, as always. He was careful to stay on the path, not to trip over anything while being so deep in thought.

One thing depended on the next thing to make everything work. There was one more thing Gunner had to resolve. He had put Butch out in the morning, and now he put him back in his stall for the evening. *Don't forget to feed him or yourself, for that matter.* There just weren't enough hours in the day. *I wish there was someone here just to do the chores.*

When Gunner was growing up on the island, he didn't need anyone, only a place to sleep. He could live off one meal a day, and Mom always had that for him. Here, there were just too many moving parts. *Cleo said things would get more complicated as I got older, but I sure didn't expect it this soon.*

Gunner was too tired to think anymore. Later that evening, he tried to read a mining book with the flashlight while frying the fresh turkey meat and studying the drawing he had made at the table.

It was useless. He couldn't focus on anything other than feeding himself.

Ten minutes later, Gunner fell into his bunk bed and was instantly sound asleep.

Both Butch and Gunner settled into a routine of getting up with the sun each day. Gunner would put together a bite of breakfast then lead Butch out to his pasture, checking the fence and surroundings to make sure Butch was good for the day.

Then he headed up to the mine, making repairs first and hauling tailings off the old tailings' pile to the crusher, stamp mill, and finally washing the crushed fines in the sluice box. A large part of the day was spent stopping leaks in the rotted-out pipe. This pipe was necessary as it carried the water to power the water wheel that powered the crusher and stamp. Most of the time, he didn't need to use the crusher because Cleo had already stamped the ore and all Gunner had to do was re-stamp the ore into fines. Then he loaded the fines into the sluice box, ran the water from the water wheel through the sluice box, and washed the gold out, hopefully.

The more water Gunner ran, the more rags he had to put on the holes for patches, wrapping a line around the spots like they did on the boats. They called the cover a "Pedro."

Gunner would come back to the cabin with more questions at the end of each day than he had left with that morning.

Today, Gunner had to rebuild the edge of the pond above the dam. It was easy to see that if he raised the pond sides, he would have a couple more hours of stamp mill time before he ran out of water. And to further complicate things, he was running low on grub and still had six days to go. The fruit was holding out but killing something for meat to eat sounded better to him.

After Gunner put Butch out in the field early the next morning, he wandered around the valley bottom with the 12-gauge shotgun, stumbling on a covey of quail. Wanting to make a single shot count, he fired into the center of the flock. As the smoke and noise cleared, four dead birds lay on the ground. Off to the side, another two were flapping around.

Gunner finished the two off by wringing their necks as he didn't want to waste the 12-gauge shells for that. Then he sat down to pluck and clean all six birds. Once wrapped up individually, he hung them in the mine, where it was cool, to cure a bit. Gunner wasn't sure how that worked, but they did it with elk and deer on the ranch, so he figured it should work the same for game birds.

He picked up his lunch at the cabin and walked back up the hill to the mine. Daylight was already burning, and he needed to get work done. At the end of the day, he would find out how he did when he cleaned out the sluice box. Tomorrow, he had to head to the ranch.

Gunner turned the water off from the upper pond and noticed some small gold flakes on top of the sluice box.

"Wow, this might work after all!" It would be nice to have something in his poke when he left. Any gold would let him go to town and buy a load of desperately needed gear.

Cleo had often reminded him to make a good plan and stick to it. He was sure now that he would not stay at Granny's anymore. This cabin would be his home. When Mother comes to visit, he would be here. He knew he was pulling all his own levers now. There would be no more old man, no school, and no town eating away at the back of his head.

He knew he would rather fight it out here for his dinner than go back to all he left behind him. Here, he didn't have a lot of those terrible thoughts cluttering his head anymore. He was too busy, and he loved it here. Here at the claim, it was a peaceful place, like the island.

Tomorrow would be his twentieth day away from Granny's. It was time to take Butch home and get more grub and gear in town. Gunner was hoping there would be a young dog in the cards for him on his way back to the claim. Company would be appreciated. He planned on getting back up to the mine before Mother and old man winter showed up.

Gunner wanted to get Mother's visit done and out of the way. He figured the better show he could make, the better the chances of convincing her that he was staying. Dealing with Mother was a job he didn't look forward to.

"Butch, this is your last day in the pasture, so make the most of it."

Gunner put a plug in the pipe up at the pond and made sure there was an overflow to keep the bank from washing out while he was gone. He shut down the stamp mill and started to clean out the sluice box.

Smiling ear to ear, he congratulated himself. *Not bad!* After cleaning up the sluice box and plastic "grass," he had a beautiful pouch full of gold. *Thank you again, Cleo. You sent me to the right place and showed me the right things to do.*

Gunner boarded up the mine to keep old bruin from making a bedroom out of it.

As he walked back down to the cabin, he realized he needed to figure out what to leave and what to take. He knew he had to return everything borrowed from Cleo. He worked up an inventory in his head, including the sawbuck pack and gun. *For tools, like the shovel and pick, I'll buy Cleo new ones.*

Most of all, Butch, his old sidekick for the last three weeks, needed to go home to his herd. That would take a lot of worry off of Gunner's mind. Putting Butch in the shed that night for the last time, Gunner gave him a rubdown. *I'll miss you, old friend.*

Then he remembered Granny. *I'll have to face the music with Granny.* He knew she would order him to stay and wait for Mother. There were no more doubts in his mind about living at the claim. He would tell Granny, "I'm sorry, Granny. I can't do that. Thanks anyway, I've got to go, the claim is my home now."

He rose before the sun, knowing what was ahead of him and not looking forward to it. He hated disagreeing with the ones he loved, and Granny was next to Mother on that list, even if they didn't always get along.

All of his gear, except his bedroll, was left in the cabin. Gunner nailed the door shut so old bruin wouldn't stop in there to rest either. *Why did I keep thinking bruin will show up?* All the time he was there, he hadn't seen any sign of bear.

The bedroll was over his shoulder and the bayonet was on the suspender of the web belt. It had become another part of him. He wore it all the time, just like Cleo had instructed him. The .22 and 12-gauge went with him too. Gunner rode Butch with the halter and the sawbuck. He wanted to be at Cleo's by noon and Granny's by late afternoon.

"Okay, Butch, we got to roll, and we will be a day early to keep Granny happy." Being a day early in returning was important to him so no one could gripe. After all, it was Granny's rule. He needed to make their place before evening, then sleep in the barn.

Cleo could come by the next morning and pick him up in the daylight to go to town and pick up his supplies. Then he would go back to the claim on foot. Gunner didn't want the responsibility of Butch on his hands anymore. If something happened to that old plug, it would be his hide.

It was a good thing the time was middle of summer, and most of the varmints were fat and happy in their homes. "Butch, we got to make time to get to Cleo's, and then we'll go on down to Granny's to face the music."

There was that gnawing pit in his stomach again. The plan was, at all costs, to keep his cool. He had been thinking of buying that young mule from Norman, and he didn't want to blow his chance by being late. A mule could do the work of four men up here.

He and Butch started toward the dogleg and up to the ridge. Butch was smart. He figured out they were headed home and picked up the pace, walking faster than his usual sleepy stumbling walk.

Gunner noticed the trail was easier to see on the way out than it was on the way in, the markings along the path much clearer. He had learned a lot about the land these past few weeks. It was such a great place to be, and he had never been happier.

Since they left at daylight, the return trip took only four hours at the fast pace of Mr. Going Home. They reached Cleo's mid-morning. Coming out to greet them, Cleo had a big smile, "Well! How did it go, young feller?"

Cleo followed as they walked to the barn to feed Butch some of Cleo's grain and unload the pack. "I want to share what I worked out of the tailings' pile," he told Cleo, smiling broadly. "I want to split my take with you. I'm planning to stay up at the claim, and I want to buy it from you."

Cleo put his thumbs in his belt. "No, I will grubstake you for working the claim, and yes, I will sell it to you when you get enough ahead."

Gunner turned from feeding Butch and shook Cleo's hand. "Wow! Thank you! That means so much to me. How can I ever thank you?"

Cleo nodded to show his appreciation for how well Gunner had done and his excitement. "What's the rest of your plan?"

Gunner wanted to show Cleo that he had thought out everything carefully. "I'm planning on getting down to Granny's this afternoon to take Butch back. I suspect she doesn't want me going back up to the mine, so I would like to ask you a favor."

"Ok, what is that?"

"Could you pick me up at daylight in front of the barn tomorrow morning and run me into town?"

"Alright. Which town do we need to go to, Elk City or Grangeville?"

"Probably Grangeville, then we could go to the Assayer's office and cash in some of my poke. I need more supplies, but not too much." Gunner paused to think. "I'm backpacking on this next trip and will have only so much space to pack things. I'm planning to hike in on a shortcut I found. That will give me an extra day to work in the mine."

Cleo listened carefully, watching Gunner talk and brush Butch down.

Gunner stopped brushing and looked at Cleo. "What are your thoughts on the shortcut? Maybe we could talk about that tomorrow on our way into Grangeville? That is if you could take me in. I'd be happy to pay for lunch and gas. I don't want to get you in trouble with Norman and Granny."

Cleo smiled again. "They came by looking for you." He paused. "I filled them in on what you were doing. I told them I thought you would be fine. Not sure if either one bought what I was selling."

"Guess they probably had to tell Mother something, huh?"

"Yes. And of course, I can run you into town," Cleo said with a big grin. "I want to make sure you get good equipment and that you don't get taken when you cash in your gold. We also need to stop and get you more clothes. It will be getting cold soon."

"I know you're right. I need to get enough gear up there before the snow starts, right?"

Cleo stared at Gunner and laughed, "Oh, so you're staying for winter now, is it?" Gunner grinned and nodded.

"Hell Gunner, I know a lot of grown men who can't make it through the winter up there. I do respect your feelings and all, but you're just a wee bit on the green side, my young friend."

Gunner felt a lecture coming. He stopped brushing Butch and leaned up against a bale of hay to hear what Cleo had to say.

Cleo cranked up the serious tone. "I think it's unusual that you would be sticking your neck out that far, wanting to stay up there for the winter, that is.

"I know you think you've figured it out by now. But the winters are harsh, and there is a lot to do just surviving, let alone caring for animals and then working the mine." Cleo took a breath. "Believe me when I say it is a cruel place up there. However, if anyone can make it up there, I think you have what it takes to do it."

Gunner stood straight up, having trouble hiding the excitement on his face. "I know! I can't help myself! I like it up there. I'm finding a lot of peace, and I've made a few dollars with the work I've done." He paused to catch his breath. "You haven't heard the best part yet. I've been making my money by going back through your old tailings' pile. That plastic turf stuff has paid off. When I get the tailings cleaned up, then I'll go into the mine and start doing some real work."

Cleo patiently listened as Gunner went on and on, talking about his adventure, unable to contain his excitement. "I'll need a drill and some powder to do the blasting to fight the rock out of there. The real problem I see coming is that I'll have to dry pan once everything freezes up. Could you help me figure that one out? I haven't got a clue about working when the water is frozen."

Cleo furrowed his brow, thought a minute, and said, "You're right about freezing up. You can't work the tailings like you are now. The snow will be taller than a tall giraffe up there this winter. It could be an easy six to eight feet where the drifts build up."

Gunner gave a loud sigh. "Guess there's lots of time to talk about that later. I need to get down to see Granny. I'll be waiting for you at daylight in front of the barn if that's okay?"

"No problem, young feller. You and that old-timer horse there get home. Give him a large helping of grain. Then let him know that he's retired, and he won't have to go chasing off with some youngster up in the hills anymore."

Gunner chuckled. "Your pack board and gear are here in the shed, and the 12-gauge is on the front porch along with the shells. Can't thank you enough, good friend. See you in the morning. If you hear someone clomping around your barn late tonight, you'll know it didn't go so well down at the ranch."

Butch and Gunner made it to Granny's in an hour. The ride was downhill, and Butch was at a trot most of the way. He knew he was on his way home. They went straight to the barn, and Butch got the first-class brushing he deserved along with a big helping of Norman's grain. The old plug was a happy horse.

When Gunner led Butch up to the pasture on the hillside behind the ranch house, the other horses whinnied and ran back and forth along the fence. They were welcoming Butch home. Gunner and Butch made it to the gate, and the herd met them.

Gunner wished he could say the same for himself. The critters knew each other and were what they call "herd bound." Probably what people do too when they're with other people they like. Gunner hoped someday he could find his herd to hang around. It didn't look so bad. He noticed the horses and mules stayed close to one another. Gunner already didn't feel welcome on this visit.

He saw Granny watching from the back window as he walked through the dried field grass down to the back of the house. She didn't come out to greet him as the horses and mules did for Butch. That told him where he stood. There was going to be something said when he got inside. *Alright, let's get this done with, once and for all.*

Gunner automatically filled his arm with stove wood and knocked on the back door. Granny was in the kitchen, stirring a pot of something on the old wood stove. "Come on in."

Gunner went in, laying the wood in the bin next to the stove. He sat down at the table, no hug, no hello, just sat there. Gunner spoke first, "How's it going, Granny?"

She said with an even tone in her voice, "We're not too happy with you. You have been gone for a long time, and we'd like to know where the hell you've been."

This wasn't what he had hoped. Gunner hardly ever heard her swear. "I thought maybe you'd be saying that. I went up to Cleo's like we talked about, and then I left for the wilderness."

Gunner paused. Granny didn't say anything. He continued, "Cleo told me you stopped by to see if I'd been around. Well, as luck would have it, Cleo sent me to his old mining claim, and that's where I set up housekeeping."

Granny kept stirring the pot on the stove. Gunner could see she was still listening, so he went on talking.

"I got to working on repairs at the claim. Butch was happy in a corral with a shed next to it at night. And he had a fenced pasture with a creek running through it during the day.

"It only took me a couple of days to fix the fence. Butch was happy all the time we were there, and I brought him in every night. I know Norman would skin me alive if anything happened to that old horse."

She was still not talking.

"I would go up to the mine every day and was able to put enough food on the table to feed myself. We were in good shape there. I got all of the equipment working and pulled some pay dirt out as well. Got enough to go to town and get more gear, then get right back up to the claim. That's what I'm planning."

Woo wee, it was out, he thought. He did it as quietly and quickly as he could with a bunch of respect thrown in. So now, the five-foot German lady with a bunch of experience in the world would be sizing him up. Gunner wasn't sure which way the wind would blow today. He did know she would rather deal with a situation calmly than fly off the handle.

Granny turned and stood there quietly, looking him over. "No, I don't think so. I think you will be staying here until your mother gets here. That should be in about three weeks. Then she'll pack you up and take you home where you belong."

Gunner could see Granny was not going to be happy when he disagreed with her. He was determined to stick with his plan. It had to be. He would do it as carefully as he could. Gunner was glad Norman wasn't in the room, or he would need to pull out of the conversation altogether. Gunner couldn't discuss anything with Norman there unless it was his idea.

"Granny, I've decided that I'll be staying up at the mine for the next three weeks. If you feel that you have to tie me to the front porch, you can." He paused to let things sink in. "I'll go ahead and chew off the ropes you tie me with, and I'll be gone before the sun comes up."

She stopped to open the oven door and the aroma of fresh baked bread wafted through the kitchen. She remained silent, but he knew she was giving him the respect to at least hear him out. "I am not trying to hurt your feelings or be disrespectful. I've decided this is the best I can do for myself. You've helped me out at every turn of the trail. You and Norman have been kind to me, and I appreciate everything you've done. Now it's time for me to go and do this on my own. I can't go back to the house or school from where I came. I'm not going to let them hit me anymore."

Granny turned, staring at the young man sitting in her kitchen chair. She could see he was stuck somewhere between being a man and a boy. A couple of minutes went by. It felt like hours to Gunner, and then he could see a small smile forming at the corners of her mouth.

"You have thought this over, haven't you?" she asked.

"Yes, ma'am, I have," he answered respectfully. "As I said, I won't go back to that school or the old man's house. I love Mother very much. I don't want to hurt her feelings, but I will do what I have to do for myself. Granny, I would like to take all responsibility for the care of me out of yours and Norman's hands. These last three weeks with Butch up at the mine have made me a better person. You'll see that as time passes."

She nodded slightly, and her smile got a little bigger. Gunner could see that she understood he was slowly becoming his own man. *I love you, Granny. Thanks for believing in me.*

"Mother will understand the fact that I did this on my own. You didn't have anything to do with me going into the backcountry. I promise you I will be back in three weeks, and I will be standing here when she arrives. Is her date for sure?"

"Well, you make several good points," Granny said, thoughtfully. "I think you should go do what you have to do. Yes, the date is firm. Your mother will be here in three weeks. You are to be here, or I will do the skinning. Do you understand that, young man?"

I'll be darned. I'm a young man now. She had to put her foot down somewhere, and it might as well be at my showing up on time. That worked for him. "Thank you, Granny," he said gratefully.

She asked, "Have you had anything to eat lately?"

Why were grandparents so wise? He answered her with a clear, "Not lately," as they heard Norman's boots stomping up the front steps.

Granny said quickly, "You go out back and get cleaned up for dinner. We will have a nice quiet dinner, I promise."

She knew a whole lot more than she let on. Thanking her with a quick hug, Gunner spun around and was out the back door before Norman got to the kitchen.

He didn't want to listen to what Norman had to say. Gunner gave Norman and Granny enough time to talk and have their plan made when he got back into the kitchen to sit down for dinner. The meal went well. Norman asked, "How is Butch doing?"

"He's fat and happy to be home. Up at the claim, I fixed the pasture fence for him, and he had a nice stall to sleep in every night."

"That's good. Was the old boy any trouble for you?"

"He was great, especially when I borrowed a pack for him from Cleo. There was a lot of gear that Cleo wanted to send with me. Leading Butch up to the claim was easy. We stopped twice so he could drink water and graze. Thanks for showing me how to hobble him. It took two and a half days to fix the pasture fence, and then we didn't have to use the hobbles anymore.

"The rest of the time we were up there, he was free to wander the pasture. He loved the sweet, untouched meadow grass. There was a good stream running through the pasture and plenty of shade trees for him to take nice, long naps. He might have gained a pound or two. And he was happy to see the herd when we came home."

Gunner kept talking. For once, Norman was interested in what he had to say.

"It was a nice place. We stayed at Cleo's old mining claim. He had started a tunnel, but his health made him close it down. There was a cabin to stay in and the shed, like I said, for Butch to sleep in."

Gunner's gut feeling was that Norman was more interested in Butch than in him. That was okay. *Sometimes, we worry about the critters and assume people will take care of themselves. We have to see that our animals are well-cared for because they do a lot of work for us.*

Gunner was starting to realize how much he had depended on Butch while they were gone.

"Sounds like you found a place for yourself, but the question is, is it paying?" Norman couldn't hold back his curiosity.

"I've been working the tailings Cleo left fifteen years ago, and they are paying more than I could make as a ranch hand."

Norman raised his eyebrows. "After they had already worked the ore, how can you get something out of it?"

Gunner explained, "After stamping the tailings for the second time, I ran them through the sluice box with new stuff Cleo calls 'miner's mat,' and it worked. I had to rebuild the sluice box to lengthen it and put in more riffles. It ran every day we were there, and I only did one cleanout just before Butch and I came out. That gave me enough to buy what I need when I go into town tomorrow.

"So, what do you need in town?"

"Guns and grub for starters, some warmer clothes, and other gear like an alarm clock, writing paper, and more books on mining. In another couple of weeks, I'll start digging in the mine. It looks like another twenty feet to go until I hit bedrock."

"That will take time, won't it, to dig that out?"

This was the game Norman liked to play. Gunner called it the cat and mouse game. Norman asked questions until he got someone cornered, and Gunner wasn't falling for it this time. A blind man could see through this old game.

"Not actually," Gunner answered. "It's soft overburden. Just a lot of shoveling and some pick work, not like the outhouse hole." Gunner didn't give him a chance to ask another question. He stood and spoke directly to Granny.

"I want to thank you for the great dinner, Granny. I'll fill the wood box and be sleeping in the barn if you will excuse me, please?" Gunner didn't wait for an answer. He went straight outside and loaded up wood for the wood box. He dropped it in the box and said goodnight.

As he started for the barn, Granny offered, "You can sleep in the house. You don't have to sleep in the barn, you know."

"No, thank you," he said. "I need to sleep in the barn. That way, when Cleo picks me up at daylight, I won't be bothering you and Norman. Thank you again for the great dinner this evening. Nice visiting with you both. I appreciate the fact that you understand what I'm doing and why."

He wasn't sure they were buying into what he was doing, and Gunner didn't much care. He wanted out of there without a bunch of hurt feelings. Still not giving Norman a chance to comment, he repeated to Granny, "I do promise that I will be here in three weeks for Mother's arrival."

CHAPTER 20

Gunner closed the front door behind him and walked across the road to the side of the barn where he had dropped his bedroll. There was still plenty of daylight, and he wasn't sleepy yet.

After laying out his bedroll on a pile of hay, Gunner went to where Norman kept the brushes for the horses. He pulled out a curry comb and brush and headed to the herd up on the hillside.

This was where he wanted to be. His heart was with the animals standing on the hillside. These critters didn't ask for anything other than pure, simple love and attention. Gunner had plenty of love and care for them. He didn't have much for most of the people back home if the truth were known. At the claim, he could feel the tension inside him melting away more every day. There, Gunner didn't have to put up with other people. That was a relief for him after hating school for so long and the old man with his bad temper. He hated living around all that. Up at the claim, all he had to think about was the everyday things, like what he had to do to survive and make the mine pay. He didn't have to think about anything beyond Ryan Creek. Those last three weeks were the best in his young life.

Coming back here for one evening took him back to where he didn't want to be. From here on out, Gunner decided he wanted to spend his time up at the claim. More than anything, he only wanted to be left alone. Now the thought about how nice it would be to have a mule and a dog kept coming up.

He was confident everything would come together eventually. He knew he just had to keep working toward his goal. He hoped someday he would be able to look back and laugh at everything he had left on the coast. For now, it was right for him to spend time with these animals. It helped him clear his head. The animals never asked him where he came from or what his grades were.

He already missed his old friend Cleo. He looked forward to seeing him tomorrow morning and going into Grangeville. *Cleo is a good friend. He doesn't make a lot of demands on me, and if he's got something on his mind, he tells a person up front.*

Butch was up in the pasture visiting with his family. The one Gunner was most interested in was the young yearling mule he had spent time with earlier this summer. He was the one Gunner wanted to buy from Norman when he came out on the next trip. That mule had a real personality and Gunner liked him from the first time they met. He was friendly, handled effortlessly, and was more than happy to please.

Gunner walked out into the field where the horses and mules stood together, stopping about ten feet away. Butch wasn't sure if he wanted to come over and say hello. The young mule remembered him and approached. He walked up and put his face up next to Gunner's face as he quietly stood there.

"I sure could use you at the mine. We could pack a lot of gear back in before winter comes and locks things down." Gunner began brushing him down from stem to stern as they say on the fish boats. The mule patiently stood there. Some animals like people, and some don't. Gunner thought this one does like people, well, him anyway. Gunner checked each hoof to see how he acted being handled. The young mule stood quietly.

By now, old Butch was jealous. He sauntered up to Gunner's backside and rubbed his nose up against him as he finished brushing the young mule.

Gunner turned to Butch, "Do you want some brushing too?" The horse rubbed his face up against Gunner's chest, so he had to give his old friend one more rub-down for the evening.

The young mule was jealous now, so he edged in closer to Gunner as he brushed down Butch. The young mule had a sister named Bunny. She was a year older and had a lot of the same markings as the young yearling. Bunny decided she wanted to get some attention as well. When he finished with Butch, Gunner gave her a brushing too.

The young mule wanted to be brushed more and got right up next to Gunner to let him know what he wanted. It was great to spend time with the critters, much more pleasant than being around people. There was nothing phony to deal with, and they made him laugh.

Bunny was calm, so he reached down and picked up each of her hooves. He was curious if she would try to kick him. "Good girl, you don't mind either." She was a beautiful mule. Gunner thought he was already attached to the young male mule, but Bunny would be his second choice. *What a team they would make. They would be ideal for someone living in the wilderness.*

The sun had passed the tree line to the west. It was getting late, and he needed to call it a day. The animals followed him to the gate. He turned to say goodnight to each one of them as he patted their neck.

Most of the animals were familiar with Norman and Granny handling them. It would be nice to spend more time out in the pasture with them, but Gunner knew he needed to get some sleep. Sunrise would come early, and Cleo would be here to pick him up.

Gunner stretched out on his bedroll back at the barn, comfortable in his nest of sweet-smelling hay. He thought how relieved he was to have the conversation out of the way with Norman and Granny.

Now, he could get on with the rest of his life without hurting their feelings. He did think about what was in store for him when Mother got here. Right now, he would be happy to go back up to the mine and maybe find a dog to keep him company this winter.

CHAPTER 21

The brown-panel jeep wagon came rattling down the road as Gunner stepped out of the barn. "You were waiting around the corner watching for me to come out, weren't you?"

"Not on your life, Sunny Boy," Cleo laughed. "You got lucky this time." Gunner was happy to see his good friend and had lots of questions needing lots of answers.

"First things first," Cleo said. "How did you do with your Granny and Norman?"

Gunner took a deep breath. He knew this would take time. "Well, Sir Norman was late coming home. That kept him from barging in so he couldn't take cheap shots at me while I laid my cards on the table with Granny."

Cleo leaned in a little closer to hear Gunner over the noise of the jeep as they rattled down the road.

Gunner continued, "Starting with Granny was tough. She wasn't letting me make my own decisions, so she forced my hand. As friendly as I could, I told her if she tied me to the front porch, I would chew off the ropes and be gone by daylight."

Cleo gave a chuckle, seeing that picture in his head.

"My mind is made up to work the claim until my mother shows up to haul me home. I told Granny we would deal with things as they come. I am tired of a bunch of emotional tension. I didn't tell her that, but I sure thought it."

"So, what will you do when your mother comes?"

"Don't know for sure. I don't want to hurt her feelings, but I need to do what's right for me."

"And what do you need to do, young person?"

"Holy smokes, Cleo! It's like we talked about. I have no use for home or school, and no, I'm not going back. I want to be left alone and get back up to the claim. All I want to do is pull more gold out of your tailing pile. Then buy that young mule from Norman. That would help me out big time."

Cleo asked again, "And then?"

As Gunner was lost in his thoughts, he had stopped talking.

Finally, he continued, "I could get better organized and have a four-legged friend to haul gear into the claim. You know, someday, I'll need to haul dynamite and other stores before winter shows up. That mule would earn his keep for what I'm doing up there."

The conversation drifted to the winter operation of the claim.

Cleo cleared his throat. "Do you realize how cold winters get up there and how much hay you'll need to keep that four-legged burner in shape?"

"Yeah, I'm guessing a bale or more a week and a scoop of oats when we're working. Does that sound about right?"

Cleo nodded yes.

"I have a question, though," Gunner said. "How do I keep working as things freeze up and I can't wash my diggings?"

"Well . . . now," Cleo started. "Most folks hunker down and hold out for spring, but I don't think that will work for you, will it?"

Dodging his comment, Gunner asked, "What about dry washing? I read about it in your books. That was in Arizona where there isn't much water."

"You still need water. Everything freezes up lock tight around this part of the country. Let's see. You could build a new shed over the stamp mill and power the mill with a gas motor. Then you could recycle the water inside the shed. But it would take a bunch of wood to keep a fire going in the shed." That was Cleo's first idea.

"How about this, Cleo? I noticed sulfur deposits in the stream that fills the pond. I haven't walked up there yet, but could that stream possibly be coming from a hot spring?"

Cleo's face lit up. "Now that you mention it, yes. I must be getting old and forgetful. There is a real small vent upstream about 300 yards. If you could tap that hot spring and pipe the water down, you could use the hot spring to keep your water from freezing. You'd need to insulate the pipe or bury it deep. The pipe could also give you hot water at the cabin, so you wouldn't have to wait until spring to take a bath," he laughed.

"Ha-ha, yeah, there you go," Gunner joked. "Just what I was worried about, taking a bath."

As they entered Grangeville, Cleo asked where Gunner wanted to stop first.

"I'd like to cash in some of my poke first. I need to buy you lunch and gas up the jeep. How about you? What do you need?"

"Just some grub for the pantry," Cleo replied. "You, however, need to pick up a sidearm and maybe an old rifle to keep you from starving. And you need warmer clothes."

Gunner frowned. "Okay, but only one set. Got to keep it light this trip. Butch is staying home. I don't want that worry anymore." Gunner thought more while staring at the road in front of the jeep. "I want to look for a young dog if we have time. One I can raise at the mine. I need a second set of eyes and ears to watch my backside. You were right, Cleo. You have to pay attention out there."

"That's a good idea," Cleo said. "Let's pick up the paper in town, and we'll go out to the pound. They say a mixed breed is better than a purebred. What do you think?"

"I'm not sure," Gunner said. "I'm a mixed breed, and the jury is still out on how I'm turning out. But that sounds good to me. Just make the dog young, so I can teach it what I want."

Cleo chuckled. "You be careful. It might be the other way around."

"Hey, I'm talking about dogs, not girls."

Cleo parked the jeep in front of the assayers' office. The sign read Gold, Silver, Coin, and Stamp Shop.

That was painless, Gunner thought, as they walked out with $267.35 for all his efforts over the last three weeks.

Next was the gun shop, and Gunner was like a kid in a candy store. The owner greeted them with a smile. "What can I do for you two today?" Gunner liked him right away, and Cleo seemed to know him from somewhere.

Cleo spoke first, "Let me introduce my friend, Gunner. He is out back working on my old claim and needs some iron to keep him company. Gunner, this is Elroy. He is the only gun shop between here and Lewiston, other than the hardware store. Elroy here can do you right, even if you need some gunsmithing."

Gunner stepped up to the counter. "I need a sidearm, sir, also a big bore long gun. Maybe an aught-six would work."

Elroy nodded. "I think we can help you there."

"I thought the aught-six could be an Enfield 303, like the one in back of the Popular Mechanics, for forty-seven bucks?"

"That's a good choice," Elroy said. "I just got a box of them in, and they're still in the preservative. They aren't Enfield, though. They're 30 aught-six 1903 Springfield. I'll get one for you to look at."

Elroy headed into the back storeroom and returned with the gun, saying he had some old military ball ammo Gunner could use for practice. He said Gunner would also need a box of hollow points for hunting game, recommending four magazines and cleaning gear for the new iron.

After handling the rifle, Gunner gave a big grin. "Okay, how much for all that? And I still need to buy a pistol."

"How does sixty dollars sound since you're buying a pistol too?"

"Ok. The pistol Cleo and I were kicking around is a large bore, maybe a .45 caliber. The bigger, the better."

"I would guess that, knowing Cleo here." Elroy smiled, glancing at Cleo.

Gunner looked down the counter, taking in all those little darlings lined up under the glass waiting for a new home. He pointed to the end of the showcase. "How about that old cannon in the end? It looks heavy enough, and it's lived a busy life already."

Elroy took the pistol out of the case and laid it on a towel spread out on the glass countertop. Gunner could see the gun had some history. He liked it and hoped he could afford it.

Cleo cautioned, "That could only give old bruin heartburn. You need the rifle for stopping power."

Describing the pistol, Elroy explained, "This here is an old Army single action .45 caliber, and you might want to shoot a 150-grain round in it. Those are old military ball rounds and cheap too."

Gunner looked at Elroy. "Where would I wear the pistol when I work? Do you have a holster that could fit the long barrel? How long is that barrel anyway?"

"They call it the Seven-Inch," Elroy answered. "I think we can find you a holster. I see you have a web belt on there and that old bayonet on the shoulder harness." Gunner had become so accustomed to wearing the web belt that he had forgotten about it.

"You could hang the pistol on the left side to balance your load. Then hang a pouch on the belt to hold the extra ammo for the Springfield. The .45 ammo comes loose. You could put that in its pouch on the belt. That might be best if you wear the gun up at the mine while you work."

"I'm working all the time," Gunner said. "Don't see any gun slinging in my future. A shoulder holster should work fine."

Elroy explained, "The pistol goes on the left strap if you're right-handed. You would pull to the right after unlatching the hammer thong that keeps the gun in the holster. I probably have some ammo pouches around here I can throw in for you."

All Gunner could see was his poke slowly draining away. He was afraid to ask but had to, "I'll take this pistol too. How much do I owe you?"

"Let's see. Sixty for the rifle and all, then the pistol with ammo and the gear to hang it on you. How does a hundred bucks sound?"

Elroy didn't look at Gunner. He looked straight at Cleo for his answer.

Cleo smiled and nodded his agreement.

Gunner answered nervously, "Okay, that'll be fine. Let's wrap it up."

"There's a shoulder sling that comes with the rifle," Elroy said. He followed up with a short history lesson. "That rifle was used as a sniper rifle in World Wars I and II and the Korean War recently. It has a fair balance, and the bolt action is trouble-free. Be sure you keep it clean."

Gunner paid his bill and headed for the door with all the "new iron," as Cleo called it.

Elroy caught them on the way out the door. "Hold up. I almost forgot. There's a sniper scope I can throw in with the rifle."

"It's hinged, so you can use the scope or the open sight on the rifle. I'm sure Cleo can explain how it works." They both thanked Elroy again on the way out then loaded the guns and gear into the jeep.

"Whew, he's a talker," Gunner mumbled to no one.

Gunner needed only rice, beans, and bacon at the grocery store, and there wouldn't be much room in his backpack.

Cleo filled his basket and visited with the store owner while Gunner bagged the groceries at the checkout and put them in the jeep with the guns.

The Salvation Army Thrift Store was their next stop. Gunner found a set of tin pants, some long johns, and a nice warm flannel shirt. Cleo told him the tin pants were made of canvas and would keep him dry in the pouring rain or while working on his knees in the mine. He also talked Gunner into a matching coat, felt-lined and not too badly worn and insisted he pick up heavier gloves to wear for warmth and a pair of leather gloves for work. Cleo wouldn't stop. He wanted to top all that off with a hat to keep Gunner's head warm.

That was the hard part for Gunner. The truth was he hated hats. He respectfully went to the hat section of the store and found a used businessman's hat for 50 cents. He tore off the band, pushed up the top to form a dome, and flattened the brim. He looked in the mirror. *I look ridiculous. Someone probably paid a bunch of money for this hat way back when.* Gunner paid the lady at the cash register $12 for the whole works. *Wow, what a bargain.* He was feeling lucky as he loaded the bags in the back of the jeep.

They drove down the street to the hardware store. There, Gunner found a Thompson pack board to get him back up to the mine. He almost forgot another flashlight with batteries and more carbide pellets for the miner's lamp. No, wait, he wanted a small block of salt to set up his lick also. They checked out and were outside at the jeep when Cleo remembered wool socks and rubber boots to work in the mine. Gunner threw his new gear in with everything else.

No sooner had Gunner said "Yes, Mother" to Cleo that he regretted it. He needed to watch his mouth. There was no reason for him to be a smart-mouth kid with this man. Cleo was trying to help him. "Cleo, I apologize for the smart comment. I need to retrain my mouth."

He went back into the store and came out with two pairs of wool socks and a pair of knee-high rubber boots.

Cleo smiled warmly on his return to the jeep. "Come on, let's get going. How about we get gas for the jeep and then lunch? We've been busy this morning. After lunch, we can check out the dog pound. There's nothing in today's paper for a dog."

The Cowboy Café on Main Street served up a hearty lunch. *Boy, was I hungry! Well, I'm always hungry.* After eating, they took off for the dog pound. Gunner was hoping to find a new partner for himself at the mine.

"Hello," Gunner said to the friendly lady at the counter. "I'm looking for a larger dog that is smart. It could be either a puppy or full-grown. I want the dog to be maybe 75 to 100 pounds full-grown."

The counter lady asked, "Boy or girl?"

"Don't care. All I want it to be is smart and to mind me."

"The only one we have in today is a Rottweiler/Lab mix female. She just came in and is about six weeks old. She has her shots and should be 70 to 100 pounds when fully grown."

"Does she need milk, and can I feed her dog food or table scraps?"

"Yes, to the milk. You would do better with puppy food rather than table scraps. You can boil some rice to mix in with cooked meat if you want to."

"Okay, let's take a look at her and see what we think."

Cleo quietly stood back and watched how the two would hit it off.

The lady disappeared into the back room and came out a minute later, followed by a bright, happy, and curious puppy.

The pup sniffed Gunner's boot. He knelt, telling her, "It's not Saturday, so I don't need a bath today if that's what you're sniffing." When Gunner laughed out loud, she started wagging her tail, and he didn't think she would ever stop.

Gunner signed a paper to bail his new partner out of jail and paid the five dollars. The lady handed him a leash and all the paperwork. He decided her name would be Bell, and he felt deep inside she would be his forever. She looked like an easy-going, happy dog and smart too.

"Okay, Cleo. Let's roll." With Bell settled among their gear in the back, they soon talked about mining again as Cleo drove for home.

He reminded Gunner to practice his shooting, especially since he had two new guns.

Yeah, I know, it could save my life, he thought to himself, but he did keep his smart mouth shut this time. Cleo was his good friend and didn't need a smart-ass attitude kid. His good friend had helped him out so much. He should be thanking him for reminding him.

"Thank you, Cleo. I'll try. How about you explain that fancy scope we just got for the rifle?"

They talked guns for a while instead of mining. That was good too. Cleo knew a lot about both, and Gunner didn't know much about either.

When the conversation slowed down, Gunner started reviewing everything in his head. He had plum forgot puppy food.

"Cleo, do you think we could stop in Elk City and pick up some puppy food?"

"Sure, I don't want you to starve your girl the first three weeks you have her."

Gunner wasn't sure how much space he had left in his backpack, but somehow, he would find room for Bell's food.

CHAPTER 22

The Elk City General Store was a white two-story building that looked more like a home than a store. The tavern next door didn't seem to fit the area. The store had a full front porch and two gas pumps out front.

Cleo told him while they drove up that it was one of the earliest businesses to open in Elk City. The town had a lot of history with mining, logging, and just everyday living. The seasonal elk and deer hunters would start showing up in the fall.

The bell on the door jingled as Gunner walked in.

Cleo waited on a bench outside with the puppy and kept an eye on things like he always did.

Gunner bought a small bag of dry puppy food and more carbide pellets for the miner's lamp. This was his last chance to pick up supplies for a while.

When he came out of the store, he found Cleo and Bell visiting with a pretty young Indian girl. They were talking up a storm and laughing over the puppy in Cleo's arms as he showed her off to the girl. Cleo set the puppy down next to his feet as Gunner walked over.

The girl kneeled to pet Bell gently on the head. She looked up at Gunner smiling and asked, "Hello. What is your puppy's name? She's so cute."

How did she know I belonged to Cleo and the puppy?

He replied, "I've been thinking about naming her Bell because her head is shaped kind of like a bell, an upside-down bell. Or we could call her 'Five' because that's what I paid for her, five bucks, that is. On second thought, 'Five' isn't a girl's name, is it?"

The girl stood and smiled at him. She was only a couple inches shorter and had the most beautiful brown eyes. They shined with warmth as she spoke. Gunner felt his face begin to flush as he looked around for a place to sit down. *What do I know about eyes?*

"Those are good names," the girl said. "I think I like Bell best. Don't you?" Her long black hair was perfectly braided and wrapped with leather strips at the end of each braid. Her denim jacket was beautifully embroidered, with colorful beaded Indian emblems in turquoise. She looked smooth in her fitted blue jeans, cowgirl boots, and a shiny silver belt buckle at her waist. *Holy smokes, I can't stop staring at her.*

She did, as they say, knock the wind out of him. It was hard to gather himself up again. The butterflies in his stomach weren't helping much either. *I'm only 14 years old, and I have a mine to work, so I can't be thinking about this girl and feeling all this stuff.*

Cleo noticed Gunner was close to stuttering and moved back to let him muddle through the conversation on his own.

Suddenly, someone came up behind him and stepped between the girl and Gunner, giving the girl a hard shove backward. She almost fell but caught her balance. The stranger kicked at the puppy. Like a real live bully, he sneered at the girl and said, "I'll get to you when you're a little older."

Gunner, with a knee-jerk reaction, planted his feet and didn't move.

The bully shoved the girl again and stood directly in front of Gunner. That left about twelve inches between their noses. It seems Gunner hadn't backed up as the bully expected. Gunner was raised in situations like this with bullies on the fish docks and even at school, where they thought they could spook you by shoving and shouting. *You don't scare me bully, you only piss me off.* And that was the look he gave the bully.

"Who are you, and where did you get that pistol you got hanging on ya?" the bully grunted. "Let me have a look at it. I had one just like that. That could be it."

Gunner calmly stared straight into his eyes, and said, "No."

"Oh, come on now, I'll give it back to you," the stranger paused and grinned, "when I'm ready to." It was just like a bully again.

The bully reached for Gunner's pistol. The holster latch on the hammer held tight so that he couldn't pull it out. While the bully fumbled with the lock, Gunner instantly reached up, wrapping his hand around the handle of the bayonet. He hit the release by the hilt, and the knife was free and clear in his hand.

He pulled straight down from where it hung on the shoulder strap with one smooth downward move and a quick upward stroke. The bully now had six-inch slit in his shirt, next to his belly. Gunner took one long step backward, giving himself a better stance and some maneuvering room.

Gunner stared a hard-straight look to the bully as to say, "Ok, all comers who want to take a shot at me, help yourself."

The bully looked down at the slit in his shirt, then at the knife in Gunner's hand still pointing at his fat belly. Gunner grinned and nodded. *Yes, that is one big knife. Fourteen inches of razor-sharp blade pointing straight at you.*

The bully looked up in disbelief and hissed through his teeth, "Hey, you just cut my shirt!"

"Yep, you bet ya," Gunner answered. "The next time you make me pull it out, I will poke another hole in your shirt and that one will have blood coming out."

The bully stood there and stared at him, speechless. Gunner obliged him with a hard stare back. *Guess you could call this an official Mexican stand-off.* Each one waited for the other to flinch. Sizing him up, the bully knew he had Gunner by fifty pounds, a couple of inches, and maybe three years or so.

This bully had been blind-sided, and that made him too late to pull his knife. Gunner had him at a disadvantage, and he knew it. And, he could see Gunner had a knife and wasn't afraid to use it. It was the best message Gunner could send.

On the porch, there was more going on behind Gunner's back. Cleo pulled the girl and the puppy back to one of the benches by the wall. Handing the puppy to the girl, he said, "Let's stand back and see how this goes down."

Cleo watched a guy approach Gunner from behind with a knife drawn. Cleo reached over to a barrel of long-handled spade shovels and quietly pulled one out. He raised the shovel up to head level and tapped the sharp end on the sneaky backstabbers' shoulder. It made him turn around to see a spade shovel in his face.

At the other end, Cleo silently shook his head "No" and motioned the guy to leave them alone. The backstabber smiled weakly, and backed off, putting his knife away.

As the standoff continued, the bully complained, "I just wanted to see your pistol, not get stabbed, okay?"

"Sure. Why did you grab for it then?"

The bully got quiet.

"Just in case you're wondering," Gunner growled, "If you're going to look at my piece, you'll have to take it off my dead body. Are we straight on that? By the way, you might be dead trying."

Gunner was figuring the cavalry would show up eventually.

Sure enough, the County Mounty Cruiser threw gravel from the dirt road coming around the corner at the bottom of the hill full tilt into the street in front of the store. Slamming on the brakes, the car skidded to a stop. Having announced his arrival, the officer unfolded himself from inside of the cruiser. To Gunner's surprise, he had a John Wayne look about him, hat and all.

The man was around six and a half feet tall and a hefty 250 or so pounds. His face was mean, and he didn't look happy with either one of them.

The officer growled loudly, "What's going on here?"

Cleo spoke first, "The girl and I saw everything, Officer Bob."

"Okay, thank you, Cleo," he replied. Then he said, pointing to the bully and his friend, "Darrell, you and Arnold go over there and stand by your truck for now. I'll be along to talk to you both."

"You, with the large knife, put it away. You won't need it here today. Go over and have a seat on that bench there while I sort this mess out."

On his way to the bench, Gunner picked up his puppy from the nice girl. He thought, *You know, the great thing about puppies is you can hold and love them because they're babies. When puppies grow up, it's a whole different story.*

The officer talked to Cleo and the girl first. Then to a lady with a small child who had also watched the stand-off.

The officer seemed satisfied with what the witnesses said, taking notes the whole time. Then he turned and walked in Gunner's direction as he sat on the bench, holding Bell in his lap, waiting for his turn.

"Do you have anything you want to add?" the officer asked Gunner.

Without hesitating, Gunner told him, "You bet. He had no right to shove the girl and kick at the dog, and if he had pulled my gun out of the holster, someone would be dead or dying right now."

"Okay, anything else?"

"Yes. I don't like bullies. They do things because they can get away with it. That's just not going to happen here, sir. That's all I got. Thanks for coming."

Officer Bob smiled, wrote something in his book again, thanked Gunner for his time, and walked over to the bullies. He listened to their side of the story.

The pretty girl sat down on the bench beside Gunner and petted Bell, who had stretched across his lap. *This dog is one laid-back girl,* he thought.

The young girl looked better by the minute. Gunner thought it would be nice to sit and visit with her for a while. *This is crazy.* It seemed like every time he was near her, he got all confused.

Cleo joined them on the bench.

The girl smiled. "Thank you for standing up to the Ferguson boys. They're the town bullies, and there's always a problem wherever they go."

"I can sure believe that," Gunner answered.

"Can I ask you what your name is?" she asked.

"They call me Gunner. I'm a guy of few words."

Her face lit up with that sweet smile again. She replied, "My name is Quiet Bird. I live in Elk City with my mother, Talking Bird. She's a teacher at the junior high school."

Gunner couldn't believe his bad luck. The teachers seem to come out of the woodwork whenever he showed up.

"I'm working a mine up the Red River, just before you get to the Ranger Station, crossover to Moose Butte Creek, and up the road a-ways to Ryan Creek," Gunner rambled on like he couldn't shut his mouth off. "Cleo here plans to sell it to me once I've pulled enough gold out of the ground."

Officer Bob circled back around to tell him he could go, but he needed to leave town and stay out for a while until things cooled off.

"Officer, why do I have to leave right away? He started it, and I offered to finish it. Like I said before, I don't like bullies, and I hate seeing them get away with anything. With you wanting me to clear out right away, they would be getting away with something. Besides, maybe I want to sit here with my new puppy and talk with this nice girl."

Gunner could see the officer's patience was wearing thin. *Maybe I needed to shut my smart mouth and mosey on along, as they say in the old western movies.*

Quiet Bird spoke up. Changing the subject, she offered, "I'll get his address for you, Officer Bob, in case you need him for anything else."

Gunner could see this girl was slick, nailing a guy down and getting his address at the same time. She could extend our new friendship another thirty minutes. Yep, she was not only beautiful but intelligent too. He liked that.

Officer Bob thanked them and said goodbye. He shook his head as he turned away and stepped off the porch.

Gunner had a feeling they would see each other again someday. Also, his gut told him this probably wasn't the end of his run-in with the troublemakers.

Quiet Bird looked at Cleo. "Could I catch a ride home with you, please? I only live up the hill by the school. I'm not feeling comfortable with the Ferguson brothers still around. There's no telling what they might try next."

"Go ahead, Cleo," Gunner said. "I'll wait here at the store with Bell. We have too much gear in the jeep for the three of us, plus the dog. I don't mind waiting, and Quiet Bird can get home safely."

He noticed the sparkle in the girl's eyes quickly fade, and then she brightened again. "You could come by when Cleo picks you up and have coffee and meet my mother, Talking Bird. She is a nice person. You'll like her."

Gunner did not want to meet a teacher. *And if we stop, there wouldn't be enough daylight left to get back to the mine today. Bell and I wouldn't get on the trail until morning.*

Cleo saw Gunner was squirming. He thought the girl liked seeing him squirm also. Now Mr. Tough Guy had backed off the town bullies and couldn't put three words together and have them come out of his mouth correctly. Cleo chuckled to himself as he watched Gunner fumble for words.

"You go ahead. We'll see, but I need to get back to the mine as soon as I can."

Cleo drove Quiet Bird up the hill to her home and was back within minutes. Gunner could tell he had more to say. "Get in. You might like a couple of minutes in a real house with real people."

No, there isn't time for a social visit. I have work to do up at the mine. But I would like to see the girl one more time before I go back to work. He opened the door to the jeep. Bell jumped in behind the seat and Gunner climbed into the front.

"What do you think?" Cleo egged him on. "The girl is really nice, don't you think?"

Wow, is this a fishing trip? Gunner wondered if the girl put Cleo up to asking him that question. She was a nice person, and she connected with the puppy almost too quickly. Bell was his new pard for the claim. *Bell will be my company when I want company, my extra eyes and ears to keep me out of danger.*

Gunner tried not to be interested. "Yeah, I guess so." Cleo took a short detour, pointing out where Quiet Bird's grandparents lived in a nice-looking home as they drove down the street.

Cleo told him that Talking Bird's dad was a retired miner, and he had a lot of used equipment in the field behind their house.

Gunner put that piece of valuable information in his memory for later use. Cleo continued to explain, "Quiet Bird's mother is Talking Bird, and she invited us in to have coffee with them. She wants to hear about everything that happened at the store today."

He gave a long pause for Gunner to comment.

"We are to come straight back to their house after I pick you up."

Cleo drove the wagon up the hill, the tires crunching on the gravel as they pulled into the driveway. The small white house set back from the street and had a look of pride about it with the neatly trimmed yard and colorful flower beds. Quiet Bird came to the door before they could get to the porch steps.

Following introductions, Cleo was more than happy to tell Talking Bird every detail about their eventful afternoon. Bell sat dead still as Quiet Bird held the puppy in her lap, and she kept glancing up at Gunner.

Gunner was a bit new at all this, but Quiet Bird had a way of keeping the conversation going. He was self-conscious about stumbling over his words but hoping it didn't show. What a great time he was having visiting with them. The ladies talked them into staying for dinner and dessert. Cleo was enjoying himself as much as Gunner.

Wow, they sure can cook in this house. The elk steak and fresh vegetables were out of this world compared to his fried turkey. The mine would have to wait until tomorrow.

The few hours he spent with the pretty girl made him feel good about himself. She seemed to like him for being him and didn't ask about his past, where he came from, or how much he enjoyed school. She didn't know it yet, but he hated school more than anything.

CHAPTER 23

Talking Bird and Quiet Bird had a "girl talk" right after Cleo and Gunner thanked them for dinner and wished them a good night.

The ladies watched from the living room window as the old miner and kid with the dog climbed into the jeep wagon and drove away.

Quiet Bird turned to her mother and quietly revealed her thoughts. "This is the man I will marry someday, Mother."

Talking Bird knew when Gunner walked into their home that her daughter had unique feelings for this young man. She sensed it coming when Quiet Bird insisted Cleo bring Gunner back to have coffee with them.

Talking Bird motioned Quiet Bird to sit on the sofa with her. "This is important for both of us," she said. "Now, how is it you know already that Gunner is the man you will marry?"

"This young man was there for me today, and I know in my heart that he will always be there for me when I need him. My Spirit Guide told me this."

Talking Bird saw that Quiet Bird was extremely serious. "Our Spirit Guides are there, but you can't depend on a stranger to be there. Even after you get to know him like I knew my Henry for so many years, things happen, and then it's out of our hands."

Quiet Bird nodded. "Henry never came back because something went wrong in his life. He had a lot of pain from somewhere. The sad part is that you were deeply hurt, and you are the one who loved him so much."

"Will you be hurt if Gunner never comes back to see you again?" Talking Bird asked. "Cleo said he is from the coast and wants to spend the winter up at the mine. That is a hard thing to do. What if Gunner can't make it up there? He might decide to go back to the coast to be with his family. You would never see him again. That is too much pain, Quiet Bird. I hope you don't give your heart away, and then someday, he doesn't want you."

Quiet Bird answered thoughtfully. "I don't see that happening, Mother. He is the one my Spirit Guide has pointed out for me. You will see it. I thanked my Spirit Guide for bringing him to me. I will be there when it's time for us to share our lives as one. I will not let him down. I promised that to myself and my Spirit Guide."

CHAPTER 24

N ight had come by the time Cleo and Gunner pulled out of Talking Bird's driveway. The ride home was quiet. *Maybe Cleo talked himself out for the day.* Before long, he swung the jeep into the barn turnout at Granny's, where Bell and Gunner would sleep for the night.

The lights were out at the ranch house, so they tried to be quiet. The new puppy and gear were unloaded quickly. Cleo drove out of the barn turnout with a wave goodbye in a cloud of dust and red taillights.

"Ok, Bell. It's you and me, pard. That's all there is from here on out."

They bedded down in the barn, with Bell curled up next to Gunner's legs. Other than a couple of puppy dreams during the night, they did fine.

Everyone was still sound asleep in the house as Gunner and Bell headed out at first light. It was Gunner's first time to take the shortcut from Granny's into the claim.

On the island, he was always figuring out shortcuts. Thinking about making a shortcut here should be no different. They were a quarter the way in and came across a burned-out cabin at the bottom of the draw.

Gunner didn't have time to explore, but he thought there was a good chance there could be a mine shaft close. *We should check that out someday, Bell.*

The puppy couldn't keep up, so Gunner picked her up and carried her in his arms. After four hours of walking, with the heavy backpack and Bell getting heavier by the mile, he decided this was *not* a shortcut.

I made a wrong turn somewhere. "Yeah, I know. I was stupid and didn't check my compass," he said to Bell. Instead, Gunner had told himself, *Trust your instincts, Gunner. You're ok.* Well, that's the last time he would listen to himself. This day will be lost due to lousy planning.

He proceeded to take out his compass and study the map to find where he went wrong. Right away, he could see that they had followed the first creek bed, which spurred off to the west.

All he needed to do was to follow the compass due south into the deep forest. That will connect them to Ryan Creek and lead them to the cabin on the western edge of the cut. Now that was so simple, and yet, here they were. Bell and Gunner, up a creek without a paddle, and it was even the wrong creek.

Like everything else in his life, when he was not paying attention to detail, life bit him in the ass. The mistake would cost them an extra day but also a night of camping out.

"Bell, welcome to the trail hotel." One good thing was that Bell didn't seem to mind camping. She was very content, mainly since he had carried her most of the day. "God, give me strength and the gold to buy a mule before I wear out," he announced.

His newly acquired iron was an absolute comfort for him. The six-shooter, snug in its holster, was a whopper and would be a good persuader for anything thinking of bothering them out here.

Dinner was straight out of the can for Gunner. He loved cold corned beef hash on bread and a long draw on his canteen of water to wash it down. He didn't mind an unheated dinner, and for sure, there were no dishes to wash.

Bell was a different story. She preferred to eat dry puppy food out of his hand. "Dinner will be fast. No fire tonight, girl. I'm going to roll out the bedroll and crawl in."

The .45 was still hanging on him, and the Springfield was on his right side, inside the bedroll. Bell snugged up to his legs and fell asleep. Gunner couldn't sleep yet. The mistake on the trail bothered him deeply. Why couldn't he let it go?

Well, dummy, you thought you had it figured out, but you didn't, so, as Cleo would tell you, "Double check yourself. One mistake, and you can be a goner." You're right, Cleo. I will slow down and double-check what I'm doing from here on.

More relaxed now, he took up a conversation with his sleeping dog. "Let's check out the stars, Bell. They sure are bright tonight. It's like when we were out on the ocean and shut down after a day's fishing. I would ice down the fish and sit on the deck to watch for shooting stars.

"The twinkling stars make me think of the twinkle in the girl's eyes. Bell, I'm not sure what's going on in my head or my stomach with the butterflies. I think I like her. Hope we see her again the next time we go to town. I know you would like to see her too."

Gunner finally started feeling sleepy. "It sure is nice out here. I feel at home with my dog and new hardware, even though we are completely alone. Guess no one else is crazy enough to be out here too. Maybe someday, that girl Quiet Bird would like to come and see what it's like."

During the night, Bell had a puppy dream and tried to put her face next to Gunner's. "Bell, you need to brush your teeth before you go to bed next time."

At daylight, they were up and dressed. Well, no one undressed. Gunner had to put his coat and boots on along with the stupid hat. Bell had puppy chow, and Gunner had a chew of a stick of jerky Granny gave him a few days ago.

They started on the trail before the sun came over the treetops. He was anxious to get back to the cabin. Mom was due to arrive in less than three weeks. He now had a calendar, thanks to those friendly folks at the Grangeville hardware store. *This beats the heck out of cutting notches in the corral gate pole.*

With all his complaining, they made it to the cabin after just a half day's walk up an easy grade. It was a snap. He had marked their way on the map and followed the creek bottom closely. He had learned a lesson and wouldn't forget it. *"Pay attention to detail." Thank you, Cleo.*

Gunner found everything at the cabin the way Butch and he had left it. Old Bruin didn't stop by for a visit or claw at the boarded-up door. *Wait a minute. Bruin doesn't have any friends. Hmmm . . . he must be related to those clods in Elk City.*

CHAPTER 25

After lunch, Gunner and Bell headed for the mine. Bell was settling in quickly, staying close to Gunner and never letting him out of her sight. Gunner could see her loyalty ran deep. The girl, Quiet Bird, was right there in the front of Gunner's thoughts no matter what he tried to concentrate on.

Ok, now knock that off. The first thing I need to do is get the stamp mill up and running, and then the sluice box working. The mine should be good. Gunner hadn't really done anything to it. *Besides, you can't do much to a hole in the ground,* he told himself. The tailings have been what he needed, and all the outside equipment was working.

Gunner remembered there was one problem he hadn't solved yet. The water would run out by noon, and he would have to wait until the following day to start up again. He thought about when he worked on the boats. They pumped water in pipes for many different things, and rather than just letting the water go, maybe he could capture it after running through the sluice box.

It would take rigging up a pump to push the water back up to the upper pond, then run it through again. *Yeah, that would be like a battery. You would only have to charge it every so often.*

Gunner knew he and Bell needed to explore up behind the mine for the hot spring Cleo had talked about. If he could open it up, it would give more water. The hot water would run the stamp mill, and the extra water would give him more stamping time. *Wow, that could help. Hold up here just a minute, Mister Big Idea. On second thought, maybe none of these hair-brained ideas will work. Well, at least I'm trying to figure something out. That's my favorite thing, figuring things out.*

Bell was turning out to be a great partner when he was working. She would lay with her back to him and keep a steady lookout for anything that might threaten them. She would sound the alarm if something didn't look right. The puppy would do a lot of quiet woofing, and then, if she felt there was more out there, she would crank up an outright bark that was loud enough to get Gunner's attention.

"Good girl, you're doing your job for the outfit." Gunner started calling the two of them "the crew" because they were like a boat crew. They all pulled their own weight, and they would be there to give a hand when the other one needed it.

With the stamp mill only working a few hours before the pond had to fill up again, Bell and Gunner walked up to the draw a few hundred yards past the creek pond. There, they explored the upper stream that fed the pool for powering the stamp mill. Following the creek, they found a small stream of water coming into it with the smell of sulfur, and the rock color showed the build-up from the sulfur.

"Come on, girl, let us check out this here, little, teeny tiny creek." Walking another 100 feet or so, they found it like Cleo had said. The hot spring bubbled and spit like the teapot on Granny's stove. Gunner stood looking at the water pouring out of the ground and the steam rising off of it, his mind churning with ideas.

They needed to go back to feed the stamp mill but would bring a shovel and pick when they returned. "Oh boy, this will be fun, Bell."

It was late afternoon when they made it back up to the newly found hot spring. Digging this hole was easier than the outhouse hole because he was working for himself.

By clearing back the sod and shoveling the dirt out another foot, Gunner hit bedrock. He could see the hot water bubbling out of the rocks. "Okay, now that I found you, what do I do with you?" Gunner guessed he'd better go to Cleo's books and see if they would tell him anything.

The evening was here, so they shut down for the night. Bedtime came early for the two in the cabin as there was no kerosene lantern to read by. Bell wanted to sleep on the bed with Gunner. "No, we won't be doing that, little friend." He had filled an old oat sack with straw and laid it by the stove for her. After a couple of tries, she got the right idea.

Then she would get up and move over next to Gunner's bed. Bell never did learn to sleep on her bed at night. Even when it was cold out, the darn dog would rather sleep close to his bedside than in her bed. Gunner finally got her an old thick throw rug and put it by the bed. That became the bed she slept on from then on.

Sometimes, during the night, she woke Gunner to let her out to go potty, then a quick look around, and right back in she came. *What a smart dog! Don't think I'll need to train you much.* She just seemed to know what to do, which would sure save Gunner a lot of time and work.

In the morning, Gunner decided he needed to practice with his new shooter and sight in the Springfield, as Cleo had explained to him. With only five days of food on hand, Gunner knew he wanted to have fresh meat to hang up at the mine for eating.

Together, Gunner and Bell went up, started the stamp mill, and checked the pond. The hot spring was providing most of the pond water now that it was late summer, and the main creek was drying up. The fresh water supply would only let him run the stamp mill for four hours or so. *How could I hitch up a mule to the stamp and get another six hours out of the stamp mill?*

"Bell, we got to do some shooting. I need to practice, then I can hit something when I have to."

There were old cans outback of the tool shed. Gunner set up a couple on the rock beside the cabin. Standing and looking down toward the can on the rock, Gunner pulled the .45 out of its holster with his right hand, pointing it toward one of the empty bean cans. He carefully pulled back on the hammer. Gunner had to cock the pistol's hammer every time he fired it, as it was a single-action pistol.

Brother said it's better to use two hands to steady the pistol. Or you can shoot like John Wayne and hope you hit something, which was not likely today. Gunner pulled the gun up with two hands, took aim, and pulled the trigger. When that hand cannon took a jump, Gunner couldn't believe it. *Woo Wee, that bucks,* thought Gunner, and he had no idea where the slug went.

Guess this will take some time. My hand hurts. Maybe I'll hold on tighter. Bell was still lying in the tall meadow grass, looking at him as if to say, *What are you doing, Dad?*

This will take longer than I thought. Two reloads later, that would be 12 rounds in total, he could hit the rock. The cans were about twenty-five feet away. *I figure them cans are safe on that rock for now.*

Moving over to the Springfield, Gunner looked forward to shooting this fine piece. He had cleaned all the preservatives off on the cabin table. The gunsmith, Elroy, showed him how to take the rifle apart and clean it. He also gave Gunner a book so he could put it back together again. That was a lifesaver, or he would be off to see Cleo for help.

Gunner laid in the grass and propped his elbows on the ground. Something felt natural about laying in the grass, holding the rifle. As Elroy said, it had perfect balance, and the bolt action was smooth when he drove the 30-aught six rounds home.

Cleo told him he needed to decide on the distance to sight it in and suggested 100 yards, basically a football field. That will be the distance you'd make a snapshot. Gunner had set the target up at 150 yards with an old brown shopping bag he had in the cabin. That should shorten his sighting time. *Quick and easy*, he said to himself.

Well, here goes, Bell. Deep breath, in then out, and hold it, squeeze the trigger, and *boom*. Then Gunner shot two more rounds and took a quick walk down to the target. *They call that a shot group,* Gunner thought. *Then you can adjust your sight left or right and up or down, whatever you need. Not one hole on the paper! We'll shorten the range to 50 yards and start over. Cleo might run this by me again.*

Stepping off 50 yards worked nicely. The shot group came out okay. Gunner changed the windage two clicks to the left and up one-click for elevation. The next three rounds were precisely correct.

Now that's more like it. Once again, 100 yards, three rounds through the center. "Alright, Bell, we will have venison for dinner tonight, girl! Let's get back up to the mine and feed Mr. Stamp Mill. This evening, we'll walk out to the valley and look for something we can eat." He needed to check on the salt lick also. Hopefully, putting out those small salt pucks he had packed in from Granny's would do some good.

Back at the mine, everything was doing fine, but the water program was a little short for powering the mill. Gunner had to shut it down to save up some water for tomorrow. *It looks like a mule hook-up or some way to send the water back up the hill. Now, that might work if I put a pond in at the end of the sluice box, then I can pump it back up the mountain every evening. I don't care either motor or mule, but I will need to get a pump in here somehow.*

"Come on, Bell, let's call it a day." Slinging the rifle over his shoulder, they started walking up the valley toward the salt lick. Gunner was hoping there would be something up there waiting for them. Stopping by the cabin, he picked up his smaller skinning knife and sharpening stone. That darned bayonet was just too big for skinning game.

They hiked out about a mile to the lick Gunner had put in a small grassy clearing. Stopping, he saw a mid-sized lone whitetail buck deer, just the right size for him and Bell, and it was only 50 yards away. Gunner hurried so not to miss the shot.

He didn't have the experience with the open sight at that range. That was mistake number one. He needed to have a bullet in the chamber already, then all he would have to do is click off the safety. But even that was too much noise at this distance. Mistake number two. These animals have excellent hearing. Their lives depend on it.

And Gunner was a greenhorn. He wanted to give the buck a fair chance by letting him know Bell and he were here to take it home for dinner. The slap of the bolt action was enough to alert the whitetail, and in about half a second, dinner was running through the brush.

There was no time to waste. Gunner immediately fired, watching over the top of the rifle. Mistake number three. He saw the buck stumble, then take off into the brush. *Every time I think I have something right, it backfires on me. My aim was for his heart, not for his left front. Now I need to track him down, and I don't want to waste all this valuable light finding him.* Gunner started running after the buck. Bell thought this was a game of some kind. She started barking and then shot out through the brush ahead of him. *Now I've gone and lost my dog!*

It is just one of those days, he thought. *First dinner, and then the dog. Not looking good, neighbor.*

Bell's bark was fading but steady for a puppy. That would be good if he could keep up with her puppy bark. It was rapidly getting dark in the forest.

"Where are you, Bell?" he called.

Coming around a big sugar pine, he found Bell, panting, barking, and wagging her tail. *The barking was to tell me, "Over here, Dad." Good girl!* The buck was down and trying to get up on three legs.

Not wanting to waste any more bullets, Gunner needed to put it down with his bayonet, through its heart.

It is more complicated than it sounds, with one wounded, scared animal being half bled out. Bell is barking, and Gunner's heart was pounding up in his throat somewhere as it had never done before.

Well, grab the bull by the horns, they say. This should work if the darn thing doesn't gore me first. By holding the horns and pulling, with a knee forced in on its side, the buck and Gunner went down hard together, and Gunner ended up on top.

He needed to do this for them to eat. Gunner guessed the first time would be the hardest, and it would get easier next time. Laying on his side, panting, he held the buck's horns with one hand, took out the bayonet, and put the point next to the deer's heart. Gunner thanked it for keeping him and Bell fed for a month.

He shoved the long bayonet through its heart and with a single shutter, it left this life. Gunner got up and went to work, as Cleo had explained to him. It was completely dark by the time he had the deer gutted and loaded over his shoulders. *Good thing it was mid-sized, or I would have had to make two trips. And no telling where the wolf pack is tonight.*

Back at the cabin, Gunner hung the buck in the tool shed. Tomorrow, the crew would haul it up to the mine to skin and let it hang in the coolness of the shaft, where it would start curing in Cleo's gauze.

"Bell, let's have some dinner."

He left the covers off the stove as it lit the cabin up to give them enough light to fix dinner. *After that colossal screw-up, there will never be any more snapshots until I have more experience from this day forward.* He promised himself he would take his time, study the situation, and double-check what he was doing.

Now Bell might have been lost out there. The buck would've suffered a slow death. And being out there in the dark was a bad idea for both of us. You never know. The wolf pack could have come in on us anytime. Gunner knew there was a resident pack of wolves, and he was competing for their food.

May the strong survive, and the weak perish, at the end of my Springfield. Brother was right, you are a product of your environment, and my environment is getting more challenging by the day. Hopefully, I'll get smarter.

The following two and a half weeks went by with no mistakes because Gunner was cautious in what he did. He was catching on and knew he couldn't afford any blunders. *Just one mistake can cost you so much, whether it be time or risking your dog's life. Besides, I'm getting to like Bell for a sidekick. Bottom line, practice, practice, and more practice with the Springfield, the shooter, and that darned knife. Cleo is correct to say practice accuracy and speed. It could save you or someone's life someday.*

Mother was due at Granny's in three days.

CHAPTER 26

Today was their last day at the mine. Bell and Gunner would pull out tomorrow morning for Granny's. On their way out, he needed to stop by Cleo's and fill up his wood box, give him some whitetail, and ask about the water problem.

There had to be a way he could coax more water out of the hot spring. Once again, whenever Gunner thought he had something figured out, something else put its big fat foot in the middle of all his grand plans.

While cleaning the sluice box, Gunner looked up as Bell woofed that something or someone was nearby.

He took a quick look down the trail. There was his mom riding Janel and brother Bill on old Butch, right behind her. As they approached, he stood up and grinned. "Hi, all, welcome to the mine."

Mother yelled (yep, Gunner believed that was a yell, definitely not a question), "What on God's earth do you think you're doing?"

Quietly, he answered, "Just working the claim, Mom."

She yelled again, "Did you disobey Granny?"

It is serious. Mom never yelled unless the old man was on the rampage.

Using a quiet, most respectful, polite tone, "No."

Mom laid it on him, "What do you mean, 'No'?"

Now's the time to choose my words carefully, and older brother is right there, ready to jump me if I'm a smart-mouth. That wouldn't be fun with him getting back from Army boot camp and looking very fit.

Gunner smiled and politely replied, "Don't know how I disobeyed her. She gave me or loaned me the gear and a horse to come up here. Then she let me come back up."

"That's not how I heard it. Yes, you were going camping. Then you came back late and said you were going back up to the claim."

His mother took a deep breath and continued, "You went to town and bought guns and gear. Granny said you would run away if you couldn't come back up to the mine. Is that true?"

Gunner was thinking fast. *Well, now that sure was a mouthful.* He felt she has been practicing the speech. *Maybe I could cool her off by getting her down off the horse. I bet she's sore from the ride.*

"How about you dismount Janel there, Mother? I'll take care of her for you, okay? Brother, if you like, I can take care of old Butch there too."

Gunner offered more, "Mom, you and brother can go to the cabin and work some kinks out while I tend to the critters here." It was working. They seemed to be cooling a bit.

Whew, that was a close one. Gunner knew Mom was more scared that something would happen to him out here in the forest. That might be most of the reason she was so upset. *Well, I didn't exactly mind Granny either.*

Brother smiled and slid down off Butch, shook his head, and handed Gunner the reins. Mom got off Janel and said, as Gunner took the bridle reins, "You had us worried."

"I don't see why you were so worried. I have everything I need right here. This place is a lot like the island, Mom. There's a lot of peace up here, and no one to bother me. I'm happy with my new sidekick puppy. Meet Bell," he said, nodding toward the dog.

He knew that was the most reliable shot he could take. Mother, without a doubt, was the world's greatest mom. In her heart, all she wanted was that all of her children be happy. Gunner thought he had unloaded half his verbal bullets in one shot with that statement.

Better save the best for last, Gunner told himself, leading the horses to the shed for a rubdown. He would take the horses to Butch's field for food and a drink that would let them cool down after the hard ride. It was August, the hottest month of the year, even at 5000 feet.

Gunner mentally confirmed his decision to be at the mine come fall if it took the last breath he drew. He was not going back to that school, but he wasn't going to tell her that.

Mother stopped in front of the cabin, turned around, came back, and gave him a big hug. "We love you."

"I know that." Gunner smiled. "Because you two wouldn't have rode these plugs up here for the fun of it. Not even for the free air conditioning we got up here. I might do it, but not you and brother."

They all three started to laugh, and things were back to where they were a family again. *God, I missed them.*

Down at the shed, Gunner started caring for the horses, and it was time to deal with brother Bill. He had stopped at the entrance, watching Gunner work on the critters. Brother was the oldest of the four kids. He looked good in his fresh Army haircut and glasses. Brother always wore glasses.

The two brothers looked a lot alike. Of course, Gunner would always tell Brother he was the good-looking one of the two, and they would laugh. Brother had five years and a couple of inches on Gunner.

Brushing Butch, Gunner looked at big Brother. "Brother, you are a good guy. A little overprotective, though, when it comes to your younger brother."

Brother fired back, "Well, hell, youngin', every time you were in trouble, I was, too, for not watching out for you."

Looking him square in the eye, Gunner snarled at his brother, "I'm no youngin' anymore. I have my place here, own my guns and grub. That dog over there is mine, and she is loyal to me. That may not sound like much, but it is a start. My start."

Brother stared at Gunner, not sure who this was standing in front of him. Gunner continued, "You're getting your start with the Army, and damn proud of it. We don't have to listen to the old man's crap anymore, neither one of us. And he will never hit me again."

While Gunner was pulling the saddle off Janel, Brother walked closer, softening some. "What are you doing up here? This is a wild country, and you can land up dead. Mom is worried about you, and she doesn't know what to do with you. Then school comes up in the same breath. You know that."

Bell wasn't happy with the visitor's tone of voice. She quietly moved between the brothers and gave one of her quiet warning woofs.

They both started laughing, and she began to wag her tail. Gunner bent down and petted her. "It's okay, Bell, this is how brothers talk sometimes, but we care about each other, like you and me."

His little visit with Bell seemed to ease the tension between them. Gunner figured his big brother was going to lean on him, but once he figured things out, Gunner was sure he would be okay with what was going on at the claim.

"I'm having a great time here. Got me a great dog," nodding toward Bell, "and a great rifle that can knock down something for dinner. Heck, my .45 cal. here, hanging on me, can shortstop most critters that might want to eat us. And this bayonet backed off a bully in Elk City."

Brother was starting to appreciate how much his younger brother had grown up. "You stood off a bully in Elk City?"

"Well, it wasn't much. That turnip head grabbed for my .45, and I pulled the bayonet and cut six inches of his shirt for him. After that, I stepped back, and the stand-off started. The law showed up, and all was well. You want to hear the best part?"

"Yea. What is that?"

"Well, sir, I met the prettiest gal with the nicest eyes, a great smile, and I think she likes me. Bell here might weigh in just ahead of me in the liking department. Cleo wasn't sure which one she liked best."

Moving his head side to side, Brother said doubtfully, "Not sure I believe everything you're saying,"

"That's okay," Gunner smiled. "I'm here in this great place, like on the island. Let's turn these critters out, then we can get some supper started."

Walking over to the cabin, Brother looked around, appreciating the rustic setting. "You know, Gunner, this place is like the island, without the water, of course."

Gunner smiled and lowered his voice so Mom couldn't hear them. "Yeah, I know. It's my new home, and I am staying here. That's between you and me, for sure. I'm staying here, okay? Even if Mom drags me back to town, I won't go back to that school. You could chain me to the handrails on the front step of that stupid junior high school, but I won't stay."

"You have your mind made up, huh?"

"Think about it, Brother. That's why you joined the Army the day you graduated high school, right? Be honest, tell me that was because of the old man and his crap, or could it be the town, with all the 'has and has-nots'?"

Brother nodded. "Maybe you're right. He is a pain, along with the town. Just don't understand how Mother puts up with him," Brother mumbled to himself.

"Must be a smooth talker, huh?" Gunner smiled.

With a tone of mixed hurt and disgust in his voice, Gunner said, "Besides, the old man has been hoping to get rid of me for years. I just wasn't part of his big plan. You know, you've heard his talk."

Mom was in the cabin checking things out, and Gunner knew this was what mothers did. He hunkered down and went in, waiting for the bomb to go off. Going straight for the cookstove, he started building a fire. "Mom, I'm thinking of fixing dinner with some quick biscuits, rice, and steaks from the buck Bell and I shot the other week."

This will be a feast for my guests. Gunner knew what his mom would say next, and sure enough, she did. "Okay, where is everything stored?"

Gunner quickly laid the fixings and stoked the fire. "Do you need more water for washing up?"

"No, thank you. Thank you anyway."

"Come on, Brother. I'll show you my mine. That's where we'll get some steaks for dinner."

"Steaks? What kind of steaks?"

"A whitetail buck donated himself for Bell's and my dinner a couple of weeks ago, and the mine is our cooler."

On the way up to the mine, the boys mostly talked about boot camp. Big brother told him how it went. Did he think he would make a career in the Army? That was a definite yes. Once they got the steaks and left the mine, Gunner explained the gold operation but wanted Mom to hear it also.

Mom had already pulled out his one steel skillet and was heating it over the cookstove. Biscuits were in the oven. They had to wait for the rice while they fried up the steaks. Gunner pulled the lid off the stovetop to get the frying pan over the direct fire.

His guests seemed happy with full tummies, and Mother had not dropped the bomb yet. He knew it was coming, but he couldn't figure out why she was dragging her feet. Gunner guessed she was waiting for him. *Okay then, I'll wade in first and test the waters.*

Smiling, Gunner started, "When are you leaving for home, Mom? Right after Brother flies out?"

The lady was smart, and she picked up on it before he could put a question mark behind it.

She shot out, "We'll be leaving as soon as we get to Granny's."

Ok, that means "You and I." Must be the German I keep bumping into around this country. There are a bunch of them. Hey, Mom, how about my way or the highway, and I'll take my road? That's how the old man would say it.

"Mother, we haven't had a chance to talk yet. It looks like dinner is over, so let me do the dishes. You two had a hard ride to get here. How about you two go out on the front porch and cool a bit?"

Mom was on it. "Cool a bit?"

"I don't mean it that way, Mom. Jeez, it's nice out there in the evening to relax for a minute. I'll be out after I feed Bell and clean up. The maid is off for the week, okay?"

Gunner got the dishes done in record time, fed Bell, came out, and sat on the steps.

"How was your dinner?"

Brother piped up, "That was some chunk of meat you had there."

Gunner waited quietly for Mom, and she knew it. He wanted to get it over with but not to rush anything. Usually, that didn't work out so well.

Mom said, "It was good. Is that what you've been living on?"

Bell was lying next to Gunner with her head on his lap as he gently rubbed her.

"Yes, and there is plenty out there. Using my new Springfield, nobody goes hungry around here. We also have fruit trees and berries out the back of the cabin.

"Food was a little lean around here that first trip. Knocked down some quail. I call them 'little chickens.' Wasn't much there once you got them cleaned. Oh yeah, I got a wild turkey. Wow, they are a tricky bird, you know. The apple and plum trees have been great. Think I like the rice the best. It will store good in a tin this winter." *Yep, two can play this game.*

Brother was sitting there watching the show. *Maybe he's coming over to my side.*

Boom, his mother flew off the handle, raising her voice, "You won't be staying here this winter, and you, young man, you're going home with me."

Gunner shook his head, "Mother, I don't want to hurt your feelings. And I don't want anyone to get mad about my staying here." Gunner was trying to stay calm, but it was tough.

Mother laid her standard line on him, "You have to graduate before you leave home." That was her rule for all her children.

Still remaining calm under fire, Gunner replied, "Mom, I won't go back to that school. I'm all done with it, the teachers and everything. The old man has had his last piece of me, not to mention the town. I'm happy here, and things are getting better all the time."

Brother finally chimed in, "You know, Mom, he does have what he needs here. Little Brother seems to be happy. He told me he wants to buy a mule from Norman when he goes in next time."

Mother was agitated, "Stay out of it, Bill. I don't want you taking sides." She knew Bill had sided with Gunner, and it hurt. Gunner thought Brother liked what he had up here at the claim.

Gunner said gently, "Mother, this is what you will force me to do. Tomorrow morning, Bell and I will be gone before you and Brother get up. You won't be able to find us. It is what we can do, just like on the island, when I didn't want anyone to find me."

Mother was adamant, "No, you'll have a problem with truant officers for not being in school." Mother gave this as her final threat, "Then you will land up in jail. Do you want that? What will happen to your puppy?"

Gunner quickly replied, "Bell can go to Quiet Bird in Elk City." He took a deep breath. "First of all, if those people are stupid enough to come all the way up here to hunt me down, I'll give them a chase they will never forget. You know that. Even the old man, with those two drunk brothers and their hounds, couldn't catch me."

Brother started to laugh. He knew that some city greenhorn would have their hands full with Gunner in the forest. He remembered how he was on the island.

Mom must have decided to lighten up. *They call it "change your approach,"* Gunner thought.

"You know, without an education, you won't do very well in the world, even out here in the wilderness." She continued, "You have a long life ahead of you. It will be an even harder life without an education."

Alright, here's the last card I have, then I'm out of cards.

"Mom, the last time Cleo and I were in Elk City, we had dinner with the eighth-grade teacher and her daughter. What I'm thinking is that I could get some books from her, then once a month or so, Bell and I can stop by to take a test and pick up a new assignment."

She paused, giving him a motherly look that a compromise might be possible. "Alright, go on, tell me more."

"I'm shooting from the hip on this, you know, so here goes. That might let me finish junior high school. Then we'll see about high school. No guarantees on high school, but I do very much want to finish junior high."

Mother asked, "Do you think I can meet this teacher? What's her name?"

Gunner said, "Talking Bird, her daughter's name is Quiet Bird, and yes, I think you can meet her. She's a genuinely nice lady, both her and her daughter. You will like them."

Mother didn't say okay, but things were looking a whole lot better.

"I didn't say we will do that. Let's sleep on it and have a talk in the morning."

Not giving things time to cool off, Gunner asked, "What time do you need to leave in the morning?"

Mom said calmly, "As soon as we can. Brother needs to fly out of Lewiston for the east coast, day after tomorrow,"

It's nice to be back on the trail of peace and family again.

"Bell and I will take you out on a shortcut we marked out. I do need to close down the mine. Then board up the cabin, so old bruin doesn't do any damage."

This is great. Now I'll get to see Quiet Bird again. Yep, those butterflies are back.

"The shortcut should cut off half the time. Mom, you take my bed. Brother, you're welcome to the upper bunk. Bell and I will sleep in the shed. I only need my bedroll and dog. Bell and I might wake up as early as daylight, and we'll head straight for the mine. Not a whole lot to do but finish cleaning out the sluice box and grab my poke."

<h1 style="text-align:center">CHAPTER 27</h1>

Come morning at sunrise, Gunner and Bell were closing up the mine. Within an hour, Gunner was back getting Butch and Janel saddled up for the greenhorns.

Bell and Gunner needed the Springfield and the Thompson pack board. When Gunner came into the cabin, Mom had made mush and baked biscuits.

It struck Gunner that she might almost be liking it here. *I think I'll invite her back next summer. After all, every mother needs to check up on their offspring now and then. Hmmm, that smells good. Our mother knows how to cook a great breakfast.*

Boarding up the cabin, he announced, "We should make Granny's by noon, with you two on the livestock. Bell and I at a fast walk can keep up."

Bell was becoming a big girl and should be able to keep up. If not, Gunner would put her on the pack board. The summer sun was rising over the top of the valley already. Ahead of them, the sight was all worth it, with a beautiful day in the Nez Perce Forest to enjoy.

Mom decided she was ok with him staying. She did need to visit with the teacher, and that was okay with Gunner. He wanted to see Quiet Bird again. There was something special there with that girl, and Gunner couldn't get her off his mind.

Out in front of the greenhorns, Gunner took time to daydream and make plans for him and Bell. They were making good time on the trail. When Gunner said trail, that was what he meant. It wasn't much more than a path, and he knew he couldn't get a wagon through. *You'd need to go to Cleo's road and follow the ridge, then you'd be at the cabin.* Bell and Gunner had kept a fast pace, plunging off into the woods when he noticed that the greenhorns were missing. He returned back up the trail looking for Mother and Brother. "What's the matter, Mom, where did you go?"

"We lost you and your sidekick there," she said, smiling.

It felt good to see everyone happy, amongst family, for the short time they had together.

"Yeah, I know. Back there, I call it 'the half-day turn.' That's where I lost half a day making the wrong turn. We know the way now. Keep close. It gets dense in the bottomland brush."

Gunner could tell both Mom and Brother were proud of him. They were surprised that his maturity and decision-making were so good. He had grown leaps and bounds since they last saw him.

Sure enough, they were at Granny's by noon. Gunner needed to care for the horses, then he could look for that young mule Granny and Norman had up in the pasture behind the ranch house. Mom and Brother went to the house to clean up. The plan was to have a sit-down visit with Granny and the rest of the visiting relatives.

It would be the first time since they arrived to have time to share with family. Mom and Granny are close. Mom's dad passed away when she was 14 and she was the oldest of the six children, so she helped raise the other five children. It was tough times, and the Depression was getting over. Mother had a problem living in poverty. That comes from growing up during the recession, Gunner guessed.

Granny had kept her family together during all the tough times, and they are still close today, thanks to Granny's hard work. Gunner said to himself, *Thank you, Granny, for all your hard work, love, and, most of all, for being the person you are!* He knew she would let him go back to the mine. It was the right choice. He wouldn't let her down.

Gunner wanted to find Norman and see if he would sell him the young mule. He still had a hundred dollars in his pocket from the last trip to town. He had been holding it back for a rainy day. The mule and Gunner had a lot of work to do packing equipment into the mine.

Gunner found Norman in the garage shop, working on a chainsaw. "How's it been going, Norman?"

"Pretty good. I need to fix Lenard's saw for him. How are you doing out at the mine?" he asked with a blank look on his face. "Wait, I better ask upfront, are you going back to the coast with your mother, or are you going to stay up there, at the claim, for the winter?"

"Well, we had quite a pow-wow over that."

Norman stopped working, smiled, and started to roll a smoke, sitting down in an old chair next to the bench. "I can imagine. Your mother wasn't none too happy when she came through here with your brother, and you were gone."

He finished rolling his smoke. "I had to saddle up the horses for them. Guess they found you, ok?" He lit his roll-me-own. "Sent them up to Cleo's. I knew he would send them in the right direction."

"Thank you for that, and they made it. A little sore, I'd guess, but in one piece. And yep, I'm spending the winter up at the claim."

Gunner leaned up against the bench where the chainsaw was. "Norman, do you think you would sell me that young mule you have out back?"

"Are you talking about the one you feed carrots to and brush every chance you got?" He smiled. "Not to mention all the grain you fed him so he would come to you."

Gunner answered confidently, "Yea, that's the one. Have you any thoughts on what you would want for him?"

"So, you want to buy that mule? He's only green broke with the pack, but he's good with the halter." Norman was a cowboy joker, and he enjoyed stringing Gunner along.

That wasn't what Gunner was there for. He wanted to buy the mule, and Norman knew it. But he had to stand there and let Norman have his fun. "How much do you want for him, Norman?"

"Probably more than you got, kid, working that played out mine like you're doing. Why are you only working with the tailings' pile?"

Norman was teasing. It was getting harder to play along, and Gunner thought he was catching on.

"Yeah, but the process has improved since Cleo worked it last like I explained the last time I was here. You know, the deeper in the pile I get, the better the pay dirt."

Norman chuckled. "At least you're talking like you're a miner."

Gunner was getting tired of the game, so he pushed back, "What about the mule, Norman? What do you think you'd want for him?"

Norman smiled. Gunner could see he was still having his fun. "Not sure. The forest service has slowed on using pack animals. So, that makes the auction price lower. Then, I have to feed the darn thing this winter. How about a hundred bucks? How does that sound? That's a lot of money, but you can pay us twenty bucks a month if you like."

Gunner tried to hide his excitement. "Sounds good to me. Do you have a halter and saw-buck pack that could go with him?"

Norman nodded. "That will cost you another forty." Norman was an old horse trader, and he was good at it. Gunner had no interest in haggling with him. He needed the mule, and Norman knew it.

"I'll take him."

Reaching into his pocket, Gunner pulled out all the cash he had in the world. He started counting out twenty-dollar bills, and there were exactly seven of them. Norman gave Gunner a surprised look and picked up the money. "Yep, those are real, Norman."

Norman, not to be short on needling, said, "I'm not sure you've been up at that mine all this time. Did you start robbing banks in your spare time?"

Moving Norman along as easy as he could, Gunner continued, "No, just worked hard like when I dug the new hole for your outhouse. Could you show me what gear goes with him?"

As they walked out to the barn, Norman asked, "What will you name your new mule?"

"I am not sure. I've been thinking, *Jack*. Do you think I could buy some hay from you once in a while?"

"Sure, if you are ever heading into town to pick up supplies, you can board him here with us. We'll keep an eye on him for you. Say, I noticed you came out of the valley behind the ranch house. Did you find the shortcut?"

"Yep, I did! It is a nice easy grade up to the cabin. The shortcut is a good one. It is only a trail now, and you couldn't fit a wagon on it. The mule will work out fine. He'll be a good partner for Bell and me."

"Yeah," Norman nodded his head, "they will keep you busy, caring for them." Standing in the tack stall, Norman pointed. "Here is the gear, halter, saw-buck, and bags. And here's a blanket for the saw-buck."

Gunner asked, "What about pack tarps to wrap things with?"

Norman was glad Gunner had thought about all the equipment he would need. "Here are a couple of old ones to get you started. You remember that mule is a teenager, like you. Don't load him too heavy or get rough with him. It could hurt him for a long time."

With that, Norman left the barn and headed to the house to tell Granny about all the new cash he had in his pocket.

Gunner grabbed the halter and headed for the pasture behind the ranch house, anxious to get his new mule, Jack. Bell was right on his heels. "Come on, Bell. I want to introduce you to your new brother."

The young mule was standing in the middle of six other horses and mules, on the path worn into the hillside. Jack was a smart mule, and he watched Bell and Gunner walking up the hillside trail.

Gunner said to Bell, "He sure looks good. His mother over there, Nugget, is a tall, beautiful bay quarter-horse, Arab bay mix. Not sure about Jack's dad other than he must have been what they call a mammoth jack." Gunner approached the mule. "You are mine now. We will make a great family, you, Bell, and me." Gunner started to rub his neck. Slipping the halter on him, he led Jack back to the barn, then brushed him and checked his hooves. Gunner wanted to handle and spend time with him. He rewarded him with some of Norman's prized grain for being such a good boy. Then, Gunner turned him out in the corral behind the barn.

It was getting close to dinner time, and he heard Mother walking over to him. Gunner was quietly watching his new crew member standing in the corral. "Aren't you coming up for dinner?" she asked.

"Yes. I was enjoying my new boy for a minute. Mother, that mule and I have been friends since I first came here. Now, he is mine forever, just like Bell there."

She smiled. "Come on, dinner is almost ready."

Cleaning up on the back porch, Gunner could hear the conversation already heating up at the dinner table. Brother was on a roll about his Army experiences in boot camp. Gunner had heard it all back at the mine. He wanted to eat and get out of there. Then, he could make up his bedroll in the barn.

Each time he came in, he felt more uncomfortable around people.

For the dreaded meal conversation, he didn't need to hear it. Everyone was sitting at the table except for a couple of young cousins seated at the kids' table in the living room.

Once Gunner had his plate of food, he headed over for the wood box where he could sit and eat his dinner in peace. He chose not to get caught up in the BS that was flying at the table.

Oh no, Mother wouldn't hear of it. He had to sit next to her in the chair she was saving for him at the large oak kitchen table. Norman sat at the head of the table, and Granny was sitting straight across from him.

Two aunts and two older cousins sat on Granny's side. Mom was sitting next to Norman, then Gunner and Brother were next. Right out of the gate, once Brother stopped to take a mouthful of food, Norman was on Gunner. Gunner knew this was coming, and he was ready. He had a new mule, and you couldn't hurt him. Bell had curled up behind his chair, never more than five feet away.

Norman took a long look at him, smiling as everyone watched, wondering how this evening's entertainment was going to play out. "Well, I see you lost your canon and machete. I think this is the first time in six weeks I've seen you washed up, and you have your hair combed to boot." Chewing on a piece of the buck Gunner brought out with them (he had strapped it behind Brother on Butch's saddle), Gunner stopped, laid down his fork, and looked at him. "You're right, Norman. It is the first time in six weeks you've seen me shined up a bit. You know you have only seen me one other time in the last six weeks. Mother is here, and I want to leave her with a good impression."

Norman was quick, but Brother was faster, and he knew how to play the game. "I liked it up there at the mine. Gunner has gotten a lot done in six weeks, combed hair or not. The sluice really works, and it's paying out for him. Didn't he buy a new mule somewhere?"

Too late, Brother, you took a breath. One of the aunts chimed in, "Will you be spending the winter up there, in the wilderness?" Not coming up for air, she stayed on it, "That is the stupidest thing I have ever heard of! A teenager up there in the wilderness. For God's sake, trying to make it in the middle of the winter in that hell hole. You know a lot of grown men can't do that. It's summertime now, and it's easy. Winters are hard up there, not to mention wolf packs on the rampage. Shoot, he doesn't know his ass from apple butter."

Boy, I didn't think she would ever run out of gas. Ok, that's it. Gunner set his fork down again and started to lean forward in his chair to pick up full-on eye contact with Auntie.

Being a mother with the she-bear's instinct, Mother put her hand on Gunner's arm to keep him from saying anything, and everyone saw it. This was the she-bear's cub, and she wasn't going to allow anyone to be slapping it around, not as long as she was in sight. With her being the oldest of her family, she had certain rights to talk about when and how she chose. It was looking like the time had arrived. Gunner thought this ought to be good. Personally, Gunner wanted to fill the wood box and go to the barn to be left alone.

Mother cleared her throat. "This is a decision that the three of us have made together. Once you have been there, you would see it is a good thing for Gunner, with his dog and the new mule." Mother continued, "He has promised both Cleo and me that if anything goes wrong, he will come out and get help." She took a quick breath. No one said a word until she was done.

"You know, this shouldn't be anyone's business but Gunner's and mine. I think he can do it, and that's why he is staying. We're making arrangements to continue his education through correspondence while he is at his claim. That's saying more than others of us can say." Mother was looking directly at the aunt running her mouth, since she had gotten pregnant, dropped out of school, and never went back.

That was a nice shot, Mother, both barrels. Gunner was done eating and had enough of the evening meal. The only reason he came up to dinner was out of respect for Mother and Granny.

This table bickering was child's play compared to the old man's table. There, you never had a chance. Gunner thought it was sad. The kids couldn't fight back when there was trouble in Dodge City.

Standing up, Gunner thanked Granny for the great meal, took his dishes to the sink, then headed for the back door and the woodshed. He gathered up an armload of wood for Granny's kitchen wood box and went back out to the woodshed to split kindling for the morning fire. As he dropped the kindling in the wood box, he bid everyone a good night and headed out to the barn, Bell close on his heels. He didn't think she was all that comfortable, either. Animals seem to know when things were not quite right. Gunner knew he did a whole lot better with his critters than with people.

Jack was standing at the corral gate, giving them a low throaty grumbling sound to say, "Here I am, just waiting for you." Gunner hooked up the lead rope to his halter and led him to his barn stall for the night.

"Better get used to this. You'll need to go to your stall every night out at the cabin. Too many things can go wrong in the dark. You, Mr. Mule, are much too valuable to let anything happen to you. Besides, you're the new member of our family."

Mom walked into the barn, and she could hear Gunner talking to Jack. With a smile, she said, "I wanted to see your new mule." Gunner thought she might be checking up on him too, letting him know everything was alright.

Mother explained, "You know, she was making a lot of noise because she could. Yes, you had better not let me down on the education. I will hold you to it as long as you live."

Guess that's why she came out to the barn to talk to me. She wasn't worried about me freezing to death or a wolf eating me. She wants me to finish that darn schooling. There is that good old German again. Boy, it runs deep around here.

"Did you say you needed to pick up some gear while we were seeing the teacher?"

"Yeah," Gunner replied. "We need to go into Grangeville if we could, please."

Mother nodded. "Tomorrow morning. I think Brother can catch a ride into Lewiston with Norman for his flight back east. It sounds like he needs some tractor parts in Lewiston."

"Grangeville is where I can sell some of my gold. Then, I need to stop at the Salvation Army for more clothes, pick up staples at the grocery store, and make a stop at the hardware store. I don't have a reading lamp for the cabin. Oh yeah, I want to buy some ammo and a new shovel too."

Daydreaming again, Gunner continued, "Later on, I want to come in and buy more hardware. I need a new headlamp with batteries for the mine, possibly a pump of some kind. Cleo will help me with that."

Mother added, "You can figure on a stop at JC Penny's too. You need more underwear, socks, and new long johns. That's a mother's requirement."

Gunner smiled. "I also need to go to the library and look up some mining books. Do you think I can use Aunt Ida's address for a library card?"

"Yes, I think she'll let you." Gunner's mother paused, choosing her words. "Are you sure you're okay out here?"

Gunner appreciated his mother's concern. "The barn is a lot safer and less hassle than in the house. Ya know, especially with all those sharks swimming around up there." Gunner paused, smiling, looking at his new mule.

"Don't want to be anyplace else other than here with my critters. See you in the morning, Mother."

Jack was quiet in his stall, and Bell curled up beside the bedroll. Gunner was wearing the .45 again, across from the knife, and the Springfield was next to the bedroll. Cleo had taught him right.

"Goodnight, Bell and Jack. We have a big day ahead of us, and I want to get it over with, so we can head back up to the mine. There is a lot to do up there," he said with a yawn.

CHAPTER 28

Mother's idea of getting up was not with the chickens. Gunner slept in the barn with the chickens, and when they say rise and shine, they meant it. First things first, Gunner put Jack out and fed Bell, taking care of his family. Washing up on the back porch, he could smell the bacon and venison Granny was cooking up. She knew how to pull Gunner in and get her wood box filled. Gunner brought in an armload to top off the wood box. She appreciated she didn't have to say anything to anyone. The chore was done.

Breakfast was farm family size. Gunner didn't think he had eaten so much for a long time. Granny kept piling the sourdough pancakes on his plate. The table was quiet. Brother, Mother, and Aunt Ida were there, the youngest of Granny's children. Aunt Ida was the one most like Gunner's mother. That was the aunt in Grangeville they stayed with when Mom brought Gunner out last spring. *Boy, there has been a lot of water under that bridge since then.*

Gunner and Brother talked lightly about his flight and going to Fort Mead, Maryland. Brother chose the Army security agency. It didn't make a lot of sense to Gunner as his mind was working on getting his gear and introducing Mom to the teacher.

Gunner wanted to see Quiet Bird again. She was on his mind more and more lately. He thought she might be the most beautiful girl he had ever talked to. He had been asking himself lately if she was for him or not. *That could be why I get nervous when she talks to me. Darn, those butterflies are starting already. Better finish up breakfast and fetch the Springfield so Granny can keep an eye on it while we're in town.*

What made Gunner decide to leave Springfield with Granny? He was guessing Mother didn't have the same appreciation for guns as he did. Taking the Springfield up to the ranch house, he asked Granny in front of everyone, "Would you mind watching my rifle while Mom and I are in town?"

Granny said with a big smile, "Sure, I'm a little surprised you would leave it here, but I see you're wearing its brother." She gave a light chuckle. "Just lean it up by the desk in the study. It is unloaded, isn't it?"

"Yes, ma'am, it's unloaded, and the bolt is open."

Mother spoke up, "Are you going to wear that gun and knife to town? You don't need it there, you know."

Gunner frowned. "We're stopping in Elk City to see the teacher, so yes, I do."

"Why would you need to take a gun to see a teacher? That doesn't sound right."

"Well, there were some bullies in town last time we stopped in at the store, and I don't want any trouble."

Mother looked straight at him. "Carrying a gun is trouble."

Gunner came back to her. "Not in that town. I think you could call it a peacekeeper or persuader. They shouldn't try anything like the last time."

Mother asked, "What do you mean by the last time?"

Uh oh, I had better play this down a bit. Everyone was tuned into the conversation at the table, watching and listening to every word.

Mother was a deaconess in the church back home, and Gunner hated church as much as he hated school. *Oh no, I don't want her thinking I'm a troublemaker with a gun.*

"Mom, it wasn't much at all," he said quietly, trying to keep the conversation between them. "Someone wanted to see my .45, and I didn't want him to. I'm glad I had the knife on me that persuaded him to leave things alone."

Gunner was not sure Mother agreed with all of that, but she dropped the subject. He figured Norman would spill all the beans to her later after he headed back to the mine. Once he got to the mine, she couldn't blast him out of there.

They were quiet, driving alongside the river to town. Mom was busy driving, and Bell was sleeping in the back seat. Gunner was doing what he did best, daydreaming about the things he needed to do. How was he going to pack Jack on his first trip up to the mine? Then there was that Quiet Bird girl again. She was still coming up in his mind. He was sure he liked her. She was quiet and very friendly to visit with.

In Grangeville, Gunner sold most of his gold and bought all the gear he needed. A stop at the library produced books on mining. Gunner had to solve the power problem for the stamp mill. Then, he would start digging in the mine in a couple of weeks and that would take some homework to boot. Mom wanted to stop at Aunt Ida's to let her know she would be stopping by on her way home.

Gunner said jokingly, "Mother, if we are going to stop at Aunt Ida's, maybe it would be polite to call Talking Bird and warn them we're coming. You never know, they might need to take the curlers out of their hair or something." Mother had no idea they had braids the last time he and Cleo saw them.

Aunt Ida's took only a few minutes, and they were off to Elk City to see the teacher and her daughter. Once again, driving along, both were lost in their thoughts. Mom was driving the twisty roads, and Gunner flat out didn't talk much. Here lately, he noticed he didn't have much to say at all. Could it be all the time he spent at the mine alone? There was no one but Butch at first, and now he had Bell to talk to, and he did all the talking. Bell would wag her tail and lean against his leg, wanting him to pet her. It was not easy for him to hold a conversation, and he didn't much care. Maybe it will be different with Quiet Bird? He was hoping so.

Elk City was only an hour away and soon, they were pulling into Talking Bird's driveway. Bell got all excited and was all over the car when she saw Quiet Bird coming out of the house. Gunner wasn't much better. He had a hard time containing himself where Bell didn't need to. That is what dogs do, show their excitement and love when they saw someone they liked.

Talking Bird was right behind Quiet Bird. Gunner got out then let Bell out so that she could run for Quiet Bird. Mother came around the front of the car and stood beside Gunner as he made the introductions. Quiet Bird was holding Bell by then. It was like they hadn't seen each other for three years rather than three weeks.

Talking Bird and Quiet Bird were both so polite and glad to see Bell and Gunner. They were very friendly to Mother.

The ladies wore long, beaded, Nez Perce dresses. *They sure look good.* Both looked freshly scrubbed, and there wasn't a hair out of place on their ponytail braids. *They both have lovely shapes,* Gunner thought.

After introductions were out of the way, the ladies invited them in to have coffee. Gunner spoke up first once they were sitting at the kitchen table. "I would like to explain why we're here. Not only do we want to stop by and say hello," he said, looking over to Quiet Bird, "this is about me finishing junior high school."

Gunner looked to Talking Bird. "This is especially important to Mother and me both. Is it possible we could work something out where I could borrow the needed books and take a test once a month?" He paused to let what he said sink in. "I will be staying up at the mine this winter, and this is part of the deal, so I don't have to go back to the coast. Would there be a chance we might do something like that?"

Talking Bird thought a moment and nodded. "I'm sure we can work something out, Gunner. I have to warn you, it's harder than if you were going to school full time."

"That's okay. The evenings are long, and I have a new kerosene reading lantern for the cabin out in the car."

Talking Bird smiled. "With you wintering over at the mine, do you think you can make it out of there once a month?"

"Yes, that's the plan right now. I have a power shortage for the stamp mill, and it will be worse when the freeze comes."

He focused on the tabletop in front of him. "This is one of many problems I have to solve up at the mine. Believe me, it is important to keep up with my studies. I want to get my schooling completed. Most of all, I want to stay here." Gunner looked over to Quiet Bird, and she smiled back at him.

He changed the subject. "Excuse me, I noticed some old mining equipment back down the road a bit. Would you know who owns it?" He already knew the answer, as Cleo had told him.

Talking Bird laughed. "Oh yes, that would be a bunch of my dad's old mining junk. He retired from mining ten or more years ago."

Quiet Bird suggested, "Why don't we walk down and ask Grandpa Oley about it? I know he would appreciate the company and would love to hear about your mine."

"That sounds like a good idea," Talking Bird said. "Gunner, your mother and I have lots we can visit about."

"Sounds great, as long as you don't talk too much about me, ok?"

"Your mother and I can visit on what you'll need to complete. You two have a nice walk. You will enjoy my father. He is quite a character."

Out the door the two went, with Bell on their heels. There wasn't much talk from Gunner. Those darn butterflies were getting in the way again.

Quiet Bird asked, "How long will you stay up at the mine?"

He was firm with his answer. "If I have a say, it will be forever. Mom would like me to come home after a year here. I'm home now and want to stay up at the mine. The cabin has everything I want. How about you? Are you going to stay in Elk City for the rest of your life?"

She laughed. "No, I am not sure what I want to do." They were quiet until they reached her grandparents' house. Quiet Bird knocked on the front door, and an older man, about Gunner's size, came to the door. "Hello, Papa," Quiet Bird said. "I want to introduce you to a friend of mine. This is Gunner Gunderson, and he is working a claim up the Red River."

Papa gave a big smile. "Would you like to go out back and look at some equipment? Whose claim are you working up there?"

"Yes, it would be great to see your equipment. The claim is Cleo Adam's, a good friend of mine. He stopped working on it about 15 years ago."

Quiet Bird smiled as she and Gunner walked behind her grandfather. "I think he is excited just to talk about mining."

She sure is walking close to me. Every so often, he could feel her arm rub up against his. As they walked around behind the shed, they saw an old, rusted stamp mill, just like Gunner was using up at the mine.

Gunner was excited. "This might make a great spare-parts stamp. I think it's just like the one I have up at the mine."

Oley nodded. "You betcha. They gave many a good year of service to a lot of us, including Cleo. I remember when he brought his through town, headed up to the mine." Oley took them into the shed where an old drill stood, all oiled, in good shape, and ready to go to work. Next to it was a gas-powered compressor with a big coil of air hose lying next to it. Gunner quickly bent down, looking at the drill. "Do you think you would like to sell all this equipment?"

Oley was excited now. "Sure, if the price is right."

Gunner asked, "How much would you want for it?" He paused as he was thinking. "I can't buy it right away. I just bought a new mule and have a lot of work to do before I start blasting in the mine."

Oley answered thoughtfully, "Seems five hundred dollars would be a fair price, and I could throw in the old single hitch wagon outback. You said you just bought a mule?"

"Sounds good to me," Gunner agreed. "Yes, I just bought a mule yesterday. I need to go back up to the mine for a while and work on it." He stopped to admire the beautiful drill sitting in front of him. "Would you mind holding on to the equipment for a couple of months for me?"

Oley laughed heartily. "Not at all. It's been here for ten years, so a couple more months won't hurt anything. My wife will be happy to see all this go. Come on out front, there are a couple of conveyor belts that go with it."

Once outside, Gunner asked, "Will the timbers they're sitting on be going with them?"

Oley nodded again. "Yes, that goes also. Anything you see for mining, you can have all for one price. So, we got a deal?"

Gunner could almost explode. He was so happy. "Yes, we got a deal. Yes, sir." They shook hands. Quiet Bird's grandpa liked this young man. He had a grip like an iron vice, finishing the deal.

Oley added, "Don't worry about picking it up. I know it takes time to get an old mine back online. You have lots to figure out and learn. Quiet Bird, you keep an eye on this young man. Let me know how he is doing." She smiled, nodding yes.

Gunner said, "Thank you, sir. You already know how much this will help at the claim."

Walking back to her mother's house, Quiet Bird could see Gunner was deep in thought. She gently asked, "What are you thinking, Gunner?"

Deep in thought, he reached over, took her hand in his, and said, "Holy smokes! I got some reading to do on all that equipment. It's exciting for me to have this equipment waiting for me and the claim."

Gunner could not slow down. "I didn't think I could be so lucky. Most times, my luck doesn't stick around long. Maybe you are my good luck. Thank you so much!" He patted her hand as he held it in his other hand.

Both were not sure who was holding whose hand, but they liked it. Neither let go until they got to Talking Bird's house. Gunner saw Talking Bird and Mother looking out the window as they were holding hands. How was he going to explain this away? *I'll act like it never happened. That'll work.* By then, they were walking into Talking Bird's kitchen and the mothers were finishing up their second cup of coffee.

Talking Bird asked, "How did the visit go?"

Gunner blurted out, "Just great! He is holding the equipment for me. He even has an old wagon that Jack can pull up to the cabin. I can hardly believe it!" They all started to laugh at his excitement.

Then, Talking Bird chimed in, "My mother will be happy to see it all be gone." And with a smile, Gunner said, "That came up also." Quiet Bird was smiling and standing close to Gunner. Somehow, that felt very natural.

"Are you happy with your visit, ladies?" Gunner asked.

Gunner's mother stood up. "Thank you for your time, Talking Bird. I want to stay in touch with you. I like to keep a check on Gunner and how he's doing. Mothers are never that far away."

"Ladies, I should be back in three to four weeks, then I can start hauling off some of the equipment."

Quiet Bird smiled. "I am looking forward to seeing you, then you can start your school studies. I'll help you if you need any." Gunner nodded to Quiet Bird, acknowledging her offer.

"Come on, Mother, I want to make the cabin before dark."

Mother asked, "Isn't that crowding things a bit?"

Gunner took a step toward the door. "Not if we get moving. Thanks so very much, ladies. See you in three or four weeks. I need to make enough to pay for the equipment. Bell, where are you? Oh, there you are, next to Quiet Bird. Getting a big hug goodbye? I think that dog might like you more than me, Quiet Bird."

Quiet Bird answered, "Well, we girls might have a better connection than you guys do."

"Maybe," Gunner smiled. "We got to get going. Mom, are you ready?"

Out at the car, Gunner so wanted to hold Quiet Bird's hand one last time. After loading Bell in the back seat, he reached his hand out as to shake hers. She also reached out, taking a quick check on the ladies. They were around on Mom's side, talking. When their hands touched, it was like electricity. It wasn't a handshake like Gunner had ever felt before. Her hand was so soft and tender, even with the electricity running through. They stood looking into each other's eyes for those few seconds, and that was enough for the connection to be complete. Gunner knew she would be with him in heart and mind. She was so beautiful. It was hard letting go and getting into the car. With a wave goodbye, he and Mother pulled out of the driveway.

On the way to the ranch, all Gunner could talk about was the new equipment and how much more work it would let him do. And having the new mule on the crew, that was his ace. Jack would be a big mule when he reached adulthood.

Gunner's mother could see how happy he was. Feeling his excitement, she could see he was heading for a great future. Gunner's life up to now had been a mess, what with school, moving off the island, then no fishing. Not much else could go wrong.

Gunner could see Mother had something to say, but that was ok. He was too happy to let a lecture get him down. While driving, Mother said, "Things are looking up, Gunner. I am happy for you. I do want you to remember that a certain young girl likes you a lot. I want you to be careful not to hurt her feelings when you are blustering around as you do at times." She glanced over to make sure he was listening. "You are a kind, thoughtful, and gentle person. Now, when you have to be hard, you're like someone people haven't seen before. We both can guess where that comes from, and I don't think you are that kind of person."

This lecture must be an important one. Mother is making it a long one.

"I like Quiet Bird and being friends with her will be the best thing you can do. I don't think she will ever let your friendship suffer on her part. She is a good person, and you can't help but see how you always need to respect and care for her when she is with you or even when you are apart."

All he could say was, "Yes, Mother, I do understand, thank you for bringing it up. I won't forget."

Darn, I am changing. What happened to my smart mouth?

CHAPTER 29

The ride back to the ranch was quiet after the long lecture. Gunner realized his life was becoming more complicated. He felt older, and someone just added a bunch of new pieces to his life puzzle. In the last six weeks, he had started working a mine, Bell became his dog and close companion, and now Jack had joined the crew. Gunner felt the new load of responsibility in keeping him fed and cared for.

What was he to do about the girl? Mother was lecturing him about "the girl," then schoolwork on top of everything else. At least, he doesn't have to feed and care for the girl, although he did have feelings for her.

Mother has decided to let me stay and get on with my life, even if I am young. Gunner was hoping the mine would help him sort things out up there. He just wanted to be left alone with his crew.

Bell and Jack are as important as the Springfield and the .45 for my life up at the claim. Guess I'd better pay attention to detail, just like Cleo taught me.

When they arrived back at the barn, Mom went in to visit with Granny. Bell and Gunner went out to fetch Jack. Tying Jack at the hitching post, Gunner thought about him being green broke with the pack. *Here we go, boy. I should have put the pack and gear on you last night for a trial run.* Loading Jack's pack bags went relatively smooth because Jack trusted Gunner from all that time they spent together earlier in the summer.

The gear they bought in town barely filled most of one pack. On the other side, he loaded grain and the salt lick block, then put in the new extra blanket Mother had insisted on. She wouldn't cut Gunner any slack. She flat out insisted he buy that darn blanket. For now, he was putting it between the sawbuck's cross. He planned to put Bell up there if she slows or starts exploring and can't keep up.

When they picked up more ammo, he had also bought a used rifle scabbard. Now, he could hang it on the cross-buck pack. Jack could carry his Springfield for him. He would pack the .45 shooter.

He would often carry the Springfield in his hand if he didn't have the .45 on him. Speaking of the Springfield, Gunner saw Mom walking down from the house with it, and Granny was with her. No one was talking, just watching Gunner get Jack loaded. Mother handed Gunner the Springfield, showing Gunner she trusted him with his life in the wilderness.

Gunner loaded the Springfield by shoving a cartridge in the chamber. He then slid it into the sheath on Jack. Next, Mother handed him his hat. With that, he could feel his throat tighten. The time had come.

With his hat in his hand, he stepped over to Granny and gave her a big hug. "Thank you for your trust. I'll be coming back through in about three weeks, maybe four. Tell Norman I will take care of our boy here."

Turning to his mother, he hugged her and had to fight back a misty eye. There were a couple of sniffs. Mother smiled her beautiful Mom smile.

She said, "You take care of yourself. I put in paper, envelopes, and stamps. Now you write to me, you hear. Gunner, I'll be checking on you with Talking Bird and Granny, so I will know when you come out." She paused, taking a deep breath. "I think with all this, there wasn't much choice. It was supposed to happen. Now you go have your adventure."

"Yes, Mother. Give my love to Sister for me. Thank you for helping out today. Thank you for trusting me to do this." He took a deep breath. "Getting away from school and town is not that important to me now. It is the dream of working the mine with my new crew. Don't worry about Quiet Bird. I'll remember what you told me."

Picking up Jack's lead, Gunner turned and started at a fast walk, calling Bell, "Come on, Bell, daylight's a-burning girl."

They headed for the shortcut. Gunner couldn't get himself to look back. It was hard as he walked away. He would miss his mother. She had always been his best support. Earlier, not saying anything to her, he had put the last of his cash, two hundred fifty dollars, in one of her envelopes and wrote on the front, "Thank you, Mother, you're the best." He then threw it on the dash of the old ford, in front of the steering wheel.

Gunner knew he could have paid for nearly half of Elk City's equipment with that money, but Mother had always been there for him. Now, it is his turn to be there for her in any way he could.

Things are thin at home, with the old man working on the boat and not making any money. This will help out around the house. I know it's not much, but it's the best I can do for now. That would be two weeks' worth of wages for the old man if he were hauling oil in the winter.

I got to quit talking to myself. Well, who else can I tell besides myself?

"Jack, did you do anything exciting this morning while we were in town? Hmm, thought not, slow day, huh? Just go ahead, enjoy the walk."

CHAPTER 30

J ack was doing well carrying the new pack. *He leads like he didn't have anything on his back. Also, nothing on his mind that I know of.* Getting out of Granny's in the afternoon had made them late, and he didn't feel like camping out tonight. There was way too much to do back at the claim and so little time to do it, especially before the snow came.

They had walked up the valley about a mile. Gunner and his crew reached the edge of the wash where the brush was a lot thicker, and he didn't want to lose Bell. "Come over here, girl, we are stepping it out, and you, my friend, are starting to drag. You get to ride on Jack here. Glad I built you a seat. Now, don't overload him." Gunner laughed making Bell's tail wag. She jumped as he lifted her, then settled in and rode in the middle of Jack's back.

Walking along, Gunner was thinking he and his crew needed to check on Cleo and have an extended visit. They needed to settle the price of the claim and how Gunner was going to pay Cleo off. Now that Gunner had a drill and compressor lined up, that could double, if not triple, the production at the mine.

When they get to the mine, Gunner wanted to get the sluice box working right away. Then, it will be time to start training Jack to pull the gondola out of the shaft. Gunner looked back at Jack. A burrow would be a better choice. Second thought, a couple of goats would be better than using Jack. He will be just too darn big to go into the mine.

The walk was good for them all. It gave the crew time to shake the cobwebs out and clear their heads. Gunner needed a dose of the wilderness after being around all those people. He thought back to the dinner table conversation at Granny's. Gunner knew what it would be like when he went in, like walking into the bear's den. The only reason he sat at the dinner table was to make Mother happy. He still didn't think it was worth the time.

What Gunner wanted was to be left alone in the barn with his critters. That sure beats any old dinner table conversation. He didn't need that, and there's a good chance he won't be involved in another one for a long time. Unless, of course, if Mother drags him into one. He would only do it for her, that's it.

Wait a minute, didn't he say he would only do it for Mother? Well, maybe the Quiet Bird girl. He wasn't sure, but something told him he would do almost anything for her, and he didn't even know the why of it.

Gunner came back from his thoughts and took a long look up ahead. It was beautiful, with the pines standing straight and filling the air with their smell. They were the tall and untouched arms of Mother Nature. He could see a few white puffy clouds floating, with beautiful blue sky behind them. Gunner was grateful to be where he belonged again. He could breathe better now and felt a lot of weight coming off his shoulders.

The sun was tipping toward the trees, and Jack is starting to sweat. "Whoa there, Jack. Let's stop for water and rest up. We might already be halfway home."

With Jack's long legs and Gunner half trotting, they were making good time, working their way up the valley for the cabin. "Bell, you can get down and wander if you like. You were a good girl, not a peep for the last couple of hours." As he took her down, she was a happy puppy, stretching her legs, then going over and putting her nose up to Jack's. "Looks like you got yourself a new friend there, Bell."

Norman had given Gunner an old canvas oat bag he could use for watering Jack. Gunner filled it halfway from his canteen, and Jack took a long drink, then put his head down to graze on the meadow grass. He seemed to like it as much as Butch did. It was hard to stop for Gunner. He would rather keep going, but Cleo had told him, "Ya gotta stop and put some gas in the tank, or they might stop running for you."

"Alright, you two, time to roll. Bell, come here." She trotted right over to him to be hoisted up on Jack's pack. Picking up Jack's lead, Gunner announced, "Next stop, home, everyone."

They made the cabin with an hour of light left for the day. Gunner didn't know for sure because he forgot to buy a clock in town. *Time doesn't matter that much out here anyway. We eat when we're hungry. Get up and go to bed with the sun. Works for me. I'll mark off the days to keep my promise in town, especially with Miss Quiet Bird.*

The cabin had not been bothered during his absence. Gunner was beginning to doubt the stories about bears breaking into an empty place. *Come to think of it, I haven't seen a sign of a bear or mountain lion yet. Guess that might be later when winter comes. I wonder how you skin and quarter a bear? They kind of look like a fat dog, maybe a little woolier.* Gunner unloaded the gear off Jack and moved it into the cabin. Then Jack got brushed, fed, and put in his stall for the night.

It was time to get out the new reading lamp and build a fire. "What sounds good for dinner to you, Bell? Think I will have the corned beef hash and two of the eggs Granny gave me. Ok, puppy chow tonight. How would you like that served? Yes, you can eat it out of Dad's hand. After all, you are still a puppy."

With feeding Bell and himself out of the way, Gunner could sit down and look over the books they had picked up at the library. All but one of the books was on mining. Mom had told him he needed to learn how to "keep" a set of books for the mine. "Keeping the books" was important to her because that was her job back home. Gunner wondered, *Why would I need a bank account, a checkbook, and keep track of what comes in and what goes out? Guess I'll chalk that one up to Mom knows best.* He suspected she was right, as usual, and he'd better get busy learning it. Not tonight, though. Bell was already on her rug, curled up and sleeping soundly.

Shutting things down, Gunner was not far behind her. Crawling into bed, he thought Cleo was right to tell him to set aside two hours every night to read about mining. He said out loud, "Cover to cover."

I do remember on the fish boat that Uncle Martin kept close track of the fish they caught, sold, and the fuel and grub they used. Hey, that's right! He did show me how he did it using one of those books with all the lines. He bought it at the drug store. It was right on the shelf and had blue pages, maybe green. I'll read Mom's book to see if I can use some of its ideas. There has to be some good stuff in there because it sure has a lot of pages. It's just as thick as the mining books, including the ones Cleo gave me.

Oh, Brother! It's back. He had that feeling that his life was getting complicated, and he had that once already in the car after the lecture. *All this thinking is wearing me down.*

Gunner was dead tired but had one last thought. *I would like Quiet Bird to give me a picture of her, so I could see her when I think of her. Yea, that's the best idea I've had since I got back to the cabin.*

"Goodnight, Bell. Keep the puppy dreams down and let me know if you need to pee, ok? We don't want any accidents."

The next morning, by the time they had breakfast out of the way, it was almost full daylight.

"Come on, Jack, let me show you your new pasture and watering hole. Butch has it all broke in for you."

With Jack in the pasture and his lead rope off, Bell and Gunner walked the fence line to make sure there had been no damage done while they were gone. Gunner looked up, and Jack was right there beside them. It made him feel good to know that Jack liked his company and would be here when he and Bell came to get him in the evening.

With Jack cared for, Gunner and Bell headed up to the mine. Everything was good. The sluice and stamp mill were waiting for them. Filling the stamp hopper didn't take long, then Gunner could turn on the water for the power. *Darn! I need to capture that water.*

"Let's go check the pond, Bell." The water had slowed, and the pond was only half full. There wasn't a rain cloud in sight, with this being August.

"This will only give us a couple of hours of operating time. A fine how-do-you-do, wouldn't you say Bell? Alright, let's see what the bubbling fountain is doing. If I could jar and tap the hot spring, that could increase the water coming out." Gunner had read about hot springs in the National Geographic once when the teacher sent him out to the foyer in the one-room-school on the island.

It's just a vent in the cracks in the rocks. The center of the earth was just a big old teapot, shoving water up to the surface to relieve the pressure. The pool and steam are free for the taking. Gunner would have to try something, or this job will be over before it got started. He thought it a good idea to stop and pick up the hand drill rod and see if he could make the crack bigger or drill a hole.

In the shed, he picked up a 10-pound maul and two hand drills. *I hope this works, or we're making a trip to see Cleo. He'll know what to do.*

Both he and Bell approached the pool of steam, and something didn't feel right. Trust your gut, Cleo taught him. The bank looked different today.

Yep. That something was a giant, fat, rattlesnake, and Bell was six feet in front of it. The snake looked like he had just had a big breakfast and took a snooze by the warm hot spring. Cleo told him rattlesnakes weren't around here that much, but in his words, "Just don't piss them off" is all he said.

Ok, that sounds good, Gunner thought. *I won't. Bell might, and she just woke it up. Dang, this was a big one. It could be over 8-ft long.* The snake was coiled up, ready to strike—his rattler chattering from side to side.

Bell didn't know what it was and froze in her tracks.

Gunner yelled, "*Bell!!*" She spun around and ran straight to him. "Good girl." She would be safe if she stayed with him. *The snake should turn, high tail it out of here, and leave us alone.*

Wrong! The snake wanted to stay its ground, head poised, ready to strike, and still rattling away. Gunner pulled the .45 out of the shoulder holster and watching the snake so close, he didn't see that curious Bell was approaching it one more time.

There was no time even to think, let alone aim, and one shot was all he would get. If Gunner missed, Bell would have one giant snake on her. He could hit Bell while intending to shoot the snake. The whole thing was rolling through his head too fast. He didn't want to kill his puppy.

The .45 was up in both hands before he knew it. He extended his arms, cocking it at the same time. Pulling in a calming breath, he held it, let out a bit, and aimed at the center of the coiled-up snake for the biggest target.

The next thought was, *Trust your shot!* It would be a twenty-foot shot. Aim straight over the top of the barrel and pull the trigger. *Firing,* he thought. He had re-cocked and was pulling on the trigger before he could see where the first bullet went.

Bell froze in her tracks again. Only this time, she wasn't going to move with the pistol going off. The snake caught the slug about 18" back from its head. *Damn, I hate snakes!* All they had was garter snakes on the coast, and all the same, he hated them. So did Bell from that day forward.

The snake was dead, not even a wiggle. Gunner had heard snakes were good to eat. Tastes like chicken, they say. No thanks, Bell, and he would pass. Gunner picked up the snake and threw it about ten feet into the brush so they could go to work. *Hell of a snake, Miss Bell.*

The snake lay there all day, and Bell never once went close to it. Gunner believed the girl got the message. Snakes are bad for dogs and people alike.

CHAPTER 31

The two-foot drill bit was shoved into the widest crack, and Gunner slammed it with the 10-pound maul. Then he gave the bit a quarter turn, hitting it again. The process was repeated over and over for a couple of hours straight. Gunner pulled on the bit to get it out of the hole. "Ouch!" He needed gloves or a rag of some kind. The drill bit was scorching from the scalding hot water. When he was just giving a quarter turn, it wasn't that hot, but a firm grip on it was too much for his hand.

"Come on, Bell. We gotta go check the stamp mill and have some lunch, and we'll see how Jack is doing in his new home."

With lunch done, a check on Jack showed he was doing fine. Gunner set up the salt lick to call in some dinner, then he and Bell went right back up to the mine. They needed the rest of the tools for his drilling project. That would be the six-foot pick bar, leather gloves, and a chunk of the chain he could wrap on the bit.

Back at the hot spring, he tried pulling out the stuck drill with his gloves on. Nope again, that won't work. Guess he'd better see if he could rig something with the chain and bar to give him more leverage.

Yea, that worked. The chain was tied to the drill, and the bar made fast into the chain. Then, he laid the bar over a chunk of rotted log he had drug up. Voila! Out she came. After all that work, it didn't improve the water flow, so he had to keep going with the six-foot drill.

By evening time, Gunner needed to shut down, and the bit was stuck again. Gunner was prying the bar out of the rock the same way. The six-foot bar was harder to get unstuck, and he had to take it in bights.

Finally! It came loose with a spew of dirty water and rock chunks flying out of the crack. The stream of hot water was spouting about twelve inches high above the creek water, more than doubling the water coming out of the spring. *Hurray for the dumb kid! Just what we needed. Now the stamp can run longer. Every little bit helps, but we do need more for the mill. I'll talk to Cleo about a pump and holding pond for water below the sluice.*

Back at the cabin, Gunner put Jack in his corral. He could step in the shed if he wanted to, and Gunner thought Jack would let him know if anything was there to hurt him. Bell and Gunner had a good dinner, the same as last night. Then he read about mining for a couple of hours and hit the rack. All that pounding on the drill took it out of him today.

The following day was the same routine. When Bell and he arrived at the mine, Gunner got the hopper filled and started up the stamp mill. They went up to the holding pond to see how much water they saved overnight with the improved flow.

Hey, this is great! Almost full! That would keep them going until noon, then the water could build a couple of hours, and they could go until quitting time. Whew, one part of his worrisome problem was solved, but it still doesn't solve this winter's problem when things start to freeze up.

In the mine, he got things ready to start digging. There was one old gondola car for mucking out the tunnel. It had small solid-rubber wheels, not on tracks, like the forklifts they had at the fish house. Gunner knew he couldn't even run over a cherry pit, or it would stop the car.

It was something else he needed to change when there was a chance. There was some old track lying out by the front of the mine. After lunch, he brought Jack to pull the track up to the mine shaft.

Now, Jack's training was something else. At just over a year, his back was darn near six feet tall. Gunner led Jack toward the mine tunnel. Oh my, he *did not* want to go into that black hole. He reared back and hit his head while Gunner was trying to lead him in. Didn't hurt him any, but it scared the both of them. They agreed they wouldn't try that again.

While watching television as a kid at home, Gunner watched a show where they covered the horse's eyes, and it calmed them for going into the mine. Well, darn, if it didn't work. Gunner was able to lead Jack into the tunnel once he covered the mule's eyes.

Now, Jack was too big to turn around in the shaft, and they very carefully backed their way out. That was the end of try number two and that was the last try. Gunner figured they had to dream up something else. This boy mule is growing like a weed.

Another idea came to Gunner. How about a rope or wire with Jack outside and using *"Giddy-up"* and *"Whoa?"* Then Jack could pull the gondola out for Gunner. Once the gondola comes out of the mine, it will hit the stops that would trip and dump the payload of rock and ore into the mill hopper. He just needed to install the tracks and change the wheels he scrounged up behind the shed. At least that was the plan.

An average day at the mine was 16 or so hours of light. The days were getting shorter, so Gunner went to the mine in the dark of morning since it was dark inside the shaft all the time anyway. The digging wasn't too hard, and according to Cleo, he figured bedrock at twenty feet away.

By now, it was late into the third week, and he was still going strong. The salt lick brought in a young whitetail deer that gave its life so they could have something to eat. They needed other provisions soon, and that would put him at four weeks. He needed to pick up some dynamite on his next trip to town. Then, he could do some blasting in the mine. Gunner had a slew of questions for Cleo on using that stuff.

I used up most of the mom's letter writing paper for my questions. I need to buy a tablet next trip.

It was time to sit down and write Mother a letter.

Dear Mother,

20 September 1962

I hope you and all the others are doing well. Jack, Bell, and I have been swamped here at the claim.

The mine is shaping up, and it's time to go to town to pick up dynamite to start blasting. I have the holes drilled and ready to go.

We've been eating very well, and I do scrub up every evening before dinner like you always told me to do at home. After supper is out of the way, I read a couple of hours before bedtime.

I hope to see the teacher when we go to town next to get started on my lessons.

Hi to everyone there at home.

Love you Mother
Gunner

Once he decided to go into town, Gunner got things cleaned up and loaded quickly. The sluice box was working great now there was more water to keep it running, and the mine was paying out better than Gunner had ever expected. He figured there was more than enough gold to take care of his trip to town, plus put some away for the equipment he had waiting at Oley's.

It was early morning, and the crew was ready to roll. The last thing was to pack a quarter of the whitetail for Cleo. He liked venison more than anyone Gunner had ever met. Gunner was figuring that Cleo needed winter wood put up as well. He planned to fill his wood box and shed even if it took an extra day. It would be worth the time spent, and always good to help a friend.

The trail to Cleo's was dry and easy to follow with no wildlife spotted. It hadn't rained for a long time and the path had become dusty. It needed a drink of water soon. There were more clouds, though, and maybe it would rain a little. *We don't need thunder and lightning, that could start a forest fire on us.*

At home, it was time for the first fall storms to start. He needed to buy rain gear, put that on the list, and an extra tarp to keep Jack's pack dry. His thoughts wandered as he led them down the trail. *While in town, we can pick a 12-gauge pump at Elroy's gun-shop. Sounds tasty, turkey and rice for dinner. Darn, I'm hungry already and have hardly made it out of the dogleg yet. It will be helpful to sit and talk to Cleo. I'm tired of talking to myself.* To Gunner's surprise, he found he didn't miss a conversation with a friend until he couldn't have one. *My crew is the best, bless their hearts, but it just is not the same. I know I sure would like to sit with Miss Quiet Bird for an afternoon. We could quietly talk about a bunch of nothing.*

"Time to rest, crew. This will be the only stop until Cleo's. Bell, you're a good girl. You've kept up with us the whole time."

The crew was out in front of Cleo's just before noon. Gunner remembered he needed to buy a clock so he could tell time. With it getting darker earlier, he was losing track of the day.

Gunner called out for Cleo from out front and it took him a while to come out to the front porch. Cleo said, "Long time no see, neighbor. That Bell of yours has doubled in size since I saw her last. And who is this? Could that be the mighty Jack?"

With a big grin, Gunner said, "Yep, he's the latest addition to my crew. Come on down here and check him out. He doesn't kick like some." Gunner was like a proud new papa showing his new son to a friend.

Coming down the steps, Cleo said, "He is a fine-looking animal. Say, I might have an old single hitch that would fit him for dragging a log or the occasional sled."

"That would be great, Cleo. I plan on spending an extra day here so that I can make up most of your winter wood. Also, do you have any heavy lifting you might need done while I'm here?"

Cleo laughed. "We'll see. Let's have some lunch. With that hoof sticking out of the pack, could that be a quarter of venison in there?"

"Yep. How do you want to cut it up?"

"You go care for your mule there and get cleaned up from the trail. I want to hear all of what has gone on. I am guessing your mother let you stay for the winter?"

Gunner nodded. "Sounds good. I'm hungry, but, heck, I'm always hungry," He led Jack off to the shed for a scoop of grain and a flake of hay." Over his shoulder, he said, "I want to settle on the claim, Cleo. You said you would take the payment in gold. I have enough in my poke to give you a good down-payment and enough left over to buy the gear I need."

Cleo was sitting in his chair at the table, ready for lunch and some good conversation. "Sure, we have time for settling the mine. Now, what I want to hear is how it went with your mother. She showed up at the claim, right? You know, I sent them your way. Your older brother sure looks a lot like you."

So, the visit started, taking Cleo through the whole stay, including holding Quiet Bird's hand. That was the best part of the two days he had been at Granny's, except for buying Jack. Cleo wanted to hear the deal Norman cut with him on the mule. That sounded fair to Cleo.

Cleo laughed when Gunner told him about buying the equipment from Oley. "You know that equipment is as good as the day he bought it. That man took the best care of his equipment, and he's a fair man too."

"Speaking of equipment," Gunner said, "You mentioned you had some lying around that you would sell me when I bought the claim."

"You're right. We'll go outside later." Still driving the conversation, Cleo asked, "Now tell me about that cute young lady you're making eyes at."

Gunner answered with a sheepish grin. "Mother made me take her to the teacher's house so she could talk to Talking Bird and set me up with once-a-month lessons. Then I could take a test. That would let me work the mine and finish junior high school. Also, Mom could call Talking Bird on the phone to keep track of me. I think there will be trouble if I don't keep my promise."

Cleo leaned back, grinning, listening to every word.

"Now, here is the best part of all. I get to see Quiet Bird once a month when I go in for gear and grub. Cleo, I'd like to settle on the claim, and I'm ready to start blasting in the old girl. That will call for some dynamite this trip. Do you think we could go into town and get some?"

Cleo liked the ambition in this young man. "Sure, not a problem. I assume you'll want to see the girls too. We should tell them we're coming. That would be the best thing to do."

Gunner said, "Yes, of course! With that other stuff out of the way, can we talk about the mine? A lot is going on out there, and I need your advice on a bunch of it. Hold on, let me go hang up that whitetail first. I almost forgot. Do you want me to cut it up for you? Then we can talk mining at the same time?"

The rest of the day went quickly, and then it was gone. It was time for dinner, with a couple of venison steaks Gunner had laid out for them.

The conversation finally turned into a thoughtful discussion of the claim.

Cleo said, "I can see you've been reading the books I gave you, and it was a good idea to check more books out of the library. Now let's see, you say you doubled the spring by drilling and letting it flush the dirt and rocks out?"

Gunner leaned forward, excited about his progress. "Yep, that cleaned it up, and I think if I drive a pipe down into it, I could send a stick of dynamite down there and loosen things some more. What do you think?"

Cleo scratched his head. "Yes, you could do that, and it might open things up a bit. On the other hand, you could close it down for good."

Gunner replied, "I hadn't thought of that, and that doesn't sound so good. Come winter I need water to run the sluice box. With that water being hot, I might be able to stamp maybe six to eight hours a day. Also, we need to talk about a retention pond just below the sluice box and then a pump of some kind to send it back up to where it had just come. There, the hot water can warm it up and send it back down the hill."

Cleo, once more, scratched his head. Gunner thought it helped him ponder. "Yea, that could work," Cleo said. "We could put a pump together with the old one-lung gas motor I have buried in the shed. We might be able to pick up a pump in Grangeville at the hardware store. Another thing, at the lumber store, they have something in a bag that's like powder, and it turns the bottom of the pond as hard as a coconut shell. Then it won't leak on you. I forget what they call it, but they'll know when we ask for it."

"That sounds great. I do need some dynamite for the mine, and could you give me a quick lesson on the dos and don'ts, please? That would make my poor mother happy."

With a laugh, Cleo replied, "Oh yeah! It will be fun to blow something up again."

They spent the evening talking about the mine, working through all the questions on the list Gunner had written back at the claim.

Later, Cleo landed up in his chair and fell sound asleep while Gunner did the dishes. After filling the stove and wood box, Gunner threw an old blanket over Cleo, went out to the shed, and called it a night.

Morning came early for the crew and they all had something to do. Jack needed to go out back on a stake. Gunner had to look for the gas motor to run a pump. It was looking like two trips back into the mine, with a box of gas and dynamite. They needed to make separate trips with the explosive and gasoline, or Jack would be a walking bomb if they didn't.

Gunner thought he could smell bacon cooking, and his stomach told him to get on in there, so they could eat and head for town. Over the breakfast table, Gunner said, "I found the one lunger and drug it out. It looks just like the one the old man used to pump water up to the water tower on the island."

Gunner shoveled in a scoop of pancakes, gulped it down, and kept talking. "I think I'll need some schooling on it. I noticed the motor was on a skid. That should let Jack yard it back to the claim with the harness you gave me."

Finishing up his plate of flapjacks and venison, Cleo said, "That should work. Let's take a close look at the hookup for the pump. You can measure the shaft and keyway before we go. Might have to stop by the machine shop in Grangeville to have a pulley bored for it, so be ready to spend some more money."

It was an hour before they were cleaned up and ready to go. The boys and the dog loaded into the jeep and headed to town. Talk never stopped as Gunner had missed his good friend. Cleo knew so much, and Gunner knew so little. It was a good partnership. The shut-up-and-listen stuff on Gunner's side of the conversation was paying off.

First, to the courthouse to sign over the mining claim. Cleo lectured Gunner about the rules and regulations for the application. That took a while. Cleo had the clerk give him a pamphlet that explained everything he had just told him. In his teacher's voice, Cleo leaned on Gunner, "Here now, read it, cover to cover! They aren't kidding about what they say and be sure you do it." He also told him to file more claims around the mine. "You just never know you might want to expand your operation someday."

The gold buyer's store was the second stop and that gave them the cash needed for the rest of the day. The gun shop was next, and that was on the way to the hardware store. Walking into the gun shop was like seeing another old friend. Elroy said, "What can I do for you two desperadoes today?"

Cleo spoke first, "Seems my neighbor here would like to do some wild turkey shooting."

Elroy, as usual, was behind the counter. "Now, that is a wily one. A long barrel 12-gauge pump should work. Used okay for you, Gunner?"

"You bet, used works for me."

Elroy turned and reached into the rifle rack behind him. "There it is. This one should fit you. Like I said, the barrel is a little longer, so you will be able to reach out and hold the pattern better."

The gun had the right balance for Gunner. "If we add a couple of boxes of birdshot and throw in a box of the double-aught buck, what's all this going to run me? Also, could you put a sling in there too? With what I'm doing, I like to keep my hands free."

Looking for a sling, Elroy said, "I heard the first day you bought the .45, it found you some trouble in Elk City."

Gunner answered, "No trouble, I just don't like bullies that shove people around. Thanks for the hammer latch. It gave me time to get the knife out next to his fat belly. I thought the bayonet was a little long. Would you have a shorter one like the Marines used in World War II at Iwo Jima?"

"Sure, we got some K-bar surplus, run you five bucks. That would be sixty bucks for everything so far, shotgun, shells, and sling."

"Sounds good. Let's do it."

Gunner could see Elroy still had something to say and was dragging his feet getting it out. Cleo could see it also. "Spit it out, would you? You have something to say."

"Okay, you asked for it," Elroy sighed. "Those boys from Elk City were in the other day buying ammo and gear. They were bragging, especially the fat one, that they had jerked a greenhorn around. He said he got the drop on Gunner here."

Cleo jumped in before Gunner could say anything, "That is a damn lie, and you know it! I was there. Just ask Officer Bob when he comes in next time."

"I already did, Cleo. Calm down, would you? Officer Bob was in, and he said the kid here had him cold with the knife and was waiting for him to make a move. Bob thought Gunner would cut him up for fish bait, coming from the coast and all."

Elroy smiled with a nod of approval. "You're getting a reputation, kid, living up in the wilderness and working a mine. Most folks figure you're meaner than a timber rattler."

Cleo said, "Reputation? Now how could he be getting one of those?"

Elroy responded while Cleo was thinking it over. "Is your memory that short? I think I remember someone a while back did the same damn thing from what my grandpa told me."

Cleo said, "Well yeah, but I never stood off any bullies. Second thought, maybe I did tap that feller on the shoulder with a spade shovel. That was to help make it a fair fight. Hell, the kid here had the bully beat before he got out of bed that morning."

Gunner chuckled. "Thanks, Cleo, it wasn't that much. He was just too slow. I'd like to see that shorter bayonet if I could. Will it fit the Springfield? How about a sheath with a latch? That worked perfectly with the bully's fat belly."

Elroy smiled again. "Yes, the sheath has a latch, and it will fit the Springfield. How is the Springfield working out for you?"

"It has good balance, and the bolt is as smooth as glass, just like you told me. Could I get a couple more boxes of ammo for it? And, the Springfield keeps meat on the table for Bell, and I'm thinking that's the best part."

Elroy looked at Gunner. "Who's Bell?"

Gunner said without looking down, "She's my dog, the one lying on my foot here."

Elroy leaned over the counter, "Nice dog. Rottweiler?"

"Yep, rot lab mix. Should be eighty pounds or so when she is full-grown. We're just getting out of the puppy stuff."

Cleo waded back in. "All right, Elroy, let's have the rest of it."

Elroy leaned back against the counter. "Now, I don't want to tell you about your business. Those boys are bad news. They come in from the hills behind Elk City. They've been raised wild-like, you know what I mean."

Elroy paused. "No one ever got the drop on them before as Gunner did, and they don't like it. The boys are always looking for a fight, even if they have to lie about it. They will be watching for you, and they *do* mean to do you harm. Don't let those good-for-nothings get the drop on you. If they get the chance to blindside you, there won't be a second chance. I wouldn't trust them to be fair about anything. Even Officer Bob has his problems with them, and he's the law up there. Just be careful."

Cleo, not liking what he was hearing, said to Gunner, "Kid, pay the man and let's go. This talk is wearing on me. Thank you for all that, Elroy. I know you're right. Gunner and I will ponder on it. Thanks again."

Cleo grumbled on his way to the door. "Elroy, there is one more thing you can pass along. When they call him *the kid*, they're wrong. He is doing a grown man's job. That would be a whole lot more than most men can do. Not only that, but Gunner is also a whole lot smarter than those boys out behind Elk City."

Elroy nodded. They could see Cleo was none too happy, and he went to the jeep to cool a bit. Gunner wouldn't want to back him into a corner. There would be a huge price to pay for something like that.

Back in the jeep, they decided the water pump was next, then the machine shop, so they could finish up their shopping while the pulley machining was getting done.

At the hardware store, they found the pulley they needed, and Cleo was right. They needed to take it to the machine shop to bore and key it. While at the hardware store, they bought an extra 36-inch hand rock drill bit and a short-handled maul for pounding on it.

Gunner asked for two cases of dynamite and enough blasting caps with fuses for what he was buying. The clerk took one look at Gunner and then over to Cleo, catching his eye. He nodded, "Yes," and they wrote up the bill.

"Thanks, Cleo," Gunner said back at the jeep. "I don't think they would've sold the dynamite to me if you weren't there."

Cleo smiled. "Next time they will. After all, you have a reputation now." They both laughed. While driving over to the machine shop, Gunner fitted the new bayonet to his shoulder harness. "How does that crap get started with a reputation and all, Cleo?"

Cleo replied, "Easy. People don't have much else to do but gossip. Now you, sunny boy, you have given them something to do their gossiping about. Believe it or not, there is excitement in that for them."

Cleo sighed and scratched his brow. "When you stood off the bad boys, you became like a hero. No one likes the bad guys. That's why they call them bad guys. Now, you backed them off where others wouldn't have the stuff to do it. People think highly of you for doing that. We could call it respect.

"Then there is the other part. They, the folks in the county, haven't had someone take on the wilderness as you have. You are all alone and going in to work through the winter. That gives them something to think about. They're watching to see if you make it or not. You know what I mean?"

"Yeah, I guess I do. I'm not much interested in all that. I just want to be left alone with my dog and mule out at the claim." They got out at the machine shop and saw Uncle Jacob out front of the big bay door. Gunner was carrying the V-belt pulley in his hand.

"Hi there, boys, looks like you need something worked on?"

Gunner said, "Hi, Uncle. I need this pulley bored and keyed to one and a half inches with a three-eighths key. How long do you think it would take?"

"Why don't you leave it here and pick it up on your way out of town? Say, you're quite the talk around here." Gunner shook his head. "Don't believe everything you hear. How are Aunt Ida and the cousins doing?"

"Mother's in the office working on the books. Go say hi to her. I'm sure she would like to hear what you've been up to." He smiled, then took a long pull on the big stogie he was always smoking or chewing on.

"Could I borrow the phone just for a minute? I need to call Elk City and make arrangements to see the teacher."

"Sure, go ahead."

As Gunner walked over to see Aunt Ida, Cleo went back to wait in the jeep, as he was feeling a bit tired today. Gunner stepped into the office. "Hi, Aunt Ida, how have you been?"

She smiled.

"I brought you some business. Could I borrow your phone to call the teacher in Elk City?"

"Help yourself. How are you doing out at the mine? It seems you've been busy in Elk City…"

She is smart that way, just like my mother. She dragged the bait across my nose just to see if I would bite.

With a laugh, Gunner said, "Don't believe everything you hear, Auntie."

Gunner called Talking Bird. She just got home from school, and Quiet Bird would be along shortly. She said, "You're with Cleo, aren't you?"

Gunner answered, "Yes, ma'am."

"Why don't you two figure on dinner and we'll have time to visit about your lessons? I know for sure Quiet Bird would like to see you."

Gunner answered, "Yes, ma'am, I'd like to see her too. Well, I want to see you both." Aunt Ida smiled, overhearing the phone conversation.

"We're maybe a couple of hours out, and then we'll see you for dinner. I don't think Cleo, or I, have ever turned down a dinner invitation. Thank you, ma'am."

Putting down the receiver, he could see Auntie wanted to talk, so Gunner sat for a minute. "Yes, Auntie, what is it that you have to say? I can see it in your eyes that words are heading my way." He learned this from his mother.

"Well, it's what's going around. You're one tough young man. You stood up for the Indian girl against the Ferguson boys in Elk City, and they didn't like backing down."

She tensed slightly behind her desk. "They're making noise that the next time you come into town, they can't let you get away with what you did. I don't want to see you get hurt, Gunner. It would kill your mother."

"Does she know anything about this?" Gunner asked. "I explained it to her, sort of, and ignored the rest. I'm not planning on any more trouble unless they are looking for it."

Aunt Ida looked at Gunner with her kind eyes, and he could see she was sizing him up. Yes, this is her young nephew, now a young man in the chair in front of her. He guessed he looked a wee bit scary sitting there with the six-shooter and bayonet hanging on the shoulder straps under his tin canvas coat, his flat brim hat on his knee, and hard-weathered face.

Auntie slowed her gaze at his work-beaten hands. She didn't stop there. She noted his torn and worn tin pants all the way to the heavy leather boots on his feet. Gunner knew he must have been quite a sight. Her eyes wandered back up past his tattered second-hand flannel shirt, taking a long look at his face one more time.

Gunner knew she had more to say. Maybe he needs a haircut. It was long and shaggy but clean. He would never come to town if he hadn't washed up at the hot spring, just short of a bath.

"I know you, nephew, you are a sight for a good fight. You may scare them with that hair of yours."

"Thanks for the advice, Auntie. I'll keep it in my secret weapon box."

Getting up, Gunner put his hat on, turning for the door. Auntie said, "Gunner, I hear that girl you stood up for is a nice girl, be good to her."

Gunner smiled. "Too late. Mother gave me that lecture on the way back up to the ranch. See you on my next trip to town. Come on, Bell, let's get going." Auntie smiled and waved her hand. Gunner thought about what she said. *I'd better lay low when I go to Elk City. Think the haircut is good advice. I would like to look clean-cut for Miss Quiet Bird.*

CHAPTER 32

Back in the jeep, Gunner said to Cleo, "Put on your best smile, pard, we've been invited to dinner tonight. If I remember right, Talking Bird has an overstuffed chair in the living room, and you can take a nap afterward. I'll need to go over some lessons and such. Also, I'd like to sit and visit with Quiet Bird for a bit before we leave."

Smiling, Cleo said, "That sure sounds good. Let's step on it. Got to pick up a couple of boxes of gas at the jobber's, don't we? One more thing, we need some of that pond liner stuff at the lumberyard for your retention pond, then back to pick up the pulley. Hope we measured those V-belts right."

The jobber was the Chevron dealership. Gunner picked up two wooden boxes. That would be two rectangle 5-gallon cans of gasoline in each wood box, giving Gunner 20 gallons total. He hoped it would last until he came out again. He planned on leaving the gas and dynamite at Cleo's. That made it handy to pick up when he needed it. All loaded, they headed back for the machine shop to pick up his pulley.

On the way, they stopped by the lumber store and picked up three bags of some powdered stuff for the pond. "The directions are on the bag," the hardware employee said. Gunner didn't think he knew much more than Cleo or him. Maybe he didn't like the way Gunner wore his hat. Could he be needing a haircut?

At the machine shop, Aunt Ida had already gone home. Uncle Jacob took his money and said he would see Gunner next trip.

They were all loaded up and on their way to see the teacher and her beautiful daughter. *"Beautiful?" Where did that come from? Maybe, it could be pretty or somewhat cute.* He did know he wanted a picture of her to take back up to the mine with him. It was a sure way to get a guy to keep up on his schoolwork.

There wasn't much talk between them, leaving Grangeville and driving down the twisting Grangeville grade with the heavily loaded jeep panel. Then, up the south fork of the Clearwater River toward Elk City.

"I can't get over the beauty of the river," Gunner said. "Now that fall is here and the leaves are turning, it's a real sign that old man winter is just around the corner. Cleo, with winter coming on, where would I get wood to cover the rest of the sluice box and the stamp mill?"

The old miner thought a minute. "Well, last resort could be to frame in the shed with lodgepole pine. Be sure to carve out the ends to fit them tight. Then, cut some shake bolts. I think I have a shake splitter you can have in the tool shed. Roof it with the shakes and split out longer shakes for the sides. It won't keep in the heat, but it will keep out the wind and snow. You realize you could get six to seven-foot of snow up there?"

"Yeah, that would get me by until spring with the wagon Talking Bird's dad was selling to me. I could haul in some lumber."

Cleo asked, "Have you done much more exploring since you've been at the claim?"

"Not really, the lick has given me all the food we've needed, and the mine has given me all the gold I've needed so far. Guess I'm pretty happy with where I'm at."

Cleo continued, "You might take a walk up the valley. Keep an eye peeled to the west side. If I remember right, Slim Gibson's place was about six miles away. He had a claim up there, and his mine petered out of any trace of gold. Then somehow, the cabin caught fire and that about killed him. All that happened after I came out and retired. After the fire, Slim came out and stayed with me for a couple of weeks, then he had me take him to his niece's place in Orofino. That's a nice town down the Clearwater River, about halfway to Lewiston. He stayed with her until he went to the home in town. Now, she stops in at the home and checks on him."

"Do you think there is any mining equipment still up there? How about lumber from old out-buildings? Maybe he would want to sell it?"

Cleo laughed, "You never stop, do you? Does that mind of yours ever take a break?"

"Well, no. That's why I landed up in trouble so much early on. I'd run my mouth because I was always thinking. Now I have the critters and mine to keep me busy."

"You can ask Slim yourself," Cleo said. "I want to make a trip to the home this fall sometime to see him anyway. We were running partners for a long time, Slim and I. Also, I want to talk to the folks about, maybe sometime later, I could move in. They might let me share a room with Slim."

Gunner said quietly, "I didn't think you were ready for the home, not yet anyway."

"Well, it has to happen sometime, maybe even as soon as this winter. Things are getting harder, and in the winter, my arthritis gets worse. It just doesn't let me get around very well anymore."

"Ok, let me know whatever I can do to help. Just don't be shy, which I know you aren't. Tell me what you need or want, promise?"

"Thanks. I promise."

Things went quiet again. Gunner was too busy thinking about Slim's claim just up the valley from his mine. Maybe there would be some equipment he could use.

Finally, just as it was getting dark, they pulled into Talking Bird's driveway.

Gunner commented, "I think we should park closer so we can keep an eye on the jeep, with all this gear. You never know with those brothers around."

"Good idea," Cleo said, pulling up closer to the house.

There was Quiet Bird, practically at his door when they came to a stop.

Gunner slid out the passenger side and he and Quiet Bird stood facing each other, looking into one another's eyes, not saying a word. Bell broke the spell by raising a ruckus and wanted out to say hello to Quiet Bird. They laughed as Bell bolted out of the jeep back door and leaned up to Quiet Bird. Bell wanted a long petting and conversation. Gunner could see the dog had missed her.

Talking Bird greeted Cleo at the driver's door, and they walked around where Quiet Bird and Gunner were standing. "Ok, you two, dinner is almost ready, and we have lots of talking to do. Into the house now. We can't stand out here all night."

Who cares about dinner? I like just standing here and staring at this beautiful girl.

"Come on, Bell, let's go inside." Gunner followed behind Bell and Quiet Bird, taking the back of Quiet Birds' arm with his hand to assist her. He only wanted to touch her for a moment. She was warm and soft, and he could tell she liked it. She squeezed her arm tight to her side with his hand next to her.

Once in the house, Quiet Bird hung up the boys' coats and hats on the back porch. Gunner wanted to do everything right. "Should I take my boots off?" Quiet Bird smiled and nodded. He sat on a chair and pulled them off, standing them by the chair in the washroom.

"Could I use your washbasin to wash up?" She smiled and nodded again, pulling a fresh towel out of the cupboard.

Quiet Bird stood watching him and holding his towel. He wasn't sure why she was standing there, but she had that pretty smile. Yes, he liked it.

Cleo and Talking Bird were in the kitchen, talking.

Gunner started washing up and looking in the mirror. He decided Aunt Ida was right. He needed a haircut.

"You wouldn't have a comb I could borrow, would you? This mop of mine needs some straightening. My aunt told me today I needed a haircut. I think she might be right."

Quiet Bird studied his thick head of hair. She reached up to his chin, turning his head sideways. "She's right. You do need a haircut." Pulling a comb out of the mirrored cabinet above the washbasin, she handed it to him.

"Maybe on the next trip to town, I could get one."

Quiet Bird suggested, "Or, if you don't mind, after dinner, I could cut it for you."

"Mind? Heck no, I don't mind. I could pay you for it."

She laughed. "No, just come back and visit with me when you come to town."

Gunner smiled, "You can count on that. You'll be my first stop, I promise."

Talking Bird stuck her head through the doorway. "Come on you two, dinner is ready."

Sitting down to the table, Gunner asked Talking Bird, "Do you like whitetail deer, ma'am?"

"Oh, yes! That is a favorite around this house. We will take whatever you can spare. I would also like to share what you bring with my parents. Dad loves his venison."

"No problem. I'll bring plenty for all. The salt lick Bell and I put together is working perfectly."

Dinner at the table was excellent, with quiet visiting, no games or BS like the ranch dinner table. The conversation drifted over to Gunner and the claim. Talking Bird asked Gunner how it was going and if he was preparing for winter. He gave short answers.

Gunner moved the conversation over to Quiet Bird and asked her how school was going and what classes she was taking. The truth be known, he wanted to hear her voice.

"School is good. I like my English and Lit classes. And in science, they're talking about computers and how they work."

Talking Bird said, "After dinner, we can sit down and get started on your first lessons, Gunner. I was able to get them laid out the other day. Quiet Bird even put her approval on them."

Quiet Bird offered, "Yes, they look good, Gunner. Not too much, but enough to pass the tests. That is the important thing. If you like, I could help you with the lessons when you come into town."

Gunner nodded. "That sounds great. I am not sure how much time I will have in town, though."

Cleo chuckled, "No problem for Gunner here. He will make time if it's you who will be helping him."

Dinner was over and Gunner could see Cleo's eyes were drooping. Gunner asked, "Talking Bird, do you think Cleo could sit in your overstuffed chair in the living room? He usually checks his eyelids for light leaks after dinner while I do the dishes."

Cleo nodded and smiled.

"Oh heavens, yes." Walking into the living room, she picked up a small blanket. Standing by the chair, she motioned Cleo to sit down. Then, she put the Indian blanket on his lap.

Gunner said, "I think he was half asleep when he hit the chair."

Quiet Bird and Gunner cleared the table, trying to decide who would wash and who would dry the dishes. Gunner started to run the water and said, "Where's the soap? You don't mind drying, do you?"

She smiled, pulling out a clean towel from the kitchen drawer. During dishes, Gunner asked, "What are your plans after high school?"

"I like school a lot. Mother has her hands full with some of those mouthy kids. I don't think they're taught manners at home. I know teaching is not a choice for me."

Gunner suggested, "Maybe their folks work, and the kids just grew up with little or no parents around?"

"Yes, maybe. I don't like rude kids. They are very mean and hurtful."

With the dishes done, they went to the kitchen table, and Talking Bird said, "I've got it all laid out for you, Gunner. It shouldn't take us long."

"That's good," Quiet Bird said. "I'll be giving him a haircut when you're finished with him." They smiled at each other. Gunner thought they had a bet going on or something.

Lessons were straightforward—complete the reading assignments, then answer the questions in the back of the chapter. Talking Bird would test him the next time he came to town.

"I can do that. It looks like a lot of reading with all the other stuff. I'm reading about the mine and all, so no problem, bring it on."

"My turn," Quiet Bird chimed in. "Let's get the clippers out. You can sit on a chair in the middle of the porch floor. I'll get a towel to cover you."

"Works for me." Gunner was enjoying all the girl's attention.

Sitting in the chair, Quiet Bird came up behind him and wrapped the towel around his neck, draping it over his shoulders. She rested her hand on his shoulder as she reached for the comb.

That feels nice. Trying to comb that mess out on the top of his head was tough going.

"Let's wash your hair in the sink. We'll put on some conditioner to take out the tangles. That should help."

"Okay, I'll get started on the washing." Gunner stood up and walked to the sink. As he bent over, Quiet Bird turned on the water, warming it up for him.

"I like the service here. Think I will come back," Gunner said. They laughed.

Once the soap and conditioner had done their job, Gunner was back in the chair again. As he started to dry his hair, she politely took the towel from him and began to dry it.

"Now I know I like the service here. Think I'll get a haircut every time I come to town." He closed his eyes, enjoying every moment of her touch. There was such a sense of warmth with her standing next to him.

Gunner thought his heart was melting. *No, my whole body is melting.*

Then came the smooth, careful combing. Cutting followed next. That lasted for half an hour. He wanted it to keep going on forever. It was just pure pleasure for them both. They could steal an occasional touch or brushing of one another accidentally, on purpose. Once done, Quiet Bird had him look at the new person in the mirror. He was surprised to see a familiar face.

"I do like you better this way, Gunner. It makes you look much older and happier." Talking Bird walked into the back porch. Quiet Bird surveyed her work. "Yes, I like him better that way. What do you think, Mother?"

Talking Bird looked at Gunner then the mirror. "Yes, I like that. Gunner, you look much more mature and clean-cut."

"Thank you both, but we won't tell anyone that I'm not all that mature." They all laughed.

It was time for Cleo and Gunner to hit the road. Gunner headed into the living room to wake Cleo up. "Come on, old-timer, time to go home so you can sleep in your own chair."

All three of them were standing around Cleo when he opened his eyes. "Who you calling old-timer?" he said with his friendly big grin.

Getting up was slow, and then the walk toward the door was more gradual. Cleo asked, "Could you drive us home tonight, Gunner? I'm pooped."

"Sure. Good thing I had plenty of driving practice on the island last winter." Talking Bird headed to the door with Cleo. Gunner stopped at the table with Quiet Bird at his side, picking up his books and the questions. He turned to face her, "I want to thank you and Talking Bird for the great dinner. Most of all, thank you for the haircut. I sure needed it. I want to make you my permanent barber here in Elk City. No, it's not like it sounds. I just like the care you gave me."

She smiled. "You're welcome. We'll do it again when you come to town."

"Boy, that's for sure! I almost forgot, you wouldn't have an extra picture I could take back up to the claim with me, would you?"

"Oh yes, you go ahead. I'll go get one."

By the time he made it to the jeep, Talking Bird had Cleo loaded up in the passenger's side. Gunner overheard Cleo telling Talking Bird, "You're always welcome to stop by the cabin anytime. Gunner is spending all day tomorrow working on my winter wood. Then, when he takes a break, we could all have a nice lunch."

"This is such a great time of year, with fall coming on. It would be a lot of fun. If we run out of things to talk about, we could watch the young couple for a while. That should keep us entertained!" Talking Bird continued, "How do we get there?"

"Gunner will draw you a map. It will be easy, you'll see."

Nodding, Gunner put the books and Bell in the back of the jeep. "I'd be happy to show you. We'll need to go back in to draw you a map." Quiet Bird was coming out of the house as Talking Bird and Gunner were going back in. She quickly caught up with them on the back porch and handed him a picture.

In the picture, she had on her buckskin leather dress. As Gunner looked at it in the dim light of the back porch, he said in a near whisper, "You are so beautiful, thank you. I will keep this close to me all the time."

She put her hand on his arm and gave a slight squeeze of appreciation. They looked into each other's eyes for a quick moment.

There are those darn butterflies again.

Talking Bird called from the kitchen table, "Come on, Gunner, I need a map if we're going to get to Cleo's tomorrow for lunch."

Gunner knew she saw them staring at each other and said that to see Quiet Bird's reaction. Quiet Bird's eyes flew open, and there was that sparkle Gunner had seen before.

"Yes, ma'am, not a problem." Gunner sat down at the table and drew the map, including written directions to Cleo's.

Quiet Bird stood behind him. He could feel her hand on his shoulder with her body next to his.

Wow, this is feeling so good. The haircut sure broke the ice for us.

Talking Bird could easily see what was going on as he laid Quiet Bird's picture on the table. She smiled, knowing she would not change the course of these two young people. In the tribe, it was the couple's choice to grow close and care openly for one another. That was the wish of the people and the young couple.

Drawing the map didn't take but a minute. Talking Bird had been to the Hot Springs before with Quiet Bird. They just had to take the bridge before getting to the Ranger station and follow the map.

With that done, Gunner headed for the jeep. Quiet Bird asked, "Mother, I would like to walk out with Gunner and say goodnight."

"Yes, you go ahead, enjoy him for the moment you have him."

Quiet Bird caught up with Gunner and slipped her hand into his. "I really enjoyed tonight and am looking forward to seeing you tomorrow."

Gunner squeezed her hand. "I can't thank you enough for this evening, and tomorrow will be just as great."

Opening the driver's door, Gunner looked in to see Cleo sound asleep. He took one more look at Quiet Bird in the starlit night. She was so pretty looking back at him. Just for a moment, he thought of kissing her. That scared him. Too much, too fast. He squeezed her hand, saying, "Goodnight, I'll see you tomorrow."

Gunner started the jeep and backed out of the driveway. He watched her standing in the headlights. *She is beautiful.*

With Cleo sleeping and Gunner thinking about Quiet Bird so hard, the driving took care of itself, going a nice forty miles an hour and no traffic in sight. It didn't take long to arrive at Cleo's cabin.

At the cabin, Gunner got Cleo into the house. He chose to go to his chair. Gunner threw the same old blanket on him, then built a fire in the cookstove to take the chill off.

"Come on, Bell, we need to tend to Jack and put us to bed for the night."

CHAPTER 33

Gunner was wide awake before daylight, turning on his flashlight while still in the bedroll. Bell was snuggled up next to him outside the bedroll. Last night, before he went to sleep, he took a long look at Quiet Bird's picture. This morning, he was looking at the picture again, setting it up on a board next to his head.

My goodness, she looks good. I want to say goodnight and good morning to her every day.

"We'd better get going, crew. We have a long day ahead of us." Just breaking daylight, Gunner gave Jack extra grain because today would be his first time in a harness hitch. *He has to pull the logs up to the woodshed to be cut up to stove-sized wood, then we'll split and stack it for Cleo's winter woodpile.*

This was also the first time Gunner would be guiding an animal in a harness, and they were both young and green. With Jack taken care of for the morning, Gunner found the chainsaw in the toolshed, gassed the saw, and sharpened the chain. One short test run, and he was ready to go to work.

There are two things the old man had taught him. 1.) How to work—no questions, get in there and get it done. 2.) How to work with tools, especially how to care for and sharpen a chainsaw. They had put up a lot of wood to sell so people could heat their homes.

Gunner hung Jack's hitch on the fence then double-checked to make sure everything was there. It needed a little saddle soap and elbow grease to fix it up like new.

The smell of bacon frying hit him hard, and his stomach was groaning. "Guess I'd better get in there before it gets cold, huh, Bell." Breakfast was quiet, with both Gunner and Cleo thinking of the upcoming day and the things they needed to do. Gunner wasn't sure what Cleo was thinking, but he was thinking of Quiet Bird and wondering what time the ladies would arrive. He asked Cleo, "Do you want me to pull out some venison steaks for lunch?"

"Yes, please. We'll feed the girls lunch around noon or a little later. That depends when you're ready to come in." Gunner filled the cookstove box then listened to Cleo's instructions on what trees to cut before heading out, leaving Bell with Cleo.

While he was falling trees, he didn't want Bell around. It was just too dangerous. The saw was running fast and reliable. The farthest trees were felled first, and then in a row of three. Gunner worked along toward the woodshed. With some quick delimbing of most of the trees, he had a good sweat worked up.

Now it was time for Jack to show his stuff. The plan was to go slow and careful. He went to the cabin to let Bell out, and she was ready. She didn't like being in there while he was outside with all that saw racket going on.

As Gunner hitched up Jack, they had a little chat. Gunner's goal was to train him to voice commands. He knew Jack wanted to please, like Bell. Getting him to back up to the first log was comfortable for Jack. It wasn't a big log, maybe twelve inches across at the butt (that's the big end of the tree).

Gunner had built a landing next to the shed out of a dozen lodge-pole pines. They were 4 to 6 inches in diameter and not so long he couldn't drag them. It would keep the firewood log off the ground while he cut them to stove-size lengths with the chainsaw.

Gunner started by using the lead rope, and that went fine for the first two logs, then he hung the lead on Jack's neck and tried only commands with the third log. Jack was excited like Gunner and ready to start pulling when Gunner said, "Get up, Jack." Jack made it to the landing in record time. The problem was he just kept on pulling, full blast. Jack rounded the cabin dragging that 40-foot log full tilt, close behind. Talking Bird and Quiet Bird had just pulled up, and Cleo was coming out to greet them.

So, here comes the mule pulling the log hell-bent for election, just missing the cabin and barely missing Talking Bird's car. Gunner was glad to see them up on the porch with Cleo as he came running behind Jack, yelling, "Wow, Jack."

They all were laughing when he finally caught up to the speed demon mule. Slowly, Gunner got him stopped. "I think it would be a good choice to use the lead. I guess maybe he's not ready for us to let go of that blasted rope yet."

Jack was taken back to the shed, and Gunner walked over to everyone on the front porch. "Good morning, ladies."

They chimed in, "Good morning, Gunner." The ladies looked nice to Gunner. Talking Bird wore a long dark beaded dress with a dark coat over that, and her hair was all braided. Quiet Bird was a different story with a slim denim jacket and a braided ponytail hanging down to her waist. Then, there were her well-fitted jeans, all the way down to the leather boots again. In her hand was a pair of leather gloves, ready for work.

My goodness, I always admired a working girl, and dressed for it too. That worked for him, especially with her friendly smile. Gunner said, "Looks like you're ready to go to work."

"Yes, I am. It looks like you could use some help with that mule." She had bent down, petting, and saying good morning to Bell. She stood up and smiled. "Let's go get some wood. Could you show me what I need to do to help you? I was only kidding about you needing help with the mule."

They walked over to Jack. Gunner asked, "You ever drive a mule before?"

"Uncle had a team of horses, and I think they are not as bright as a mule. Let me try. Could you hook me up to a log, please?" Gunner thought she made it look easy. Gunner stayed back in the woods, delimbing the rest of the trees and hitching Jack up to the logs when Quiet Bird came back for another turn of wood.

She would skid the logs with Jack to the woodshed where the landing was, unhook the logs, and be right back for more. Just like clockwork. The following seven turns were only twelve-inch pine at the base, not one problem. *She has a way with that mule. Shoot, I can't get Bell away from her either.*

Gunner was a lost cause for sure. He was thinking the girl was stealing his heart, his mule, and his dog to boot. By noon, everything was lying in front of the shed. He removed the hitch from Jack, hung it on the fence, and let him out to graze.

"I'll saw and split the blocks to firebox size. If you would like to stack, we might get it done this afternoon, and maybe there would be time for a short walk and visit."

Talking Bird came around the woodshed. "Lunch is ready. Come and get it."

Lunch was relaxing, and they talked about a lot of things. Quiet Bird and Gunner would steal looks at one another. He wasn't sure how this worked, but he was sure it was nice to sit and look at her.

Cleo would shake his head then ask Gunner about the mine. That was a natural subject for him. Gunner only wanted to sit close to Quiet Bird for the time they were at the table.

The afternoon went by faster than the morning, and all the wood was soon cut and stacked. *Must be getting on to 4 o'clock and still plenty of light.* Gunner washed up and asked Talking Bird if she would mind that he and Quiet Bird went for a walk. "I don't think I could stop her if I wanted to. You two have a nice walk. Cleo and I will figure out some dinner when he wakes up."

Once out of sight of the cabin, Gunner took Quiet Bird's hand and the electricity from the warmth of her hand surged through him. He wasn't sure where her hand started, and his ended.

Their talk was light. Quiet Bird said it was fun pulling logs with Jack, and Bell was right there to help her. Gunner explained how he planned to use voice commands to train Jack to pull the gondola out of the mine. She laughed. "I think there will be more training for that, don't you think?"

"Jack is young like me, and we'll grow together." He looked at her. "Maybe like you, Bell, and me." She squeezed his hand and smiled. It was time to go back to the house for dinner, and the ladies would be going home soon.

Dinner was quieter. Gunner thought they all had a busy day, and it was nice to sit with good friends and eat the meal peacefully. Cleo was ready for his chair, heading into the living room and saying his goodbyes to the ladies. He thanked them for coming to the cabin and especially for all their help. Gunner covered him with the old blanket.

Rolling up his sleeves, he started washing dishes. Quiet Bird picked up a dishtowel for drying while Talking Bird sat at the kitchen table and flipped through the pages of a National Geographic magazine.

Quiet Bird said, "Thank you again for the walk. It was nice to spend quiet time together. Someday, we'll have to go fishing together. That would be fun."

"Holy smokes, you like fishing? That is my most favorite thing, next to my crew and you, of course."

"I saw that you put my picture next to your bedroll in the shed."

"I like to say good morning to you every morning, then goodnight to you every night."

"Gunner, that is very thoughtful of you. Thank you for thinking of me that way."

Quiet Bird smiled. "So now I need a picture of you to set next to my bedroll."

"I don't have one. Maybe Granny has one I could get from her. I'll ask the next time I come in."

"When do you think that will be?"

"Not sure. The next three days, I'll be packing in the gear we bought in town. Then I'll need to be doing some blasting, so three, maybe four weeks would be my guess. I want to buy the drill and compressor from Oley. You know, the time gets away from me up there. I promise I'll stop to see you first on my way out."

"I was hoping you would say that."

With the dishes finished, it was time for the ladies to leave for home. Gunner walked them out to the car. It was early evening and still light out. He reached for Quiet Bird's hand as he opened the car door.

"Mother taught me it was a polite thing to do when you get a lady's door for her." He lightly squeezed Quiet Bird's hand, "Thanks for coming. I'll see you soon."

Watching the dust as they drove away on the dirt road, Gunner had many thoughts going through his head. It was like a nonstop movie. He started going back over every detail of the last two days with Quiet Bird. It made him happy that no one was standing there saying, "You can't like a girl, you're too young." That would come from the fire and brimstone of his mother's church back home.

He was happy for his mother if that was what she wanted. Too bad she wasn't here. It is looking like he had a life of his own. Gunner was not sure what was going on, but he liked having a good friend, living in the wilderness, and not a long way from home. He reminded himself, *Hey, I am home, just a few hours down the trail.* He said out loud, "Don't worry, Mother, I will never do anything to hurt her."

Back in Cleo's cabin, Gunner started shutting down for the night. Cleo had his feet up on the ottoman and was sound asleep, snoring lightly. Gunner filled the cookstove wood box and backed the jeep around to the shed so he could unload the gear they bought in town yesterday.

It was time to fit the pulley and put the pump together. Then, Gunner got it ready so Jack could pull it on its skids tomorrow. As Gunner kneeled to install the pulley to the pump shaft, Bell came over from where she was lying by the door of the tool shed. She leaned up against him as if to say, "Dad, I miss Quiet Bird. She is so kind."

"I know, Bell. I miss her too. What a great friend for both of us. Now I got to get this pump done, ok?"

Gunner began fitting the pump to the motor and needed a couple of bolts to hook it up to the old brackets. Bolting the pump up and putting on the belts was easy. *The v-belts fit exactly right, so why am I worrying so much about them? Sometimes, I worry too much about stuff. Cleo is right. My mind never stops. The pump and motor are all ready to go for tomorrow's walk back into the mine.*

Putting Jack away, he brushed him down, giving him a scoop of oats. Bell was right there next to Jack. Gunner sat on a bale of hay and brushed her with Jack's brush. Smiling, he thought, *both of us can daydream about our new friend, Quiet Bird.*

Gunner woke up sore in the morning. *That's to be expected with all the wood we put up yesterday.* Standing in his stall, Jack looked at Gunner over the sideboards, with Bell sound asleep tucked in next to Gunner.

Gunner looked up to see Quiet Bird's picture and said, "Good morning. What a nice face to wake up to." Then to the crew, he said, "All rise and shine. We have a long hike ahead of us. We are going home, boy and girl." The animals could hear the excitement in his voice. Both were getting worked up to be ready for another adventure.

Feeling the coolness of fall approaching, Gunner headed for Cleo's kitchen where all the great breakfast smells were coming from. He picked up an armload of wood and found Cleo at the stove cooking up a mountain of venison, eggs, and the usual sourdough flapjacks. Gunner still had a million things running through his mind. There were so many questions, he didn't know where to start.

Cleo said, "What's new there, partner? Cat got your tongue?"

Gunner shook his head, trying to put a sentence together.

"Now tell Old Cleo what you got on your mind."

"Cleo, I see what I need to do ahead of me. That is easy. Why does it get mixed up with the girl coming into my life? That doesn't make sense."

Cleo smiled. "Go on, you're making sense to me."

"I'm too young to let it make me feel this way about her. My life is getting complicated real fast with the mine, Jack, Bell, dynamite, more machinery, and schoolwork to deal with. Then, the bullies in Elk City to boot. All the talk we heard in Grangeville is a bunch of BS. I wasn't looking for a reputation. Guess maybe now I got one. The crazy thing is that I didn't do anything I wouldn't have done on a fish boat dock back home. I don't need any of this. I want only to be left alone and work the mine with my crew."

"Go on, you're doing fine."

"Now, our new home is the cabin, and we like it there. It suits the three of us. It might be a little one-sided on the conversation. Well, that would be on my side. There is no better place in this world for us. With all I went through with Mom and Granny to convince them I needed to stay, I had to hustle to get things up and running. Now all this comes along. Will it ever stop?"

Cleo served up breakfast. "Is it okay to talk now? I didn't think you were going to come up for air. So, here's how I see it from an old man's eyes. You eat your breakfast. It will take a minute to explain. Are you okay?"

Gunner was staring at his eggs and venison, but not seeing them. "Yeah, I'm okay."

"Don't worry or let the Elk City stuff get to you. Like I said before, people like a good story, and yours has drama in it for them. Just leave it be. It doesn't cost you anything, and they're having fun with it.

"I will tell you one thing, though. Those boys are bad news, and they don't like what's going around anymore than you do. You watch your backside. Those rotten varmints will blindside you if a chance comes up. You know you won't get the drop on them so easily the next time. When they come at you, you come back at them twice as hard and faster than they can believe. One last thing, they mean to hurt you, so you hurt them first. As Elroy said, there won't be a second chance for you. Gunner, with that kind, you gotta reach down deep and get mean like you have never been mean before."

"Thank you, Cleo. I understand what you're saying."

Cleo continued, "So, here's what I'm thinking for the girl. You can take your time. She will be there, trust me on that. It appears to me she'll be happy to wait for you while you're roaming all over the wilderness looking to find your fortune. She cares for you, and that's ninety-nine percent of the game.

"You be sure you don't do anything to lose her trust. I can't say this loud enough, Trust is everything, no matter who or what it is, man or animal. Once you have that down, the rest of your life is easy. Look at your mule and dog. Jack and Bell trust you to give them both food and love. You watch out for them and never let anything hurt them. Well, that's what they give back, their loyalty, trust, and love. That's all they bring to the table, and it is plenty. I know you love them for it."

Gunner sat there, nodding, finally chewing on his breakfast. Cleo wasn't slowing down any. He hadn't even dished up his own plate. He sat down in the chair across from Gunner and started laying it on some more. Some lectures are precisely correct. Gunner thought this is one of the best. He needed this one this morning.

"So, this is not a major responsibility. Having people and animals in your life, it's a partnership. That's not a hard job, taking care of your partners."

Cleo paused. "Young feller, they are there for you as much as you are there for them. Now, going back to the girl . . . I slid off the track a bit there. She has no demands on you. Truth be told, you're putting it all on yourself. Just load up your equipment and get it up to the claim. Work your three to four weeks, then come out and enjoy your short break before going back in.

"You keep that mind of yours working overtime, and it will take away from what you need to be paying attention to at the claim. More than anything, Quiet Bird is a real gem, and I mean twenty-four carats. You need not screw that up. She will go to hell and back with you. I think she will back you, even if you are wrong. She might tell you you're wrong, but she won't leave you or love you any less for what you're doing."

Cleo sighed. "Is any of this getting through to you?"

"Yes, it is. That is a mouthful you got there. Don't worry about my crew. I depend on those two as much as they depend on me. Is that what you're telling me? Just don't let them down and keep their trust."

Gunner looked out the kitchen window. "I do remember a couple of times where Bell was in danger, and it was my poor judgment that put her there. I let her down those times. Now, the girl is in my head, and I don't have a clue what's going on. Cleo, I get butterflies, and my heart races when I'm around her. Might she be a little ahead of me on the relationship stuff? I'm not that clear. Did it make any sense to you?"

Cleo chuckled and looked up at the ceiling. "Maybe you're getting some of it. The girl thing will work itself out. Give it time. You're right on track. That's how it works."

"What part are you talking about?"

Cleo smiled. "Oh, brother, you have it bad. Listen to me. You are good with all that girl stuff you got stuck between your ears. She's a wonderful girl, and I'm sure she likes you a lot, so take your time. This is not a race, you know."

"Yeah, I know this is not a race, but what if she finds someone else, and I'm up at the mine? Guess I'm out, how about that?"

Cleo looked solemnly at Gunner. "Yeah, you could be out, and that's how it works. You want a job at the grocery store where the Ferguson boys always come into town to kick dirt in your face?"

Cleo frowned. "Well, what are you going to do? Keep on going like you are, or just shut down and move to Elk City?"

"You got a point there. I couldn't do that. No way, I'd go home and get a job on a fish boat first."

"Do you realize how young you are?" Cleo asked. "You have a long and wonderful life ahead of you. If you play your cards right, you could have a great fishing partner for the rest of your life."

Standing up to clear the table, Gunner said, "You said a lot of good and humbling things to me. I need some time up at the claim to sort it all out."

"Good man. Remember this, I think the girl was yours the first time you met. She will be there for you, hell or high water."

Breakfast was over, and Gunner had to get going. "Do you need help with the dishes?"

Cleo laughed, "Go get that mule hitched up and come on back tomorrow. You have a lot of work to do."

"Thank you, Cleo. You know all we talked about didn't go in one ear and out the other. You made a lot of sense, and I'll sort it out up at the mine."

Jack was patiently waiting in the corral for Bell and him. After yesterday, the hitch went on quickly. Gunner took him around to the tool shed, backed up to the skid, and shackled the harness to the engine skid.

Jack was ready to go to work as he leaned into the harness. He had enough of sitting around, and thinking was not good for any of them. *All three of us need to head for the cabin.* Gunner couldn't help thinking how easy Quiet Bird drove Jack with the logs yesterday. *Wish she was here now with her smile and always something nice to say.*

"Okay, Jack, easy does it. Giddy-up, be a good boy for me today."

Jack pulled the skid easily. Gunner stopped him in front of the stall where they slept, tied Jack up, and started putting his pack and bedroll together.

Cleo came out to say goodbye. "Are you okay?"

"Yea, I'm okay."

Cleo said, "We talked about a lot of stuff over breakfast. I don't want to make you mad, and I don't want to hurt your feelings."

"Cleo, you did talk about a lot of things. Remember, you're my friend, and I trust you with everything I have. That includes my feelings. Don't you ever worry that you've made me mad or hurt my feelings. I need you to let me know these things."

Gunner paused. "I need to know what you're thinking, you have so much in your head, and I have so little. Thank you again, partner."

Cleo smiled and nodded.

"You have helped me so much, and I have no real way to ever repay you."

Cleo smiled again. "See you tomorrow for the next load."

CHAPTER 34

Gunner and crew walked out to the trail, and there were many mixed feelings in the back of Gunner's mind. Once Jack got his stride pulling the pump, Gunner got into step alongside. Bell was out front, keeping an eye open. They started making time, and things began to peel off the backside of his mind as they put on the miles.

Bell was still up front, quietly woofing and running ahead. She would run back to check on them occasionally. Jack would give a friendly snort to say it felt good to be going. Two hours out, they stopped for a break. Jack took a drink. Bell was not interested, she only wanted to keep going. Gunner sipped on his canteen, thinking it was best for all of them to get home to the claim.

When they arrived at the cabin in the early afternoon, the sun was warm on their backs, and more leaves were starting to turn to their fall colors. Gunner let Jack graze for a minute while Bell and Gunner checked out the cabin, then the outbuildings.

Gunner and Bell headed up to the mine where he wanted to drop the pump, next to the sluice box, out in front of the tunnel. Looking over to the mine, Gunner could see some of the boards he had put up across the entrance had been torn off, and the big heavy door was shoved open.

Gunner thought of the whitetail deer meat he had hanging in the mine. "What do we have going on here, Bell? Do you think old bruin stopped by for dinner on us? This doesn't look right, girl."

Gunner pulled the Springfield from Jack's pack sheath, checking to make sure there was a round in the chamber. He walked up to the open door, kneeling to take a close look at the tracks. *It certainly looks like bear, and the darn thing is still here.*

The busted boards and torn-out timbers had long, deep claw marks on them.

"Bell, I suspect that old bruin could be inside. Keep quiet, girl, and stay right here. He might be a big one."

Moving silently, Gunner hugged against the tunnel rock wall, careful not to get into the light. Just before all the light ended, the smell of bear hit him.

Gunner could hear grunting and growling coming from further in the mine. Still, on his knees, the Springfield was pointed into the mine. He couldn't make out the bear in the dim light.

It was scary being in a dark hole with an animal the size of a small truck. He thought it could weigh up to eight hundred pounds or more. There wasn't enough light to take a safe shot and Gunner did not want to wound it. Then, the terror would really begin. He could tell it was time to leave because his heart was speeding up, and his mind was screaming, *Run. Run like hell!*

Gunner thought the bear didn't know he was there. It sounded happy chewing on the last quarter of deer.

How am I going to get rid of the damn bear?

Gunner carefully backed his way outside. Bell was waiting at the mouth of the mine.

"Let's go back to the cabin, Bell, and think this over a bit. We have to be careful. This thing could eat us."

Gunner wanted to get his critters safe first. That would be getting Jack and Bell back to the cabin. The bear might think the whitetail quarter wasn't enough for him. Then, in the night, he could decide to do some exploring and sniff out Jack or Bell and himself in the cabin. Then Gunner would have to take it on in the dark, and that would be harder yet. There wouldn't be any advantage for him. That bear could run faster than his mom's old flathead ford. The crew and him wouldn't stand a snowball chance in hell to take the bear on in the dark.

No, that is out. Gunner knew he would have to flush it out of the mine. It would have to be a daylight show. Hopefully, it would spook and run away. Most likely, though, he would have to kill it. One way or another, it would be on Gunner's terms if it did choose to stay and fight.

Gunner was good for the fight, and if there was a fight, one of them would die. Cleo had told him there is no such thing as a dumb animal. They have to be smart to survive in the wilderness. Gunner knew he needed to be ready for anything.

Back at the cabin, Gunner put Jack in his stall with hay and a scoop of oats, then locked the door. *Maybe I should put him in the pasture where he can run if the bear gets me and I'm dead.*

Whoa there. I'm not going to let anything kill me.

Bell was a problem. She wasn't having any of this being locked up in the cabin idea. *She is hard-headed. She must have some German Shepard in her. No wait, she's a Rottweiler, and Roman soldiers would take their dogs into battle with them in those days.* That's what the lady at the dog pound told him, and they are fiercely loyal. She would lay down her life for him.

"Okay, girl, you'll have to fend for yourself." Gunner had heard that dogs were a natural enemy of a bear, and hopefully, she could keep its attention while he pumped lead slugs in it. That is, if it decides to stand and fight. There was a good chance it will, so he would need Bell's help.

The bear will think they want to take the whitetail away. You never want to mess with a bear's food. "Ok, Bell, you can come. Just play it loose for me and don't get in too close."

They started walking back up to the mine. It was later now, and Gunner figured they had only a few hours of daylight left. At the mine, he could hear the bear in there, still grunting and growling.

How am I going to get it to come out? I need to get a couple of shots through his heart when he rears up on his hind legs, if I am lucky.

As he thought things over carefully, a plan came to him. If he turned on the stamp mill, the bear might not like the noise. That should bring him out to take a look around. If that didn't work, he would use a trick from the Alaskan Indians. Gunner had read in a National Geographic where they would crawl in a hibernating bear's den and wake it up. He thought the bear would be plenty cranky and still groggy from his nap after a big dinner.

Once the Indians got the bear out in the open, they get it to rear up on his hind feet. *Not sure how they did it. Could be they run a bunch of dogs around the bear, Bell?*

Dogs are a natural enemy of bears, and maybe they don't like the barking. Heck, he knew he got tired of it. That will keep the bear distracted. Then the natives would take a pointed stick and put it up against the bear's chest, where his heart is.

When the bear came back down on all fours, the stick drives through his heart, and he falls over dead.

It sounded like a long shot to Gunner.

1-This bear is wide awake.
2-He thinks they want his food.
3-I don't know if I'm as brave as those folks up in Alaska.

Yep, this is one hell of a long shot, last resort deal, that's it. He would put the bayonet on the Springfield anyway. It won't cost anything extra. Fourteen inches of the old blade sounded good. Pulling the bayonet out of his harness, Gunner snapped it to the barrel of the Springfield. "Okay, Bell, looks like it's showtime. Let's go turn on the stamp mill and make some noise."

As the stamp mill started crashing and banging, they waited quietly next to the big pine tree twenty feet from the stamp mill. The Springfield had a round in the chamber and a fully loaded magazine.

Gunner's heart was up in his throat, making it hard for him to breathe. He was scared and he knew it. *It is him or me. No damn bear is running us off of our claim, and that's final.*

The mouth of the cave was twenty feet from the stamp mill, so there was forty feet between them and bruin. *If he decides to rear up at the mouth of the mine, that will give me three or four shots to put in him as fast and smooth as the Springfield bolt is.*

Deep breaths. *Take your shot carefully. There won't be any time to go back and do it over again.* Bell was a good girl, as always. She was lying right next to him, waiting. She knew there was something in there.

That didn't take long. Out came old bruin, lumbering, sniffing, holding its head up high, and walking on all fours.

Watching it carefully, Gunner could tell its sight wasn't that good, and it hadn't seen them yet. Leave it to Bell. She started barking, running right toward the bear. When she was next to the stamp mill, she turned and scampered back next to Gunner. Gunner thought she as much as hollered to the bear. "Hey, over here, Mr. Bear. Here's my dad, and he has a big gun he wants to shoot you with."

Thanks, Bell! Maybe you're not that much help.

The bear watched the dog, and now it could see Gunner as Bell sat down next to him. That certainly took the surprise out of what they were doing.

The bear walked out by the stamp mill, started to rear up and gave a roaring growl.

This thing is enormous! Ok, easy. Take the shot right into its heart, get as many as you can. Make them count, damn it.

Bell had run up the bear, barking up full tilt as she'd never barked before. The bear paused, looking at Bell. It was Gunner's chance to get a clear shot.

The bear looked ready to chase Bell and take a swipe at her with his huge paw. *Be careful with your shot.* It was mangy for being at the end of the season. Gunner's guess the berry picking wasn't all that great this summer.

Now the bear was fully raised on his hind legs, growling and howling as loud as he could. *Damn, it is enormous!* Gunner figured he had about one, maybe two, seconds to get his shot.

Things were so intense he wasn't scared anymore. It was life or death for the dog and him. Boom, Boom. Gunner got two shots off before the bear dropped down to all fours and started running straight at them.

Gunner cranked in another round as he dropped the rifle butt to the ground, readying the bayonet to slam into the bear on arrival.

He had no idea where Bell was until he looked down in front of himself. She was about three feet in front of him, with her tail sticking straight up and barking the meanest, loudest, snarling, barking growl he had ever heard out of her.

Gunner felt the tree with his right foot. That was his way out, where he could get around it, then planned on drawing the .45 to do more damage. If the rifle came up missing with this freight train of a bear coming straight for them, he knew he couldn't lose his balance or trip. If he did, it would be the end for him.

Right there, between the bear and Gunner, Bell did the job. The bear stopped and reared on its hind feet just like before. Bell had backed up next to Gunner, still snarling and barking like crazy. The bear was only three feet in front of them. Now, the time for a last resort shot had arrived. Gunner was glad he had put the bayonet into the Springfield.

He was still on one knee and shoved the bayonet up against the bear, where he had drilled two holes with the 30-aught six earlier, hopefully into its heart. He shoved the butt end of the rifle to the ground and pulled the trigger hoping for another shot at its chest, all the time holding the rifle.

There was no time to think. He had to stay low and hold the rifle steady. The bear dropped down to all fours and drove the bayonet into himself. Gunner was still holding the butt of the rifle on the ground. The bear swung violently to the left, swinging its giant right paw at Bell.

The sudden move tore the rifle out of Gunner's hands and smashed the rifle butt up against the sugar pine. The bear's momentum and body weight snapped the bayonet off inside him, and the busted rifle stock was lying smashed up against the tree.

Damn, this was one hard-ass bear to kill. And now it's also a mighty pissed-off bear.

On hands and knees, Gunner darted out from under the bear, crawling around the tree on his hands and feet, reaching for the .45 a breath later.

Bell was still barking like crazy off to the bear's right side, keeping its attention. Now the bear had spun around still on all fours and swinging its huge paws toward Bell. She was staying just out of the bear's reach. It looked like she was trying to keep its attention on purpose.

Once on the other side of the tree, Gunner stood on both feet and was automatically aiming at the right side of the bear. He emptied the .45 into the bear with a clear shot as it was lunging for Bell again. It took two steps on all fours and fell over on its side.

The bear appeared to be dead. *You never know. We'll wait a minute, girl.* Gunner was reloading as fast as he could, his hands shaking. He was sure his adrenaline level was somewhere around his eyeballs. *That was a total of nine shots, three from the Springfield and six from the shooter. But who's counting?*

Gunner figured all of that happened in less than 90 seconds. *Darn bear sure did a job on the Springfield, I'm not sure if he didn't bend the barrel to boot.*

Walking toward the bear, Gunner could not see any breathing or any other sign of life. It appeared the bear was good and dead. Gunner walked to the stamp mill and with his hands still shaking, shut it off.

That was a lot of noise he didn't want to listen to for now. Both Gunner and Bell slowed down and started breathing deep. *Jesus, that took a lot out of me.* Sitting on the edge of the sluice box, Bell came over, sat down, and leaned against his leg. Gunner was glad she decided she could stop barking now.

"Bell, this place can get crazy, real fast. Thank you. Without you, I have no idea what would have happened here today. I hope we don't have to do that kind of work around here very often. I'm no bear expert, but it looked like a grizzly. From what Cleo told me, grizzlies don't live in this country. Maybe he's a stray on his way through to Montana or Canada?"

As he sat watching the bear, making sure it was dead, he thought about what had to be done next. *I'll start by bleeding it out and thank it for feeding our friends and us.*

"We'll take all the meat we can carry on the way back out tomorrow, Bell, and save a quarter for us. Cleo can have the rest, and then he can share with whoever he likes. Okay, let's get Jack. We need him to pull the bear up by a tree limb so we can get to skinnin' it."

Gunner sliced the bear to let the blood run out, and he and Bell went back to the cabin and rigged the harness on Jack so they could hitch him to a rope. Gunner would throw the rope over a branch on the big sugar pine they were standing by when the bear charged them.

I need to fix something to eat and take a break for a minute. Gunner needed to collect his thoughts. Digging through the backpack, he found the short bayonet he would use to skin the bear.

Fixing himself some lunch, he took out the new 12-gauge shotgun. That would be his backup for the next few days. *You never know, there might be something else lurking around the corner, or maybe bruin has a friend that might want to come over and visit Bell and me while we are trying to skin this one out.*

Pulling the bear up was nothing for Jack, using his harness. Gunner tied the line off with one hitch and untied Jack, letting him graze next to them. Gunner didn't have to tether or hobble him. He just stuck around and liked being with Bell and him.

Now that he thought of it, Jack and Bell had pretty much bonded. Gunner noticed they liked being near each other. They would talk, in whatever way animals communicate that is.

Once Gunner skinned out the bear, he put the innards on the hide, tied a rope around the bear's head, and threw a loop around Jack's hitch.

Jack pulled it down the valley for them. The bayonet was lodged in some ribs that went with the innards. Now, the wilderness varmints could have dinner thanks to Jack, Bell, and Gunner.

Getting the bear meat wrapped was a wrestling match for one person. Gunner hoisted a quarter at a time across his shoulder and took them up to the mine. There, he was able to hang them all on a crossbeam where it was nice and cool. He had wrapped each one with a cloth, so the meat would cure properly. He was a big bear, maybe 800 pounds, could be more, walking weight, and once skinned out, it looked more than a hundred pounds per quarter.

Finally, back to the cabin, it was dinner time. After taking care of Jack, then Bell, Gunner cleaned up and made a big dinner. Tired but happy that the bear work was finished, he didn't have to lie in bed worrying that darned bear was going to come to visit them. Bell was sound asleep, lying next to the bunk bed on her rug.

Gunner didn't even feel like reading. He laid on the smelly old bed and woke up in the middle of the night cold, after the stove fire had died down and cooled off.

Bell needed to go outside. Gunner got dressed, let her out, then waited for her to come back in. Once she did, he crawled between the blankets of his bedroll. It was one of the best things he could have done in a long time, just lying there. So much had happened in the three days he was gone.

Of course, Quiet Birds' picture was by his nightstand, and he told her goodnight. Thinking about the bear and how vicious it fought for its food, then it's life, was almost shocking to him. Those few moments made him feel older, knowing death is only a breath away. Gunner knew he would fight that hard and harder anytime his family or his life was threatened again. This experience would always be with him, the rest of his life, the day he killed the bear.

CHAPTER 35

Waking up with the sun already coming up, Gunner fed everyone, then put the packs on Jack. Picking up the new 12-gauge shotgun, he shoved it in the sheath attached to Jack's cross buck pack. They made a quick stop at the mine, as he loaded Jack with two of the bear quarters, then headed out for Cleo's cabin.

Just like yesterday, it was the cool of a fall morning with a clear sky to walk under and all the forest to enjoy on their way to Cleo's. Gunner thought it is nice to be alive. He knew he would not take so much for granted from now on.

In step behind Gunner and walking close, Jack seemed at ease with the meat on his back. Bell was out front, enjoying her role of watchdog.

Gunner thought Cleo would be happy to see what they brought in. But then again, perhaps he wouldn't be so surprised. Gunner had to talk to him about that. Gunner still thought it was a grizzly and he had two of the bear's paws in the pack, so Cleo can tell him what it is. He guessed after the forest critters get done cleaning up the carcass, he could get the skull and bring it to Cleo as well.

As before, a couple hours from the mine, it was break time for the crew. Now, they had their favorite stopping spot where they watered Jack. Again, Bell wasn't interested in the water.

Cleo was sitting on the porch in his rocker, in the early noon sun, waiting for their arrival. Gunner led Jack over to the front porch, turned him sideways, and said, "Look what I got for you."

Cleo had a surprised look on his face. "What is that in the bags?"

"Old bruin visited us yesterday. That darned bear was quite at home living in the mine, and he didn't want to leave." Gunner waited while Cleo walked up and eyed the pack on Jack.

"Not only that, but he also had dinner, lunch, and breakfast on Bell and me by eating the last of the whitetail deer. Woo-wee, it's quite a story on how we made him go away. And he ruined my Springfield rifle to boot. Guess we'll have to take it to the gunsmith on our next trip to town. Cleo, I am glad we bought the 12-gauge. Just like you said, it definitely gave old bruin heartburn. But I do have a question."

Gunner took the bear claws out of the pack and unwrapped them. "I brought these claws in for you. Maybe you can tell me what kind of bear this is. It didn't look like any black bear because there was not a black hair on it. It was blonder in color with some dirty gray. I'm guessing he's a grizzly?"

Cleo took the paw. "That sure looks like a Grizz to me."

"I know you told me they didn't come around here anymore, and it has been years since anyone has seen one. Do you think that bear came all the way up from Yellowstone?"

"Maybe. That's where bears like that live, other than up in Montana and Canada. I wouldn't think he would come down this way. Up toward Canada is where a lot of them are, just trying to stay away from people."

"I need to get this unloaded. I brought you two quarters. Maybe you want to give them to the neighbors or even run some to Talking Bird and her dad, Oley. It's yours to give to whoever you want. Tomorrow, I'll bring another quarter in for you to keep. I'll keep one for Bell and me at the claim."

"Let's go ahead and load them in the jeep, then I can run them over this afternoon when you go back up to the mine."

Gunner put the quarters in the back of the jeep, then headed to the side of the shed where the boxed gasoline was stored.

Cleo followed him, watching him pull the cans out and getting them ready to load on Jack. "Aren't you even going to take a break?"

"I'm taking a break right now while I'm starting to load this gear. Jack's fine. I'll give him some water and a bite of hay. I want to get back up to the mine. I got a lot of digging to do up there."

Cleo brought up their last conversation. "Looks like you thought a few things over. How's that working out for you?"

"Well, old friend, I'm going to be okay. All I want to do is go to the mine and work. I don't want to get tangled up with a bunch of crap in town. Exceptin' Miss Quiet Bird, of course. I do like her a whole lot, but that'll have to keep. For now, I've got work to do. She will be there when I come out. That is if she wants to be."

Cleo stood next to Jack, a kind smile on his weathered face. He knew Gunner had made the bend in the road of his young life, out there working the claim.

Gunner thought about the bear. "To take that bear's life was a job for us. It did take something out of me. At the same time, something came into me." He paused to think about what he wanted to say. He knew it was important to him to use the right words, even if it was a kid loading his mule while talking to an old sourdough miner.

Gunner continued, "I had to fight for the mine, and with it, I had to kill to keep it because no damn bear is going to tell me I can't work my mine." He smiled at Cleo. "Once he was dead and it was over with, I sat there on the sluice box pondering for a minute and thought about what I'd just done. For me, the mine's worth fighting for, and so is my dog, my mule, even someday, maybe a woman."

Cleo encouraged the young man. "Yes, go on. I see what you're saying."

"Right now, I see I have work to do. Once I get this gas loaded, and Jack has had a drink, I'll give him some grain and jerky for Bell and me. Then we will be heading back up to the mine. I'll be back tomorrow and get the last load. If not, I'll make another trip, I guess. Cleo, it feels good to be back at work. I'm getting things done. I'll be fine."

Cleo nodded and kept that warm, friendly smile of his.

"The dynamite will help a lot. I think I'm getting closer to the hard rock, which will put the brakes on for me. I need the powder as soon as I can put it to work. And I need to get the cash up to buy that drill and compressor from Oley."

"Well now, young man," Cleo said. "It sounds like you got things worked out. I figured once you got back up there, things would settle down for you. I would never have guessed you'd have to take on a bear to do it."

"I guess you just got to kill a bear now and then in your life to see what's going on." Gunner laughed. "I'm happy, Cleo. I like the way things are in my life. I still figure I'm going to enjoy my time with Quiet Bird when I have a chance. Until then, I'm going on about my business and keep doing what I'm doing."

Cleo was keeping quiet, just smiling and nodding as Gunner talked.

"I need to better myself, study on the mine, and keep my schooling up. That's what I want to get done. I want to finish it to make my mother happy and be proud that I finished it. Does all this make sense to you?"

Cleo smiled from ear to ear. "That makes a lot of sense to me. You'll be fine, take your time. Don't get in a hurry, make good decisions, take care of your critters, and care for the woman when you can."

The gas cans were loaded and tied up on Jack's pack. Gunner loaded up his backpack with small things and turned to Cleo. "Seems like I'm always saying hello and goodbye to you. I thought about you going to the home, and you would be sorely missed, old-timer. Cleo, you are such a good friend. Thank you for all your time and advice one more time."

"We better stop gossiping, and you can get going. See you tomorrow," Cleo said.

"Enjoy the meat and tell everybody hello, whoever you see. As I said, I'll have that last quarter for you tomorrow when we come in."

Gunner turned and looked at Cleo's wrinkled smiling face. "If you drop off some meat to Talking Bird and Quiet Bird, would you tell Quiet Bird that I am thinking of her morning and evening with the picture she gave me? She'll know what I'm talking about."

Taking Jack's lead rope, Gunner and Bell started walking toward the trail. Now that Jack and he have been together for a while, they quickly fell into a comfortable stride, making good time.

"Bell, out front," Gunner called out. She was growing more every day. She could stay ahead of them now, losing a lot of her puppy stuff.

It was warm enough for Gunner to take off his wool shirt and stuff it in the backpack when they took their break. The sky was still blue as he looked up through the pine trees. *This is a good day.*

The crew made better time with Jack hauling gasoline in his packs rather than pulling the skid. It was mid-afternoon as they passed the cabin heading up to the mine. Gunner tied Jack up by the stamp mill and he and Bell walked up to the mouth of the mine shaft.

The boards he put up in the opening were still in place. Going in, Gunner didn't have his flashlight, so he could only see as far as the light would let him. It was silent and untouched, other than where the bear had been living for a couple of days chewing up the leftover whitetail deer. Gunner could smell that he needed to clean that mess up and get things organized so he could start digging again.

He unloaded the gas next to the pump they had dropped off the day before. Jack knew he was going to his pasture and pushed Gunner along as they started walking back down to the cabin. Mules were smart that way.

The air was brisk and sharp, being late September already. *Midthirties I'll bet.* As he walked, he was creating a plan for the next month. He guessed they would need to go back out for supplies and take the test for schooling around the 25th of October.

It would be nice to see Quiet Bird sooner than that. He knew he needed to get this work done before the snow came. A lot of things would slow down after that. *Yes, everything will work out, but the weather is changing.* Gunner noticed he was wearing his long johns more. Even Bell was getting her winter coat, and Jack's mane was filling out along with his chest and legs. His coat was getting thicker too.

Bell led the way into the shed, and Gunner pulled Jack's pack gear off, brushed him down, and took him out to the field where he started grazing.

Gunner mumbled, "Good, now back to work."

He found the old spade shovel in the tool shed, a couple of square nose shovels, and the pick he had used at the hot spring and he and Bell headed to the mine to mark out where the lower pond would go.

The mining book called this a retention pond, just big enough to hold the water needed, then pump it back up the hill to reuse.

Cleo and Gunner had gone over the one lunger engine. Gunner should be able to start and get the maintenance done on it. He needed to put a pump pick-up pipe in a pond that caught the water when it came off the sluice with that setup.

Gunner chose to put the pond about 10 feet away from the end of the sluice box. The water would fall out from the rocks, then travel down in a spillway built with old boards that he had set aside for the pond. The lower pond would have to match the upper pond size. He would shift the valves, start the pump in the lower pond, pump the water back up to the upper basin using the same pipe that sent the water down to the crusher, and stamp. They called this setup a manifold on the boats, using the same pipe for two or three different jobs.

The problem now was where he could get the pipe, valves, and plumbing material to go from the lower pond to the sluice box's pickup, where the water came down from the upper millpond.

Gunner had a trip over to Slim Gibson's claim in the back of his mind. Maybe he could find what he needed there. For now, he'd start digging on the lower pond until he couldn't stand it anymore. Thank the Lord, the lower pond would not be another toilet hole like he dug at Norman's.

Now according to the side of the bag and his books, the sodium bentonite clay or vermiculite had an expansion rate that will go from 1 part out of the paper bag to 18 times that when mixed with water. *That's hard to believe. I wonder if that yahoo at the lumber store ever read the bag?* Gunner still felt the guy didn't like him.

Gunner planned on putting on a thin three-quarter-inch layer of vermiculite on the walls. The ground looked relatively soft, not hardpan, and that should speed up his digging.

The hole would be 10-foot in diameter by 2 feet deep, which would make it about a 4-foot-deep hole with the berm from the digging dirt. Tonight, Gunner planned on using his calculating book from mining engineering to figure out how much water the pond would hold.

Gunner dug all afternoon and into the evening, and by five o'clock, it started getting dark. Bell had been lying down, her head resting on her legs, watching him dig the hole the entire time, so when he threw the shovel out over the side of the hole, she knew it was quitting time.

"Come on, Bell, we got to get Jack, give him a snack, and put him to bed, then we'll call it a night."

Jack was glad to see them with his throaty nicker. By early dark, he was happily in his stall.

In the cabin, Gunner got the cookstove fire going and cooked a healthy dinner of leftover rice and meat for both he and Bell. They had started on the bear meat today when he took off a piece at lunchtime. Even though he cooked it a little too long, it was good just the same.

Gunner pulled out the kerosene lamp to light up the cabin, dark earlier every day now with winter fast approaching. This was his first chance to look at the study work for school. It was nice of Talking Bird to put this together for him. After reading for school an hour and a half, Gunner decided he needed at least thirty minutes for reading his mining books to figure the size of the pond he was digging.

He filled the stove with wood to burn into the night. Bell and he would keep warm for a while. She was sound asleep on her rug next to the bed as Gunner piled into his bunk. He had been calling it his old smelly bed, but changed the name to bunk, like on the boat.

Reaching over to the small dresser by the bed, he picked up Quiet Bird's picture and said, "Goodnight, pretty lady," then blew out the lamp and fell into a deep asleep.

Gunner woke just before dawn, got up, stoked the stove, went out to Jack's shed, and fed him. As he talked to Jack, a one-way conversation, Jack seemed to nod in agreement. Back in the cabin, Bell was ready for her breakfast too. Gunner cooked up some of the bear meat for both of them in a small pan, and he had another bowl of mush.

Bell knew they were doing something, lying by the door, making sure that Gunner didn't leave without her. She is not only the best company, but Gunner enjoyed her more every day.

As Gunner walked into the shed, Jack started talking in his low, grumbling voice.

"What are you talking about, Jack? It's time to go, boy. We got a big load today, and don't you fail me now with this dynamite on your back."

He threw the packs on Jack and tightened the cinch, then tucked Jack's lead in his harness. With the 12-gauge in his hand, Bell automatically headed toward the dogleg, knowing where they were going. "Not yet, girl, got to go up to the mine and get Cleo's quarter of bear, so he'll have some meat to eat."

The crew hiked up the hill to the mine shaft. The quarter was hanging quite nicely next to Bell and Gunner's. He pulled it down, put it on his shoulder, carried it outside, and tied it over the middle of Jack's pack.

"Okay, girl, let's go to the road now. You know the way." Bell ran to the dogleg and sat, waiting for them to catch up, then ran ahead as usual.

The walk was comfortable, although Gunner could see his breath in the early morning. Gunner talked a little to his crew, and the rest of the time, everybody was quiet. Sometimes, he got tired of talking to himself but still enjoyed his animal companions.

They stopped at their usual place two hours into their trip. This was about the fifth time they had been there. Both animals knew what to do. Gunner dropped Jack's lead rope on the ground and got his water. Of course, Bell wasn't interested. She would get a drink when they got to Cleo's.

Cleo was on his front porch in his rocker. Gunner thought he caught him taking a nap as he took his chin off his chest. "You look like you are taking a nap there, old-timer. We didn't mean to interrupt you."

"Who are you calling old-timer? Not me. How are you doing today? Looks like you're ready for another big load."

"It's a big day today. Jack gets to haul the dynamite, and I get to carry the caps. We should be okay though. He's getting pretty sure-footed, and everybody's used to the trail now. Did you get all your bear meat delivered yesterday?"

Cleo knew what he was getting at. Gunner wanted to know if he had talked to Quiet Bird. He smiled. "Yes, I got all the bear meat delivered yesterday, and I happened to see this one pretty young girl too. She certainly had a lot of questions as to how this guy killed a bear. Both Talking Bird and Quiet Bird had to hear all the details of you and that bear. I told them as much as I knew about it. I said it was a real experience for you. I think you could have grown five years in those ninety seconds."

"It was a real humbling experience for sure. I'm glad you got to see the ladies. Did Talking Bird have enough to share with her dad?"

"Yes, she did, and she was very appreciative. I'm hoping you brought another quarter today?"

"You bet, I got it right here for you in Jack's pack. The next time I come out, I'll try to pick up a large whitetail to share with everybody. Did you drop some meat off to Norman and Granny also?"

"Yes, and they're doing well. I gave them a full quarter, and they were happy to see it. That will give them some fresh meat until elk season."

"You want your meat hung in the shed?"

"Yes, that would be appreciated. Those darn things get awful heavy when you're rapidly approaching eighty plus years old." Cleo always had something funny to say and a smile on his face.

Gunner pulled the bear quarter off Jack onto his shoulder, carried it to the shed, and hung it on one of the hooks hanging from the rafters. Then, he led Jack to the tool shed where he had stored the dynamite. Cleo followed them and chatted as Gunner pulled boxes of dynamite out, ready to load in Jack's pack bags.

"Don't you have time to stop and have lunch?"

"Well, I could, but I think that we need to get going. I've started digging that hole for the lower pond already."

"Young feller, at least you can stop and have a sandwich and a cup of coffee before you go. You need to eat."

"Okay. Jack, you got yourself a free lunch on the grass over there, and Bell, you come with me. We'll have lunch with the old-timer here. Let's go in and see what we can scare up for grub with our good friend."

Cleo scoffed, "Old-timer. I do have some whitetail lying around."

"That must be the last of the whitetail because we were chewing on that last week, weren't we?"

Cleo chuckled. "You're right, that's been around a while, but now we can break into the fresh stuff. That would be bear a good friend of mine just killed."

Stopping off at Cleo's woodshed, Gunner got an arm full of firewood and dumped it in the cookstove box, then opened the lid on the stove and filled it to get the fire built up.

"Cleo, how are you feeling with this cool air we're getting? I forgot to ask the other day."

Cleo said, "Well, sir, it does make my arthritis sit up and pay attention. Hopefully, I can keep enough fire going to keep things warmed up around here. If you don't mind, I think you and I will be making that trip to Orofino to find a warmer place for me."

It didn't take them long to get some food out and warmed up in a pan. They sat down and started visiting again.

"Cleo, if I went up to Slim Gibson's mine and found some parts that might work for my pump, you think he would mind if I borrowed them or paid him or worked something out?"

"I don't think he would mind at all. I think he'd be happy to have somebody put that equipment to good use. When we go down to Orofino, we can visit with him and see if you could buy his claim."

"That sounds great. I could use some parts for my pump setup. Here's what I have planned. I'll set up the one lung pump at the bottom and dig a hole for the pump suction and foot valve. With all that done, I'd like to pipe it over to the valve that spills the water into the sluice box. Piping the pump into that, I'll be able to shut off the sluice box and push the water back up the hill to the upper pond in the same pipe."

"That might work. That's a perfect idea, Gunner. Wish I had thought of that. If you can't find the parts, come on out, and we will go to town and get them."

"I need to get packed up now. There is a lot of digging to do when I get back home. Jack is doing great, and Bell, she's becoming less of a puppy every day. She did a hell of a job with that bear we killed. I think she saved our bacon."

"I'll be here when you get back tomorrow if you need to go into town and buy parts. I wouldn't worry when you go over to Slim's place. He would like to sell the whole shebang. It hurt him when the cabin burnt down, just like if I were to lose this cabin. It's all I got in this world. It's not much, but it's all mine."

Gunner gave Cleo a wave as they were getting a little farther away just to let him know they were thinking of him.

Gunner's crew had gotten used to the walk, so it went by fast. He thought they made better time today than any earlier trips.

Maybe we could run a wagon down the trail. I'll bet Cleo used this trail as a road to get the stamp mill to his mine. I'll ask Slim if this was the road he used to get equipment into his claim as well.

CHAPTER 36

Before Gunner knew it, they were back at the cabin. Jack and Gunner walked straight to the tool shed to unload and store the dynamite.

For the second day in a row, Gunner turned Jack out into the corral, took off his packs, then lead him to his pasture for grazing. Jack hadn't even worked up a sweat on this last walk. The dynamite was light for him, and he did a smooth job.

Gunner thought about what Cleo said about going over to Slim's place. He did need the parts.

"Bell, we should take a quick walk up the valley. Let's bring the 12-gauge along in case we run into dinner on the way."

They went down to the cabin and picked up the Trapper Nelson Pack Board in case they found tools and equipment he could use. Gunner threw in a pipe wrench, screwdriver, and a couple of crescent wrenches as well.

It was late afternoon, perfect for a pleasant walk through the Nez Perce forest. Gunner told himself this was one of the benefits of living here. It wasn't overly warm, and the cold weather was coming.

The squirrels were storing pinecones that have started to drop. The forest floor was covered with pine needles, and their steps were muffled. The sky above was full of high clouds, but it was clear to the west. Gunner knew it would get cold tonight. Mother Nature was telling him winter was on its way.

Cleo said Slim's place wasn't that far, six miles or so. Gunner hoped he could make it in a long hour if he and Bell walked fast. *Guess I could ride Jack.* Gunner decided a walk sounded better.

When they arrived, Gunner figured he only had thirty to forty minutes to look around before they had to head back to make it to the cabin before dark. They would need to come back another time with a full day to explore.

Bell was the best partner for taking a walk, and she moved along with him. She was now three months old and doing what she needed to do.

Gunner could see the charred remains of a cabin up in the trees to the west of the canyon. According to his map, that was where Ryan Creek came down through the valley and over to Cleo's claim. As they got closer, he could see the foundation was burnt and crumbling, also destroyed by the fire. *It must've been scorching.* The only other identifiable thing in the remains was an old metal sink.

Out back, Gunner could see the tool shed, and to the left, a small barn with stalls. Behind those buildings, he could make out an overgrown trail leading up the hill, perhaps going up to a mine.

Remember, it's been ten years since anybody's been here. Gunner was running out of time. He walked quickly up the trail about three hundred feet and found the mine, a big wood door across the mouth of the tunnel.

It was a lot like the one Cleo had built for his mine. It would take some work to get this door open so he could look inside. The equipment Slim used for the claim could be in there. He needed to bring a crowbar and sledgehammer next time. He had to remind himself he was just looking for plumbing hardware and a quick look around this trip. At the tool shed, Gunner found the door locked with a hasp. All this time, it hadn't been bothered by anybody since Slim set the lock.

Gunner gave a shove to the door, and it swung open, falling off its hinges. Gunner leaned it up against the handrail on the front of the shed. Equipment and tools were everywhere, and to his surprise, three boxes of old plumbing parts. There were lots of things to make repairs. *Remember, you're not close to town.*

"Look at this, Bell. There's an old one-lung engine underneath the bench, and it has a generator hooked to it." He was excited. Everything he saw would help him out on his claim. If Slim would sell it to him, he would sure like to buy it.

Gunner would only be borrowing a few plumbing parts for now. Taking his backpack off, he leaned it against the bench, kneeled, and started picking through the boxes under the benchtop. He wanted to tell Slim what he had picked up. Sure enough, there were plenty of the inch-and-a-half fittings he needed.

Gunner also found some old firehose up underneath one of the shelves to the right. That would work to get the water from his new one-lung pump, and as long as he can keep everything from freezing, the sluice and stamp mill could work all winter.

"Bell, looks like we've hit a real gold mine here. At least we found the parts needed, and we won't have to make a trip to town. Shoot, I bet both you and I would like to see a certain somebody in town, but that's okay. We decided we got a job to do and we're going to do it."

Looking outside, Gunner could see it was starting to get dark. "Hey, girl, it's going to be late by the time we get back. I don't like leaving Jack outside in the dark. We gotta hurry up."

Gunner grabbed the pipe fittings he needed and the fire hose to load in the backboard pack. He didn't take time to look in the barn stalls. That would wait until the next trip.

Bell and Gunner took off after re-hanging the door on the tool shed. At a half trot, they headed down the trail and made it back to Jack in record time, arriving just as the night shadows covered the shed. Jack was standing at the gate, waiting for them to come to get him and say goodnight.

Gunner and Bell got into the cabin as full darkness settled on the cabin. Gunner started the lamp, then the stove fire, planning on frying up some of old bruin for dinner. He knew the meat wasn't seasoned enough, but it would put winter fat on the two of them. Bell didn't complain. She was fine as long as the meat was cooled down. Gunner mixed in some of the puppy chow he had left. For him, he was happy to cook up rice, mixing it in with his fried bear meat. He wanted to get his heels propped up for the night and read in the lamplight.

The stove had a friendly fire to keep them warm. Bell was sound asleep as soon as she finished her dinner. Gunner got things cleaned up and put away, then it was time to sit down with his schoolbooks for at least an hour. Finally, he picked up the mine books and read up on drilling and blasting. *This is just like last night, Bell. It is turning into a natural routine.*

When Gunner got ready for bed, he stripped down to his long johns, and sat on the edge of his bunk. He paused to pick up Quiet Bird's picture and couldn't help but say goodnight.

"I do miss you. I hope you feel the same for me."

It was still confusing for him to feel like a good friend, then some other interests. *What is my other interest? Well, I am thinking there must be the man and woman stuff we will talk about.* He was hoping she would see it the same way as him. He knew there is a lot of life ahead of them, and he wanted them to enjoy it together.

Gunner reminded himself that now was not the time to get wrapped up with all those feelings. "For darn sure, I'm not going to Elk City and get a job at the grocery store. Goodnight, Quiet Bird, I'll see you in the morning." After he set her picture on the dresser, he crawled in between the blankets in his bunk to fell fast asleep.

Early the next morning, in the dark, still in his bunk, Gunner told a sleeping Bell, "Bell, we need to get up and get going, better say good morning to Quiet Bird. Then we got to get to scooting for that last load. Someday, I'll get around to making biscuits and pancakes. We don't have the time right now."

Gunner got up, dressed, and headed to the shed to check on Jack. That mule was happy as always. Gunner fed and brushed him, then took him to the corral and mounted the pack gear on him.

Stopping by the cabin, Gunner picked up the backpack they had come in with last night.

"Crew, this looks like it's getting to be quite a routine for us. I'm figuring this should be the last trip until next month."

Making their rest stop repeated the same routine as before, Jack got his water, Bell happy without it. As they approached Cleo's place, Gunner didn't see his friend on the front porch. That bothered him. Cleo was always there when they came in. Getting within 10 feet of Cleo's front door, Gunner gave a holler.

"Hey, Cleo, we're here. Are you hiding?" He started to worry. Cleo was always here, unless he was out in the toilet. And if he were, he would have hollered back at him, but Gunner didn't hear anything.

Gunner walked up the porch steps and through the front door. There was Cleo, sound asleep in his chair.

"Hey, old-timer, are you okay?"

Cleo's eyes opened slowly, and he looked up at Gunner, "Is that you, Gunner? Aren't you early?"

"Cleo, are you okay? Is there anything I can do for you?" Gunner asked, trying to keep worry out of his voice.

Cleo answered, more awake now, "Yeah, I'm okay. Just taking a little nap before you got here. You know an old guy can do that."

"I was just worried about you. I'll go outside and get things pulled out and loaded up so we can get going. I'll come and check on you before we go, okay?"

"Hey, don't get in a hurry now. I just woke up and will get moving shortly. You are going to have lunch and visit, aren't you? I look forward to seeing you when you come in."

"You bet. I'd love to have lunch with you. It will be nice to have a good visit. I find one-way conversations with Jack and Bell get old out there at the mine. At least, you will argue back with me when you think I don't have my head screwed on straight. We'll have lunch together. I'll come in and cook, okay?"

"Alright. Things are just running a little slower for me today. You already know this, but I think maybe this winter, sometime, we need to go down and see Slim. By the way, did you get out to his place yesterday?"

"You bet we did. It was late, but we made it. We'll have to talk about it over lunch. Got lots to talk about."

Gunner headed outside, collecting up Bell and Jack. They went to the corral, putting Jack out into the small pasture area. Bell was at his side as he went back inside, stopping to pick up an armload of stove wood.

In Cleo's kitchen, Gunner found everything in place and Cleo was sitting in his kitchen chair. It bothered Gunner that his old friend still looked dead tired.

"Okay, old-timer, tell me, do we need to do something now? You going to be okay?"

Cleo looked up with his tired eyes and smiled, "I might be dragging a bit, but I'll be fine. Sure nice to see you. I appreciate the company. Nice to have you here for lunch."

"Cleo, it's nice to be here with you. After lunch, I'll get that old mule out there, wait no, he's not ancient, we'll get going and leave you in peace."

Cleo smiled and sat in his chair, quietly waiting for Gunner to dish up lunch. Gunner thought the old guy was still waking up.

"When you talked to Quiet Bird the other day, did she say anything else? Did she want to send me a message? I forgot to ask you that," Gunner said sheepishly.

Cleo perked up. "She wanted me to tell you hello and that she is looking forward to seeing you when you come into town next."

"Thank you, I appreciate the message."

Gunner enjoyed being in Cleo's company, and Cleo felt the same.

After lunch, it was time for Gunner to load up for the trip back to the mine. He was planning on digging on the lower pond when they got there. Cleo followed him out to the barn as Gunner explained what he found and what he had brought from Slim's mine. He would use it all to get his pump running.

Cleo agreed that should work.

Getting Jack loaded meant throwing the bags of pond liner inside the big pack bags and tying them down.

Turning to Cleo, he said with a serious voice, "Cleo, we won't be back until late October. Are you going to be okay if I don't come to check on you?"

"Oh, sure. The folks down the road, they'll come to check on me. You and Quiet Bird put up plenty of wood, so I'll be good until then. Now, make sure you stop by when you come out next time. I like to see you. We always have a good time."

"There is no way I'd miss checking in with you. And, as always, Cleo, thank you so much for everything."

Gunner and his crew headed out, turning back to wave before stepping off into the woods. He thought about Cleo and finding him sound asleep like he did. Cleo was right. Maybe he's getting drained. It could be his arthritis taking it out of him. The home might not be a bad idea after all. It was not safe for him to be alone up in that cabin. He needed somebody checking on him regularly.

Gunner and crew were back at the cabin early. He took Jack over to put the bags in the tool shed, then a rubdown, and to the pasture. Looking over at Bell, Gunner gave her a nod, and she followed as he headed up to dig on the lower pond. He knew it had to get done before he could start running the stamp mill, or it would be filling in as he was trying to dig.

It's one of those things you got to get done now. Gunner, you need not mess around and take your time.

Gunner worked on the lower pond for the next three days. Finally, it was time to mix the bentonite with water and fill it in and around the upper edges of the pond. That would hold the water in as he started filling it up.

He was able to dig a sump hole to place the suction foot valve in it. That's what they called it in Cleo's book. Between the old tools Cleo had given him, the ones found in the shed on his claim, and the plumbing parts he had picked up at Slim's, it all came together.

Next was a problem with the firehose fittings. They wouldn't fit the pump parts, so Gunner cut the pipe fittings off the hose, slide the firehose over the pipe, and put hose clamps on to hold the firehose. Gunner discussed the plumbing with Bell and decided they would wait until morning to test run everything.

It had been a long day, and he was ready for a break. First, dinner, reading, and then studying his schoolbooks. Gunner refused to flunk the test Talking Bird would be giving him.

Getting ready for bed was the same routine as before. Gunner held Quiet Bird's picture up to the lamplight and said goodnight, then blew out the lamp, slid under the covers, and immediately fell asleep.

CHAPTER 37

Gunner woke up excited to get back to work. This morning, they would turn on the stamp mill and test the lower pond and piping for the water return system.

With the tailings' pile all gone, Gunner had to start digging in the mine. He was looking forward to drilling and blasting. Finally, production from the mine would start soon.

It was a beautiful morning as he and Bell headed up to the mine. The squirrels were still working on putting everything away for the winter, and the dry pine needles crunched under Gunner's feet. Bell was twenty feet ahead of him, making sure everything was safe.

Turning on the stamp mill was like music to Gunner's ears, as if he had never turned it off. He started shoveling the last of the tailings in the hopper, and the water from the sluice box ran into the new lower pond. *Looks like it'll run until noon, then I'll fire up the one-lung pump and shove all that water back up the hill to the upper pond.* He figured he could work the mine twelve to fourteen hours a day now. *Maybe even more. No, I'll be too tired by then.*

Gunner and Bell ate on the bear meat, so Gunner didn't need to hunt whitetail. That became the routine for the next twenty-two days.

Daylight averaged about fourteen hours now and shorter every day, so Gunner went to the mine in the dark. It was dark all the time in the tunnel anyway. He wished he had a regular hanging kerosene lantern, like they used on the inner tube at the end of the fishnets back home.

Gunner refused to bring the kerosene lantern out of the cabin. He was afraid it would get broken with some flying rock. It had a glass base as well as a fragile glass lens. If that happened, he would be out of a reading lamp and that would not work.

"Bell, when we go to town, I'll buy one of those old blue lamps, maybe two. That will give us a spare so Jack could use it in his mule hotel. Better put another 5 gallons of kerosene on the list. I've used up all of the kerosene we had for the cabin lamp."

The new pump set up for the lower pond was running perfectly to power the stamp and sluice. Gunner would crank up the one-lung engine when needed, and usually, by the time lunch was done, all the water would be pumped back up to the upper pond. Then, he would run the stamp and crusher until he needed another pump out on the lower pool.

The water was warm, and Gunner thought, hopefully, it wouldn't freeze this winter. He still needed to put up a shed to keep some heat around the pump, sluice, and stamp mill.

The mine is another story. It's a mess, and there is a whole lot of work to get the track straightened out.

Gunner had to pick and bust rock to get a bed smooth enough for the ties to lay down. Then, the track went on top of that. He was unsure what size the track gauge was, but he knew it was awfully small for the itty-bitty gondola he had to push in and out of the mine by hand.

Gunner was still hoping to get Jack up there by using voice commands. Jack could pull the gondola out of the mine, then after dumping the gondola, he would tell Jack to back up so the gondola would go back into the mine. He decided trying to train Jack would take more time than he wanted to spend. It was easier to push the gondola out himself, trip it to dump into the crusher hopper, then push it back in the mine. Gunner figured he would think about that problem later.

Bell was getting better every day. She knew their routine and knew what to expect at certain times. That made Gunner's job a lot easier as Bell was his alarm clock, amongst other things. She reminded him when it was time to knock off and go back to the cabin for dinner with a friendly, but insistent, woof.

The digging wasn't all that bad after removing the loose dirt and glacial rocks. According to Cleo's figuring, bedrock was only twenty feet away. *Good call, Cleo, 43.5 feet exactly from bedrock to the mouth of the mine.*

This is where the six sticks of dynamite would come in. Cleo had given Gunner a good talking to about all the finer points of blasting caps, dynamite sticks, and everything that could go wrong.

Gunner felt he had a handle on the process. Using the short, 48" drill, he pounded six holes in the mine walls. Then, he packed one stick of dynamite per hole, with the old idea that more is better. Besides, he figured, he wouldn't need to stamp it so much with the dynamite doing the stamping for him.

As this was the first time Gunner had ever used dynamite, he laid a long fuse to give him plenty of time to get the heck out of there. The part he hadn't given much thought to was he wasn't blasting entirely in hard rock. There was a lot of glacial rock and dirt included.

Gunner locked Jack in the shed. He didn't want his prized mule around, not even close. He knew even the hillside could slide down. Anything could go wrong, and he wasn't taking any chances.

Gunner lit the fuse and high-tailed it out of the mine shaft. Suddenly, the light snow and pine needles lying on the slope above the mine lifted almost a foot off the ground, followed by a huge BOOM!

This is not good. The shaft opening belched out smoke, dirt, and dust, followed by half of the supports and ceiling timbers flying everywhere.

"Oh, crap! I'll need a sawmill to replace all of that! Maybe two sticks would have been better than six. Guess I should do more reading," he told Bell.

The cleanup took him three days, and that included putting all the support timbers back in. At night, he studied up on blasting in the mining books. *You are right, Cleo. Slow down and make good decisions. Yes, six sticks was not the right decision.*

Gunner thought it was around the first part of October. No snow yet, but it looked like it was coming. Bell faithfully watched outside, keeping an eye peeled for danger as work continued in the mine.

Fill the gondola cart, push it out to the hopper above the stamp mill, dump the cart, push it back into the mine. Do it all over again.

Gunner's system worked well. He trusted Bell to let him know if somebody or something was coming around for a visit. Keeping on the alert was especially important out there in the wilderness.

He always seemed to be watching over his shoulder, and maybe that came from Cleo's schooling. Cleo had said, "You have to be ready and quicker than the next thing that you will have to deal with."

The bear incident is still in the front of his mind. Nearly losing Bell had been a rude wake-up for him. *That dog has a lot of value. Most of all, we're good friends.* That day, Gunner had found what depth a person had to go when it came to killing or be killed and protecting the ones you love at any price.

A heavy frost covered the ground in the mornings now and it never seemed to warm up. The clouds were heavy and dark grey today. *Looks like snow, too cold for rain.*

This morning, Bell was lying out in front of the mouth of the mine, as she had done from the first day, and he started working in the tunnel. Mid-morning, she came into the mine and stood staring at Gunner. He was busy shoveling dirt and rocks into the cart he had finally gotten fixed. She gave one of her low, quiet woofs, then another, then a third, louder now. Her tail was not wagging, and her woof was to tell Gunner there is something out there, and it needed his attention. "Now!" They have been together for three months. Maybe he needed to learn that when she said something, she meant it.

The back of the mine was completely dark, with only the carbide headlamp to give any light. Turning toward Bell, Gunner could hardly see her. Her coat was mostly black now that she had lost her puppy brown. She had a little bit of white under her chin, some whisker white on the sides of her nose, and two touches of white above her eyebrows. The feathers on her chest above each front leg were gray.

Gunner asked, "What is it, girl? Do you hear something?"

Bell turned just a little and looked back at him and woofed again. Not looking back a second time, she started walking for the mouth of the mine. Gunner followed behind her, knowing something was there.

The .45 and knife hung on a nail halfway down the shaft. Gunner hurriedly slung the harness on and buckled the web belt, picked up the 12-gauge pump, and cradled it under his arm.

Gunner looked around as he reached the mouth of the mine. He checked the dense black clouds as they continued a snail's crawl across the sky.

Bell didn't go down toward the cabin. She had stopped just outside the mine opening. She started moving right, above the trail, in the thick pine-covered forest floor. Gunner followed, walking above the path in the shadowed trees. They had fair cover there and high ground. That would be choice number one if there was going to be a fight of some kind.

If it were a person coming up the trail, they would never see Gunner and Bell. Bell sat down and watched the path as voices floating up to them. Familiar voices to Gunner, especially one, Norman's son Ned.

Gunner could see the two riders now. The one behind Ned was on a familiar horse. Gunner had heard the man's voice before, but he couldn't place it. Ned was in the lead with his big bay horse. Gunner remembered admiring it last summer.

Behind Ned, Gunner recognized Officer Bob. He could tell by his County Sheriff hat and coat. But the thing that warmed Gunner's heart was that he was riding old Butch, and Butch was his old cranky self, snorting and walking slow. *Dang, I miss that old plug.*

The men were quietly talking, and Gunner could only make out part of what they were saying. They thought they would be coming up on the mine any minute as they could hear the stamp mill. Gunner had left it running just in case it needed to cover any of the noise Bell and he would be making.

Gunner was surprised the horses didn't smell Bell and him sitting above the trail as the riders passed them. Gunner walked silently down the twenty feet to the tail, coming in behind them.

The riders looked at the mine operation with the stamp mill still running and mentioned that Gunner must be in the mine. When they came to a complete stop, Bell and Gunner also stopped, standing in the middle of the trail. Gunner called out, "Now, what can I do for you boys today?"

They both jerked, quickly spinning around in their saddles. They knew someone had the drop on them. Gunner could see the surprise in their eyes, not to mention disappointment with the 12-gauge shotgun laying across Gunner's arm with his right hand deep into the stock and trigger guard.

With a big smile, Ned spoke first, "Well, I'll be damned, here he is. We figured it wouldn't take much to get you flushed out." Gunner liked Ned. He was a good man, kind of a Hoss sort of a guy, and he had a crazy girlfriend. But that didn't make any difference. Ned was kind to Gunner. He always had good words to say, and Gunner was happy to see him.

Officer Bob, he was a different deal. Gunner was not sure why the law was here.

They met that one time when there was trouble with the Ferguson brothers in Elk City. "Hello, Officer Bob. What brought you all this way out here today?"

The first thought that shot across Gunner's mind was that someone wanted an attendance officer to come out here and drag him into juvenile hall for not going to school.

Officer Bob spoke up, "Gunner, we heard the rumor and thought maybe we should come up and check it out."

"And what would that rumor be, Sir?"

"We heard that there was some bear killing going on up here."

"Sir, you heard right. Things got down to a point where it was me, Bell, or the bruin. I'll be damned if I'd give my claim, and most of all, my dog, up to that smelly old bear. You see, old bruin had been camping in the mine, and having him around wasn't what you would call comfortable for me and my critters."

"Gunner," Officer Bob asked politely, "would you mind if we got down off these horses, stretched a bit, and ask you how it happened?"

"Sure thing, we'll go down to the cabin. I can give the critters some hay. Then, I'll fix coffee and get you warmed up. Ned, did you come by the shortcut through the valley out back of the ranch? Or did you go up to Cleo's and then across on the ridge and down the dogleg?"

As Ned and Officer Bob dismounted from their horses, Ned replied, "We came by way of Cleo's. That was a long hike in here coming from the ranch with the horses. We took off from the ranch at six this morning, and now it's darn near noon."

After Gunner shut down the stamp mill, the group walked toward the cabin. Gunner was in the lead and looked back at Ned. "I'll give you shortcut directions to get back to the ranch that should save you two to three hours if you hustle. Hopefully, you can make it back before it gets too dark. That, of course, depends on how long you want to hang out up here with Bell and me." Walking over to the shed, Gunner dug out two coffee cans of grain and suggested everyone throw their saddles over the corral fence. Gunner gave them the grain and dished up a can for Jack.

"When you have company, Jack, you're entitled to what they're having," Gunner said, walking over to the pasture where Jack was standing.

"Boys, you can put your critters in this pasture, and I'll get the stove stoked up to make coffee."

Officer Bob said, "That would be appreciated. Gunner, we brought lunches in our saddlebags, so we won't need anything to eat. All we want is to hear about the bear killing, then we will be on our way."

Shortly, Officer Bob and Ned came through the cabin door and Gunner gestured for them to have a seat at the table.

Gunner sat on the bunk bed with his leg over the top of Bell. He wasn't sure how Bell felt about having strangers in the cabin. He didn't want her to make any noise.

Officer Bob took off his hat and tossed it over to the foot of the bed. "The reason I'm here is that we heard you killed a bear that appeared to be a grizzly. There is not a question of whether it was right or wrong. It's a question of did it happen that way?"

When Gunner began talking, Officer Bob took a notepad out and started taking notes. Gunner smiled. He took notes just like he did in Elk City when the bully and Gunner had it out in the street.

"Oh, yea, it did happen. It was one tough job. Would you like me to explain how it happened?"

"Well, yes, that would be appreciated. How did you first stumble into the bear, and we understand it tried to attack you?"

"Yes, it did try to attack us. We found it in the mine. You can pretty much guess what the rest of the story is. The only thing I can tell you, Officer Bob, is that it was an experience I don't want to repeat. Don't know how many bears you've killed in your life, but I've had my share and don't want any more. That was a very humbling and scary experience. The one good thing that I can say is that this dog lying next to my feet here most likely saved my life. The meat was there, and I didn't want to see it go to waste, so I took three quarters into Cleo, and he shared it with the neighbors."

Officer Bob stopped writing, thought for a minute, and reached out to sip some coffee. "That's quite a story. What kind of bear do you think it was? Do you have any remains?"

"Yes, to all the above, I think it was a Grizz. I wouldn't know a grizzly if it was sleeping next to me, but from everything Cleo explained to me and what I've seen before in magazines, I'd say yes, he was. That was one mad bear, and he was in rough shape. Yes, I do have some remains, unless the wild critters have dragged them off. I put the carcass out in the forest after the bear dressed out. I left the busted bayonet inside the carcass. You can have that if you like."

Officer Bob nodded. "I'd like to see the remains. Could I see the bayonet handle, and do you have the rifle that got smashed up?"

"Yes, would you mind dropping it off at the gun shop in Grangeville when you go through? The handle for the bayonet is still on the rifle."

"I can drop the rifle off with Elroy. Let's go see the remains, then we'll leave you alone."

They walked down through the valley to find the bear's innards laying out by the salt lick. The critters had picked them clean. The rib cage was still intact and, sure enough, the broken knife was sticking out.

"I don't think you could pull the bayonet out of there without getting some pliers," Gunner said. Bell and Gunner retrieved a pair of pliers out of the tool shed then came back down.

Ned and Officer Bob surveyed the rib cage, shaking their heads. "What do you think that bear weighed, Gunner?"

"Well, sir, I'd guess it was around eight-hundred or more, and then dressed weight would have been around four hundred, maybe four-fifty. He did dress out easy. I left the rib cage with the carcass because I didn't want to fight the bayonet out of it. When skinned out, he just looked skinny, but the meat was good. I think he was older. Like I said earlier, his eyesight was terrible, and he seemed to be having a tough time getting food. So, that led me to believe he was going to defend the meat in the mine. You know that put me on the other side of the fence where I was going to defend my mine and critters. And just in case bruin decided to come down to have dinner on us during the night, we short-stopped him."

Ned took the pliers and pulled on the bayonet, with no luck. Officer Bob kneeled down and held the carcass as Ned gave a big yank on the blade. It finally came out with the tug and weight of those two behind it.

"That should do us for now, Gunner," said Officer Bob. "Thanks for your time and hospitality. We better get going if we're to get back by dark."

Ned added, "Hopefully, that shortcut of yours will cut those two hours off for us."

"I'll help you get your critters rounded up. I'm sure Jack enjoyed the company while he had it."

The group went up to the pasture, got the horses, and Gunner took a minute to say hello to old Butch. *He's such a cranky old horse.* Gunner didn't know if Butch remembered him very well, but he remembered the old plug, and he had been a lot of help getting the claim started. And, of course, Jack had to come over and get his muzzle in the middle as Gunner talked to old Butch.

The horses saddled quickly as Ned had packed for his dad for years. He knew what was needed and how to do it and soon, Ned was up on the big bay horse. Officer Bob was a little slower but not far behind.

"Just a minute, Officer Bob, I got to go get that darned Springfield. Could you tell Elroy that if it's not worth fixing, don't worry about it? I want to buy another one from him just like it when I come in. The bayonet was a little too long and I've gone to a shorter one now."

Officer Bob replied, "I'd be happy to drop it off for you. Next time you come to town, hopefully, I'll see you. You know there's a lot of talk about somebody killing a bear out here by themselves."

"I don't get out much, and I don't want to, so I'm not much concerned with people's talk. If they got a problem with me killing the bear, they're welcome to come up here and take care of it for Bell and me. I've had my fill of them."

"That wasn't quite what I was getting at, Gunner. You're becoming somewhat of a folk hero around the county with you living up here and working the mine and all. I can see you want to be left alone."

"Sir, let them have their fun. I just want to make it through the winter, care for my crew, and keep us alive. I'll be coming into town in a couple of weeks to pick up some equipment I bought from Oley Benson, Talking Bird's father."

Gunner turned to Ned. "Ned, you take care, say hello to your dad, and give my love to Granny when you get home."

Officer Bob thought of something else. "Gunner, one last question, where did the paws go? I noticed they were missing from the remains."

"I took two of them to Cleo so he could identify if the bear was a grizzly or not. I think maybe he gave them to Quiet Bird. She asked him if she could have them. I have the two hind paws if you would like to have them?"

"That would be appreciated, then we can piece some of the stories together. I know Elroy would be interested. He was asking me a lot of questions and, of course, the wildlife people will be asking me if I have something to show them. Thank you."

With that, Gunner nodded, walked over to the tool shed, and took down the hind paws hanging in the rafters, handing them to Bob. "Let me go get a piece of rope. We can tie those claws to the backend of old Butch here. He won't mind a bear claw rubbing on his butt," Gunner laughed. "That will help keep him moving for you."

The riders were ready to head out. Gunner hoped they could stay on the path to the shortcut. He explained it carefully and even drew a map on the back of a brown paper sack. The men turned away slowly and started their mounts down the trail. He waved goodbye as they rode down out of sight below the tree line.

It was mid-afternoon already. "Come on, Bell, let's get some lunch, then we'll get back up to the mine and back to our digging."

That night was the first snow of the season. Jack was tucked away in his mule hotel and Gunner hoped Ned and Officer Bob made it to the ranch before the snow started to fly.

CHAPTER 38

It had been a couple of weeks since Officer Bob and Ned had come visiting. Gunner woke up this morning out of a sound sleep and sat straight up. *Oh no, it's almost the end of October.* He had lost days somewhere and was frustrated about what day it was. He got up to look at his calendar, and for the life of him, couldn't figure out exactly what day it was. Thinking it over carefully, then having a visit with Bell, he decided it would be best to get their gear gathered and go into town. He thought they had enough in their poke to pay for the air compressor and drill.

"Bell, you and I will go up and shut the mine down. We'll be back in a few days. We need that drill now." Bell, being Bell, knew something was going on, and was happy to do it whatever it was. She camped out by the door so she wouldn't be left behind.

Outside, the snow crunched under his feet, the six inches frozen hard as a rock. There hadn't been much snow since Officer Bob and Ned left. The sky was gray, and silence surrounded him. As he tromped up to the mine, he thought about how to prepare the mine and equipment. He had to pump all the water back up to the upper pond so it wouldn't freeze in the lower basin, then service the gas engine and drain all the water out of it. The hot spring at the upper pond would keep the water warm and, hopefully, keep it from freezing while they were gone.

Gunner boarded up the mine with the gondola inside, then covered up the stamp mill and sluice equipment with an old tarp. Good thing he cleaned the sluice out yesterday. Maybe he was thinking it was time to go.

Gunner and Bell went back to the cabin and went through the same process, ensuring everything was put away neat and tidy for their return. He studied his shopping list: food, dynamite, tools, writing paper, critter food, gas, kerosene, books, and . . . *This darn list keeps growing.* He wanted to bring home the compressor and drill with the ten-foot star bits. *Don't forget oil and gas.*

His schoolwork was packed, and the books he had read needed to be traded in for more at the library. Gunner realized he did miss school, even though learning the mine and all that was interesting. He wanted to finish junior high school. As the days had gone by, the good side of school made more sense to him. That was why he worked every night on the lessons Talking Bird had given him. He wanted to be ready for the test.

Outside of the mule hotel, Gunner pulled Jack's pack and gear out. Oley said he had a single hitch for the wagon to pull back into the claim with the compressor and drill. That would be a new experience for Jack. The mule had matured and grown over the summer and was standing by the gate, talking to Gunner in his low rumbly voice.

"Bell, you must have told Jack we were heading to town. Look, he's waiting for us. Jack, we got to get you loaded up, and the first stop will be Cleo's. I want to check on him and see if he can give us a ride to Grangeville to sell some gold and pick up more gear tomorrow.

"Dang, I almost forgot, first we have to go back up to the mine. Bell, you and I have that whitetail deer we shot two days ago hanging in the mine. We'll take all four quarters with us. Then, we will drop some off with Cleo, Talking Bird, Talking Bird's parents, Norman and Granny, and whoever else Cleo would like to give some to."

Cleo likes fresh venison. He might want to keep an extra quarter for himself. "And once we get to Cleo's, we can figure out what our schedule will be."

The whitetail had been small, and it didn't take long to load the deer quarters in Jack's packs. Gunner knew it had been at least a month since they had made the trip from Cleo's.

As they arrived at their regular rest stop, it was like they had been there just yesterday. Only now the snow was there. None of it had melted off since it snowed two weeks before. The squirrels were scrambling, digging out pinecones, and getting more food put away for what Gunner suspected would be a very cold winter.

Picking up Jack's lead, Gunner called over to Bell, "Let's go, girl. The next stop is Cleo's cabin."

Gunner didn't see any activity at Cleo's, although smoke was coming out of the chimney as they walked up to the front porch. Gunner called out, "Cleo!" He tied off Jack, went up on the porch, and stomped a couple of times to shake the packed snow off his boots. *That should wake Cleo up if he's taking a nap.*

Gunner still didn't hear any movement, so he knocked loudly on the front door. He waited. It took a while, but finally, he could hear Cleo coming to the door.

As the door opened, Gunner greeted his old friend, "How are you, old-timer? Have you been napping?"

Cleo was bent over more than Gunner remembered, but his weathered face and kind eyes still showed a friendly smile. "Gunner, how have you been! I see you still have that spry young mule and the very pretty dog with you."

"It's nice to see you again." Gunner was genuinely glad to see Cleo was ok.

"I'm doing good, and things are just moving a bit slow for me with arthritis and the cold coming on the way it does."

"Well, sir, I come to check on you, and I think I've got enough dust saved up to buy that compressor and drill from Oley. I could sure use it up at the mine. You are right about how far the bedrock was. It came in at 43 ½ feet from the mouth of the tunnel." Gunner realized he was rambling on and wasn't even in the front door yet.

"Would you mind if I put Jack up in your shed? Then Bell and I can come in and visit with you for a while."

"You're sure welcome. Just come on in. You'll need to get warmed up with some food in you." Cleo paused to look over to Jack. "What's sticking out of Jack's packs? Is that deer hooves?"

"Yep, I got all four quarters. I'd like to give some to Talking Bird and Oley and Lisa when I go to buy the equipment. The rest is yours, whatever you want to do with it. Maybe we could drop a quarter off to Norman and Granny if you wouldn't mind?"

"We can drop off whatever you think. It will be nice to have some fresh venison around the old cabin. Go take care of your mule and get back on in here."

"Will do. Got lots to tell ya, partner."

Gunner hung the quarters in the shed like last time. It was early afternoon, and he knew Jack would be happy in his stall munching on hay and having a scoop of grain. Gunner left him in the open horse stall so he could wander into the corral if he liked.

Walking by the woodpile, Gunner saw it was time to split up more wood and load up Cleo's wood box. He told Bell, "I think that's what we'll do before it gets dark." *Nowadays, it seems like it gets dark earlier than ever.*

Gunner picked up an armload of stove wood on the way in the back door to the kitchen. Dropping the wood into the wood box, he automatically opened the lid to the stove and filled it up.

Cleo was by the sink putting meat in a pan to fry. The eggs were already out on the countertop to round out lunch.

Cleo's cabin smelled so good, Gunner realized he had been gone too long. He sat down in one of the chairs at the table. "Tell me, old-timer, how has your health been? I know, I know, I'm not supposed to call you old-timer. I do say it with all due respect and reverence."

They both chuckled. Gunner knew the next thing he was going to do is call him a young feller. That was their private joke, and they both liked it.

Cleo said, "I've been doing okay, but I think I'd like to go to a place where someone else has to pack all the wood in, and maybe they could do all the cooking too. I want to be someplace where I can visit with other folks my age, then play cards with Slim like we used to."

"Cleo, tell me the truth. Do you think maybe you want to go visit with those pretty blue-haired gals too?"

"Now that you mention it, it would be nice to play some cards with the ladies too. I know you'd much rather be down there visiting with Quiet Bird than being in this kitchen visiting with me."

"You have a point there. We need to take care of business first. If I can talk you into running me into town, I'll buy you lunch and gas as usual. I need to pick up enough supplies to put in the wagon when I bring home the drill and compressor from Oley's. That's the main reason I needed to come out. I'm into the hard rock, and that old sledgehammer just isn't quite getting it when I know the drill is in Oley's shed.

"Also, I need to stop and see Talking Bird to take a test for my schooling and get a new assignment from her. Of course, then I'll have to sit and visit with Miss Quiet Bird. I think I'm doing okay with all this now. It was confusing last time when I left."

Cleo had filled up their plates and sat down, quietly waiting for Gunner to let his mainspring run down.

"Killing the old bruin and the scare he threw to me, I had a chance to do a little more growing."

Cleo continued listening, nodding his head, not interrupting.

"I will enjoy my time out and then get back up to the claim. I've been able to get a lot done up there. The mucking out of all that rock and soft overburden from the glacial days is all done. Now, I have the gondola set up, and I'm working with it. Once I start drilling, and I think you're right again, I'll find the vein, because there is too much good sign."

Cleo perked up with Gunner's excitement. "I've always held that in the back of my mind. Never let go of it. You keep digging, boy, and you'll find it just waiting there for you."

Between bites of fried venison and easy-over eggs, Gunner laid out his plan. "Right now, if you don't mind, I'd like to go out and work on your woodpile for a while. Then, I'll cook up some dinner. I would like to sleep in your shed tonight with Jack and Bell. Can we go into Elk City first thing in the morning, drop off the whitetail, then go on up to Grangeville?"

"Yes, and working on my woodpile would be appreciated."

Gunner cleared the table and headed out the back door, Bell right on his heels. She laid down to watch him split wood, and Jack was just a stone's throw away standing in the corral, watching the two of them. The rest of the day was spent putting up the split wood for Cleo.

Jack got fed and brushed, then Gunner fixed dinner for the two of them. After he got the kitchen cleaned up, he threw a blanket over Cleo as he headed out to the shed for the night. Gunner crawled in his bedroll, next to Jack's stall, with Bell snuggled up next to him, and daydreamed about seeing Quiet Bird again.

He wondered if she would look the same after being gone a month. Pulling her picture out of his backpack, he looked at her and said, "Goodnight, pretty girl. I'll see you tomorrow, I promise."

Gunner woke up early, with Quiet Bird still on his mind. He was sure looking forward to seeing her. Taking care of Jack, he decided to load the meat in the jeep.

By the time Gunner got three quarters loaded, the lights were on in the kitchen. Cleo was up and moving around, trying to dig up some breakfast.

Gunner picked up an armload of firewood, went through the back door, and filled up the wood box. It was already full, though it didn't hurt to have a little extra. He sat down at the table and asked, "Are you ready to go for the day?"

"Yes, but we need to figure out for sure what we're going to do, so let's talk about our plan, and then we can just do it when we take off."

Gunner knew Cleo was a good planner.

"Now, what do you want to do with Jack? How do you want to work this out, picking up the drill and compressor?"

"I can take Bell and Jack to Norman and Granny's and put Jack up in their barn until we get done with town. Then, fetch him and ride into town. Would there be time before it gets dark?"

Cleo scratched his head. "Don't think you'll have time to get into Grangeville then back to take Jack into Elk City. Don't forget you have a test to take and need some time to visit with Miss Quiet Bird."

Cleo and Gunner discussed the best way to accomplish everything Gunner wanted to get done. Cleo suggested he stay another day so he could spend more time with Quiet Bird.

Gunner wanted to test Jack with the wagon as this would be his first time pulling a wagon.

"Sometimes, you think that mule is more human than mule," Cleo chided. "You expect the mule to know things automatically like people." Gunner grinned and nodded in agreement.

With all their planning, it looked like three days before Gunner could head back to the mine.

Gunner furrowed his brow. "It still might take a couple of trips. I don't want to overload Jack. He is awful young yet. Sometimes, Cleo, I think a team would be better, but I can't afford it at this time. Let's get rolling. I want to get things done, and today is Saturday, isn't it?"

"Yes, it's Saturday. Quiet Bird will be home," Cleo answered, smiling. He could hear the excitement in Gunner's voice.

"That's good. I've got the meat all loaded, so we're ready to go."

"Whoa there, slow down now. We have to feed the old man before we go to town. We old folks just aren't built like you youngsters."

It looked like breakfast was in order, so Gunner took over. He washed the dishes so they could get it done "quickly."

Gunner took care of Jack, as they had agreed to leave him at Cleo's. He could wander in the corral or stand in the shed if the weather took a turn for the worse.

There was still three inches of snow on the ground as Cleo warmed up the jeep. Gunner and Bell loaded into the jeep, and Cleo started driving. Gunner was thinking about seeing Quiet Bird and Cleo was holding the steering wheel as the old jeep wagon rumbled down the road.

Cleo said, "Let's stop at Norman's and Granny's to drop off this quarter first."

"Sounds good. I'd like to say hello and ask if I could sleep in their barn tonight with Jack."

"That would let me get a little closer to Elk City with an early start. I can make it back here by evening tomorrow night."

Granny and Norman were up and moving around as the jeep rolled in. *Norman doesn't look very healthy.* Gunner asked Norman how he was doing, and he mentioned he didn't feel all that great. Gunner thought the quarter of whitetail cheered him up.

Granny said, "That was quite a story that you told Ned and Officer Bob. Those bear stories get pretty scary, especially if you're living them. I'm glad you're okay, Gunner. And we thank you for the bear meat. We' re still eating on it, and this whitetail will come in awfully handy."

"Thank you, Granny, I'll be back sometime this evening hopefully, although I could be late coming into the barn from Cleo's.

That will let me get an early start tomorrow morning to go into Elk City and pick up the equipment I'm buying from Oley."

Granny said, "You're welcome to sleep in the barn. Come in and have dinner if you're not too late."

Just as daylight was breaking in the crisp early morning, Cleo and Gunner climbed into the jeep and took off.

Gunner thought about the next stop, Talking Bird. *Hopefully, they'll be up, and we can give them a quarter too.*

The old jeep rumbled into the driveway, and all the lights were on in the kitchen. Bell and Gunner got out quicker than Cleo and headed straight for the back door. Quiet Bird was standing at the door before Gunner and Bell reached it. She smiled at him through the back-door window and opened the door. "I see you've decided to come back out of the mountains. Besides that, you're getting quite a name for yourself, you know. Do you have time to stay and visit?"

"We don't have a lot of time today. We need to get into Grangeville and pick up supplies. We do have a quarter of whitetail deer for you and Mother Talking Bird. And, we have a quarter for Oley and Lisa."

By now, Talking Bird was standing over Quiet Bird's shoulder at the back door. "Did you say you brought some whitetail for us?"

"Yes, ma'am, we did. And a quarter for your folks. Would you like to come with us while we take it to them?"

"That would be fun," said Talking Bird. "We will need a minute to get ready, and you can take the quarter that you're leaving here to the garage, please."

Going to the jeep, Gunner pulled out the ladies' quarter, threw it on his shoulder, and took it to the garage to hang up. Cleo was already inside, having a cup of coffee waiting for the young guy to do all the work.

Gunner went back over to the back door and knocked to see if somebody would let him in. Even Bell had left him outside. *Sometimes, that dog forgets who feeds her.*

Quiet Bird let him in, and in a few minutes, they were ready to go after Talking Bird called her mother and told her they were on their way.

Everyone climbed into the jeep. Bell and Gunner shared the back with the quarter of meat as there was no back seat. The ladies got to ride up front with Cleo. Oley and Lisa were standing at their back door to welcome them.

Before Gunner went in, he asked Oley, "Where would you like me to hang your quarter?"

Oley replied, "Just over there in the shed. You'll see some hooks hanging on the rafters. Thank you for thinking of us."

Gunner went out to the jeep, got the last quarter, and hung it in the shed. This time, Quiet Bird was waiting for him. She watched him walk toward her. Gunner's heart warmed thinking how nice it was to see her again, and he had a feeling she felt the same way.

She asked, "You said you're going into Grangeville to get supplies?"

"Yes, we got a lot of gear to get and not much time to do it. I need to get it back up to Cleo's tonight. What we're hoping is that we can stop and see Talking Bird later tonight so I could take a test on our way back from Grangeville. That would give you and me a chance to visit."

"Good. Would you mind if I go along with you to Grangeville? Then I could spend the day with you and Cleo."

"No, I don't mind. It would be fun having you along. I think it would be up to Talking Bird and Cleo more than me. But if you were wondering what I'm thinking, I'm saying yes."

CHAPTER 39

Quiet Bird and Gunner went into the house. She got permission to go with Cleo and Gunner to Grangeville. Cleo had to finish his cup of coffee before they could leave. Soon, all three were in the front seat of the jeep headed to Grangeville and Bell was in the back. The ride was quiet.

Finally, Cleo started talking to Quiet Bird, "Don't mind him. I think the cat's got his tongue."

Gunner grumbled, "Don't pay no attention to him. He doesn't know what he's talking about."

Quiet Bird started laughing, and then all three of them were laughing. From then on, the jeep was filled with friendly talk and laughter as they enjoyed each other's company.

Quiet Bird filled them in on the talk in town about Gunner killing the bear. It had been many years since a grizzly bear had been taken. Gunner informed her there was no taking going on. It was flat out to kill, or he and Bell would be dead.

Quiet Bird was proud that Gunner, her friend, had killed the bear. He had earned the respect of the community. Gunner decided all the commotion was ok, as long as it kept Quiet Bird's attention on him.

The first stop was Elroy's gun shop in Grangeville, and he was behind his counter, working on a gun again, the parts laid out on a towel on the countertop. He looked up with a big grin as he recognized the visitors.

Elroy waved his arms and announced, "Ladies and gentlemen, it is the Great Bear Killer of Idaho County, accompanied by his closest friends. Now, let me ask you, Gunner, would you be looking for a new rifle today? I happen to have one." He reached behind him and pulled a broken rifle off a special mounting on the wall. "This particular stock is slightly used. By the way, the handle of a bayonet is still locked in at the end of the barrel. Think you might like it?"

"Okay, Elroy. Yes, I'm here to buy a new rifle. I think the one you have is not repairable. I believe it has a bent barrel to boot. I want one just like it, nothing better, nothing worse, exactly like that one. So, what have you got?"

"Yes, I've got one here, all shined up and ready to go for you. I knew you were coming in. Officer Bob dropped off the old one. He also gave me the bayonet and the two rear claws. If you wouldn't mind, I'd like to make a trade with you."

"Sure, what would that be?"

"I'd like to trade you the bear claws, the busted-up rifle, and one snapped off bayonet for a brand-new, just out of the case, 30-aught-six 1903 Springfield Rifle."

"That's quite a deal. What's the catch?"

"No catch. I would like to keep these items and put them someplace where I can show them off. Gunner, it would be good for my store. Think about it. This is one big story when people come in and want to hunt bears. And they might want to talk about the 14-year-old miner who is meaner than a young mountain lion. I will need to take your picture before you folks head back out, of course."

"Do you really think people would care to hear about that story? Would it really help you to sell guns and bullets? By the way, I'm 15 now."

"That is correct, I think it would be great. I don't think you want to use that rifle anymore, do you? That's the first grizzly in this country since the late 1800s, over sixty-two years ago!"

Gunner thought about Elroy's offer. "You got yourself a deal. I need a box of the 45s for my pistol and a box for the Springfield."

"What about a new knife?"

"I bought an M1 from you last time I was in, with the fourteen-inch blade. It was just too long to do anything worthwhile. Now I can use the M1 to skin my game with."

All this time, Bell was leaned up against Quiet Bird's leg instead of Gunner's. Cleo was leaning up against the counter, just smiling.

Gunner thought Cleo was having more fun with this bear killing than he was.

They finished up business at Elroy's after some picture taking. He insisted on taking one of the three of them. Gunner thought Quiet Bird was so beautiful standing between Cleo and him.

At the next stop, Gunner sold his gold, and the group headed straight to the lumber store where Gunner bought more vermiculite for the lower pond. At the hardware store, he picked up two blue kerosene lanterns, batteries for his flashlight, and other odds and ends.

The grocery store was next for food, buying just enough to give Gunner staples for another month. Cleo ran them to the drugstore, where Gunner could buy one of those lined record books for keeping books. It was just like the one his uncle had used on the fish boat.

It was getting close to noon, and Cleo announced he could hear his stomach grumble. Gunner offered to buy Quiet Bird lunch, as he had to feed the old guy. She smiled and nodded yes. *A woman of few words, that works for me.*

They stopped at the Cowboy Cafe on Main Street and had a large lunch of hamburgers, fries, and milkshakes for all. Quiet Bird wasn't saying much, but Gunner thought she was enjoying herself. After that, they picked up dynamite and caps. The last stop was the jobbers for oil, gasoline, and kerosene.

With all the running around done, it was time to head back to Elk City. Gunner wanted to stop at Oley's to look at the equipment and talk to him about loading it up. Gunner asked Quiet Bird if she would like to go back to her mother's or stay with them when they visited Oley.

"I think I'd like to stay with you and Cleo. It is much more fun than going home. I would like to see Grandma Lisa. I visit with them a lot, and they are very nice people."

"Okay, then we're off for the equipment and Oley, but you might want to call your mother and let her know where we are. We'll be heading her way shortly."

The jeep was hardly in the driveway, as Oley came out the door and headed out back for the equipment.

Gunner caught up with Oley, and Cleo followed close behind. Quiet Bird and Bell brought up the rear.

Oley said, "I'm pleased to see somebody buying this equipment. I know you'll take care of it and use it correctly. I've just been waiting for the right person to come along that wanted to buy it. Now, don't go telling my wife that because she would accuse me of that very thing."

Everybody chuckled and knew what he was talking about. Gunner got down on his knees and examined the equipment, asking Cleo and Oley questions, who were both more than helpful. The two old miners told him how the engine would work, how to check the oils, and how to keep things running when they didn't want to run.

Patiently, they showed Gunner the drill and bits, how they hooked up and worked. Most importantly, they taught him how to get a bit out when it got stuck in the rock. They went on for about an hour, and then, it was time to go into the house.

As they headed back to the jeep, Gunner pulled out five hundred dollars, already counted out, and handed the money to Oley. He reassured Oley he would take care of the equipment, just as Oley had. That was because Gunner cared for it just as much.

"Cleo, we need to check the wagon. I need to see if Jack's hitch will fit. Let's go back over and decide how to load the gear while we're at it."

Oley said, "That shouldn't be a problem, I've got all the skids. Once we get it loaded, it will slide right out of there when you have your mule walk away with the wagon. I have a team hitch I'll throw in with the wagon too. It's hanging in the barn next to the old four-wheel wagon. I'm sure you have more use for it than I do."

"Thank you, Oley, that would be appreciated. And hopefully, I'll be here early tomorrow to get everything loaded up. I need to keep the load light because my mule is young, and I don't want to hurt him."

They walked out the driveway to the jeep after checking the wagon and said their goodbyes. It was only up and around the corner, not half-a-mile, to Talking Bird's house. She was glad to see the group as she met them at the back door. She thanked Quiet Bird for calling and was happy her daughter had such a great time.

Gunner sat down on the back porch, took his boots off, went to the sink, and started washing up.

He grinned at Talking Bird, "I don't want to act as I've moved into your place, but I've been here before. Didn't want to come in dirty or wear my boots on your clean floors."

Talking Bird replied, "That's fine, Gunner, you make yourself at home here. We are a pretty friendly bunch. You go over and sit down at the kitchen table. Quiet Bird and I will get your books pulled out so we can go over your lessons, then you can take your monthly test. Did you have a chance to study while you were up at the claim?"

"Yes, ma'am, I did. I tried to study for at least one hour each night. I did start with two. That didn't work out so well, with working in the mine fourteen hours a day, then caring for the critters, then reading my mining books to make sure I knew which direction I was headed. I made it so I had a chance to do my studying, complete my reading assignments, and I'm here ready and willing to take the test."

"Good, let's get started. Here is your test and a pencil. You may use the open book method for the first test. That will help you understand the test process and become comfortable with it."

Gunner quietly started on the test. It was familiar because he had read everything and remembered what he had learned. Gunner thought that was unusual for him. Back at home, when he sat down to take a test, all he could do was stare at the paper, and it might as well have been blank. That brought on the frustration, and it would build in him.

By the time Gunner finished the fifty-question test, he felt good with his answers and handed it to Talking Bird for correcting.

Right away, she sat down at the table across from him and started checking his answers. Gunner waited for her to start making marks with a red pen. Remembering the one-room school, he thought of the red pen as a painful experience.

She's not making any red marks. Maybe she has the wrong answer sheet? I know I must have missed some.

Talking Bird looked up at him and smiled. "Congratulations, Gunner, you made 100 percent. You got all the answers right."

As Talking Bird was writing "100%" across the top of Gunner's first test, she looked over to her daughter. "So, Quiet Bird, what do you think of this young man now?"

Quiet Bird said, "I knew he could do it, especially if he could take time and read the books. I noticed he didn't use the book on an open book test. I'm very proud of you, Gunner."

"Thank you, I wanted to do good on the test. Being able to study every night worked for me, and I'm looking forward to finishing school someday."

Talking Bird gave Gunner his new lessons and traded books for the following lesson. She took a few minutes to show him some of the exciting parts coming up in the new text.

Thanking her, Gunner was quietly proud to have gotten that far with school without hating it. *This might work.*

Looking out the window, he could see the weather was clear and cold. It would be a good time for a walk.

Gunner looked over to Talking Bird and asked, "Would you mind if I take Quiet Bird for a walk, ma'am? Not far, only so we can visit, just her and I. Then I won't have to entertain the old guy, but I will have to leave him with you."

Talking Bird laughed. "Ok, you two go have a nice walk. Gunner, don't you have to get your mule and start bringing him back this way?"

"Yes, ma'am, I do."

Gunner looked up to see Quiet Bird putting on her coat and handing him his as he stood up.

After he slipped his boots on, Quiet Bird took his hand as they headed for the door. Talking Bird and Cleo both watched as she pulled him toward the door. They smiled, giving a nod of approval.

Outside, Gunner was glad she wanted to take his hand even in the house in front of everyone. She was a beautiful person, and he was happy she still wanted to be friends. The walk only lasted thirty minutes, but long enough to talk about what they were going to do tomorrow.

It was dark early with the cloud cover and the cold was settling in for the night. They decided Gunner would stop at Talking Bird's first thing tomorrow morning, pick up Quiet Bird, then go to Oley's to start loading equipment. That would take the better part of the day, but it was okay with Gunner. All he wanted was to spend more time with her. She always gave him a nice warm feeling when he was around her.

Back in the house, Gunner told Cleo, "Got to go, partner."

Quiet Bird walked with him to the passenger door on the jeep. He took Quiet Bird's hand, warm, soft, and such a pleasure to hold. Looking at her, he could see forever in those clear, deep, sparkling brown eyes.

"I guess I'll see you tomorrow?"

"Yes, I'll be here waiting for you. Be sure and come early, so we will have more time to spend together. I'm looking forward to you being here."

About the only thing he could get out of his mouth was a half croaked, "Goodbye."

Cleo had the engine running in the old jeep as Gunner climbed in. There was not much to say on the way home. Gunner wanted to sit and get lost in his thoughts about Quiet Bird. With Cleo, that didn't last long. He had things on his mind and wanted to talk about them. "You know, I was thinking that compressor and the drill with all the bits and the conveyor would be too much for your poor young mule. What we might think about is me loading the compressor with the drill bits in the back of the jeep and the old single axle trailer. We could put the conveyor belts on top of the trailer. Then you can take the rest of the equipment in the wagon with Jack. And didn't you want to stop and pick up some hay from Norman on this trip out?"

"You're right, Cleo, that would be too heavy a load for Jack. I thought I would lead him back up to the mine."

"Good thinking, but I still think that compressor is just too heavy for one mule. Maybe if you had a team, that would be different."

"That's a good idea. Let's do it. I still think Jack and I need to make a head start tonight. I'll have a chance to sit down with Granny and Norman."

Laughing, Cleo agreed, "Okay, then it's settled. I'll take off tomorrow morning about eight and meet you at Oley's with the trailer. Or wherever I see the mule tied up." They both knew what he was laughing about. He guessed Gunner would pick up Quiet Bird, then go down to Oley's and load the equipment.

"The more I think about it, Cleo, I think you should show up around noon. By then, I will have the wagon loaded. Then all we have to do is load the jeep and trailer."

"Sounds good to me. Noon it is, and I'll see you there at Oley's."

They pulled into Cleo's with only an hour and a half of daylight left. Gunner unloaded the jeep as quickly as he could, then put his backpack together with the bedroll and some personal gear. He shoved the new Springfield rifle in the holder on Jack's pack, double-checking that he had Jack's single hitch harness loaded.

Gunner turned to Cleo and shook his hand. "Many thanks, old friend, and someday, I will repay you for all the help you've given me."

"Now you go on there. You've done plenty for me. Besides, it would be boring if I didn't have you around. You take care of getting to Granny's and I'll see you at noon tomorrow."

Gunner pulled Jack up close to swing a leg over the sawbuck pack. Bell was at their side, ready to trot along beside them. Jack was loaded light and seemed to be okay with Gunner on his back. They started at a fast pace toward Granny's, hoping to be there within the hour.

The weather would turn colder when dark came, and Gunner wanted to have Jack inside the barn at Norman's mule hotel. They were making a good pace as Gunner got lost in his thoughts, thinking about the drill and compressor. The new tools would increase his production, and that put him closer to the vein of gold. Like he had told Cleo, the sign was good with all the quartz in the rock.

Granny saw Gunner, Jack, and Bell trot in the gate as she stood on the front porch. She called down to him, "You be sure and get up here. Dinner's ready in thirty minutes. We want to hear all about what you have been doing. So, you hurry up and get up here, young man."

CHAPTER 40

Granny knew Gunner too well. He would rather lay low in the barn with Bell and Jack, and never to come up to the house. She had been waiting and caught him before they could sneak into the barn. Gunner didn't think it was so obvious that he didn't want to be around people.

The only people I want to be around anymore would be Quiet Bird, Talking Bird, and of course, Cleo, my best friend. These are not only my good friends, but also the people I feel most comfortable around. The rest of the time, Gunner was quite happy being with Bell and Jack. Like he had said before, "The conversations were one-sided, but they are good friends and patient listeners."

"Okay, Granny, I'll be right along. I got to take care of Jack. Would you happen to have an extra bit of dog food I could give Bell? I forgot to hold back some when I was unloading Cleo's jeep."

"Yes, we've got plenty. You hurry and get cleaned up. Dinner will be sitting on the table when you get here."

Gunner gave Jack a quick brush down, throwing him a couple handfuls of grain with a flake of hay. He went up to the back of the house, washed up, and grabbed an armload of firewood. Granny had him trained right. Before he went to the kitchen, he always picked up an armload of stove wood.

Bell was ahead of Gunner as they went through the door. Granny had already fixed a bowl of food for her, and she was talking and petting Bell. Bell looked up at Gunner and asked permission to eat. It is something she had done when they had been to other places and wasn't sure if she was supposed to eat the food or not. She would give him a look, and he would nod yes. It took some training, but it was well worth the time.

Norman was sitting at the head of the table. His faded flannel shirt had the sleeves rolled up. Gunner could tell he had just washed up, his hair wet and slicked back.

Ned was sitting next to Norman with a big grin on his face. Gunner wasn't sure why that was, other than Ned might have told Norman and Granny the whole story of him and Officer Bob up at the mine. Granny came over next to Gunner, put her hand under his left arm, and said, "You sit here next to Norman."

With that order, he sat down. Gunner forgot he still had his shooter and knife on him. He got back up, walked into the living room, took the halter and weapons off, and laid them on the couch. He returned to the table and quietly sat down.

Granny said, "Thank you for doing that. I don't think we'll need any guns at the dinner table tonight." Everyone gave a big laugh, and that started the evening meal off on a good note.

Gunner was figuring he would get grilled over the bear killing and anything else they wanted to drill him about. That was the way it worked around there before. *How does it work now?* he thought, naturally on guard.

Norman said, "Ned here told us all about Officer Bob's visit with your bear killing. Did it happen that way?"

Gunner set his fork down, took an exaggerated deep breath, and explained, "Norman, you don't have to believe a thing if you don't want to. You don't have to question everything everybody says. Ned there told you straight up how it came down. I trust him for that. And you'd be welcome to go to the Elroy's gun shop in Grangeville. You can see the rifle with the bayonet handle at the end and two bear claws. That might help you make up your mind on whether it happened that way or not."

Gunner finished dishing up his plate. He hoped the evening was going to be a short one. He needed to eat and clear out.

Norman said, "Now, hang on, Gunner, I didn't say you didn't do it that way. I was only asking if the killing of the bear happened that way. Did you stab him with that bayonet as he said, with it on the rifle? I think that would be one hell of an experience."

Gunner tried not to answer curtly. "Yes, it happened exactly the way I explained. I think if you talked to Cleo when he brought you that quarter of the bear, he said exactly the same thing. Guess the only thing I can tell you is it was the bear or Bell and me. Be darned if I'm going to give up my mine, dog, or life to some mangy old bear that couldn't see straight." Gunner needed to change the subject. This wasn't going anywhere.

Granny was sitting on the edge of her chair and Gunner could see she wasn't happy. He asked Granny, "Did you get your quarter of bear, okay?"

Granny nodded yes.

"Have you tried any of the whitetail? It's a little fresh yet. I got it three or four days ago and hung it in the mine."

Granny replied, "Yes, we did, and thank you. That extra meat comes in real handy now. Ned is going to get us a couple of elk to put up for the winter. Is there anything you need up at the claim that we can help you with?"

"Well, yes, there is. When I bought Jack, Norman said it would be okay to buy hay from you now and then. I want to put in a wagon load of hay, so six or eight bales if I could buy that much from you. That would feed Jack up to the first of the year."

Norman jumped in the conversation. "Not a problem, you would be more than welcome. Do you need more than eight bales?"

"I have a little shed up at the claim that Jack can live in when the heavy snow comes. Your hay would hold us over. If it would put you out any, I don't want to bother you. Maybe I could buy some from Wayne across the way. He seems to have had quite a hay season last summer."

Granny quickly answered, "Like Norman said, no problem. You take what you need. What will you haul the bales with?"

"I'm buying a wagon, actually a team wagon, from Oley Benson in Elk City as well as a compressor and drill tomorrow. The wagon is fairly light. I figured Jack could pull it. Like you told me, Norman, he is young and needs time to grow like me. Maybe I can find another mule someday. Then he will have a teammate I can put with him on the wagon."

"I'm not worried about you hurting him," Norman said. "I figure he's probably got better care than some people around here."

Gunner noted the compliment Norman had just given him. Those were few and far between.

"You know, Gunner does have it pretty good up there," Ned interjected. "That little cabin he lives in is a real Taj Mahal." Ned gave a loud laugh. "The field runs down by the creek and plenty of mountain grass there for his mule. That's a nice place up there, Gunner. I'm kind of envious of you living there on your own."

"Thank you, Ned, it was nice to see you and Officer Bob the other day. You will have to come back up and spend the night some time. Not much room, though. As big as you are, I'll need to give you the lower bunk."

"Thank you, I'll take you up on that invite next spring sometime. I bet you have good hunting up your way if things get slow down here. You think it would be okay if I came up and do some hunting out in your backyard?"

"Not a problem. I don't much like having anybody else around though. Farther up the valley, I have a salt lick. Cleo coached me to set it up in the right place. That's been giving me plenty of food on the table. I don't want to waste any. I try to use everything I take. Maybe next spring, I'll build a smoker then make some jerky or hams. Just got to outsmart the wild boar."

Ned said, "Most mornings, there's a herd down by Moose Creek in front of the barn. We should get a couple of elk there, then drag them up to the barn with the tractor. If we get short down here, I'll come your way."

"You're always welcome in our camp."

"Granny, have you heard anything from Mom lately?"

"I got a letter from her the other day. Sounds like your father left for Alaska about three weeks ago. The other kids are doing good in school. She asked how you were doing. I wrote back and said we didn't get to see you much, but we did hear a lot about you on occasion."

Granny gave Gunner a big smile. *Okay, I know what that smile's about, so let's get it over. I knew this was going to happen.*

Granny asked, "We heard you had a little run-in in Elk City. There was even a young girl involved that you were standing up for. Then, of course, the bear killing. That put you up to the head of the conversation list around Idaho County. Not that your age, or working your claim up in the wilderness by yourself, doesn't put you there already."

"Thank you, Granny. I think Officer Bob said it best. He could see I just wanted to be left alone up at the mine. I don't want to bother anybody, and I don't want anybody to bother me. If I have another run-in with those bullies, that'll be their problem. I don't like bullies, and I don't like what they get away with. Guess maybe that comes from being raised by the old man. He is the biggest bully of them all."

They finished dinner and Granny dished up fresh baked pie for everybody. The conversation fell quiet for once.

It is nice being in a warm kitchen with good smells and family. I don't get this when it's just me doing the cooking. That's because I have to cook to survive.

It was time for him to go to the barn. Tomorrow would be a very long day. "I want to thank you for dinner. It was nice to sit down for a home-cooked meal and have a visit with you all. Bell would like to thank you for dinner, too, also Jack. Let me pay you for those bales of hay, and I'll be heading out to the barn. Hopefully, I'll be back tomorrow night, if not the next morning. We decided Cleo would haul the compressor and conveyor belts back up to his cabin. That would lighten the load for Jack, where we will only have the drill and extra gear, then I can pick up the bales."

Gunner paused. "That still might be too much. I might have to come back later for the bales, but we will work that out with you."

"Thank you for coming," Granny said. "We've enjoyed having you for dinner. When I write to your mother next, I'll tell her you were here. By the way, how's your schooling going? I know she will ask."

"Granny, you can tell Mother that I completed my first lesson, and I got 100 on it. I try to study for at least one hour every night. I was running short on kerosene for my cabin lamp, so that slowed me up a bit, but I still got it done. You might mention to her, for a good laugh, that my life is getting more complicated by the minute, and that wasn't the plan."

Everyone chuckled and Gunner stood, went out to the living room, picked up his .45, slung the harness on, and headed for the door. Bell was right on his heels, not letting him be more than eighteen inches from her. They headed straight to the barn and found Jack already half-asleep.

Things felt more natural out in the barn. He was with his crew, and it was quiet. Gunner preferred things this way, living alone. It wasn't that bad, after all.

Gunner woke up before daylight, wanting an early start to allow spending the extra time with Quiet Bird. He and Bell chewed on some jerky for breakfast. Outside, he felt the finger-numbing cold and crystal sharp air. No snow, no clouds, nothing but crisp, clean, icy-cold sky, not even a moon.

Leading Jack for a while rather than riding him, Gunner found it easier to see the road, walking, as dark as it was. He hoped it would start breaking light before they got on the main road. Trucks and cars are always coming along. Since today was Sunday, he hoped the traffic wouldn't be so bad.

Soon enough, they strolled into the front yard of Talking Bird's house.

It was daylight now, and Gunner could see smoke lazily coming out of the chimney. The air was so still, the smoke stayed in a narrow column. Quiet Bird was looking out the kitchen window.

As soon as she saw him, she left the window, coming out the back door as she put her coat on. She came straight over to Jack and put her arm around Gunner. "I'm so glad you could come early."

"My thinking was to be here early, so we could have more time to visit and quietly be together. I like spending time with you, Quiet Bird. I don't think I need to talk all the time either. I just like being around you. You make me feel good."

"Thank you, Gunner, I feel the same way. I did miss you when you were gone last month."

"I missed you too. Now for business, where should I tie up Jack?"

She gave a light laugh and said, "We can pull Jack's pack and tie him up out back in the old woodshed. He'll be fine there. Then we can go into the house and get warmed up. Have you had any breakfast yet?"

Gunner smiled. "No breakfast yet. I just chewed on some jerky, sharing it with Bell."

"I'll make breakfast for you."

What a nice girl. She can cook too and so young. This is crazy. We are too young to have an interest like this. I would like to be friends, and if I'm correct, that's what it is, we are just friends. But, we do like being together, we do like holding hands, and we do like looking into each other's eyes. Now, that's close enough for me. I think we need to have that talk. Maybe pull back on the reins a bit, as they say.

Talking Bird joined them for breakfast. It was fun, and Quiet Bird made enough for the three of them. Even Bell got a second helping. Gunner had to tell them about the dinner conversation at Granny's last night and the plan that Cleo was going to meet Gunner at Oley's, and they would load the compressor in the back of his jeep to lighten the load on Jack.

They all had a good time laughing and talking. Together, Gunner and Quiet Bird washed dishes, then Quiet Bird got her coat to go down to Oley's house.

Talking Bird said she would be along soon as she wanted to visit with her mother. Gunner helped Quiet Bird mount Jack. He wanted to see how she looked on his prize mule. She looked terrific, and he said, "You should have a mule in your garage someday."

The walk to Oley's was short, not much more than a half-mile down around the corner. On the straightaway, Oley and Lisa were in the red house on the left. Oley was already outside watching for them. He had been looking at the equipment, figuring things out.

Gunner and Oley got right to work. Gunner told Oley they had decided Cleo was to haul the compressor, drill bits, and conveyor using the jeep and trailer and he would be along at noon.

They pulled out the wagon and backed Jack into the harness, adjusting it to fit correctly. The drill was light enough for the two of them to pick up and set in the back of the wagon, followed by the timbers.

"Oley, do you think all this gear will be too heavy for a single hitch on Jack? He is a young mule, and it worries me."

Oley replied, "I think it would surprise you how much that mule can pull. You see, a mule is smart. They only work as hard as they can. They won't hurt themselves, whereas a horse will keep pulling and damage themselves."

"I might have him on a lead for a while, but we can try on the harness. Once Cleo arrives, we'll get the jeep loaded, then I can get going."

Oley, Gunner, and Quiet Bird spent time going over the equipment. Oley explained more about the drill and drill bits, what things to look for, and reminded Gunner to lube them regularly. He also explained what to look for when things didn't work. He was very thorough, explaining everything in complete detail for the second time. Gunner needed the education, especially with the compressor, so he took even more time. They went over all of that one last time.

Quiet Bird quietly waited and watched. Gunner suggested that she go into the house and warm-up so she wouldn't be standing out in the cold.

She said, "I'll do that. I want to go in and talk to Grandma anyway. She's so much fun to visit with."

Talking Bird had rolled up in her car and went into the house, with Quiet Bird right behind her. Oley and Gunner loaded the rest of what they could.

By now, it was lunchtime and Quiet Bird came out to tell them lunch was waiting. They needed to come in now or the food would get cold.

Oley seemed like he wanted to stay outside talking about equipment rather than go into the house to sit with the women and have lunch. Gunner didn't question it. Lunch sounded too good to him, and his stomach agreed.

A group of ladies sounded even better, so Gunner headed in. He figured Oley could stand out here and talk to the machines by himself if he liked. They all had a friendly lunch, and halfway through, Cleo showed up. He sat for lunch with the rest of them.

Gunner was thinking it was getting late in the afternoon. They had to get things wrapped up to get him on the road. The boys went back outside and started loading the compressor using skids and timbers. By evening, the old jeep had a sag to it when Cleo took off down the driveway, dragging the trailer loaded with two conveyors behind him. Oley and Gunner laughed, and Oley thought he would make it home in one piece. Besides, Cleo never drove fast anywhere, he commented. If there were a problem, Gunner would find him on the way home and help him out with whatever broke down.

Quiet Bird was back out with Oley as Gunner pushed the last of the timbers into the wagon. Talking Bird had left to go home a while earlier. Shortly, Lisa came out and said that Talking Bird had called and wanted Quiet Bird to come home before it got too dark.

"Thank you, Grandma," Quiet Bird said. She turned to Gunner, "I'd better get going. Are you going to stop and say goodbye when you come through?"

"You can count on it. I shouldn't be much more than a few minutes behind you. Are you sure you don't want me to walk you home? It would be no trouble at all and it's starting to get dark."

"I am fine. I do this all the time. I like coming down to see Papa and Grandma."

"Okay then, I'll be right along."

CHAPTER 41

Gunner didn't think it was another fifteen minutes before they had the last of the equipment loaded and Jack hooked up and headed out the driveway. Gunner didn't like Quiet Bird walking alone on the dark road at night. It was something his mother taught him when he was at home. If his sister went to the movies, Mother made sure he always walked her home, just to be safe.

With the lead in Gunner's hand, he walked in front of Jack, with Oley beside them. Both watched Jack, and they decided he was doing fine. Gunner hurried up on the seat and took the reins.

"Oley, thank you ever so much for lunch and for selling me your equipment. I promise I'll take good care of it, just like you did."

Oley had enjoyed talking to the young man. "You take care, Gunner, and don't be killing no more bears. Thanks again for all the meat you have been sending our way. Lisa and I appreciate it."

Jack and Gunner were out on the road with Bell sitting next to him in the wagon seat. Jack was doing fine for his first time in the harness. He was smooth and comfortable at a fast walk. Gunner looked up at the sky, and sure enough, there were clouds up there, and to his surprise, it started to snow. *Come to think of it, it's been snowing all afternoon.* Trying to get all the equipment loaded, Gunner had been too busy to notice.

It looked like an inch of soft powdery snow already on the road. *That's okay. The wagon's heavy enough, and it doesn't look slippery, so we will be good to go.* Gunner was so happy with his new equipment. Now, he had a genuine real live compressor and drill. What a beauty, built in the 1930s, like a huge one-lunger, and it worked.

As Jack pulled the wagon up the hill for Talking Bird's house, a dilapidated pick-up truck roared by them. *Jeez, they darn near sideswiped us!* Gunner remembered the truck from town the day he had the run-in with the bullies. It was the Ferguson boys and Gunner had not forgotten them. They were the bullies that hassled him the day he met Quiet Bird. Cleo warned him against them. "Gunner, you never give any slack when it came to their kind. Hurt them first and make it hard enough they remember you. They will think twice before they come back at you."

Hopefully, Quiet Bird is already home with her mother. Gunner had a sick feeling in his gut. "Get up, Jack! Something's wrong, Bell, get up, mule!" Jack strained into the harness and pulled as hard as he could the last hundred feet of the hill. As they rounded the corner, Bell stood and started barking, and Jack kept pulling. Gunner saw the Ferguson brothers, and they had Quiet Bird.

The truck lights were shining on a terrible sight. Quiet Bird was spread-eagle in the middle of the snowy road. Two of the Ferguson boys were each holding a leg. Another one had Quiet Bird's hand held above her head and her dress was thrown up over her head. The fourth one, the fat one Gunner got the drop on, was standing above her, unbuckling and dropping his pants.

They couldn't hear Gunner coming or even Bell barking, with the noisy truck idling to keep the headlights on. Jack knew what to do. He trotted up beside them and stopped as fast as he could. Gunner locked the brakes on the wagon. He flew out of the seat with his .45 already out of the holster, knowing what had to be done.

He landed flat-footed, standing over Quiet Bird lying on the road, his feet firmly planted on the ground. Gunner shoved up against the slob that had his pants down around his knees and shoved him up against Jack. Jack didn't move. Gunner's .45 was already coming up for his face with all the might and anger he could muster. He heard the thud of the shooter slamming into the side of the brother's face with the snapping of bone.

Gunner was sure he had busted his nose and cheekbones. The gunsight raked across the right side of his face, tearing the skin, making a wide gash full length. His head snapped to the left away from Gunner and the .45. With smashing his cheekbone into a bunch of pieces, Gunner was hoping that not only had he done damage, but it was a knockout blow.

The bully went down hard on his side, out cold. He landed between Jack's feet, curled up, with his knees pulled up close to his chest, his pants still down around his knees.

Gunner swung to his right wanting to destroy the hand holder above Quiet Bird's head. That one still had most of his right side to Gunner. The fool was in shock, looking around, trying to figure out where Gunner had come from.

Gunner could see these boys must have been drinking all day and that slowed them down considerably. This brother was on his knees and that had him at a sizable disadvantage, as Gunner stood over him, his arm coming back from its first victim with a backhanded swing. Gunner was cocking his gun in one rapid motion. The pistol laid up to the brother's ear as Gunner pulled the trigger.

Gunner didn't much care if he caught the bullet in the ear or through his head. Blood and chunks of his ear flew everywhere with an ear-splitting boom. With a shove from Gunner and his .45, the hand holder spun away from Quiet Bird. He gave an ear-shattering scream, blood covering the side of his face as he reached up to where his ear should be. He fell over to the shoulder of the road and rolled into the ditch. He laid there moaning and calling for his mother.

The other two let go of Quiet Bird's legs, backing up fast on their hands and knees. Gunner spun around, facing straight at them, pointing the pistol and cocking it at the same time. He planned to drill them square. They were crawling fast enough into the darkness that Gunner couldn't see them for a clear shot.

Aiming the .45 a little more to the left, he decided to slow their getaway by putting two bullets into the truck radiator. That made a lot of noise with steam and water going in all directions. *Those shots might bring some help for us.*

Gunner yelled, "If any of you ever touch this girl again, or even come around her, I will hunt every one of you bastards down. Then I will kill you, every last one of you. I promise you that and you damn well best believe that you will be dead!"

Gunner kneeled down on one knee, pulling Quiet Bird's dress back down. He could see her face in the truck lights. She stared straight up toward the sky, not one tear, no noise, no fear, only determination on her face.

Bell came over and laid next to Quiet Bird, growling at Gunner when he reached down to pick her up. "Easy, Bell, it's me. We're going to help Quiet Bird now." Bell went quiet and stayed close to her.

As quietly and carefully as he could, Gunner said, "Come on, Quiet Bird, let's get you home."

As he stood her up, Gunner cradled her in his arms, holding her close, her arms folded up against his chest, helping her feel safe. They stood there for a while. Quiet Bird didn't say anything, not one word.

Gunner wasn't kidding when he said he would kill the Ferguson boys by hunting them down one at a time. The one in the ditch was still moaning and calling for his mama. The fat one was still out cold, lying next to Jack's hooves and Gunner's feet.

A siren could be heard in the distance. Gunner hoped it would be Officer Bob and he could take these two away.

Gunner was still holding Quiet Bird as the sheriff patrol car roared up, slammed on the brakes, and skidded to a stop in the coating of snow on the road. Officer Bob climbed out of the driver's seat, quickly looking over everything in the headlights of his cruiser.

The truck lights were still working, water draining out of the radiator, and the engine was running rough. Officer Bob studied the situation and figured the damage had already been done. He came around the wagon and saw Gunner holding Quiet Bird with Bell at her side. Bell started growling. Gunner told her it was okay. He was here to help.

Officer Bob walked up to Gunner as he held Quiet Bird. "What happened here?"

Gunner said, "Sir, looks like you're a few minutes late for the fireworks, but these bastards here tried to rape Quiet Bird. It took some convincing, but they will be glad to go with you. I would like to file charges for what they did. The other two scumbags crawled over by the truck and ran off into the bushes. That's when I had to shoot the truck so nobody could make a getaway in it.

"They looked young, but I would guess they're part of the Ferguson family. I did notice there seemed to be some heavy drinking going on earlier. They even have a jug over there where Quiet Bird's feet were. The dirtbag in the ditch might be missing a chunk of his ear, and I'm sure that my .45 took care of his eardrum.

"He's been trying to find his mother down there in the ditch. This drunk by our feet has his pants down around his knees, as you can see. He hasn't spoken to me once, and that might be because my .45 smashed up his face. I'm glad they left the headlights on so you could see all of this.

"I informed them that if they ever came around or said anything to this girl, I would hunt them down and kill them one by one. Now, if you don't have anything else, I would like to take Quiet Bird home. When you get done with whatever you want to do with them and would like to talk to us, we'll be at Talking Bird's."

"That would be fine, Gunner, and I'm sorry about this, Quiet Bird. We're fortunate that Gunner came along when he did. I'll catch up with you at the house. Gunner, you be sure that you stay there. Don't be going back up to the mine. I need to talk to you both and it might be late by the time I get back to you."

"Yes, sir, I'll wait until you get there. I'm more than happy to sign a statement. And if you need a hand to hunt down those other two varmints, you can come get me."

"No, I don't think that'll be necessary. You've done enough this evening already."

Gunner guided Quiet Bird to the front of the wagon and got her loaded up in the seat. He scooped up Bell and set her next to Quiet Bird. She put her arm around Bell and held her close.

Gunner walked around the wagon, checking to make sure everything was still secure. As he came back around to the right side, he grabbed the brother with the pants down by the collar of his jacket, jerked him about 6 feet from where he was lying between Jack's hooves, and dropped him on the ground.

Bob looked up from the ditch, trying to give some first aid to the one down there. "Alright, what's going on up there?" he asked.

Gunner said, "I just had to move the garbage from between the wheels. Would you want me to run over him? That wouldn't be a bad idea, sir."

Not waiting for an answer, Gunner climbed into the left seat and picked up the reins. "Get up, Jack," he said quietly. Quiet Bird still hadn't said a word. She just sat there and hugged Bell.

It didn't make much sense to say anything at the moment, but Gunner felt this was his fault. He should never have let the girl walk home alone. Gunner didn't know how he could apologize or make it up to her and Talking Bird for what happened tonight.

Gunner's anger was white-hot, and his guts churned with the thought of what those slime bags would've done if he hadn't come along. And now he didn't know how to protect Quiet Bird when he had to go back up to the mine.

The wagon turned into the driveway of Talking Bird's house. She came running out into the driveway, putting her coat on as Gunner stopped Jack. Talking Bird could see something was wrong with her daughter. "What on God's earth has happened? Gunner, I could hear shooting and sirens. Was that you doing the shooting? Quiet Bird, are you alright? Come into the house, let me help you down." Talking Bird reached up to help Quiet Bird down. That alerted Bell and she growled at Talking Bird. She was not going to let anyone touch Quiet Bird, not even her mother.

Gunner got down off the wagon and walked around to stand beside Talking Bird. He reached up to Bell, "Bell, Quiet Bird needs help. Now let her mother and I help her down. You can come to the house and stay next to her."

Bell jumped down from the wagon, stood there, and waited. She watched Talking Bird and Gunner help Quiet Bird down off the wagon. They both took an arm and walked her into the house. In the living room, they set her down on the couch.

She hadn't said a word, just stared straight ahead. Talking Bird sat down next to her and asked softly, "Are you okay? Did somebody hurt you?"

Quiet Bird said, "No one hurt me. Gunner was there in time to save me. I don't know what would've happened if he hadn't come along when he did." She looked up at Gunner standing in front of her and said, "Thank you, Gunner. I knew you would be there. I just didn't know when. When I heard Jack's hooves, I knew it was you. It could only be you. Thank you."

Gunner dropped down to one knee and took her hands in his. He looked into her face, emotions and adrenaline surging through him. All he could see were white flashes of light in his mind. Gunner paused to calm himself. "Quiet Bird, I let you go home alone, and you were in danger. I can't apologize to you enough. It is all my fault.

"I promise you, if you'll forgive me and give me a chance, I will never let anything like this happen to you while I am around." Quiet Bird looked at him, not saying anything. Gunner thought she needed quiet time. Maybe he could catch the other two that ran off. He knew that was crazy talk, and being mad would lead to stupid decisions.

Gunner looked at Talking Bird. "If it would be okay with you, I'd like to go take care of Jack and tie him up in your shed. Then, I'll sit out front in case anybody comes around that might want to get back at us. Those low-lifes might come looking for me, and I'll be ready for them."

Talking Bird replied, "Yes, take care of your mule and then come into the house. We all need to slow down."

Jack was waiting quietly when Gunner went outside. Bell decided she wanted to stay in the house leaned up to Quiet Bird. Gunner un-hitched Jack, put him in the shed, and gave him a small bag of grain. *Jack, it is very hard. My good friend was in a terrible situation, and I was almost too late to help her.*

Gunner didn't know how to make it safe for her or others. Maybe he should hunt down the garbage that did this. He pulled his backpack and the Springfield out of the wagon, hefted them over his shoulders, and went through the back door of the house. He took off his hat and coat, hanging them up, then took his boots off and walked into the living room.

"Talking Bird, Officer Bob asked that I stay with you until he can get here and talk to the both of us. Would you be okay with that? I would be happy to go back outside if you prefer."

Quiet Bird tipped her head up to look at Gunner. "Would you please stay? Come sit next to me if Bell will let you." He thought he detected a slight smile on her lips. He sat down on the couch next to Quiet Bird. Bell moved out of the way, then moved back in, wedging herself between their legs, making sure that they knew she was supposed to be there.

Gunner reached over and cupped both Quiet Bird's hands with his hands. She didn't pull back. He thought that was the best thing he could do at the time. He didn't know if she wanted a man's touch around her.

They sat there for what seemed a long time when headlights came into the driveway. They could tell it was Officer Bob's cruiser.

Talking Bird let Officer Bob in, and they spoke by the door. Sitting in the living room, Gunner and Quiet Bird could hear talking. Gunner could hear Officer Bob explaining to Talking Bird the details that he knew. Officer Bob came into the living room and sat across from Quiet Bird. "How are you doing? Are you going to be okay?"

"Yes, sir. I think I will be. It's going to take some time, and they scared me. Do you have any questions for me?"

"I do. This shouldn't take long, and if we miss something, I'm more than happy to come back. The thing I worry about most is if you're going to be alright. I know being here with your mother, you're in excellent hands. If at any time you need anything, be sure and call Estelle or me. We will be here for you and your mother."

Bob started asking questions, but Quiet Bird wasn't talking much. She would nudge Gunner to answer when Bob would ask her a question. Gunner wasn't shy. He was still mad and told Bob. "This is crap. A bunch of drunks running around the countryside trying to rape girls is not working for me."

Talking Bird could see Gunner's anger wasn't helping Quiet Bird. She came over to him, asking him gently if he would go into the kitchen with her.

Talking Bird asked Gunner to sit down at the kitchen table. She looked at him sternly. "Gunner, you're not helping. I know you are very angry about this, and it is not going away. It might be better if you had some time to cool off."

"Okay, I got it." Gunner abruptly stood up and walked back into the front room, stopping in front of Bob and Quiet Bird.

"It appears I'm not helping very much with all the anger I have stoked up in me." He took a breath. "Talking Bird thinks it would be best that I go cool off someplace." Gunner took another short but deep breath. "Bell and I will get Jack and leave.

"Quiet Bird, I'll come and check with you before I go back up to the mine to make sure you're okay. Come on, Bell, we need to go, but we will be back." Gunner sat on the porch chair to put his boots on.

Bell came up in front of him with a questioning look as if to say, "Dad, are you sure we need to go? I don't think we do. She needs us now."

Standing up, Gunner slung the rifle over his shoulder, picked up his backpack, and waved his hand to Bell. He went out the door to hitch up Jack, with Bell at his side.

In the shed, Gunner worked on hitching Jack up, his anger and confusion showing in his shaking hands. He said, "Bell, we were told to leave, so I guess we had better go."

CHAPTER 42

Gunner said, "Damn, I'm sorry, Jack! I plumb forgot you had that feed bag hanging on you." He took off the feed bag and carefully eased Jack into his hitch. The heavy snow-filled clouds made the night especially dark. Gunner thought it was a good thing Talking Bird had a circular driveway so he could drive Jack all the way around to the front road.

"Bell, we're heading back up to Cleo's. I'm sure I can talk him into making one more trip to town tomorrow so we can check on Quiet Bird."

The crew, wagon, and gear traveled down the road about a mile. A car came up behind them, and Gunner had to ease Jack over to the shoulder as much as he dared to let the car drive by the wagon.

As it went by, Gunner could tell it was Officer Bob. The car drove slowly up to the corner, turned around, and returned as Gunner pulled Jack to a stop.

"Good evening, Sir," Gunner started. "Is there something I forgot tonight? Or could I've done more damage to those boys and gotten away with it?" Gunner paused. "I think I'll rest my smart mouth and shut up now."

Smiling, Bob said, "It's okay Gunner, I understand the hurt you feel. Yes, I know you'd kill them if you had another chance. There won't be a second chance for them, will there?"

"No sir, that about covers it."

"You need someplace to go tonight?" Officer Bob asked. "This road is no place to be when it's so dark. And it's starting to snow again. I want you to follow me to my house. The brothers were shipped off to the hospital and will be locked up after they get patched up. You can sleep on the floor in front of my fireplace. And there's a warm, dry place for Jack to sleep tonight."

Gunner was struck with Officer Bob's generosity. "Thank you, sir. That will give me a chance to check on Quiet Bird first thing tomorrow morning. Then I can drive the wagon to Cleo's during the daylight and you won't find some logging truck stacked on top of my poor wagon here."

Bob lived close to the backside of Oley's place, not far away. As Gunner followed him to the driveway, Bob got out and waved Gunner over to the shed. It was more like a small barn than a shed.

The shed had two ponies Bob kept for his daughters. "Oh, Jack, your luck is improving. You get to share your roof with a couple of ponies tonight. You'll enjoy the company."

Once Jack was taken care of, Gunner headed to the house where Bob was waiting. Gunner asked, "Do you mind if I wash up a bit here in your porch basin?"

"Go right ahead, and we're all in the kitchen. Come in and have hot chocolate with us."

Gunner washed up with Bell next to him. He thought her loyalty was always with him, but he was glad she was loyal to Quiet Bird as well.

Officer Bob, his wife Estelle, and their two daughters, Rebecca and Linda, were sitting at the kitchen table. Rebecca looked like she was older than Gunner, and Linda looked close to his age. They both had the same light blond hair, fair skin, and good looks as their mother.

Bob looked at Gunner as he came through the kitchen door, nodding to the empty chair to join them at the table. Gunner was guessing that meant to go over and sit in the chair. He didn't look forward to getting the fifth degree as it had been a long day already.

The family was very welcoming, and yes, they had a lot of questions.

Rebecca asked first, "Gunner, is it?" He nodded yes. "Did you come from the West Coast? What was it like living out there with all that water?"

"I was raised on an island until the folks moved into town. That was a shock for me where I preferred living on the island. You could compare that to the wilderness here. Guess that's why I'm so happy to live up there alone."

Linda asked next, "Did you kill that bear? How big was he, like how many pounds? I heard you had a dog that helped you kill the bear. Is that the dog? What's her name?"

Estelle spoke up, looking at her daughter, "Linda, sometimes you just ask the darndest questions. Gunner is a guest in our house, and you will treat him as a guest. That means no questions that he might not want to answer. What I'm trying to say is no direct questioning. It is very uncomfortable for people."

Estelle looked at Gunner and smiled. "I'm sorry. Gunner, sometimes you try to teach them good manners, and it just doesn't stick."

"It's okay, Mrs. Summers, I'm fine, and you can ask me almost anything. If I don't want to tell you, I won't. There's nothing that Linda asked I wouldn't answer."

Estelle smiled, "Please, call me Estelle."

"Yes, ma'am. And Linda, yes, I killed the bear, and I'd say its walking weight was about 800 pounds. When your dad came out and saw me, he saw the carcass. I think he would say the same thing. My dog and partner here is Bell. She's a rottweiler-lab cross I got out of the pound in Grangeville. I've had her since she was a puppy. We've had some exciting experiences and I wouldn't be here if it weren't for her.

"Bell wanted to stay with Quiet Bird after what happened tonight. I think she is a loyal dog. For now, she should stay with me, and I am proud of her for that."

"What happened tonight? We heard gunshots, and Dad drove away real fast."

Bob said, "Gunner, Estelle and I are open with our girls. When something is going on in the world, we don't try to hide it from them. Out of respect to you, if you don't want to discuss it at our table tonight, you don't have to."

Gunner smiled, "I prefer that you explain it. I could say something the girls wouldn't understand. I'm sure you or Estelle could explain things way better than I could. We are close to the same age, the girls and I, I mean."

Bob nodded in agreement. "Linda, tonight was a bad situation on the other side of the road near Talking Bird's house. It appears the Ferguson brothers had been drinking, and they came across Quiet Bird walking home."

Rebecca said, "I know her, Dad. She's in my class at school. She's nice, mostly quiet, a kind person. What happened?"

"Well, the Ferguson brothers tried to rape her in the middle of the road. Gunner here came across them as they had her down." Bob described what happened, and ended with, "After I got there, Gunner took Quiet Bird home and that's where I talked to them."

Rebecca asked, "Is Quiet Bird okay?"

"Yes, I think so, but it's a very traumatic experience for a young girl. Let that be a lesson to you. Don't be wandering around after dark. She had just been on the road for a few minutes, heading straight home, and it was barely dusk. This could happen in the daylight or any time. It doesn't matter if it's day or night. You remember that you are to be careful."

Estelle said, "Okay, girls, let's let Gunner have some time to visit with Dad, then we will get ready for dinner. You go find something else to do."

Estelle looked at Gunner. "Gunner, I'm sorry for you to relive that. We feel it is essential that they know the truth, and we hope that it will help educate them by not holding back."

"I understand, ma'am. I'd like to go back out to check on my mule if you don't mind." Gunner needed to get some air and headed out to see Jack. He didn't think about it, but he must've looked a shamble in his raggedy flannel shirt, flat brim hat, the .45, a bayonet hanging on him, and his hair sticking straight out like a scarecrow. Gunner thought he would like to sleep in the barn with Jack, check on Quiet Bird in the morning, and go back to the mine for a month.

This had not been good for him. He was still mad, but not as much as right after it happened. Quiet Bird never bothered anybody. She didn't mean any harm to anybody, and those no-goods wanted to violate her. He cared for her a lot, and he hoped she could understand his anger. He didn't want to lose her as a friend.

Gunner looked up and saw Bob quietly watching him brush Jack. Gunner thought Bob expected him to talk but he didn't have much to say.

Bob cleared his throat, "I'm not going to apologize for the questions in there. There won't be a long explanation for what happened tonight. I think you're tougher than that. What it does for Estelle and me is the conversation gives our daughters some insight on what really can happen out in the big world. That is one thing I can't help. I think, as a father to those two girls, them knowing what you did, how you did it, and why you did it will be a lesson they'll never forget. I want to thank you for that."

"Bob, if you wouldn't mind, I'd like to sleep out here with my mule and dog tonight. I got my bedroll, and I've got some grub in my pack. I'll be fine. You have a beautiful family there and a warm house to share with them. Where I'm at right now, I need to sleep out here with the mule in the shed. This is pretty much where I belong."

"I don't think you'll need to do that, Gunner. How about a hot shower, a good dinner, and you and Bell can sleep next to the fireplace? You'll feel better about things in the morning. Then you can go see Quiet Bird. I think that's what you want to do more than anything."

"Yes, Quiet Bird has always been kind to me since the day I first met you and we have become friends. It's nice to have a friend when you're a long way from home." Gunner paused and sighed.

"My home is not back on the coast anymore. My home is here with the mule and dog, and someday, with the girl. Do you get what I'm saying?"

"Gunner, I understand where you are. Come see what a shower and a hot meal will do for you, then a night's sleep in front of a warm fire."

"Okay, you talked me into it. If I get up in the middle of the night, to go out and hitch up my mule, don't stop me, okay? I should have stayed up at Talking Bird's and slept in my wagon. I know it's cold out, but it doesn't matter to me."

Bob smiled and nodded. They walked together into the house. Bob handed Gunner some clothes. "Here are some old duds of mine you can put on while yours are getting washed. Go down the hall, and you'll find the bathroom and fresh towels."

Bob walked to the kitchen, watching Estelle work on dinner while the girls were in the front room watching television. He said, "Estelle, that is one tough young man. He's done more good." He paused to collect his thoughts. "By kicking those Fergusons around than a lot of people have done in years. You know I couldn't do it as part of the law. It's a real tragedy though, that the young girl got caught up in the middle of it."

Estelle said, "Don't you go fret over that. You know you can't do anything with those boys. Everyone knows you've tried to reel them in. They have been up to more no good than anybody in Idaho County. Ever since they came out from West Virginia and so young at that, they were no good. I don't think it's safe for our girls to be here on or off their horses alone on the roadside. Sometimes, I think this is not where we need to be raising them."

Estelle was on a roll. "I'm going to change the subject. Did you notice your oldest daughter this evening at the table? No, I didn't think you did. I hate to break the news to you, but she is smitten with that young man. She's just at the age where it's going to stir something in her to take notice of somebody like him."

Bob smiled, slowly shaking his head. "Then she better get in line. When the word gets out what he did to those brothers, that boy could run for governor and probably win. Not to mention that he lives up in the wilderness by himself with the mule and dog. He's fifteen-years-old, Estelle, and he's killed a grizzly bear already. The kid is almost a folk hero around here. Then the time he cut Darrel's shirt in town and squared off with him. Everybody talked about how the kid got the drop on him.

"If our daughter wants to make eyes at him, you be sure and tell her there's going to be a whole lot of competition out there. No, on second thought, I don't think there will be any competition. I do believe he has been spoken for."

Estelle gave Bob a questioning look.

"That would be one Miss Quiet Bird. They are meant for each other. Just watch them together when you get a chance. Here's the bottom line, I like him. I think he's a good young man. He is a stable person who is growing into a man in a man's world, and he will be perfect for it. He'll do a lot of good for our community, our children, and our children's children if somebody doesn't kill him first. You realize they'll try to knock him off the block, just like the old days. I'll put my money on the kid. No, that's wrong. The kid is already a man, and he has paid his admission fee to become one. He is one tough young man already."

After Gunner showered and dressed, he found Bob sitting at the kitchen table, and caught the last sentence. "Thank you, Bob. I only got the last part of what you said. It was nice of you, and it's not often people get around to calling me a man even if you do a man's job." Gunner gave a big smile and held out the sides of the colossal shirt hanging on him.

"I think you've got a shirt here that could fit over a 55-gallon drum. Estelle, I believe you'll be going to what my old man used to call 'a tent and awning company' to get his clothes made."

The three of them laughed, easing the tension for the evening. The girls came in and wanted to join in, asking what's so funny. Estelle said, "Gunner here has one of Father's shirts on, and I think maybe two Gunners could fit in that one shirt. He accused Dad of having a chest the size of a 55-gallon drum, and I'm not so sure if he isn't right."

After dinner, Bob dug out some blankets and threw them by the fireplace. Estelle had all his clothes washed up, even his poor, dirty long johns.

Gunner thanked Estelle multiple times. She said his clothes did need proper washing, and apparently, he didn't have a machine up at the claim. He turned to Bob. "Thank you for everything. I'll be here in the morning when you get up."

"I was hoping you would be. We'll have breakfast, then you can go check on Quiet Bird."

As everyone headed off to bed, Gunner changed into his own clothes, including his worn red long johns. Digging into his backpack, he found Quiet Bird's picture and told her goodnight. Bell had snuggled up next to him and was sound asleep. Gunner was warm and dry next to the fireplace. Most of all, he was happy knowing that Bell and he will be checking on Quiet Bird first thing in the morning.

By morning, the fire had died down, and no one was up in the house yet. The clock on the living room wall said 5:30. Gunner got dressed and went out to check on Jack who was happy with his two new friends. On the way back in, Gunner picked up an armload of firewood and filled up the fireplace.

Sitting in the rocker, he felt good remembering the old rocker his mother had in the living room at home. Some of those home times were good times. Some of them were not so good. For now, it appears he was making his trail here, not worrying about waters gone past. All he wanted was to be left alone and go back up to the claim. There was lots of work to do up there, making a living with what God gave him. He didn't depend on some half-crazy old man who yelled over the dinner table or grabbed him by the collar with his hand raised to smack him.

About then, Bob walked out in his County Sheriff uniform. For Gunner, it was a surprise to see a policeman coming out of the hallway. The lights were dim other than the fireplace, with the flames licking up toward the damper.

Bob said, "Good morning, Gunner. How did you sleep?"

"I'm okay this morning. Thanks for the warm place to sleep last night and the wonderful meal your wife fixed. I'm glad I had time to rest and think things over. It seems like Cleo is always asking how I'm doing, and I'm always answering him that I'm okay. Do you ever know if you really are okay?"

Bob paused. "That's a big question. Probably not. We all operate out on an edge somewhere. I want to keep my sanity intact for my family and the job I have. Now, you might have a different perspective. You live a whole different lifestyle than me. I know you're more settled than you might appear to be. That's because I've been up to your cabin. I've seen what you're doing. In a way, I'm somewhat envious of how you're doing with your life. Compared to us flatlanders down here, as you call us, you live a whole lot different than us."

"I know you're coming up against your first winter, and it's going to be tough. My money is on you. I think you can make it. You are a skillful young man, and you can do the job."

Gunner smiled. "Thank you. That means a lot to me. Right now, all I want to do is check on Quiet Bird and go back up to my claim. When it comes time to testify against those cowards, you know how to get a hold of me. You and your family are always welcome to come up to the cabin and spend time if you like. Could you thank Estelle and the girls for me? I'll go get Jack hitched up and head out to check on Quiet Bird before Talking Bird has to leave for school."

Bob nodded as Gunner headed out the door with Bell at his side.

With Jack hitched up to the wagon, Gunner and crew headed out. Talking Bird's house was less than thirty minutes away, once he and Jack were on the road.

Gunner had worried about both Talking Bird and Quiet Bird last night. He didn't know what he could do other than find the ones that did it and kill them. He knew he had to get that thinking out of his head, especially when he was so angry. Cleo is right. You need to be calm to make good decisions. Right now, Gunner knew he was not doing well with decision-making. Getting back up to the claim would help.

CHAPTER 43

The night before, soon after Gunner left Talking Bird's, Officer Bob drove out the driveway.

Quiet Bird said, "I wish you wouldn't have sent Gunner away, Mother. You are right, he is outraged. He has a right to be angry.

"Gunner feels responsible for what happened to me tonight. I have already forgiven him. Before I left Papa's, he asked me if I wanted him to walk me home. I had come home hundreds of times from Papa and Grandma's, especially when they watched me while you were teaching school.

"Just this one time, this had to happen to me. I knew Gunner was right behind me. I knew he would be there. He would never let me down. I know this to be true."

Quiet Bird took a deep breath to collect her thoughts. "Mother, don't you see his anger is genuine for a good reason? I laid there on the road in the snow, sensing, more than hearing, Jack's hooves pounding on the pavement over the engine running. I knew Gunner was there, and he was going to help me. If Gunner wasn't the man he is, I don't think he would have had the courage to jump in the middle of them and do what he did. I know it takes a lot of courage to be able to pull a gun out, smash somebody's face to pieces, then shoot another one without hesitation.

"Yes, Gunner was angry, justifiably so, and that's what saved me. Those Fergusons don't scare him. He showed that before in town, and he has shown it again tonight.

"I think he will be showing his courage for the rest of his life. I can see it bothers you when he is so angry. Then at the same time, he is trying to be so careful and gentle with me. In my heart, I know he was only doing what he could do. Mother, that's the place I feel the safest, next to him. Thank you for letting me speak. I have been waiting to say this."

Talking Bird replied slowly and quietly, "I feel your concern, but it is my responsibility to protect you. Calmness is what you need, not somebody sitting next to you, boiling over. It is not good."

"But Mother, he was not boiling over, he was sitting next to me holding my hand. It was very calming for me. It gave me great comfort to know he was next to me. Mother, these are bad people, and they scared me deep inside. I know it wasn't Gunner or anything about him that did this to me. My spirit guides were there, and they told me to wait. Gunner was coming."

Talking Bird started, "We are back to the spirit guides now, are we? I don't think the spirit guides will keep those terrible people from doing something vile to you. What we need to do is talk about where you're going to be safe. I'm sure those terrible people will get out of jail. They will be a threat to you here in Elk City. This town is too small for you to be safe."

Talking Bird continued, "Does Gunner know they'll come looking for him and try to do him harm? I think you need to go to the prairie and spend time with your Auntie or Uncle Bill. You can safely live and go to school there. These are evil people, and they will go to any lengths to stay out of jail. You and Gunner are the two that can put them there."

"Mother, if they're going to come after Gunner, then you shouldn't send me up to the Prairie with Auntie. I should be beside Gunner, where we can fight them together."

Talking Bird blurted out, "What do you mean you should be beside him?"

Quiet Bird had an idea. "I mean, I should go back up to the mine with him. We both would be safer there, together, until springtime."

Talking Bird rolled her eyes, shaking her head to indicate this was a terrible idea.

Quiet Bird continued, "They won't know how to get up to the claim in the dead of winter. Things are so cold and unsafe up there. I don't think they have the guts to try anything in the winter. In the spring, they might want to, but Gunner and I together can fight them. You will see."

Talking Bird was getting frustrated. "God, I think this is some warrior Indian fight or something going on here. Is this something spiritual for you? Could there be something more to this for you?"

Quiet Bird spoke calmly. "All I can think of is, this is the person I want to be with, to be safe. If there's going to be a fight, he is the one I would choose to be close to. I feel he is the one for me. My spirit guide told me this when we first met."

"Do you realize how young the two of you are?" Talking Bird asked adamantly. "Not that age has anything to do with what happened tonight. You do understand there is a point where two young people can only do so much?"

Quiet Bird loved her mother but had her mind made up. "You said it, Mother. After tonight, if they come for us, I have all the confidence that Gunner will kill them to protect me. We need that confidence to be who we are. You know we will stand together."

Talking Bird was starting to give in. "You have a point. How do you feel about being with Gunner in a cabin in the wilderness all alone? He is a young man, and young men have thoughts, you know. I think he is a good person, but is he that good? You need to think it over. This is a big step. I'm not sure if it's the right one. I think Auntie would be a better choice."

Quiet Bird said, "Gunner can fend for himself. If they go up into that forest, they don't know who they are dealing with. He's proven himself by killing a bear and surviving up there on his own. No, Mother, this is what I need to do. I only feel safe near him. We will be good together, and he is a smart man. Yes, he is a polite person, and I think he is a good man. We need to catch up with him tomorrow.

"Mother, I need you to talk to him and tell him that he needs to take me with him. Then, I will talk to him and tell him what I can do to help us work together. We will work as partners and friends, nothing more."

Talking Bird shook her head again. "I don't think you know what you're getting yourself into. You're going up into a wilderness that you know nothing of. Gunner barely knows enough to survive up there himself. How is he going to care for the both of you, as well as his mule and dog?"

Quiet Bird moved to the edge of the couch. "In my heart, I know we can do this. If we come through the winter being friends, it will be a good experience for both of us. Remember, the Nez Perce tribe has a pre-marriage agreement where two people can live together to see if they want to be man and wife? That would keep tongues from wagging. You know that Mother. The other thing we have is mutual respect and trust for one another. It is the basis for our friendship."

Mother Talking Bird feared the brothers would undoubtedly come back from jail for Quiet Bird. She decided they each needed to pack a small overnight bag and go to her folks for the night. There, they could tell them what was going on and listen to their thoughts.

When Talking Bird and Quiet Bird arrived at her folks' house, Talking Bird explained everything. It was late, and everyone was exhausted. They agreed to continue the discussion in the morning.

As she sat on the guest bed, Talking Bird said, "I've been thinking your idea over. You do have a point, but let's sleep on it tonight. Daughter, you know this is a huge decision for both of us. If this is what you want, I will talk to him, but I'm not sure I can convince him. He might not want to take on the responsibility of another person. I think he has his hands full putting the mine together, and now you want him to take a young woman with him? I still do not think this is the best plan. But whatever happens, I will respect your choice.

"Once you make up your mind, I realize I must let you do what you feel in your heart. You must promise me that any time you feel uncomfortable, you will leave. Get on that mule that Gunner so cherishes and come home to me."

"Thank you, Mother. I knew you would understand. Now I can only hope that Gunner will understand."

CHAPTER 44

Gunner pulled into the driveway of Talking Bird's house. He noted Jack's breath was freezing on his nose hairs. An inch of new snow had fallen, and black clouds packed in above, telling Gunner more snow was on the way. He was sure the temperature was below freezing because his fingers were numb.

Taking the Springfield out of the sheath, he slung it over his shoulder and walked toward the house. *Bad sign*, he thought, as there was no smoke coming out of the chimney. Bell was at his side as he looked up at the kitchen window. It looked frigid and empty. There wasn't a light on anywhere in the house.

With no one home, Gunner's heart sunk down to his socks. He walked to the garage. Tipping up on his toes, he wiped frost off the garage door window. Just as he guessed, no car.

Gunner thought they must have gone to Oley's and Lisa's for the night.

Can I go down and see her there? No, probably not. They would have left me a note to find them. Maybe they didn't want anyone to know where they were.

Gunner walked back to Jack, brushing snow off his roached mule mane. "Well, Jack, we are not needed here."

Gunner picked up the lead rope after putting Bell up on the driver's seat and had Jack pull the wagon out onto the main road. With Talking Bird's warning about the Ferguson family, he kept looking over his shoulder. There was a possibility someone could come looking for them on Red River Road.

Walking slowly, Gunner had a massive lump in his throat to match the pit in his stomach. *Quiet Bird is gone, and you did it. The old man was right. You are a stupid dummy. Quiet Bird deserves better, not some clunk of a muck bucket like me.*

The road had a fair shoulder for pulling the wagon along and Gunner was alert when anyone drove by. Soon, it was time to rest Jack and give him water. Gunner pulled the Springfield out of the wagon and hung the sling over his shoulder. This was the only road Gunner could take to the mine, and the Fergusons knew it.

It was slow going for Jack with the wagon. They had been grinding along and, by mid-morning, they were halfway up the river bottom to Granny's. The morning was cold and dismal, with an occasional snifter of light snow falling, just enough to make the snowy road very slick. Behind him, Gunner could hear an engine rev up, its tires spinning.

Gunner looked back as something smacked the back of the wagon, followed by a ping in the roadside bank. Gunner saw a pickup truck spinning its wheels, coming hard as it could, heading straight at them. Someone was hanging out of the passenger window.

This fool is shooting at us with a handgun. Without thinking, Gunner kneeled on one knee, pulling the .45 Cal. out of his holster in one quick move, cocking it as he gripped the handle with both hands. Taking in a breath and holding it, he looked down the sight of the pistol. He patiently waited for the fifty feet to close between them. He only had six shots and wanted to make them all count.

Squeezing the trigger, the .45 bucked back with a loud boom. Gunner quickly re-cocked it, pulling the hammer back. The person hanging out the window slumped down and hung halfway out the passenger door window. The pistol dropped to the middle of the road. The truck couldn't get much traction on the slick road, and it was just now picking up speed. Gunner slammed three quick shots into the front windshield. He needed to convince the driver to stay away from Jack and the wagon. *Good thing I put Bell up on the driver's seat. She's safer up there. I just hope she stays there.*

The truck roared by as Gunner holstered the .45. He was thinking he had two rounds left. He pulled on the sling of the Springfield as he stood up. He had it in the ready position in both hands, pulling the butt up tight against his shoulder and cheek. He took careful aim down the long-familiar barrel through the open sights, aiming at the front end of the pickup. As the truck spun around, it crossed the center line again heading straight for Jack, Bell, Gunner, and the wagon. With certain death for the three of them, Gunner drove a round home into the chamber. He aimed low on the hood, at the steering wheel area, and in rapid succession, fired five rounds as fast as he could. He hit a tire on the last shot. The truck crossed back over the centerline of the road, leaving Gunner and his crew in the safety of the roadway shoulder.

The truck was forty feet from Gunner when a front tire let go. The truck took a sharp right turn and augered into a sugar pine stump on the opposite side of the road from the wagon.

The stump killed the truck. A plume of steam and smoke poured out from under the hood as Gunner walked toward the driver's side of the pick-up truck. He could see the driver slumped over the wheel through the door window. His partner was still hanging out of the passenger window, not moving.

Gunner reached the driver's window holding the Springfield in both hands. A forest service truck approached, slowed, and stopped. The passenger rolled his window down, and asked, "Everything okay?"

"Oh yeah. Could you call Officer Bob when you get to town? I would appreciate it. You might tell him they need an ambulance for the driver here. And the mortician for the rider hanging out of the window over there."

Gunner turned the Springfield around, pulling the gun's butt back about twelve inches, then busted out the driver's side window with two quick smacks of the rifle butt. He rehung the Springfield on his shoulder with its sling and pulled the .45 from its holster. Reaching in the driver's window, he grabbed a handful of the driver's greasy hair, and shoved the barrel of the .45 to the side of his head. Just like before, he cocked the gun on the way out of its holster. The pistol was ready to go, and so was Gunner.

It seems that was enough for the forest service truck. The truck eased away, not wanting to see what would happen next.

With a gravelly voice, Gunner said, "I told you last night if you come around the girl, or me and my crew, you would find yourself dead. Now, you get to live this one time because I want you to go back to whoever is pulling the levers on this mess. You tell them that when I find out who put you up to this, they are dead and that is a promise. Do you hear me?"

Gunner was not getting the answer he wanted and tightened his grip on the driver's hair. He pulled his head farther through the busted glass, making a lot of minor cuts to his face and neck.

"I said, do you hear me, you bastard?"

The driver gave a quick nod as he looked at Gunner with frightened eyes. He slumped back into the driver's seat when Gunner let him go. Gunner walked back to the wagon. Bell was stretched out on the driver's seat, wagging her tail, patiently waiting for him.

"Good girl, Bell, you did just what you were supposed to do."

Gunner opened his pack, pulling a jerky treat out for Bell and himself. He put water in the nose bag for Jack who was due for a good drink and maybe some calming words. As he hung the nose bag on Jack, he talked in a low voice as Jack calmed down. Gunner could hear the calvary on its way from town. Bell sat up, wagging her tail. She was used to the sound of the siren and knew it would be Bob climbing out of the cruiser. He pulled in behind the wagon, making a sharp swerve to miss the pistol lying in the middle of the road. The cruiser came to a stop, all lights flashing. Bob climbed out and walked toward Gunner and his crew. Gunner was chewing on jerky with one hand and holding the water bag bottom for Jack in the other hand.

"Morning again, Bob," Gunner said with a nod.

"Looks like they found you," Bob said with a sigh.

"I'm thinking they're regretting that about now. The shooter is hanging out the passenger window, and he is gone. You dodged his pistol coming in."

"Yeah, I saw that."

Bob walked toward the pickup truck, steam and smoke still coming out from under the hood. Gunner could hear the ambulance wail in the distance, guessing they couldn't go very fast with the slick roads.

As Gunner was taking the nose bag off Jack, Bob walked back over to them. Gunner said, "I got to get going, Bob, daylight's burnin'."

"Give me a quick rundown," Bob asked.

"Well, sir, I was on the shoulder of the road right here. They come up behind us, shooting at my crew and me. I killed the shooter hanging out the passenger window with four rounds of the .45. The driver went up there," Gunner said, pointing, "and turned around. He started back, straight at us in one of those Japanese kamikaze runs. You can see the tracks there. I used the Springfield, five rounds total, into the hood and windshield. Got me a tire for the last shot and that put him into the stump over there."

"What about the door window?" Bob asked.

"You don't miss anything, do you?"

"The forest service people told me on the phone." Bob smiled.

"Well, sir, I had to have a little chat with him. The person pulling the levers on this stunt will be dead as soon as I can get around to it. I needed to send them a message, or the driver would have been dead also."

Gunner continued, "It is a long way to Cleo's. I want to rest Jack at Granny's. I'll be there if you need me."

The ambulance had arrived, and the medics were unloading the driver and the body on the passenger side, waiting for the coroner.

"You can go. I'll catch up with you if I need any more."

With Jack's lead in his hand, Gunner said, "Get up, Jack." The wagon and crew pulled away headed for Granny's. There was still a long, cold walk to go.

Gunner thought about what had just happened. *Killing the person hanging out the passenger window took less emotion than that mangy old bear up at the mine. It looks like we're into it now, crew. I promise to find the person putting them up to this.*

Gunner and crew walked into the barn turnout just before dark at Granny's. Norman came out of the shop and walked over in the evening light. He walked along the left side of the wagon, stopping to look at the damaged wood from the morning's shoot-out. Gunner was busy tending to Jack. The light was slipping away with a cold evening coming on, the cold digging into Gunner's backside, where he had been sweating.

Norman gave a long whistle. "We heard there was some shooting out on the river road today. Just never figured it would be you."

"Well, if they want to shoot at my crew and me, then they got to be willing to pay for it."

"When you get Jack cared for, you and Bell come up to the house. I think Granny has an extra plate for you. Maybe you could fill us in then. Wasn't there more shooting in town yesterday?"

"Yeah, that was me again."

Gunner had an enjoyable visit during dinner, including answering all their questions. Norman said, "I would never have guessed you were that mean."

"Norman, you threaten my friends and family, like the bear or those clod hoppers did in town, and I'll do what I need to. I have nowhere to go, and they weren't any different than the bear wanting to kill Bell and me. Fighting back is all I can do. Being raised by the old man, you need a mean streak to survive his dinner table."

Both Granny and Norman knew the old man from when he was a young wild jerk.

Gunner thanked Granny for dinner and excused himself. Outside, he gathered an armload of stove wood, and Bell followed him back in again.

"Thanks again for everything. Jack needed the rest. He is a hell of a mule. You bred him right, Norman."

"Thank you for that, Gunner."

Gunner got ready to leave for Cleo's. Once Jack was in his harness, he backed him into the single hitch under near darkness. The only light he had was a lightbulb over the front of the shop and another one up on the front porch of the house. The yard was blacker than a chunk of coal.

The snow started coming down from the black clouds, and the temperature was still dropping. Gunner's hands were numb as he hitched up Jack. He had left the wagon up on Forest Service Road 1150 by the ranch shop.

Gunner walked Jack out of the yard, stopping to open the cattle guard by-pass gate. He hoisted Bell up to the driver's seat of the wagon then hitched Jack to the wagon.

Granny and Norman came out to stand next to the shop to say goodbye. Gunner thought they were in shock with all that had been going on with him.

CHAPTER 45

Granny called over as he was swinging the gate open, "Gunner, are you expecting anyone? Those headlights are coming down the road fast over there by the bridge."

Immediately, Gunner ran to the wagon seat where Bell was lying. Without hesitation, the Springfield came out of the sheath next to the driver's seat.

Gunner quickly shoved the bolt home, putting a bullet in the chamber as he called out to the folks, "You best go up to the house. I don't think they've had enough today."

Granny and Norman hurried up the walk to the house.

Gunner walked to the back of the wagon to crouch down on one knee, pulling off his glove to uncover his trigger finger. With a firm grip, he pulled the rifle stock up tight to his shoulder. He leaned his cheek against the rifle, taking careful aim on the car's driver side with the safety off.

The car headlights were blinding. *Easy now, Gunner, don't shoot till they start shooting.*

Gunner's trigger hand was getting cold, being out of the glove. The increasing cold of the Springfield's blue steel barrel was turning his hand numb. The car pulled up just thirty feet away and stopped, engine running.

Slowly, the driver's side door opened. He knew they could see him crouched down by the wagon wheel, ready to start shooting. A woman stepped out slowly and stood by the door. She called to him over the idling engine. "Gunner! Gunner! Don't shoot. It's Quiet Bird and me. We need to talk to you, please."

With his half-frozen hand, Gunner fumbled to switch the safety on. He pulled back the rifle with a quick motion, as it went to the ready position on his shoulder. By now, both ladies were standing in the headlights' beam.

Bell could see it was Quiet Bird and started barking. Gunner set her down on the ground and she ran to Quiet Bird. Gunner had no idea why Talking Bird wanted to talk to him. *Maybe she's still mad I let Quiet Bird walked home alone last night. I apologized to them both. I can't do anything else. Is she going to lecture me about anger again?* "What is it you want, Talking Bird?"

Talking Bird didn't keep him waiting long. "Gunner, are you better now?"

"Yes, ma'am, my anger has gone down some. I still feel terrible about letting Quiet Bird go home alone last night. I knew better. My mother taught me better. I know I will never let her be alone in the dark like that ever again."

Granny and Norman had moved down next to the shop so they could listen.

Talking Bird spoke up with a firm voice so Gunner could hear her. "Gunner, Quiet Bird, and I had a long talk last night. At first, I didn't agree with this idea of hers. But the more I thought about it and considered all the facts, I think it is the right idea."

The ladies were still 30 feet away from Gunner, and the car continued to idle. Talking Bird raised her voice, "Gunner, do you see? That Ferguson family will hunt both of you now. You will testify against them in court sometime this winter. In the meantime, there is only one safe place for either of you to be. I thought of sending Quiet Bird up to her aunt on the prairie. She also has Uncle Bill up there where she could stay. I don't think either place would be safe, though. Those brothers could go down the river and talk to people. They could find her. Not even the town of Nez Perce would be a safe place for her. We heard what happened today. You were right, those nasty people want to kill both of you. As you saw today, they don't care how or where."

I see why they call her Talking Bird. She sure is doing all the talking. Maybe it's because she's a schoolteacher. Those kids can't tell her, "Okay, you've talked enough now. Would you let someone else speak?"

Talking Bird continued, "Gunner, you're not safe either. You might be until spring. I don't think they have the nerve to come up to your mine in the wilderness. And you were right by being so angry. I was wrong."

Well now, that's a first.

Talking Bird had finally stopped talking and Gunner could speak. "Okay, what are you trying to say, Talking Bird?"

Gunner had worked his way closer to the car and was ten feet from the car's headlights. The snow was coming down steady now, in big white clumpy flakes.

"Gunner, you are the safest place for Quiet Bird." Mother Talking Bird raised her voice to stress the importance of him doing what she wanted him to do. "You and your cabin in the forest is the safest place for you both. There, you will be safe until springtime."

"So just come out and say it." Gunner was now face-to-face with her. "Here, let me help you out. You want me to take your daughter up into the backwoods of the Nez Perce forest in the dead of winter?"

"Yes, that is it exactly," Talking Bird said. "They don't know about your background or who you are. Those people have run into you three times now, and know you intend to hurt them seriously. Gunner, I am guessing they want to kill you if you don't kill them first."

Now that is a good guess, with what happened this morning.

Talking Bird continued, "In our conversation last night, Quiet Bird and I decided the best thing she could do is go up to the cabin with you. The both of you can hold up there most of the winter without worry. Other than when you have to come out for supplies and the trial, it would be safe. Do you see what I am saying?"

Wow. I can't believe she's asking this.

Mother Bird kept talking. *The lady does not stop.* "I think I know both of you well enough where this could work." Talking Bird didn't take a breath and repeated herself. "What we thought about is this, could you consider taking Quiet Bird back up to the cabin with you? Quiet Bird could watch out for you, and you could watch out for her. No one knows when or where the Fergusons are going to come after you."

Gunner stood there, almost overwhelmed with the enormity of her request and the responsibility he was being asked to take on. He didn't want to be shoved into anything. "This is hard. Yes, we are friends, but I don't think I have the what-with-all to do this."

He paused to collect himself. "Talking Bird, I would be taking on the responsibility of a woman up at the mine. It would change everything. Now, don't get me wrong. I care a lot for Quiet Bird."

Gunner looked over to Quiet Bird. "The mine is one hard place. The dog, mule, and me, we do just fine there. But I don't think it is any place for a young girl, or I should say, woman. I would have to double my supplies and most likely make changes in the cabin. I'm just not sure how it would work out. That cabin is tiny." He was quiet, thinking it over and dreaming up more reasons why he should not do this.

Cleo talks about knowing what your plan is. Talk about a stampede. Well, sir, I am being asked to make a huge decision here in the middle of the road. This is reckless thinking.

"Talking Bird, there is no one in the world other than Quiet Bird that I would like to have come up to the cabin." Gunner stopped to take a breath and think for a minute again.

Talking Bird started to raise her voice one more time. "Gunner, don't you see that there is no other way to do this?"

Gunner tossed an idea to Talking Bird, "You could send her to my mother on the coast. No, never mind, Quiet Bird wouldn't do that. Her home is here. She would make a stand here like I am."

Gunner looked over to Quiet Bird again. *Damn, I look at her and lose my argument.*

Gunner took a deep breath and blurted out, "Neither one of you has any idea what it's like up there. Not only do you have a good chance of freezing to death, but there are a whole bunch of creatures that want to eat you for dinner."

Both ladies smiled. They hoped this was a sign of him weakening.

Gunner was fumbling for words now. "As I said, I don't know anything about taking care of a girl up at the claim. Didn't I just say that? Now you got me repeating myself. Hell, it's hard enough to care for Bell and Jack."

Quiet Bird approached them both. "Mother, would you leave us, please? I want to talk to Gunner alone."

Gunner's resistance was building. *Quiet Bird wants to calm me down with just the two of us talking.*

Norman started to chuckle. Granny put a hand on his arm and shook her head.

Quiet Bird led Gunner back to the wagon to be alone.

"Gunner, we like each other's company, true?"

"True."

"We respect each other, true?"

"True."

"We could be good working partners." Quiet Bird continued as Gunner started to object. "Let me explain. I can care for the animals and the cabin. That would give you more time in the mine, true?"

Gunner paused and thought over her statement. *You know she is right about that. It would be a lot of help. I know I would love a home-cooked meal. She is smart and knows the way to me is through my stomach.*

"But can you skin and clean game?" Gunner asked.

"You kill it. I will clean and cook it."

"Now, you're talking." Gunner gave a cheek-to-cheek grin.

"Gunner, I think this is the best thing we can do for both of us. You and I know what Mother is saying. They are mean enough to come after us. We could go up to your cabin and work together. I will help you a lot and be safe there from the brothers at the same time. Don't you see that?"

"Quiet Bird, I like you. I think it would be wonderful to spend time together. Up at the claim, I work fourteen hours a day. Then I spend another couple of hours just taking care of the critters and myself. After that, I study for two hours every evening. On top of that, sometimes, I have to kill and dress game to eat. You know all of this takes time."

Quiet Bird looked into his eyes and smiled. With a calm voice, she said, "I don't want you to do this unless you want to. Remember, you know I can help you. If you shoot it, like I said, I will dress and cook it for us. That will save you a lot of time. I can clean the cabin, keep meals on the table, and care for the critters while you're up in the mine. If you need help with the mine, I can help you train Jack to pull the gondola like you were talking about the other day."

Quiet Bird paused to let what she said sink in.

Gunner's protests were getting weaker. "You can cook. I've had a chance to sample that. Are you sure you can dress game?"

"Yes, I can dress game. I even know how to smoke it. These things were taught to me early in life by my grandparents."

Gunner asked, "How long do you think we will have to stay up there together? When the snow comes, I'm figuring it's going to get quiet and dark for a long time. We might not be back out for six weeks or more. If the snow is too deep, it could be spring. Are you sure you are ready to do that?"

Quiet Bird looked up at him with her beautiful brown eyes. *Oh no, I'm doing a lousy job here.*

"Gunner, I can do it if you can do it."

They stood there a full two minutes as Gunner looked into her warm, beautiful brown face. *Damn, this has all switched around. This morning I thought I had lost Quiet Bird. Now, I'm going to be responsible for her, full-time, and at the claim to boot.* "This is until things quiet down with the Fergusons, right?" Gunner was still thinking about how not to do this.

Quiet Bird smiled that warm, steady smile, thinking he was going to say yes. "Yes. Thank you, Gunner, you'll never regret doing this for me."

Gunner called over his shoulder. "Talking Bird, can you come over here, please?"

Talking Bird walked to the wagon. "Yes, Gunner."

"I agree to do this, but there are a couple of conditions."

Both ladies waited and for once, Mother Talking Bird was quiet.

"This is only for Quiet Birds' safety. She can stay at the claim only until the Fergusons are in jail or the threat is gone. Does everyone agree?"

Both ladies said "Yes" at the same time.

"Talking Bird, we will need more provisions. Clothes and books for Quiet Bird. Could you bring them to Cleo's sometime tomorrow? If we're not there, you can leave the supplies with him. I'm not sure if I will go back to the cabin right away or not. Everything depends on the weather."

They talked for ten minutes more. Gunner fetched Quiet Bird's bag and the blanket she had brought.

The girls hugged, and again, Mother Talking Bird thanked Gunner for taking this responsibility.

Gunner hoisted Bell up on the wagon seat, then helped Quiet Bird to the driver's seat next to Bell. He wrapped a blanket around Quiet Bird, fashioning a hood with it to cover her head. Taking a small piece of rope, he tied it all together by wrapping it around her waist.

"Here, use my gloves. I have an extra pair in my backpack."

Quiet Bird smiled that shy, beautiful smile.

No words. I like that about this girl. Thank God she doesn't talk like her mother, or this show would be over before it started. He still wasn't sure what to do with a girl other than he figured they get cold just like boys do. *Guess I better try to keep her warm.*

I thought my life was getting complicated before. Shoot, this is confusing and complicated! Guess I should have killed those bastards when I had the chance.

"Pull, Jack." Gunner had Jack's lead rope in his hand, and they slowly move through the gate.

He looked up to the sky and noticed the snow had stopped as he turned to close the gate. An opening appeared in the clouds with a sliver of a new moon to help light their way to Cleo's cabin.

The End